BOOKS BY E.M. SMITH
The Agent Juliet series
Broken Bones

BOOKS BY TIM MCBAIN & L.T. VARGUS
The Violet Darger series
The Charlotte Winters series
Casting Shadows Everywhere
The Scattered and the Dead series
The Clowns

LONE

WOLF

LONE WOLF

A VICTOR LOSHAK NOVEL

E.M. SMITH
L.T. VARGUS & TIM MCBAIN

LONE WOLF

PROLOGUE

Andi Wayland wrestled the Rubbermaid tote from her hip onto the railing of the stairs. The podcast mail was crazy heavy this week. Inside the tote, the envelopes and packages bumped and slid around, making it awkward as hell, too.

She felt like Sisyphus shoving the tote up the railing, but it was better than having the thing bumping against her thigh the whole climb. Last time it had left bruises.

When she made it up the first flight of stairs, she paused to catch her breath, her internal monologue spewing out a stream of sarcastic complaints.

Who cares if it's a three-story walk-up, they said.

The apartment is amazing, they said.

Such a great neighborhood, they said.

They were half-hearted gripes, really. Because being forced to lug a giant bin of fan mail up these stairs every few days was a good problem to have. *All Murder* had started out with one listener, and that had been her dad. Nowadays, the podcast had close to a million subscribers, an active community, and incredible organic growth every quarter.

Thinking about her passion project in terms of quarterly growth made her feel just a teensy bit soulless, but hey… Patreon and ad reads were what paid the bills. And living in the hip area of Denver's world-famous Dairy Block did not come cheap.

1

She was huffing and puffing by the time she got to the third floor. Sweating through the delicate, gauzy material of her shell top. Definitely needed more cardio. Or better yet, she needed to start sending her assistant to get the mail.

Andi pinned the tote to the wall with her knee while she unlocked her door, then swooped over the threshold with it, letting its momentum carry it inside and barely missing her overweight tabby.

"My bad, Sanford, look out. Lots of snail mail today."

She caught a whiff of something rank and initially assumed the culprit was Sanford's litter box. He had a habit of taking a crap without burying it, though it wasn't for lack of trying. He'd spend a good five minutes scraping his paw against the wall and the floor and the side of the washing machine — anywhere but the inside of the litter box itself, really — before deciding his work was done.

But after a second sniff, she determined it was definitely not cat shit she smelled. This odor was more putrid.

That was when she remembered cleaning out the fridge that morning, and the ancient container of refried beans she'd discovered, way in the back, tucked behind a jar of marinara.

She'd tossed the beans in the garbage and taken the bag straight down to the dumpster, but apparently, the stench had been powerful enough to linger even still.

There was a candle warmer on the small table beside the door. Andi reached over and turned on the switch, hoping the fragrance of the candle would banish the enduring stink of the rotten beans.

She squinted at the label, which declared that the scent

was called "The Zodiac Killer" and listed the notes as "a dark and enigmatic blend of amber, sandalwood, vetiver, and vanilla." Andi didn't know what any of those had to do with the Zodiac and found the scent to be kind of "generic cologne," personally.

She also couldn't help but wonder if there was a big market for serial killer–themed candles, but since it had been made and sent in by one of their fans, she mostly just felt appreciative that their listeners cared that much.

The short hall to her kitchenette was lined with posters from old horror and grindhouse movies. Vibrant shades, delivering violence and gore in high contrast. The bold lettering spelled out titles like *Children Shouldn't Play with Dead Things* and *I Drink Your Blood*.

With a grunt, she heaved the tote onto the table and dropped her keys next to it. Leaned over and slapped the paddle switch on the wall. The natural light in this place was practically non-existent. Sometimes it felt like living in a cave. Next on her upgrade list was an apartment with a huge bank of windows, in a location where the buildings next door didn't block the sun.

The tabby twined around her legs, his big belly actually forcing her to spread her feet farther apart. His vet had used the term *alarmingly obese* at his last appointment. Not very nice, but not an inaccurate description, either.

She stooped to scrub her fingers over his face, thumbs sliding over the soft, glossy *M* pattern on his forehead. He really was a pretty cat, he just liked to overindulge a bit too often.

Apparently, attention wasn't what Sanford had been looking for. He let out an impatient, rolling meow and nipped at her hand.

"Dude. I fed you before I left."

He really drew out the next complaint. Sometimes she swore he actually understood her.

"Do you want to die early? Because that's what will happen if you keep eating like this."

Sanford waddled to his bowl and loafed there on the floor, yowling.

"God. Fine. Let's just find out what's in the box first."

Maybe if she kept pushing back the feeding times, they would eventually get to the once-a-day feedings the vet recommended.

Tuning out Sanford's hangry squalling, Andi upended the tote, spilling out large envelopes, both the manila and white variety. Some padded mailers. A few small boxes. Letters in standard-size envelopes. Brightly colored stationary, a weird number of them neon pink.

All Murder did have a disproportionate number of female listeners. Something about serial killers really drew in the ladies.

She skimmed a few letters and a thank-you card from a woman who was disturbingly grateful for highlighting Chad Daybell.

That episode was already a few years old, but still the most popular one to date. Before that one, Andi had just been glad to get an occasional affiliate commission or two from one of those companies peddling make-at-home subscription meals. But within six months of Episode 24, which was titled "One Foot in the Grave," the *All Murder* Patreon had enough subscribers that she could afford to quit her job and really focus on the show.

Sanford's wail wavered, then broke off. Ran out of air. He licked his chops, then got back to it.

"Maybe you're the one who needs cardio, Sanfy. Did you ever think of that?"

Was it any wonder that she overfed him when she had this diva attitude to contend with? The fans loved it when Sanford made his occasional appearances on the podcast; the audio tech did not.

Andi added the Chad Daybell thank-you card to the Standard Response pile for an assistant to deal with — maybe send some stickers and a newsletter — and moved on.

The padded mailers and manila envelopes were mostly fan art. Those would need to be scheduled for spotlights on the social media pages, mentioned in the "Shout-Outs" segment of the show. There were a few sketches of the podcast crew, some really awesome reimaginings of the *All Murder* logo, and several portraits of the infamous killers they talked about every week.

She paused over a photorealistic drawing of Richard Ramirez done entirely in blue ballpoint. A shiver rolled down her spine. Something about the eyes really got under her skin.

Even for someone as deeply entrenched in the true crime world as she was, it was slightly disturbing to think somebody had spent hours rendering the Night Stalker in such loving detail. There was just no other way to describe it. Nobody with a mere passing interest could've captured that predatory gleam in his eyes.

And she wondered what she always wondered when she opened these homages to the most violent criminals in their nation's history: Who were the people drawing this stuff, and were they OK?

She kept a few pieces of really top-notch fan art framed and scattered among the horror and true crime posters, but they weren't there for her. The apartment was basically the studio/work room for the podcast, set up to be "on brand." They'd brought in a legit interior decorator to help design the place back when they started filming the video version.

A sharp pain in her calf made her yelp.

"Hey!"

Sanford meowed and trundled back to his bowl.

"Asshole," she muttered.

She had one mailer left to open, the biggest one of the pile, all bulging and thick, but clearly she wasn't going to get any peace and quiet until the monster in the room was dealt with.

She abandoned the last mailer on the table and grabbed the plastic container of cat food off the shelf. The kibble jangled into the metal bowl, tiny nuggets of compressed chicken and rice or salmon and some other grain. She couldn't remember which flavor she'd bought him this time around. It was one of those top-of-the-line science diets, though. Maybe if she bought something cheaper, he wouldn't love it enough to gorge on.

With a chirrup of satisfaction, Sanford stuck his face in the bowl. The phrase "set to with a will" came instantly to Andi's mind. No idea where she'd heard that one. Sounded like something from a regency romance.

She shook her head.

"The things I do for you."

Back at the table, she reached for the remaining mailer.

Paused.

Another trace of stanky bean smell assailed her nostrils. Jesus, how long was that stench going to hang around?

She *had* taken the garbage down to the dumpster, right? She distinctly remembered doing it.

She toed open the under-sink cabinet, confirming that not only was the trash bin empty, she hadn't even put a fresh bag in yet.

Is it me? she thought. *Maybe the bean funk is clinging to my skin, permeating the fibers of my clothing.*

But when she lifted her blouse to her nose and inhaled, it just smelled like fabric softener.

She cracked the window over the sink and picked up the final mailer, still puzzling over the persistent odor. The large envelope crinkled with bubble wrap, both built into the packaging and filling the interior. Whatever this fan had sent must be fragile. They got non-paper art now and then. Ceramic plates made to look like the ones old ladies hung on their wall, except with idyllic scenes of pastel axe murder, or Blair Witch–style stick creations.

This… this she wasn't sure about. There was so much bubble wrap that she couldn't see through to the thing at the center, and she couldn't tell anything by feel. The bubbles rustled and bulged beneath her fingers as she unwound layer after layer.

Whatever this thing was, it definitely wasn't getting damaged in shipping.

Color became discernible through the layers as she unwrapped. A whitish-yellow-gray on one side. Something reminiscent of melted cheese. Gruyere, maybe, or a slice of American. Grab some turkey and rye, and she could have lunch with Sanford.

The other side was mottled with a darker brownish-pink. Kind of like old hamburger. Much less appetizing.

The end of the bubble wrap fell away to reveal a layer of cling wrap, the thin film sliding under her fingers on the red side, sticking a little better to the pale. She still couldn't tell what she was looking at. It didn't make any sense.

It was the mouth and eye holes that gave it away.

"Oh, duh. Mask."

That explained the rubbery feel and Jell-O-like wiggliness whenever she flipped it over. Somebody had sent in a Halloween mask. Maybe even homemade — that would be pretty original as far as fan art went. They would have to feature this one in the next "Shout-Outs" for sure.

She skimmed her nails over the Saran wrap until she ran across the little bump that indicated the fold. Picked at it. It was really stuck on there.

Finally, a corner stripped away from the rest, something weirdly reminiscent of dropping a piece of bacon into a pan in the sound. Maybe she was hungrier than she'd realized.

As the plastic wrap came away from the mask, the putrid stink she'd been smelling wafted up from it. Stronger now. A mix of roadkill and sushi. Juice dripped out of it, pitter-pattering like rain on the forgotten bubble wrap.

At the back of her mind, Andi realized she was gagging. The stench. The dripping. The feel of that thing against her palms.

It wasn't latex. Wasn't a mask at all.

It was skin. Human skin.

The flesh shook wetly in her hand as she started trembling. The tote, envelopes, and piles of letters appeared and disappeared through the mouth and eye holes.

A face.

She was holding a human face in her bare hand.

CHAPTER 1

Camera flashes glinted against the plastic wrap stretched over the detached face. Techs circled around, photographing and filming. Documenting every detail.

Somehow that splayed flap of human skin seemed to take up the entire table. A wad of discarded bubble wrap sat nearby, opened letters stacked to either side, a big gray and green tote behind.

But the face was the showpiece. The main attraction. Everything else faded into the background.

Loshak stood at the edge of the remodeled kitchenette, watching the CSIs work.

"So did you have to do a lot of fancy talking to get the top brass to let you come out here?" Spinks asked from beside him.

"Not at all." Loshak smirked a little. "ASAC Morris took one look at the case notes you sent me and agreed the FBI should offer assistance due to the quote, 'unusual nature of the package.'"

"'Unusual nature of the package,' huh?" Spinks repeated, glancing over to where the techs were working. "That's a bit of an understatement."

"I'm just lucky Morris didn't barf on my loafers. Desk jockeys like him tend to have weak stomachs and are only too glad to have someone like me between them and the really weird cases."

They parted to make way for a tech with a clipboard.

"OK, so… Dahmer," Spinks said, lifting one finger from his cardboard coffee cup and pointing at the poster on the wall. "Then you've got your Bundy. And don't forget Green River's Gary Ridgway. I didn't even know you could get his poster. I could've had him up on my wall in twenty-four by thirty-six this whole time."

Loshak tipped his head left and then right as if he were considering the options.

"You've got to have a specific palette to pull off this look."

He glanced away from the techs documenting the scene long enough to indicate the color choices in the kitchenette-cum-podcasting studio. Reds. Blacks. Garish colors that spoke to the ancient parts of the human mind. Colors that screamed danger, violence, death.

Spinks shook his head.

"Honestly, I'm a little disappointed in the lack of Leatherfaces. No monument to horror is complete without one."

"There was one in the hall as we came in," Loshak said.

The reporter let out an *aha,* eyebrows stretching up toward his smooth brown scalp, and strode back out into the hall.

Loshak turned back to the whirlwind of activity. Spinks was playing it cool, but he also hadn't so much as glanced in the direction of the face since they had come in. Loshak understood. There was something deeply disturbing about being in the same room with an object that had once been a part of a human. Recently, too, if the coloration and apparent lack of significant decomposition was any indication.

Just last month, Loshak had been in an antique store with Jan when the owner had taken them aside to show off her pride and joy — the scalp of a cavalry soldier from just after the Civil War.

But the scalp hadn't had the same power of place this face had. Loshak had already walked by it twice when the proprietor pointed it out to them. He had glimpsed the small handwritten index card in the corner of its display case, filed away the information, and dismissed it. Jan had been looking for CorningWare, not mummified scalps.

The face, however, couldn't be ignored. Even when Loshak squared his shoulders in the opposite direction, he could feel it there, like a constant low vibration or a radiator putting off heat. It was almost like the face itself was dangerous. Like for his own protection, he had to keep track of where it was at all times.

So what was the difference? he wondered. Why had he been able to casually brush the scalp aside but not the face? Because it was so fresh?

He shivered a little at the word.

Fresh meat.

"Alright, I've figured it out," Spinks announced upon his return. "They went with the Dewey Decimal style of interior decoration. In here we have the Non-Fiction section." He indicated the walls covered in posters of serial killers, then pointed at the stub of a hallway. "And out there we have the Fiction section. It's a simple, yet bold style that makes a statement. Some might say the ultimate statement."

The reporter was doing one of his bits. Loshak knew the pause was meant for him. You couldn't have a comedy duo without a straight man. Since he also knew it made Spinks feel better to joke around at a time like this, he obliged.

"And what statement is that exactly?"

Spinks raised his hands, coffee clamped between his thumb and forefinger, and spread them in the air like he was framing a lit marquee.

"*Scare me.*"

Loshak grunted.

"I was thinking something along the same lines."

He hooked the flaps of his suit jacket back and stuck his hands on his hips before he went on.

"Podcasts like this *All Murder* one have become incredibly popular in recent years, but they're just the latest iteration of the cavemen telling scary stories around the fire. The danger is removed, but the thought of it still sends a shiver down the spine. They offer a look at death from a safe distance."

"Ah yes. Living vicariously through the death of someone else." Spinks took a sip of his coffee. "I'm going to find a way to use that when I write the book about how you solved this one."

"If we solve this one."

"Come on, partner, don't be modest. Special Agent Victor Loshak always gets his man."

Loshak shook his head.

"You're forgetting one very important detail: This time, we've got a face with no body. That's a new one."

"Yeah, but how hard could it be to match it to a body? It'll be the one missing this area."

Spinks made a circular motion around his face.

"Ah, see, you've been spoiled by our previous cases,"

Loshak said. "Those bodies were more or less handed to us by killers who either explicitly wanted us to find them or at least made no attempt to hide their crimes. It's a different puzzle altogether when the killer doesn't *want* a body to be found. There are an infinite number of hiding places to choose from. Landfills. Condemned buildings. Lakes and rivers. Remote wilderness. And that's not even taking into account the possibility of it having been buried, fully dismembered, or otherwise altered and disposed of in an attempt to keep us from ever IDing it."

He couldn't help but picture it: Somewhere out there was a dead body with its face cut off.

The question was: where? In a dumpster, surrounded by rotting trash? At the bottom of a reservoir, weighed down with cement blocks? Tucked into a shallow grave in someone's crawlspace?

The truth was, it could be hidden anywhere. And yet he understood the reporter's presumption that the body would have to be found. It felt deeply wrong — impossible, even — imagining that a crime this grotesque and shocking might go unsolved. That they might find a face and nothing else.

"I'll tell you what we need," Spinks said, barely hiding the grin behind his coffee cup. "More information."

Loshak snorted.

"That we do."

CHAPTER 2

"I downloaded a couple episodes of the podcast," Spinks said. "Listened to one on the way over."

The reporter's coffee was long gone. So was the face. Carefully documented, bagged, and stowed in the refrigerator of the mobile crime lab van to slow the breakdown of any blood or tissue evidence they might glean from it. Piece by piece, the mundane paper and plastic mail followed — photographed, processed.

The operation dragged while the tension mounted. Every now and then, Loshak caught a tech side-eyeing the serial killers on the wall. Something upsetting in seeing this neat, clean, commercialized worship of the darkest urges in human nature juxtaposed with the real thing.

"I can see why it's popular. The podcast, I mean."

Spinks was a little less desperate to make jokes now that the face was out of the room. He'd let the silence build over the last half hour, forty-five minutes before breaking it.

"The details of the crimes are so… striking, I guess. And then the podcasters are sort of insightful. This Andi Wayland especially. I'm not saying she could be a profiler, but she knows her stuff. They've got the comic relief, too. One of the guys — Jack? Jim? Yeah, it's Jim, because she's always calling him Jimbo. Anyway, Jimbo's pretty funny, considering the subject matter. He's got this shtick where he hears one detail that sticks out — for some reason, there's always one ridiculous detail per crime — and he goes off on a rant about it. Calls it his 'OK, imagine this' section. Like, 'OK, imagine this: You're the courthouse guard on duty for Ted Bundy, a man already convicted of kidnapping one woman and suspected of killing a dozen or so others across five states, and you're in the library while he's researching, and you see him pick out this book on horses, and you're like, everything seems fine here. I should go get a drink from the water fountain and leave him completely unguarded...' He goes way over the top, though, really sells the ridiculousness of it. It's hard to recreate out of context."

Loshak canted his head.

"Makes it accessible to a wider audience — the people who want the scare, but who need the break in tension to keep listening. Jan's like that. Can't watch a scary movie unless there's an element of comedy in it. Or like some ironic angle."

"Otherwise it gets too overstimulating?"

"No, I don't think so. She says it gives her something to hang onto when she gets scared in the middle of the night. Like a point of ridiculousness she can refer back to. It lets her think, 'Wait, that couldn't have been scary, because I laughed here, here, and here.'"

Loshak shrugged. Took a lukewarm coffee sip. Then he went on.

"*All Murder* didn't have that in the first couple seasons. It was just Wayland by herself, really delving into the horror of the crimes." Loshak thought back to the episodes he had listened to on the flight. "She brought in Jimbo somewhere around the end of season two, beginning of season three."

Spinks grinned at him.

"Somebody's done their homework."

Loshak shrugged.

"I had a layover in Chicago. Seven hours."

"Ouch. Not my favorite airport, either."

"Decent podcast, though, right?" Spinks stuck his hands in the pockets of his khakis. "I'd listen to it while I did the dishes."

Loshak shrugged again.

"I'd listen to it if I forgot my readers on a long layover."

"Readers? As in reading glasses?" The reporter snorted and shook his head. "You're really getting into this old man thing, huh?"

"I am old."

Over near the table, plastic crinkled as a bunny-suited tech splayed the bubble wrap flat to make sure they weren't missing anything. Empty. Another dug into the empty mailer with mini tongs and released the tension that held them closed. They sprung open, separating the sides and allowing her to peer inside.

"So am I," Spinks said, "but I invested in bifocal contacts to retain the illusion of youth and vitality. I don't wear a pair of reading glasses on a pearl chain."

"Neither do I. That's how I forgot them."

If Loshak remembered right, they were sitting on his night table.

"So, what, did you have to do the trombone with the case file?" Spinks demonstrated holding reading material at various distances from his face while squinting. "Or did you just—"

"Hey!" the tech with the mini tongs yelled. The shout

wavered a little, maybe surprised by her own volume. She dialed it back to standard inside voice. "We've got something here. In the envelope."

Spines around the room jolted upright. Hunched Tyvek suits straightening, heads turning to reveal faces. Something in the motion reminded Loshak of those paintings of hunting dogs at sunrise, their heads turning toward their owners, giving the impression of excitement and eagerness and earnestness all at once.

The chatter picked up as the swarm descended on the tong-bearing tech. A few stray questions rang out of the throng, and a few people reminded the tech of proper procedure. Sounded like she was a newbie to the team. Hell of a first case, if so.

At the center of it all, the tech took a deep breath, then slowly pulled her tongs out of the mailer. Her hands shook a little, making the folded paper at the end of the metal tool quiver.

She swallowed, went to say something, then stopped like her mouth had gotten stuck. One of the other techs made the announcement for her.

"It's a note."

CHAPTER 3

Loshak and Spinks stayed back while the note was photographed and documented. From across the room, the agent could see that it was just a few words scribbled in red pen on a piece of notebook paper. He had pretty decent distance vision, but he couldn't make it out just yet.

Anxiousness settled into Loshak's stomach while he waited to get a look. Acid reflux climbing his throat. A subtle sting ascending all the way to the back of his tongue. It tasted like bad pizza sauce. Sour and cloying.

The process of logging the evidence dragged on, the tech confirming every step with her superior before committing to it. It was the right move for a newbie, to do everything within her power to cut down on possible chain of custody errors. The kind of things that might seem small after twelve hours of combing a scene, but that could destroy an otherwise airtight case when the defense presented it in a courtroom.

Loshak's arms wouldn't stay still. They were restless, a little jumpy. He crossed them, contracting the muscles like some kind of reptilian constrictor that could squeeze the antsy feeling out.

But that only moved the restless sensation to his legs. He shifted his weight from foot to foot and exhaled. There was a hint of frustration in the sound.

He wanted to see that dang note. Get an idea of what they were working with. The fact that this killer had sent a note at all told them a lot.

With a jolt of sudden awareness, Loshak realized Spinks was talking, and he wasn't listening. He turned toward the reporter.

"What was that?"

"I was just saying, it's always notes with these serial killers. Zodiac, Son of Sam, BTK…"

Loshak thought about it.

"I was going to say we didn't know yet whether this was a serial killer, but the note is significant. You rarely see it with a single homicide. Except in outlier cases like opportunistic copycats trying to cover up a murder by disguising it as another in a string. Legitimate attempts to convey messages to the authorities are almost exclusive to the attention-seeking type of serial killer. The act itself poses an extreme risk. It's innately aggressive."

"They're like the Letters to the Editor of the violent crimes world," Spinks said. "Never anything nice to say, but they just can't keep it to themselves."

"Exactly. In some ways, it's advantageous for us that they do it. That drive for attention and acknowledgment often leads to these killers getting caught. But there's a negative side, too. The attention-seeking types tend to rack up the body count quickly."

Spinks dragged his attention away from the flurry around the note to lock eyes with Loshak.

"You think there'll be more?"

Loshak hesitated. There was always the possibility this would be it. That it was all a fluke, and the note was some kind of confession. Or it could also be that the guy would disappear for years before surfacing again, like BTK.

But he knew those were unlikely scenarios. None of the statistics pointed that way.

He nodded.

A raised voice cut through the hushed atmosphere of the apartment, something sharp in the formant.

"Agent Loshak."

The lead CSI waved them over.

The sea of bunny suits parted, allowing the agent and the reporter to belly up to the table.

The note had been slipped into a numbered evidence baggie, splayed open like a euthanized moth in a collection, wings pinned out wide so the pattern was on full display. The message took up the full spread from left to right in dark, slanting letters.

IT BEGAN LIKE ANY OTHER DAY...

CHAPTER 4

The fervor over the note had died off slowly but surely, and the cataloging eased back to the usual lumbering pace. Someone in a bunny suit noted that it was after two and suggested an intern go for Subway. The motion passed unanimously.

Loshak turned to Spinks.

"I think it's time we talk to Andi Wayland."

A few uniforms had been hovering around the edges of the scene, keeping the stairway outside clear, checking credentials, and moving residents along, while a local detective sat with the podcaster in a side room on the other end of the apartment.

In theory, they would have kept the woman in a nice, quiet room where she could give them a report and calm down from what she'd seen. If what Loshak heard as he headed past the bathroom to the back bedroom was any indication, though, the detective and Andi Wayland were locked in there with a bunch of angry banshees.

Loshak grabbed the handle and opened the door.

"Wait!" A man's voice shouted from the other side. "Don't let the—"

A striped ball of fur shoved its way between the agent's legs, knocking him off balance and leaving a thick patch of cat hair on the cuff of his black pants. He bumped against the wall.

The cat gave a rolling chirp as it darted toward the

crime scene on feet almost hidden by its gut.

The detective who'd yelled from inside the room scampered through the doorway. Broad shoulders. Dark features. His head swiveled as he hit the hallway, and his eyes narrowed when they locked onto the loose cat.

"Shit, grab that thing!"

The detective lunged past Loshak and snatched at the overweight monster.

Loshak twisted and reached for the beast at the same moment. His head cracked against the detective's.

The agent hissed and jerked away, pressing his fingers to the pain sinking into his brow ridge. Embarrassment followed hard on its heels.

The detective dropped the rest of the way to the ground, kneeling with his hand pressed to his temple.

"Aw, who's this little guy?" Spinks's knees cracked as he crouched and effortlessly scooped the massive cat into his arms.

"Sanford." A young woman in a gauzy top appeared in the doorway, arms wrapped around her stomach. "Sorry. He wants his food bowl. We gave him some food in one of the cereal bowls, but he won't touch it."

She looked at the floor, blinking rapidly. The quiet seemed to swell in the hallway in the few seconds before she spoke again.

"He likes his routine. He can't understand why we won't give him his bowl until the whole kitchenette's been… you know… processed. Sorry," she repeated.

"You're a chonky boy, aren't you, Sanford? Yes, you are."

Spinks bounced the ball of fur on his hip like a baby,

ignoring its attempts to wriggle its way out of his arms. He scratched the cat's chin.

The downed detective stabilized himself with a hand on the wall and pushed back to his feet.

"Son of a bitch, that was a hit." He jerked his chin at Loshak. "What are you, a lineman for the Broncos?"

Great way to open a working relationship with the locals. Loshak took a step back and relaxed his posture, hoping to subconsciously diffuse some of this guy's hostility.

"Unfortunately, I remain undrafted," Loshak said.

He guessed the detective was somewhere in his early forties, late thirties; he might react best to the "old man" excuse, even though Loshak was only ten or fifteen years his senior.

"Sorry about the collision. I don't catch runaway pets the way I used to."

He stuck out a hand, subtly leaning his upper body back as he did. The brain tended to interpret forward motion as aggressive.

"Special Agent Victor Loshak, first string profiler, fourth string tackle. This is Jevon Spinks. He's a consultant with the FBI."

The detective shook Loshak's hand. A knot was already forming over his eyebrow.

"Detective Jason Aque, Denver PD. So, are you feds here for something besides letting the cat out of the room?"

"We also provide cat-catching services," Spinks said, raising the head and arms of the now-purring ball of fur a little as if to back up his claim. "You might say our net footprint is cat-neutral."

He offered the calmed monster back to its owner.

Andi Wayland took it with fingers stained black; she'd been printed to rule out her prints from the package. The muscles of her arms bulged a little as she caught the tabby's full weight.

"We were hoping to speak to Ms. Wayland."

Loshak framed it as a request, both for the detective's and the podcaster's benefit. To varying degrees, both had been thrown into situations where control had been yanked out from under them. The illusion of being able to refuse might lessen the feeling of helplessness and disorientation.

Detective Aque nodded. Then he swept his hand toward the open doorway.

"Room's yours. I'll be right out here if you need me, Ms. Wayland."

"Thanks."

She gave the detective a weak attempt at a smile over the bulk in her arms. A spasm of the lips. She looked like she might throw up at any second.

Loshak mirrored Aque's gesture toward the bedroom.

"After you."

She walked into the room on legs that looked slightly wobbly. Loshak and Spinks followed, the reporter shutting the door with a quiet *click* behind them.

Immediately, Sanford the cat pushed off his owner's chest and ran for the closed-off exit, yelling and stretching his wide body until his paws almost touched the door handle.

"Not a happy camper, that one," Spinks observed. "But neither am I when I'm hangry."

The girl made a sound that wasn't quite a laugh and smiled more convincingly.

"He's always been that way. I'm trying to help him lose some weight. Cut back a little on the overeating, but it's hard, you know? One, you want to give your pet whatever he wants, but two, there's the noise."

"The shrill squawking *is* hard to ignore."

Spinks managed to put her at ease with the cat talk, but it didn't last. As soon as he stopped speaking, the podcaster went silent, holding her elbows and looking around the room like she wasn't sure where she was.

"You can make yourself comfortable," Loshak said, keeping his tone light, making it a suggestion rather than an order. "This isn't anything formal. We're just here to ask a few questions about what you found."

Two chairs had been pulled into the bedroom and a night table commandeered to act as a desk during the report process.

She swallowed.

"I don't think I've been called Ms. Wayland before in my life," she said. "That definitely makes it feel formal. Like I got called into the principal's office or something. Uh, but I guess you're being polite, right? You can call me Andi. Everybody else does. Even people I've never met. Like when they recognize me in the grocery store."

She plopped onto the edge of the bed. Shook her head.

"God, that sounded conceited. Sorry. I don't think I'm an A-list celebrity or anything. *All Murder* does really well nowadays — for a podcast. We've got upwards of a million regular listeners at this point, even though not all of them are subscribers. But we've also been doing the video thing for a while now, so we get recognized sometimes in public. Not just me. Jim, me, Mel does less frequently because she's not on a lot, but she has tons of followers on Insta."

Andi made that not-quite-laugh sound again.

"Even Sanford's got a fan club at this point."

"I can see why." The reporter pulled his chair over to the door and started scratching the angry cat behind the ears. "I'm already a fan, and we just barely met. I love a big personality."

Loshak took a seat on the opposite side of the night table.

"So, with that size of community, you must get a lot of fan mail."

"I mean, most of it comes in the form of emails, ats on social media, that kind of thing. We don't get a ton of snail mail, but it's a lot compared to…"

Her voice wavered and she stopped. She pressed her fingertips to her eyes.

"Augh! This is so stupid. I read about this stuff all the time. I tell millions of people about it every week."

Tears slicked her eyelids and wet her lashes as she continued to rub them. Her voice quavered when she finished her thought.

"It's just so different when it's you."

Loshak gave her a second to calm down. When she was breathing normally again, he went on.

"Have you ever gotten anything creepy before? In the mail, I mean."

Her eyes met his, but she couldn't maintain the eye contact for very long. She stared at nothing as she spoke.

"Well, yeah. It's part of the job, right? Not like we ask

for people to send us this stuff, of course, but there's an air of general creepiness to the whole true crime sphere. I think that's what draws them in." She hugged her elbows with her ink-stained fingers. "But yeah, I guess there have been a handful of notable items. This one guy sent a tooth that he claimed he got from Bradley Michael Jessup — you know who that is?"

Loshak nodded.

"Serial killer from Idaho."

"Oh, duh, right. FBI. God. Sorry, I'll stop treating you like a kindergartener."

"Don't worry about it," Loshak said. "Jessup's definitely among the lesser known of the cases I've seen. So, you said a 'handful' of creepy items. What else have people sent you?"

He sensed she was feeling conflicted if not outright guilty — as if the podcast were somehow to blame — so he made it a point to emphasize the *sending* of the items versus the *receiving* of the items. The last thing he wanted was for her to feel like she was being accused of something.

"Things like a tuft of hair taped to an index card, supposedly from Charles Manson's beard," she said. "Someone bought us a John Wayne Gacy clown painting. An Ed Kemper signature on some notebook paper. I don't know if any of it's legit. The painting could be; Gacy did tons of them. We never got any of that stuff authenticated or anything. It's not real high on the priority list. But like… hair taped to an index card is sort of creepy no matter where it came from, right?"

She shrugged and squeezed her arms tighter around herself. Then she swallowed.

28

"There was also a video of Leonard Lake and Charles Ng. It was fairly benign — no gore or violence or anything — but still disturbing somehow. And we get a couple of authentic serial killer letters a year. A lot of these guys like to correspond with their 'fans,' and the letters go for a stack on eBay."

"Did you feel like any of the items sent to you were threatening, either to you or another member of the podcast?"

"No. Our community is really supportive. Every now and then someone will pass through pulling a bullshit prank or trying to be edgy, but they get booted pretty fast."

"Do you happen to have any information on any of these pranksters? Names or emails?"

Andi nodded.

"Mel keeps a record of everybody blocked or booted. She's our secretary, administrative assistant, whatever you want to call it. She keeps track of everything on the back end so Jim and I can focus on writing and prepping the episodes."

The podcaster pulled out her phone.

"I can get you her number."

"Thank you."

Loshak noted the trembling in her fingers as she found the information for her assistant.

Based on what Wayland was saying, this was going to be a lot to sift through. Her initial impressions were probably right — most of the pranksters probably had nothing to do with the case. But one might. They couldn't rule anything out yet.

"So, Andi," Loshak said once he had the administrative

assistant's number saved, "about the note in the package..."

Her eyes got bigger, and she sounded faint.

"A note? I didn't see anything inside but the— I couldn't see past *it*, you know?"

"There was a note still in the mailer. It said, 'It began like any other day.' Does that have any significance to you or maybe to anybody else at the podcast?"

"Oh, God."

Andi pressed her hand to her mouth, breathing noisily through her nose for a second. Her eyes teared up again, and her whole body started shaking. She let her hand drop onto the bed beside her.

"Do you think he did it because of the podcast? He killed somebody because of us?"

Loshak shook his head, though truthfully, they couldn't rule that out with an attention-seeker. But he needed to put her at ease if they were going to get any more information from her.

"Do you recognize that turn of phrase? Does it mean anything to you?"

"Yeah."

Her voice cracked, and she cleared her throat.

"It's the intro we recorded for season five. *It began like any other day...* then slasher scream queen. Then we go straight into me talking about our first victim. We always start with the victims because, like, we want to put the emphasis on these being human people whose lives were cut off in the middle, unthinkably. But also because listeners can identify. There's a level of suspense knowing it's always going to be the victim there at the beginning, and a level of 'what would I do?'"

She sniffed and scrubbed at her nose with a white-knuckled fist.

"But what if we got some sicko all hyped up to kill somebody?"

Loshak glanced around the room. No tissues he could offer.

"Andi," he said, locking eyes with her so she would know he was sincere. "There's nothing you could have done to push somebody else into murder. That is always a choice they make. I'm sure you've read cases where the killers blame their upbringing or their environment or even a barking dog—"

She gave a half-hearted laugh at the reference.

"But lots of people live through horrific abuse and brutal circumstances, and they don't go on killing sprees. Serial killers make a choice, and that choice is on them, no one else. Not you. Not *All Murder*. Just them."

"You can say that, and maybe it's even true, but none of this exists in a vacuum. If something we said on the podcast served as some kind of inspiration… if we were the catalyst… how are we *not* partially responsible?"

Loshak didn't think pointing out the flaws in that logic would be very effective. What she was feeling wasn't tied to rationality. There was nothing sensible or reasonable about getting a disembodied face in the mail, about holding that piece of human skin in your hand knowing there was a body somewhere with its muscle and bone and nerves open to the sky.

But Spinks slipped into the conversation before Loshak could formulate a response.

He put a comforting hand on the podcaster's shoulder. His voice was soft but filled with the kind of determination that came through loud and clear at any volume.

"We're going to catch this guy. We're going to go through every last piece of evidence we can get to do it. Whether that's the human evidence, video timestamps, physical puzzle pieces left behind… Whatever it takes to get a clear picture of this guy, we'll use it. We will stop him."

He paused a second, and the quiet in the room seemed suddenly bigger.

"We'll stop him so he won't do this to anyone ever again."

CHAPTER 5

Spinks drove them toward the station after a quick stop off at a Dunkin' Donuts for Loshak to grab his customary offering. They weren't the fancy, gourmet breakfast pastries lovingly hand-crafted by a struggling small bakery owner that he preferred, but after a few times showing up to task force meetings empty-handed, they were better than nothing. The box balanced on Loshak's knees as they coasted along with the afternoon traffic.

Out the window, Denver's neighborhoods passed by in layers, like a drive-through history. Denver had been founded by prospectors back in the late 1850s and quickly bloated into the third-largest city in the West with the arrival of the railroads a few years later. All that had fallen apart when the government passed the Silver Purchase Act in an attempt to close the gap between the value of silver and gold, and Denver had been forced to diversify to survive. The stockyards and breweries sprang up — Coors being the most notable and long-lived of that group — creating neighborhoods like the Dairy Block where Andi Wayland lived.

Gas and oil companies started moving in after World War II, but it wasn't until the 1970s that the skyscrapers started growing up, marking Denver's next big boom-and-bust businesses — telecom and energy. They'd left their mark on the city, both in the skyline and the surrounding urban sprawl that spread out for miles when the price of oil plummeted in the late 80s.

The city was like a living, breathing thing that kept adapting and changing. First the Arapaho settlements were destroyed by the cavalry, leaving the remaining prospectors to build up their little shantytown on their own. Then the railroad boomtown had been built over with Victorian houses that had probably been the height of wealth and status at the time. Now the architectural survivors of that era were being torn down and replaced with twenty-story luxury condos. Geographical sociologists would say that it never ended, it only shifted.

"You ever see that movie *Shazaam*?"

Spinks's question came out of nowhere. Loshak had to rack his brain for a minute to get it back from the ever-changing landscape of Colorado.

"Uh, maybe?"

"It's the one with the kid who gets a genie. Sinbad was in it."

"I might've watched it with my daughter." Loshak frowned. "But didn't Shaq play the genie?"

Spinks shot him a knowing look.

"Shaq, huh? You're from here, then."

That definitely had the ring of a setup.

"Nope."

Loshak rubbed dry eyes. His lips were starting to feel dry and tight, too. He knew Denver was technically semiarid high plains, but the lack of moisture in the air snuck up on a person. One minute you were fine, the next you were human jerky.

"I'm from Virginia."

"I didn't mean you were from Denver, I meant you

were from this universe. The one where *Kazaam* was the original genie movie — starring Shaq — instead of being just a cheap knock-off of *Shazaam*, which everybody knows starred Sinbad."

Loshak grabbed his water bottle out of the cup holder.

"Alright, I'll bite. What do other universes have to do with movies?"

"Have you ever heard of the Mandela Effect?"

"Yeah, it's the thing where people misremember when Nelson Mandela died."

Spinks stuck up a finger.

"Or it's the thing where people remember when Mandela died in *their universe.* In this universe, he died in 2013 from complications from cancer, but in other universes, he died in the 80s in prison. Millions of people around the world remember watching his funeral on TV. Some of them can quote his widow's speech — that's how well they remember it."

"Has anyone ever gotten two people who've never spoken to one another to say the same lines from her speech in separate interviews?"

Spinks grinned.

"I knew you'd be skeptical, partner. Let's come at this from a different angle. Remember those kids' books about the Bear family? With Papa Bear, Mama Bear, Brother Bear, and Sister Bear?"

"Yeah, Shelly had a couple. She wasn't big on them. She liked the Mercer Mayer books better."

"Well, Davin loved those damn Bears. I read him one of those books every single night, except when I was on location. Now, riddle me this, Special Agent Loshak:

Would I have forgotten the name of a book series I read every night?"

"Depends on what kind of long-term memory you've got."

Spinks grinned.

"Excellent is what kind I've got, and I wouldn't have made up the name Beren*stein* Bears after ten years of reading the Beren*stain* Bears."

"Maybe you've been mispronouncing it this whole time."

"I think I know my E-Is from my A-Is."

"Alright, Old MacDonald. What's your point?"

"My point is, millions of people besides me independently have the same memories. There's your independent corroboration."

Loshak took a slug of water. He couldn't get behind it.

"Humans as a race are too good at forgetting details and replacing them with new ones. When you have eight billion of them consuming the same movies and news bites and books, you're bound to get a scattered percentage who patch their incorrect memories of the same things in the same ways."

"We're not talking a scattered percentage here," Spinks said, taking a hand off the wheel to gesticulate. "We're talking probably fifty percent of people who remember it as 'Berenstein' instead of 'Berenstain.' And you want to know what else?" He shot Loshak a sidelong look out of the corner of his shades. "I've seen a VHS tape labeled *The Berenstein Bears,* not Berenstain. E-I. Right there on the worn red and yellow face label. Probably the only piece of evidence that came over with us Berenstein truthers."

Loshak snorted.

"And I've seen entire police departments with the city's name spelled wrong on their insignia. You wouldn't believe the kinds of things people don't double-check before they ask for a print run. Case in point: My dad grew up in this little town where a guy on the city council didn't double-check the spelling of the street names when he ordered new street signs. Rutherford became Rutheford, Owensby turned into Owenby, North Stillings became North Stilings, things like that. Dad made fun of that guy until the day he died — all the old folks in town did. But now that generation's gone. There's no city record saying John Doe screwed up in the late seventies when he reordered the street signs, and there was a fire back in '68 that destroyed most of City Hall and the surveyor's office next door."

Loshak shifted the donut box on his knees, checking to make sure the grease wasn't leaking through onto his suit pants. He didn't want to have to waste time looking for a dry cleaner.

"Someday, someone in the generation after me is going to think, 'Hey, my grandma always swore that street was *Owens*by Street, not *Owen*by. Must be the Mandela Effect!' Then they'll look and realize that there aren't any town surveys in the computer before 1968. Suddenly it's evidence for the conspiracy. The records must've been left behind in the other universe."

Spinks raised his eyebrows.

"How do you know they weren't, and everyone in that little town didn't just create memories of the guy screwing up the forms so they could cope?"

Loshak leaned back in his seat.

The station was just down the block, a blocky red brick building with banks of black tinted window banks and a courtyard gated by an almost Medieval-looking spiked iron fence.

"OK, let's say for a minute it's true. If so, what are all these people from another universe doing in my universe? How'd they get here?"

Spinks checked his mirrors and flipped on his blinker to pull into the turn lane.

"There's some debate on that, but the most popular theory has to do with CERN. See, most people who have alternate timeline memories have them before the first time they fired up the Large Hadron Collider — to the day."

"So they're saying it, what, tore a hole in the space-time continuum?"

"Don't be silly. It just shifted half of the population here from the other universe."

The light turned green, and Spinks swung them around the corner. On this side, the brickwork had been painted over in a mural of people crossing the street, some with skateboards in hand, others in wheelchairs or walking dogs. *The streets belong to the people* was emblazoned across the top.

"I assume that means that somewhere there's an alternate Jevon Spinks and Victor Loshak arguing about how it's actually Berenstain Bears, not Berenstein."

"Bingo."

Spinks guided the rental down a narrow back alley and into the station parking lot. Smile lines crinkled around his eyes as he went on.

"But since they're versions of us with everything the

same except the Berenstain Bears, they're probably not getting anywhere, either."

Loshak huffed a laugh. Most of the time, he couldn't tell whether Spinks believed his own riffs, but the reporter was definitely enjoying himself.

Spinks shut the car off and craned his neck to look at the other parking lot entrance across from them. It opened directly onto the street, without any one-way squeezes.

"Well, that was a convoluted way to get us here. We could've turned a block back."

He shut off the map on his phone, took it out of the holder, and pointed it at Loshak.

"So you're telling me there's no way in hell you'll ever admit that the Mandela Effect is more than people screwing up the details in their memory?"

"I'll tell you what would make me believe it," Loshak said. "When someone goes through every one of you alleged 'other universe' people and records all your Mandela Effect stories. If they can show that you've all got the same memories of Berenstein and Sinbad and Nelson Mandela's death, and everybody from this universe has the same memories of Berenstain and Shaq and Mandela's death, *then* I'll believe it."

The reporter bounced the keys in his hand.

"So basically, you need more evidence?"

"If I'm going to believe something as crazy as that, yeah." Loshak swung open his door, grunting as he climbed out. "More evidence never hurt anybody."

CHAPTER 6

Loshak snagged a bottle of water from the coffee counter, then took a seat with Spinks near the back of the room. From there, he could keep an eye on the refreshment area at the center of the outside wall. A uniform was busy pulling the shades behind it, blocking out the piercing afternoon light and making it easier for Loshak to see who selected which type of donut.

The crullers were by far the most popular. Within the first five minutes of their arrival, all eight of the ribbed, airy concoctions were gone.

Although the Denver Police Department had authority over criminal investigations under Denver's Division of Public Safety, there were a few Deputy Sheriffs present as well, milling around and talking. They had shown up too late for the crullers, though. Poor bastards had to settle for a Long John or a powdery jelly-filled donut.

Spinks nodded to the front of the room.

"There's not even a podium up there. What is this madness? Who holds a task force meeting without something to stand behind?"

Loshak shrugged.

"It's a new one on me."

"Authority demands division from the rabble, a clear visual separation. At the very least something between us and them. How are we even supposed to know whose turn it is to talk?"

"My guess is they'll be the one standing up there."

Spinks shook his head.

"This is bloody anarchy."

An officer with a single star on her collar stepped inside and scanned the room. When she saw Spinks, she smiled and made a beeline for them.

"There's our informant." Spinks planted both hands on his thighs and stood. "Kate!"

"Jevon, hey, thanks for coming."

She shook hands with the reporter, then turned to Loshak.

"This must be the infamous Special Agent Loshak. District Six Commander Katherine Belte. Thank you for taking time out of your busy schedule to come out to Colorado. I know a dismembered body part isn't much to go on, but I've listened to lectures of yours detailing the different types of multiple murder cases. As soon as I got the call, I was positive we were looking at a thrill seeker type."

Loshak nodded.

"Based on what we've seen so far, I'm inclined to agree. Thanks for having us, Commander Belte. This is something of a first for me, getting invited to join a case by a friend of Spinks's. I didn't realize anybody else in law enforcement could stomach members of the press."

Commander Belte chuckled.

"Well, the truth is, I almost made the same bad call Jevon did. We started out in journalism school together, but I dodged the bullet at the last minute, switched my major to criminal justice."

"You know, a lesser man would take a whole lot of

offense right now," Spinks said. "But I think I'll let your student loans decide which one of us made a bad call."

"Ouch." She grinned and turned her wrist over to check her watch. "I'm going to get this meeting going before I take any more hits like that. Make yourselves comfortable. We've got a lot of tedious procedural stuff to get out of the way up front, then we'll hear from a representative of the post office. Then, if you're amenable, Agent Loshak, I'd really love for you to talk to us about what you've gotten so far from the scene."

Loshak was a little thrown by Belte's choice of words. *What he'd gotten from the scene* made it sound like he was some kind of psychic receiving transmissions from the other side. Not the sort of language he was used to hearing from higher ranking law enforcement. But then journalism school to law enforcement wasn't exactly a standard career track, either.

"Shouldn't be a problem. I've got some preliminary thoughts I can share."

"Great."

The task force meeting got underway. The division of labor breakdown, chain of command, communications procedures, and prohibition on disclosing information to outsiders were all standard points Loshak had heard in a thousand different meeting rooms over the years. What got Loshak's attention was when Commander Belte started talking about HALO, the High Activity Location Observation surveillance cameras set up at intersections, tourism hotspots, and other public spaces around the city.

"Thanks to the speedy response of the USPS, we've got a mailing location — a post office in Globeville." She glanced at Spinks and Loshak. "A working-class suburb of Denver near I-70. We've got somebody retrieving HALO footage from the date on the package as we speak, and the Postal Inspection Service assures me that we will have access to their internal footage as well. I don't have to tell any of you how effective HALO's been over the last fifteen years. If we can get a quick ID on our mailer, we can wrap this up before he offs somebody else."

Loshak had followed the successes of Denver's HALO cameras off and on. The city was particularly proud of the rise in drug convictions and subsequent drop in criminal activity their installation had caused. What didn't get mentioned as often was the shift of that activity to new, less monitored locations, and the constant additions of new cameras required to keep up the conviction rate. Still, like Spinks had told Andi Wayland, if it got this guy off the streets, Loshak would take any evidence they could get their hands on.

"With that in mind," Commander Belte said, "let's hear from Postal Inspector Randall."

A heavyset balding man with a thick handlebar mustache took the commander's place at the front of the room. Rather than the standard postal service blues, he wore a badge and suit jacket with an obvious sidearm bulge. All in all, he looked more like a detective knocking on the door of retirement than an employee of the USPS.

Spinks shifted in his chair, leaning closer to whisper to Loshak without taking his eyes off the inspector.

"They let postal workers carry guns now?"

"The United States Postal Inspection Service is technically a federal law enforcement agency."

"But imagine the 90s comedian jokes. Stuff about expediting postal worker mental breakdowns and going postal." Spinks turned his palms up and jerked them back and forth, mimicking an *are you seeing what I'm seeing?* gesture. "There'd be a lot of this going on, on stage."

Similar whispered discussions seemed to have sprung up around the room. Postal Inspector Randall cleared his throat, bringing them to a standstill.

"Like Commander Belte said, my office tracked the package's origin back to the US Post Office location in Globeville, on 46th Avenue. That's significant because it means the guy actually walked onto federal property to commit mail crime."

Spinks slapped a hand over his mouth, his eyes watering.

When Loshak raised an eyebrow at him, Spinks whispered, "Mail crime!" his voice wavering with a barely contained snicker.

Up front, Randall went on, oblivious.

"The timestamp in the code puts mailing at four days ago, nine sixteen A.M., just after lobby opening. We're having the interior and exterior footage from eight to ten sent over as we speak, in case our criminal spent some time casing the joint."

Spinks choked. A few people twisted around to look at him, but he clamped his mouth shut and put on an overly studious frown.

"He paid cash for the shipping."

Randall's face was slightly flushed now, white spots standing out here and there beneath his thinning hair, but he went on as if he didn't notice Spinks going into hysterics in the back.

"No insurance on the contents, no signature required for delivery. It was sent by two-day mail and then sat in the recipient's post office box another two days waiting for pickup. According to the superintendent of the Globeville location, it's normal for the owner of the PO box to come in once per week, at most, to collect their mail, so nothing strange about the delay."

"But it does put us several days behind our perp," said a sheriff's deputy near the front.

Spinks cleared his throat and added in a surprisingly serious tone, "It also means he might already have mailed again."

Inspector Randall nodded. The corners of his mustache twitched.

"As soon as we have him nailed down in the footage, we'll get the description out to each of the area post office mailing locations so inspectors can begin going through their own footage. See if we can't get ahead of this guy." He looked to Commander Belte. "That's all I've got for you for now."

"Thank you, Inspector."

She checked something on her phone, then returned to the head of the room.

"This is a predominantly commercial area, so we're not going to get a lot of private doorbell footage, but I spoke to the DC of District 1. He's sending officers to canvas the area in case somebody saw something or has security footage from their storefront. I also just got word that we've received the HALO footage from the intersections on either end of the post office block, so we'll add that to our evidence to sift through. Maybe we can get a hit on a vehicle, or at the very least see which way he came from and where he went when he left."

Loshak scratched his jaw. He'd told Spinks that more evidence never hurt, but the truth was, too much unrelated data masquerading as legitimate evidence could definitely slow them down. With Denver's love of surveillance, it was looking like they would have a lot to wade through. And considering that the guy could have driven from anywhere to mail the package, there was every possibility that this would turn out to be a cold lead.

But any information was better than nothing. They couldn't dismiss anything before they checked it out. Something might shake loose.

Belte consulted her notes, flipping through pages.

"On top of the surveillance footage, we've got to go over all the weird stuff our podcasters have received through the mail over the last few months—"

Inspector Randall raised a hand, three fingers up like he was about to say the Boy Scout Pledge.

"I'll have USPIS agents working with your officers on that."

"Alright." Belte scribbled something on her paper, then went on. "Heading up the fan mail, email, and online communications the podcast received in the past six months, we've got Benally and Johnson."

She looked at the officers in question and shook her head.

"Spoiler alert: There's a lot."

A Native American officer wearing a white cowboy hat shrugged.

"Hell, I wrote to 'em last month. Their podcast is the bomb."

"Jesus, Benally," his partner said. "Nobody still says 'the bomb.'"

Benally shot him the finger.

"Like you'd know."

"Moving on from Benally's terminal uncoolness," Commander Belte breezed ahead, "we've got two other members of the podcast to speak to — a Melanie Rivera and a James Nez-Kelly. Schrader and Aque, that's you."

The detective Loshak had the head-on collision with at Wayland's apartment stuck a thumbs-up in the air.

"Further assignments as details warrant," Belte said, letting the sheaf of papers drop to her side. "OK, I'm sure you've all noticed a couple of unfamiliar faces in the room. Special Agent Loshak is here on loan from the FBI." She nodded at him. "Agent, would you mind sharing your initial impressions of the killer?"

"Sure thing."

Loshak didn't have any paper notes with him for once. Just as well considering the lack of anywhere to set them. He did take his water bottle up front with him. It only had a swallow or two left, but it would give him something to do with his hands besides stick them in his pockets or cross his arms.

He looked out across the conference room, taking in the faces.

"I'm sure you've all heard of the organization of serial killers by types — organized versus disorganized, and you've got your visionary, hedonistic, power, or mission-oriented types. In reality, it's not always as cut and dry as all that, but they give us a good frame of reference to start with. Someone who mails a body part to a popular podcast along with a cryptic note would best be described as an attention-seeker. The Zodiac and BTK killers leap immediately to mind, but we may be looking at something closer to a Luka Magnotta here."

A female sheriff's deputy jerked her chin at him.

"The YouTube cat-killer guy?"

Loshak nodded.

"Magnotta started out uploading videos of himself torturing and suffocating kittens — a guaranteed way to attract attention."

"And tons of hate," the deputy said. "You can do a lot of sick stuff on the internet, but you don't want to mess with cats. The internet will lose their shit."

"That may have been the point for Magnotta. With this type of killer, they crave fame and recognition any way they can get it. If that means being hated, well… at least people are paying attention to them. And anything is better than being ignored. It's the epitome of that old adage that 'no publicity is bad publicity.'

"Understand that this is someone who feels a deep sense of separateness from other people. He sees himself as an outcast. A loner. Pushed to the outermost edge of society. But humans are social animals. To be completely solitary is against our nature. So he still seeks connection — perhaps only subconsciously — and bizarre acts like this stem from an urge to reach out to his peers. To communicate. It's backward and twisted, but there's a logic to it.

"If you followed the Magnotta case, you know that he

later went on to murder and dismember a Chinese student living in Canada. He uploaded the video to a gore site, mailed several body parts to different government buildings, including two elementary schools, then went on the run. Magnotta was finally apprehended in an internet café in Germany while googling his own name."

"Talk about an ego," Detective Aque muttered.

"While it's true that there's a level of narcissism involved, there's often a proportional level of self-loathing." Loshak tapped the water bottle on his palm. "There's some disagreement in professional circles about whether Magnotta was an organized or chaotic type, but it's likely we're looking at someone who sought psychiatric help in the past. There's a high probability that our unsub is a twenty- to thirty-year-old white male, with what he considers a major failure in his personal life. Job loss or a ruined relationship he can't get over. Things like that.

"He may have compulsive behaviors, such as nail-biting, hair-pulling, or hoarding. He likely struggles with social relationships and probably has few friends, if any, and limited contact with family. Frequently we find comorbidity with things such as insomnia, drug use, and antisocial tendencies, including an inability to stomach authority. As such, it's unlikely that he has stable employment. He's the type to move from one entry-level job to another, likewise for his place of residence, either moving from town to town, or even building to building within the same city. A nomad, if you will.

"But all that doesn't mean our killer is incapable of functioning within society. After all, the mailing shows signs of organization and planning — which is the main reason my colleagues still disagree about Magnotta's classification. The fact that nobody in the post office found our unsub any stranger or more memorable than the other people mailing packages that day means that he has enough social skills to go largely undetected in public. It's something of a contradiction, this hiding in plain sight while trying to attract attention, but mailing body parts in a city famous for having HALO cams on every public space points to thrill-seeking behavior. It could be that the risk of being caught is part of the fun for him."

Benally shook his head.

"Sick fuck. Swear to God, if we find out this asshole is killing cats too…"

"I mean, isn't that a given?" an officer asked. "All serial killers start out killing animals, right?"

Loshak pushed back his suit jacket and put his hand and water bottle on his hips.

"While it's true that many serial killers have a history of 'practicing' on small animals, that's not a certainty. Animal abuse is generally seen in those who want to exercise power over someone weaker. In many cases, that graduates to the abuse of another person, either a spouse, child, or elder, but always someone perceived as physically weaker than the abuser. The only time Ted Bundy supposedly attacked another male was when he was in his early teens, twelve to fourteen years old. He claimed he killed another boy, significantly younger than he was at the time, but that was never confirmed. Bundy didn't go after anyone who might be able to take him. So you most often see animal abuse in power-focused killers, but you occasionally get it with other types as well.

"Obviously this profile will develop as we get more evidence." Loshak did a final scan of the room. "Unless there are any questions, I think that's it."

A few beats passed in silence. Commander Belte stood up.

"Thanks, Agent Loshak." She clapped her hands together. "Alright, get out there, and get on your assignments."

Chairs screeched and papers shuffled as officers, detectives, and deputies headed for the door, some pausing to refill their coffee or snag one last pastry before leaving.

Belte gestured at Loshak and Spinks to wait. She spoke to Postal Inspector Randall, then Detective Aque and his partner Schrader, getting them to hang back, before joining Loshak and Spinks.

"Randall just got the footage from the post office," she said. "Would you two mind sticking around to review it? See if we can get enough to pick this guy out for when the HALO footage is ready?"

"Not a problem," Loshak said.

Spinks nodded.

"Let's take a look into the face of a murderer."

CHAPTER 7

Commander Belte led the five of them — Loshak, Spinks, Randall, and the pair of detectives — into a side room where another officer had the footage queued up for them on a widescreen monitor. The room wasn't small, but neither were Loshak, Spinks, or the postal inspector. There was a lot of shuffling and squeezing around office furniture and file cabinets before everybody had a spot.

"We don't normally have this many people in here," Belte said by way of apology. She patted the officer at the desk on the shoulder as she sidled past. "Suck it in, Danno."

As one of the taller entities in the room, Loshak ended up behind Randall and Belte, his body tucked awkwardly between a file cabinet and the wall. He rested an arm on the top of the file cabinet and angled his shoulders toward the screen.

"I've got the HALO footage pulled up, but the post office videos are password-protected."

"On it."

Inspector Randall leaned over Danno and brought up the USPIS portal, keying in a long sequence of letters and numbers. It took some clicking around and, Loshak thought, a pretentious number of passwords, but eventually the player opened up to show a split-screen view of a post office interior.

Folks waited in line or stood at the counter. A hand

reached for the post office door, someone out of frame grasping for the handle.

"There we go, that'll be our perp," Randall said, tapping the motionless hand. He started the footage and backed up.

Lurching into motion, the hand yanked the door open. A woman stepped into the doorway, carrying nothing, and passed from the first half of the split screen to the second to stand in line. She dug out her pocketbook and started counting out cash.

"Money order," Spinks guessed. "She's not our mailer."

Randall cleared his throat, a little red creeping up from beneath his collar.

"Well, they told me it was cued up to when our perp walked in."

"There," Detective Aque said. "We missed him. Roll it back."

The officer at the desk tapped the keyboard and restarted the footage.

The woman yanked the door open and went to stand in line while she dug out her cash. The door started to swing shut, the arc slowed by its soft-close mechanism.

Someone in a black zip-up hoodie shouldered inside before the door shut. They had a padded mailer envelope tucked under one arm.

Loshak stared at the bulging manila envelope, and something in his gut went icy cold. Inside that package was a human being's face. This guy had peeled it off somebody.

It was an eerie feeling, knowing what lay inside that thin veneer of air-padded plastic, knowing that a bit of tape and adhesive was all that held it in. Around the room, the shifting weight and darkening expressions of his fellow watchers said they felt it, too.

Loshak forced himself to look away from the padded envelope, dragging his eyes up the unsub to search for distinguishing characteristics.

Most public spaces were equipped with height strips at entryways to help law enforcement and eyewitnesses better identify suspects. The strip on the post office's doorway showed their mailer at just under five-nine, but the head stayed down, hunched a little until he passed off the first screen and into the second.

Their suspect took a spot behind the woman waiting to get her money order and finally lifted his head. Big black sunglasses hid half the face, and an obvious wig poked out from beneath the hood and hung against his cheeks. His sleeves were pushed back to reveal bony, birdlike forearms. The limbs looked pale, papery white in the grayscale of the footage.

"So that's him?" Commander Belte said, a slightly stunned quality to her voice. "Are we positive?"

"The timestamp on the camera should prove it."

Inspector Randall reached over the desk officer again and jumped the footage forward until the mailer was at the counter.

"Watch the clerk print out the packing label. See?"

He stabbed the button to pause it, then pointed at the numbers in the upper corner.

"Nine-sixteen. He's the only one getting a label printed at that time. That's our mail perp."

"And, if you will," Spinks said, "a *male* perp."

"Hey, that's great wordplay," Aque sneered. "Do you guys mind if we get back to catching a murderer who cut somebody's face off now?"

His partner, Schrader, nodded at the screen.

"Well, the scrawniness shoots holes in my conspiracy theory that it was the other podcaster, James What's-His-Name. Jim's a big boy, so unless he lost a lot of weight since his Facebook profile photo was taken, it's not him."

"Let's get screenshots from a couple angles here," Aque said. "Maybe we can't get a clear look at his face, but it'll give us something to go on with the HALO footage. Send those pictures to me and Schrader, too. Maybe the podcasters have seen somebody creeping around wearing a crazy wig and sunglasses."

After the screenshots had been dispersed to the task force, Commander Belte had the desk officer pull up the footage from the city's cameras. The HALO film was in higher definition and full color. Something about seeing the range of different hues splashed across the screen made what they were looking for feel less threatening, almost fake. Like watching a movie rather than security tape.

Even with plenty of leeway around the post office mailing time, the southeastern intersection yielded them nothing but a steady stream of foot traffic devoid of black hoodies.

They switched to the camera at the northwestern intersection. Everyone leaned in unconsciously as the people on the screen started moving.

A sea of bright colors paraded along the sidewalk. A jogger ran along the bike path to avoid the crowd. Three people in mismatched layers of clothing hauling tarp-covered carts shuffled by.

"Homeless shelter around the corner must have let out

just before this," Belte said.

The seconds ticked by, and then Spinks lurched forward.

"That's him," he said, pointing at the upper left corner.

The black hoodie was still pulled up, the wig and glasses in place, but there was something about getting a better look at his stride, his posture. The way he carried himself was different from in the post office. More relaxed maybe. Maybe a little less aware that he was being watched.

The shirt poking out of the zipper was a pale yellow that looked somewhere between faded and dirty. His feet skimmed the sidewalk so obviously with every step that Loshak could almost hear the soles scraping.

It seemed like he was the only one headed southeast that day. All around him, the brightly colored clothing of his fellow pedestrians streamed past the black hoodie. He was swimming upstream, headed in the opposite direction of everyone else.

He paused for a moment in front of the hardware and locksmith shop across the street from the post office. Tucked the package under one arm and slipped off his sunglasses, reaching up with his other hand to rub at his eyelids.

Everyone in the room stiffened. Commander Belte's mouth made a quiet popping sound as her lips formed a surprised O. No one breathed.

The hand came down. They got a perfect look at their suspect's face.

Loshak twitched, a jerk of the shoulders, a slight pulling back. Another wave of cold washed up from the pit of his stomach.

Even at this distance, he could see that the guy's expression was utterly blank. Empty, like there was nothing behind it. Slack mouth. Dead eyes.

As the suspect slipped his sunglasses back on and started walking again, Aque spluttered.

"Stop it! Run it back and get a photo!"

"On it," Danno said, banging keys.

It wasn't perfect, but it was damn sure better than their post office screenshots. And even if it couldn't make for a positive ID in court, they could circulate it. It was enough that someone might recognize the guy.

On the screen, he hopped off the sidewalk and walked between the slowed traffic. Stepped up to the closing post office door and shouldered his way inside.

Belte pulled out her phone.

"I'll get on the horn with my media contacts, get this video out to all the local channels."

"You've got half an hour before the five o'clock broadcast starts," Schrader said.

"Then I'd better move ass, huh?" She scrolled through her contacts. "Go warn the tip line, will you? See if they can't call in a few extra bodies to man the phones for the next couple days."

The detective nodded and ducked out.

Left untouched, the HALO footage restarted, reverting to the beginning of the clip. Loshak watched, eyes glued to the black hoodie swimming upstream in that aggressively bright rainbow of color.

The scrawny outsider engulfed by the crowd.

CHAPTER 8

The group spilled out into the hall, everyone bustling off to work their piece of the investigation.

Loshak swallowed. The sound was unnaturally loud in his head.

Those dead eyes seemed to swallow up his memory of watching the HALO footage. Like a pair of black holes every other detail was trying to claw their way free from. The moment they had come into view on the computer monitor felt like a sucker punch. Even thinking back to that split second in time refreshed the cold feeling in Loshak's middle. There had been something inhuman about that emptiness.

It wasn't the first time in his years of interviewing and interrogating killers that he'd gotten a glimpse behind the mask of normalcy so many of them wore. No matter how slick they were, there were slips here and there, minute fractures in the façade, and then suddenly he wouldn't be looking into a face but into a void. A place where life had maybe been at one time, but where now there was a missing piece, a chasm.

"Whoops."

Loshak pulled up short of running into Commander Belte. She had stopped in the middle of the hallway, still on the phone.

"Yep, that will be perfect. I'll send it right now. Right. Will do."

Loshak turned his body and squeezed past her to catch up to Spinks.

In twenty minutes, their killer's face would be circulated all over the local Denver channels. By this evening, it would run national.

There was a twinge of excitement in his gut. They had some truly promising leads considering they were still only in the beginning stages of the investigation. Usually this early in a case, it felt like they were just running around behind the murderer cleaning up the bloody messes of the lives he'd destroyed. Waiting for that critical piece of identifying information that only came after another body instead of before.

But this time they had video of their unsub. Now they just had to hope that someone recognized him from the TV broadcast and called in a tip.

"What're you thinking, partner?" Spinks asked, slowing his pace to let Loshak catch up.

"Trying to decide where we can do the most good. Helping out with the tip line or sorting through the podcast correspondence. Either one is bound to be a slog."

Spinks rubbed his chin.

"The footage seems like a sure thing, but I'm guessing you don't want to put all your eggs in one basket?"

"You remember that convicted murderer who escaped from a prison in Pennsylvania a while back? He was making national headlines every single day, and it still took two weeks before they managed to get him back in custody." Loshak shrugged. "Sometimes these guys go to ground, hide out, family and friends get a warning out to them whenever the cops get close."

"*If* they have family and friends who'll do that for them," Spinks pointed out. "You were saying this guy might have cut all ties. In my humble experience tagging along with a profiler, I've noticed lots of these killers are grade-A loners."

Loshak nodded, acknowledging the correlation.

"There's also the possibility that he sees the broadcast and gets excited. We're talking about someone who wants attention."

He lowered his voice then so no one beyond Spinks would overhear.

"Seeing his face on the news might amp him up to kill again sooner, keep the publicity wave rolling. Ultimately, we're gambling on the footage leading to his capture before that happens, but there are too many variables here to know how the dice are going to land. I don't want to get overconfident just because we have his face. Not until we have him, and everybody's safe."

A door burst open down the hall behind them. Someone shouted something Loshak didn't catch.

The agent swung around, and Spinks stepped up beside him.

Aque strode down the hall, phone still pressed to his ear. Schrader was on his heels, face tense and drawn.

When Aque yelled again, Loshak finally made it out.

"We've got another package."

CHAPTER 9

Loshak, Spinks, and Aque followed a uniformed officer through a dumpy building in West Colfax. A staticky voice trilled on the uni's radio, then suddenly several voices, something spiky in their tangle of responses bursting out of the speaker. She had the volume turned low, just above a whisper, but Loshak could pick out snippets of chatter between the dispatcher and the officers. Domestic in progress. Nearby units responding.

This building was dingier than Andi Wayland's, in a neighborhood better known for a game locals played called "Fireworks or Gunshots?" than its hip breweries and restaurants. The carpet reminded Loshak of something you would have found in a Holiday Inn circa 1982. It had a faded, undulating pattern of gold, brown, and blue, and was worn so thin in places that the supporting meshwork of thicker fibers showed through like ribs. Brown water stains marked the ceiling and had seeped down the walls in places. Everything seemed hazy, like some kind of interior gloom dimmed the hall lights.

It also smelled like French onion soup. The second they opened the door on the ground floor, the scent had hit them like a wall of the stringy brown liquid.

Loshak could picture a bowl of it, that crust of cheesy bread on top. He was hungry enough that he wasn't immediately repelled by the nose-shock of finding a smell in the wrong place at the wrong time.

Somewhere in the building, a baby bawled its lungs out, a howling series of cries without end. Nobody seemed to be in any rush to help.

Loshak considered giving the parents the benefit of the doubt, the possibility that it was colic and the baby would be crying from now until midnight no matter what anyone did, but he didn't hear the telltale hiccups and wavers in the wailing that would mean a parent was pacing the floor with the baby over their shoulder, patting, swaying, and trying to comfort the poor kid.

Ahead, cameras flashed through an open door. The back end of a bunny suit poked out for a second, the techs inside shuffling around in the small space.

"There she blows," Spinks said. "That must be our destination."

"What gave it away?" Aque muttered.

The reporter caught Loshak's look and rolled his eyes. Becoming buddy-buddy with the locals was usually a specialty of Spinks's, but Aque wasn't having it.

Luckily, the uniform escorting them was a little less abrasive.

"Home of Jessica Caine, twenty-six," she said, hands hooked in the armholes of her body armor vest. "Caine called it in a couple hours ago."

"And we just now got word?" Aque asked.

"There was an apartment fire over in Villa Park, and we didn't have the units to spare right away. It didn't get to the top of the priority list until the dispatcher heard about the, uh, package from earlier."

The detective sighed and pushed his way into the apartment.

The uniform shrugged, looking at Loshak and Spinks.

"Sick as it may sound, a box of body parts isn't top priority when you've got whole, living people who're gonna die without your intervention."

"Believe me, I get it," Spinks said. "I grew up in an area where a baby in a trash bag full of coke or an arm in the incinerator weren't even the top gossip."

Loshak nodded.

"You've got to save who you can while you can."

The apartment was small, a studio, with new snap-together vinyl tiling that looked strange in contrast with the dingy wallpaper and water-stained popcorn ceiling. There were only three techs in all, but in their Tyvek suits, they seemed to take up the majority of the space.

Aque hovered at the edge of the activity, craning his neck to watch over their shoulders.

A few paces inside the door, there was a small dining table. A circle of wood veneer over pressboard. The box sat on the edge.

Loshak wove through the techs, closing the distance.

Just another cardboard cube indistinguishable from any of the two-to-three hundred million packages the USPS delivered every day. No company logos. No handwritten labels.

The flaps of the box stood upright, reaching toward the ceiling like outstretched arms.

A hole opened in the wall of techs, more shuffling that allowed Loshak closer. It wasn't until he stood right over it, however, that he could look down and see what lay inside.

Ears.

A pair of them wrapped in more Saran wrap. Side by

side, slightly flattened. The plastic wrap covering them gave the whole tableau a glossy film that seemed to remove it from reality a little.

Still resting in the box, they almost looked like vacuum-sealed food items. Seemed like there should be a block of dry ice in there to keep them frozen. Omaha Ears. A delicacy in some places.

Loshak let the random thoughts flow. Though the wounds were turned downward, faint traces of blood were visible along the edges and in the wrinkled parts of the cling wrap. The ears were nestled in there like eggs in the bird's nest of bubble wrap that obscured the bottom of the box.

The room seemed suddenly very quiet. Still. And somehow unreal.

He blinked. Slow. Blacked out the image with his eyelids, then reopened them, trying to see the scene afresh.

Ears.

Not easy to process, just lying there like that.

Spinks appeared at his side.

"So do we think…" The reporter's voice was low, like he could feel the oppressive quiet in the apartment, too. "I mean, does this pair match the, uh, face from earlier?"

Loshak blinked again, this time more rapidly as he turned the thought over. He couldn't look away from the severed body parts. It was like some kind of electricity held his gaze there. Static cling adhering a dryer sheet to a sweater.

"I think we can assume it's one victim. At least until we get evidence to the contrary. Which wouldn't shock me at all."

He swallowed, and the sounds in the apartment gained definition, the pressure in his ears equalizing, as if the elevation had been the trouble.

Spinks nodded slowly.

"Right. Yeah."

They both stared into the seashell curls of the ears, the contours of skin and cartilage that spiraled into holes where the canals should have been but instead led to a thin sheet of plastic and a boxful of bubble wrap.

Another swallow, and Loshak forced himself to step back to give the techs room again. His body went rigid at first, neck and shoulders stiff like the image wanted to hold him there, keep him trapped in its grip.

But then he was far enough out that the cardboard flap obscured his line of sight. Without the gore directly in his view, the image lost its hold on him. Releasing him all at once.

He slipped back through the techs to an empty bit of floor near a window and one of those long baseboard heaters. Toed up to the cracked place where the window stood open a few inches.

The breeze coming in wasn't necessarily cool, but with all the bodies crammed into the small apartment, it felt fresher, at least.

All at once, a big breath seemed to open his throat, force its way into his lungs. Fresh night air, clear of the polluting force that seemed to hold sway over the apartment, rushed for the interior of his chest cavity, opening it wide.

He stood there, breathing a few more times. Eyes closed. Nothing real but the wind.

It felt good. Seemed to clear his thoughts. Something cleansing about knowing it came from outside, not from within this building of screaming babies and soup smells and dismembered ears lying on beds of plastic.

"So…"

Spinks was there again, popping up seemingly out of nowhere, still speaking in that low voice like a loud noise would make the whole apartment shatter.

"They said the tenant is ready to talk to us… if you want."

Loshak opened his eyes.

Out the crack of the window, he could see the parking lot below. Colorful cars drained to a gloomy gray-orange by the flickering streetlight.

He turned to Spinks. The reporter was watching him from behind a closed-off expression.

"Let's go."

CHAPTER 10

Jessica Caine waited for them in the farthest corner of the apartment, near a window that led out onto a balcony. Her hair was dyed green, short and a little crinkly. Watercolor tattoos covered her forearms and disappeared into the pushed-up sleeves of a woolly sweater wrap that she was hugging around herself as if she needed the comfort but couldn't deal with the heat of all these bodies invading her space.

Her eyes were big and sad, both where she sat on the small loveseat and in the few pictures with friends she had scattered around the apartment. Beneath the wrap, and in all the photos, Caine wore black t-shirts. All of these were screen-printed with white, the logos of what Loshak assumed were bands. He'd never heard of any of them.

No shock there. The last time he'd been up-to-date on what the kids were listening to had been sometime in the eighties, back when he had still been trying out the standard cop 'stache. That was about the time he started to realize he wasn't going to keep up with any of it, the music or the nose cozy.

Loshak spotted the thousand-yard stare in Caine's big eyes before they made it to her. She looked somehow both zoned out and on high alert at the same time.

When they introduced themselves, however, she blinked and straightened up.

"I know you guys."

She looked back and forth between them. Blinked again. Spoke.

"Special Agent Victor Loshak and Jevon Spinks, crime reporter and independent consultant with the FBI."

Her voice was airy and vaguely distant. It made Loshak think of a cartoon version of a good fairy, though the cadence was more in line with someone in shock.

"You… you guys played a huge part in my most popular episode. You were everywhere when I was researching it."

Spinks raised his brows.

"Episode?"

"Oh, sorry."

She wrapped the sides of her sweater tighter around her. Her mouth quirked as she searched for the right words.

"I'm a podcaster. Not like as a job. I also have a real job. The podcast is just sort of a side thing. I've only got thirteen episodes out so far. Most of them barely get any attention. But my episode about the Kansas City sex trafficking conspiracy has like twenty thousand listens. It completely blew up."

"Interesting," Spinks said. "So, would you call this a serial killer podcast?"

"Well, true crime. I try to find the weird, unusual stuff. Stuff that hasn't already been done to death, and to be honest, most serial killer stuff is way overdone. Some of my episodes aren't even specifically about murder. Like that bank heist in…"

When she didn't come up with the place name, Spinks prompted, "Which bank heist was this?"

"Huh?" She blinked. "Oh, sorry."

She reached up a hand covered in woolly sleeve and rubbed at her eyes. Then she squinted.

"This is so weird. I can't remember what I was saying. Can you repeat the question?"

"It's alright," Loshak said, keeping his voice gentle. He'd seen victims and eyewitnesses dissociate like that before, just sort of drop off the map in the middle of conversation, and he didn't want to push her too hard. "You were just telling us about your podcast. Have you ever received any strange or threatening mail before this?"

"Not really. I don't get a lot of real mail, to tell the truth. I mean, we've got a small contingent of die-hard listeners, but the community is all online. This is *Scene of the Crime*'s first package. I thought it would be…"

She trailed off again, eyes going unfocused.

Loshak cleared his throat.

"Were you expecting something when you got today's package?"

She jumped a little.

"Not specifically."

"You were saying that you thought it would be something."

Another eye rub.

"Oh. Yeah. I thought it was cool that we'd finally gotten something in the real mail. I guess I figured it was fan art or maybe a book from my wish list or… I don't know. Stuff like big-time podcasters get from their listeners. I didn't think it would be…"

Her face washed out, going from pale to gray. She swayed forward. Loshak moved closer to her side and put a hand on her shoulder.

"Keep breathing," he said. "Put your head down for a few seconds if you need to."

Caine leaned forward, planting her elbows on her knees and her face in her hands. Her shoulders and back heaved, muscles flexing and releasing spasmodically. She was starting to hyperventilate.

Loshak made slow, calming circles with his palm on the girl's back. He looked up at Spinks.

"Do you see a paper bag? Something she can breathe into?"

Spinks hopped to his feet.

"On it."

The reporter flitted around the studio, checking in cabinets and leaning into the bathroom. The search reminded Loshak of those old shows where a woman went into labor and the man lost his mind looking for hot water and towels.

While Spinks searched, Loshak sat next to Caine and spoke in a low, controlled voice.

"Jessica, count with me while you inhale. Breathe in, one, two, three, four. Now hold your breath. One, two, three, four. OK, breathe out, one, two, three, four…"

They went a few rounds before she could manage the full count.

Spinks came back shaking his head.

"Not so much as a cloth tote bag."

"That's alright."

Loshak kept up the count.

Gradually the color came back to her face. She sat back on the couch.

"I'm so sorry. I'm not like this in real life. I think I was going to pass out just now. It was getting hard to hear, and then it was like this reddish black was creeping in at the edges... That's not me."

"You've been through a serious shock," Loshak said. "That can trigger a vagal response completely outside of your control."

"That sucked. That feeling of not being able to do anything to stop it was so... I'm not normally some helpless baby."

She was starting to sound angry, but her big eyes were still stretched too wide.

Loshak gave her a reassuring smile.

"I've seen hardened criminals twice your size hit the floor over this kind of thing. You're actually doing pretty well, considering all you've been through today."

"I want to help catch this guy."

She balled a fist around a wad of woolly sweater material before she went on.

"It's sick. *He's* sick. And he needs to be stopped before he hurts someone else."

Her voice gained strength while she spoke, until it sounded less airy and distant than it had since they'd started talking to her, as if the frustration were giving her something to anchor herself to. She locked onto Loshak then, her gaze meeting his and holding, something fierce in it.

"What else can I tell you? What would help your investigation?"

Spinks cocked his head.

"Earlier you said you don't get much 'real mail' and

most of your community is online. Does that mean you have had some threatening or strange stuff sent to you online? Email, social media, that kind of thing?"

She shrugged.

"Just the usual. You're bound to get some weirdos in the true crime sphere."

Then she tilted her head as she thought about it again.

"But there was one guy… Darren Bowden. He's kind of internet infamous in the true crime sphere. Like he would post these long off-topic screeds in the middle of a podcast comment section or someone else's Reddit thread. And he has this insane website where he puts up tons and tons of material a day. Most of the connections he makes aren't even real connections, they're just like, 'these two words sound similar, that must mean *X*.' He thinks he's the only real person and the rest of us are just malicious computer programming out to get him.

"But then he started DMing me pictures of himself in, like, weird skimpy outfits. Like a maid's dress obviously from some sex shop. You could see everything… down there. He was basically taking upskirts of himself, from the front and the back."

She stuck up a hand.

"I don't care what people do on their own, but when I asked him to stop sending them to me, he got really mad. He claimed I was the one asking for this stuff so I could blackmail him — that he could hear my messaging being implanted in his brain whenever he listened to the podcast or read one of my comments.

"There are these people he's always talking about in his rants called 'the remnants,' who I guess are supposed to enslave the human population and take over the world or maybe already have. I don't know. He's got this whole delusion built up, and it's pretty elaborate. Anyway, he said some threatening stuff about how I'm part of them, and we would see what our evil got us. But none of what he said was like, 'I'll kill someone and send you their ears.'"

Loshak jotted down the man's name in his phone.

"Are you still in contact with him?"

"No. This is kind of dumb, but it took my friend telling me that I didn't have to take harassment from anybody, let alone some jerk on the internet. Like it wasn't my responsibility to cater to this guy. After that, I blocked him everywhere I could think of. I mentioned the whole thing to a couple other podcasters at the local true crime convention here in town, and they said they'd had trouble with him, too. Like I said, he's kind of well-known in this circle."

She pulled her sweater tight around herself again.

"I guess I wouldn't be that surprised if it turned out he was the one who sent this. He always seemed like the kind of person who could just snap."

CHAPTER 11

"What do you think?" Spinks asked as they left behind the tiny studio apartment still crammed full of crime scene processing personnel.

Loshak nodded.

"This Bowden guy sounds like a good place to start. We should see if the *All Murder* podcast had any run-ins with him."

They came to the rental car, and he circled around while Spinks unlocked it. Instead of getting in right away, however, the reporter leaned his arms on the roof.

"I don't know, partner. My gut is saying he isn't our guy."

Spinks scratched his jaw with the key, the metal rasping on the five-o'clock shadow he was working on.

"You run into weirdos like this a lot on the crime beat. People often point at them the second something bad happens, but usually it turns out that they're just paranoids who work everything they hear into the web of delusions they've built."

"That's a definite possibility," Loshak said. "We can't jump to any conclusions one way or the other. For now, though, we'll check him out, see what shakes loose."

They climbed into the car, both of them taking a moment to arrange their long legs. Spinks turned the key.

"The fact that Caine's podcast hasn't gotten as big as Wayland's is good for us, though," Loshak said. "Smaller pool of listeners and comments to sift through. And we can check for crossover — anybody who might have sent something to both *All Murder* and *Scene of the Crime* in the last few months."

Spinks shook his head as he put his hand on the gear shift.

"That's like the number one rule of keeping your sanity while surfing the internet, you know. *Don't read the comments.* You ever dig through a random comment section on YouTube? Facebook?" He made a face. "Cesspools."

"Better put your gaiters on, then," Loshak said.

"Ha! A full rubber hazmat suit, more like it. But before we start wading into the filth, what do you say we get some food?"

◆　　◆　　◆

They found a sandwich place named General Pickled's a few blocks from Caine's apartment with curbside pickup.

"Sounds like the name of a drunk cat," Loshak said, studying the menu on his phone.

If his partner Darger were there, that would've shown her that it wasn't just the young kids who were hip to technology. And he would've said it like that, too. *Hip.* Just to make sure she was getting the full impact of the disconnect.

"Wow. There's a lot of booze on this menu."

"It's the evolution we were all waiting for in sandwich dining." Spinks read over his shoulder. "After all, what's better with a sandwich than a Fuzzy Navel?"

"I'm not big on drinks named after body parts."

Loshak had meant for the comment to be a joke, but as

he said it, it brought the weight of the case back, the reality of what they had witnessed in those packages settling around them and filling the car.

He shifted in his seat. He wished he'd kept that little bit of stupidity to himself. There was something about it that felt more wrong than the usual blowing off steam.

Spinks seemed to sense the change in atmosphere. He cleared his throat.

"I'm leaning toward the Reuben and the Saint Paddy. You don't think they'll mind if I come in sloshed when I help sort the creep mail, do you? There's a lot of good Irish whiskey in this Paddy and not much else."

He sighed before he went on.

"Better not chance it. Don't want that postal inspector to come down on me for not taking my job as a consultant seriously enough."

Loshak smirked.

"I guess you heard Randall say he was rousting his people out of bed to get to work on tracing that second package?"

"I did happen to hear that particular turn of phrase used at seven-thirty this evening."

They called in their order to General Pickled's, then pulled into one of the curbside pickup spots to wait. Spinks fiddled under his bucket seat, and then the whole thing ratcheted back as he made room to eat there in the car.

"So are we assuming they were mailed from the same place?"

"That seems pretty likely," Loshak said. "We should know for sure soon."

Spinks pursed his lips and pointed to the dash clock. It

was a quarter to nine.

"In the middle of the night like this?"

The silence slid back in, both of them staring out their windows at the fresh darkness beyond the glass.

Caine's neighborhood didn't have the vibrant, energetic feeling of movement the area around their first podcaster's apartment had. Wayland had been situated in the hustle and bustle of tourist dining and clubs. On this block alone, Loshak could see a pawn shop, an empty lot with a graffitied *For Sale* sign, a payday loans place, and a liquor store. The sandwich shop was the most upscale business on the street.

That was what finally made the connection for him, why he'd felt so much more disturbed by the discovery of the second package. Jessica Caine's big, dark eyes reminded him of Sandra Marsden from primary school.

God, he hadn't thought about Sandra in years. Maybe not since they all went off to different high schools. Sandra had had those same big, sad eyes as Caine, beautiful but somehow slightly wounded, even when she was smiling. Sandra's family had lived on the wrong side of the tracks — literally. The roughest neighborhood in his hometown had been situated opposite the railroad yard.

Not like the Loshak clan had ever been wealthy, but there was a pretty big difference between the "respectable" poor and the "never made it out of the tar paper shack_ poor. Loshak might have come to school in old clothes with the occasional patch, but Sandra always came to school dirty, sometimes with bruises or fresh scratches.

And of course, instead of realizing that compassion might bring out her better qualities, the kids had done what kids do — ostracized the one who didn't fit. Sandra had been a pretty little girl, and he'd had a hell of a crush on her, but he had been careful never to let it show. Even young as he was, he'd known that would have gotten him cast out, just like her. He had never come out and made fun of her like everybody else, but he hadn't had the sense of self yet to stand up for her, either.

A teenager with his General Pickled's visor on upside down brought out their sandwiches and drinks. Arid evening air flowed in through the window.

Almost immediately, Loshak felt the skin of his face drying. It was a tightening, almost itchy sensation.

Outside, the kid licked his upper lip repeatedly while he swiped their cards on a point-of-sale tablet, emphasizing the chapped red banana of skin just above his mouth.

Loshak took a big sip of virgin Bahama Mama and made a mental note to grab some lip balm at a gas station. He wasn't big on putting greasy, waxy stuff on his face, but he also didn't want to end up with a cherry-red clown mouth and a bad lip-licking habit.

He and Spinks ate for a while in silence — the reporter had forgone the Saint Paddy's in favor of a virgin daiquiri — the reporter putting to use every extra napkin from the sandwich bag. It never failed that he ordered the messiest thing on the menu, then spent the majority of his time meticulously cleaning his hands and face between each bite.

"So, do you think we'll get some more footage of this guy from the HALO cameras?" Spinks asked, dabbing Russian dressing from the corner of his mouth. "Maybe something of him leaving the area, heading back to his house?"

"It's a definite possibility."

A wedge of pickle spear slipped out of Loshak's Cuban and bounced off his chest. He picked the escapee up, poked it into a ham-heavy spot in the sandwich, and wiped the grease spot it had left on his tie. That looked like it was there to stay.

"Tell you what I want to know." Spinks's napkins rustled. A glance his way revealed the reporter's pale, Easter-green polo was still spotless in spite of the condiment overkill in his sandwich. "Do you think Caine is her real name or do you think she changed it to better fit with her aesthetic? Intentionally referencing the O.G. murderer? The one who started it all?"

"Her podcast is so new, I can't see that happening."

"Not necessarily with the podcast in mind. I mean, with the tattoos, green hair, suicide-girl-next-door thing she's got going on. Going with 'Caine' when you could pick any last name is kind of an edgelord move, but it would line up with her preexisting interest in the dark, depraved, and deadly."

"But a legal name change?" Loshak shook his head. "What if next year you're really into surfing instead? Or western wear? Do you go through the whole process again?"

"Well, I can't speak for the whole world, partner, but I've known a few folks who've made more permanent decisions on the spur of the moment. Face tattoos and suchlike. Not exactly what you'd call long-term planners."

Loshak shrugged.

"Can't argue with that. I've come across a few of those

myself, I suppose."

"That's the narrative I'm going with until proven otherwise," Spinks said.

The reporter took a gargantuan bite of corned beef, sauerkraut, rye, and a heaping helping of dressing, then went to work napkinning off while he chewed. When he finished off the last of his Reuben, he started up again.

"Here's something nobody's pointed out yet. I've been waiting since we got the call about Podcaster Two for someone to say it, but it's like nobody wants to. Like if we say it out loud, we make it real for whoever becomes unlucky True Crime Podcaster Number Three."

He paused dramatically, completing the last step of his cleaning ritual by neatly folding his final napkin and tucking it into the empty bag before going on.

"Our guy's only sending these packages to women. Thoughts?"

Loshak frowned and balled his own napkin in his palm, letting it come to rest on his knee.

"Two points don't make up a reliable set of data. But yeah, it had occurred to me that we might start to see that as a pattern. Especially if this is his way of reaching out to the opposite sex when he's otherwise felt unable to approach them. It's something to keep in mind, but not necessarily something to pin our profile on yet."

"I'm watching for it anyway," Spinks said. "Maybe if we find a ne'er-do-well or two in common between *All Murder* and *Scene of the Crime*, we can take a look at other ladies they've been creeping on in the true crime community."

"Maybe," Loshak hedged.

"But you don't think so?"

"What I think is that we're looking for a needle in a haystack. It's a smaller haystack now that we've got Caine's smaller audience to compare to Wayland's, but it's still a haystack."

Spinks was already nodding, a knowing grin on his face.

"And you don't want to jump to any conclusions."

"If I can avoid it…" Loshak shrugged. "No, I'd rather not."

CHAPTER 12

Sam Crozier came awake shivering in the dark with no idea of where he was or how he'd gotten there. His heart thundered like an overworked kick drum, and his panting laid down a panicked counter rhythm. His eyes were open too wide, so wide they stung.

He was in an alley, slumped in a corner made by an overflowing dumpster and an apartment building. A yellow glow from the streetlight silhouetted the brickwork of the building in front of him and shined in the myriad puddles that somehow continued to exist in spite of it not having rained for over a week. The scent of motor oil rose from the pothole closest to him, its edges glinting with a rainbow sheen.

He sat up. The material of his jacket scratched against the stone as he shifted. Too loud.

He went still. Felt a wave of panic he couldn't quite explain. Sensed somehow that he wasn't alone.

And then he heard it.

The footsteps that had jerked him awake. Whoever they were, they were headed his way.

Trying to make as little noise as possible, Crozier pulled his knees up, drawing himself into a ball so the shadow of the dumpster would fully conceal him.

You couldn't be too careful sleeping on the streets. Denver liked to think of itself as a friendly town, but when the sun went down and the streetlights came on, all bets were off. The nine-to-fivers, the normal humans, they went into their houses or climbed the stairs to their fancy apartments and locked themselves in, all the while telling themselves how safe it was.

Crozier knew better. He'd only been on the streets for a few months now, but it hadn't taken him long to see how the game really worked out here. He'd learned to sleep with an ear open, not let anybody sneak up on him.

It wouldn't be so bad if he wasn't alone.

In the dream, he hadn't been alone. He'd felt Siobhan with him in a way that was so full and complete that he couldn't comprehend it in the waking world. The only way he could experience it was in the feeling of loss after the footsteps had torn him out of her presence. That lack lay inside his chest and at the back of his throat, as heavy as the day he'd found Shiv dead in their apartment. A sudden negative space that somehow had more density than the presence of any living person he'd ever been around.

The footsteps crept to the end of the alley. Stopped.

Crozier held his breath.

Silence. On his end, on the footsteps' end. No one wanted to make the first sound.

The dumpster occluded Crozier's view of the mouth of the alley, but in his mind's eye, he could see a hulking figure, a shadow in the yellow streetlight. The stretching black length of an arm. The spiky point of a knife clutched in a fist. Violence etched into the posture of the shape, an eagerness to leap out and kill.

Crozier was dying to peek out. Bend around the protection of that blue metal box and look death in the face.

His lungs ached. Too much saliva filled his mouth, needing to be swallowed, but it would be too loud. Any sound would be too loud.

The predator was out there waiting. Ready to spring.

And then the footsteps trailed away, moving on down the street.

Crozier let out a tremulous breath. His whole upper torso shook with the relief of a narrow escape. He eased his head back against the dumpster and let his eyes fall shut.

Without the fear to distract him, the full measure of Shiv's negative space rolled back in. He'd been dreaming about his lost love. Most nights he did, one way or another.

His dreams seemed to run her back and forth through time, unconcerned with staying accountable to the chronology of their relationship, presenting different eras night by night. Sometimes Shiv would have the dyed pink hair from when she was twenty, barely down to her chin, other times she would have the curtain of long, black hair she'd died with, hanging down to the middle of her back.

Her tattoo was another piece that came and went. Sometimes she had the elvish lettering slanting across the inside of her wrist, the black so much blacker against her pale skin, the Tolkien quote about how she would rather spend a lifetime with her love than face the ages of the Earth alone. Other times, there was nothing there but the faint blue crisscrossing of her veins beneath the skin.

Tonight, he'd been with her on the crooked futon in the old apartment they'd had on Walnut. Shadows had seemed to reach through the windows, drawing charcoal smears on their walls as night settled over them. But they were warm and quiet there together. Just being with each other. He'd

84

felt that presence again, felt her inhabiting space with him, and it was as if she had never really gone.

He wished more than anything that he could bring that feeling fully into the waking world. Experience the sensation of her being there with him again. But that reality was only available to him in dreams now.

The final image of her thrust itself into his brain like an ice pick.

Her pale face gray, eyes gone empty, froth trailing out of one side of her mouth, bubbles the color of straw. His last look at her somehow bigger and more vibrant than anything he'd seen of her while she was still alive, pulsing in his skull like a hemorrhaging vein.

Overdose. Overdose on the drugs he'd gotten for her, drugs that had slowly broken down her body, her cheeks going hollow, her teeth spacing out from the bone loss, her glowing pale skin turning papery and taking on a yellow tinge, all of it right before his eyes.

Crozier shoved himself to his feet. He needed to move. Walk. Get some distance.

His head spun a little. A black flutter of dizziness swooping over him, spiraling weakness into his legs. Probably from not eating anything today. Maybe he hadn't drunk anything either, he wasn't sure.

He grabbed the corner of the dumpster, fingers fumbling against flaps of flattened cardboard boxes, and waited for the headrush to subside. Balancing. Waiting.

It was the image of the dumpster with those flattened boxes poking up, the metal box painted industrial navy blue, that reminded him of Bodie's Last Ride.

Bodie had been a local legend, the old man who'd

haunted the streets of Denver nearly all his life. Crozier had run into Bodie once, just in passing, but he'd seemed like an alright dude. He'd shared some of his forty, even though he'd mostly just had backwash left.

They'd talked music for a bit. Bodie was a big fan of Gordon Lightfoot. Claimed he could take or leave Dwight Yoakam, then went on to sing "I Sang Dixie" to a tune that didn't fit Crozier's recollection of the song at all.

Bodie's Last Ride had happened maybe a month back the way Crozier figured it, though time got hard to keep track of out here. Back when winter was still giving way to spring, anyway, when the nights were still cold enough to give you frostbite.

Bodie had been sleeping in a dumpster and hadn't woken up when the garbage truck came. Technically, the drivers were supposed to check each one for vagrants before they dumped it, especially on cold nights, but this driver must've been lazy or in a rush, because he hadn't.

Crozier ran the pad of his thumb across the straight edge of a cardboard flat. Had Bodie woken up when he dropped into the back of the garbage truck?

Probably better if he hadn't.

Crozier had been surprised how easily the rest of the folks on the street had accepted the loss of a living legend. According to them, it happened a few times a year. Bums sleeping in dumpsters wound up dead in landfills. Sometimes a cop came by to ask about them. Sometimes nobody came by. It was the nature of the beast. Their attitude about the whole affair left Crozier as sure as ever that life or death or nothing, none of it mattered.

Unable to shake that feeling of wariness, Crozier crept

toward the mouth of the alley. He took it slow, careful. The glow painted there by the streetlights, the various bulbs spattering brightness across everything like a Jackson Pollock laser light show, seemed somehow predatory. Hungry.

It felt like he was moving in slow motion. He rolled up on that threshold, that interplay of artificial brightness from the street and natural dark of the nighttime alley. An estuary of light.

He sniffled. Wiped his nose. Touched the heel of his hand to the bulk tucked down in his waistband.

Someone lurched out of the shadows then. Grabbed for him.

Crozier panicked. Saw again the flash of that bulky silhouette with the spike of the knife extending from the end of the long, snaking arm.

He fought. Couldn't tell whether he was actually hitting his attacker, but he kept at it. Once he felt something rake across his face and neck. Something else — a head or an elbow — hit his cheek.

They went down. Hit the ground together, rolling around on the uneven asphalt. Grunting. Harsh, desperate breathing.

Crozier's foot kicked down, splashing oily water from a pothole. The ragged hem of his jeans flung droplets everywhere as he struggled.

Then Crozier was on top, stabbing. Ripping the blade down into a chest. Again, again.

Wet resistance. The occasional scrape of something harder.

Light seemed to flash over him all at once.

It was a girl underneath him. Bloody. Eyelids still fluttering. He could smell the alcohol on her breath. See the glittery gloss on her opening and closing lips.

She was no one. Not a threat, just some random pedestrian trying to find her way home after a party or maybe a night at the club.

When he pulled up the knife, he saw its reflection in her swollen pupils. Twin versions of the dripping blade glinting there.

The body underneath him went still quickly. Less than a minute.

He stayed sitting on it a while, straddling the hips. His own lungs heaving. Cold, dry air in. Hot, wet air out.

No thought. Blank. Void.

Finally, Crozier moved. He leaned over her face, bringing the bloody knife to her jaw, and got to work peeling the skin from the bone beneath.

He knew exactly who to mail this one to.

CHAPTER 13

In the task force conference room, Loshak pincered open his hundredth envelope of the night, the gloves the DPD had provided sticking and tugging weirdly at his skin as he did. The paper mouth gaped in his hands, ready to bare its contents.

This one contained a collage of printer paper photos of Elizabeth Short, the Black Dahlia crime scene, the letters to the police, the suspects from the 1947 investigation, maps of LA, and ruler-straight marker lines connecting the photos in a variety of colors. The whole thing was reminiscent of a certain string board he'd kept in a storage unit just a year ago. A letter accompanied the collage, making the case that there was no possible other murderer than the doctor, George Hodel.

Loshak had to admit the sender made a compelling argument. He turned to the laptop set up at his station and began entering details like the sender's name, mailing date, and a few pertinent keywords. This piece of mail got tagged with "physical mail," "no threat," "Black Dahlia case," and "armchair detective."

He and Spinks were sorting through the physical fan mail while Johnson and Benally, the officer earlier dubbed terminally uncool, combed the various online communications with the podcasts. The postal inspector's team had apparently been there before Spinks and Loshak showed up but were pulled to work on tracing the origin of the latest package.

Each piece of communication was carefully logged so they could cross-reference them later if they got a hit. It had taken about twenty minutes to go through all of Caine's *Scene of the Crime* mailings. They'd been working on Wayland's *All Murder* fan mail for over two hours, and they still had five totes of physical mail left to go. God only knew how many pages of comments, emails, and messages the PD officers had left to sift through.

Some of the fan mail was disturbing. Not necessarily in a this-was-their-murderer type of way, though Loshak had found two that he'd tagged as "high threat" to dig deeper into later. Rather, disturbing in a way that made him want to take a step back so he could shake off the sender's desire to revel in darkness.

He knew that humans were naturally drawn to darkness, to taboo. It was encoded deep in their DNA to see how close to the flame they could get without getting burned. But some of these podcast listeners clearly got off on what the killers had done, on the details of the destruction of another human life, the senseless pain and torture the victims had suffered.

For the most part, the mail was coming up "no threat." Some of it was funny, in a pathetic way. Some was congratulatory, telling the podcasters what a great job they'd done relaying this case or how hilarious Jimbo's bit on this serial killer had been. One letter had even come from a relative of one of the victims, writing to tell Andi Wayland that her handling of their cousin's murder was the most tasteful of any of the podcasts and news bites on the subject, to let *All Murder* know that they felt heard and seen in a way they hadn't before.

The work oscillated from long stretches of tense, focused silence to lighthearted conversation. The latest swing had come from Spinks mentioning the Mandela Effect again.

Detective Johnson stuck up a hand to stop Spinks's explanation of the conspiracy. He jabbed an accusatory finger over his laptop at Benally.

"I don't want to hear about no Effects. I get enough of that conspiracy stuff from this guy."

Benally scratched a thumb across his dark hairline. He'd taken off his cowboy hat for the sorting and hooked it over the back of an empty seat to his right.

"Forgive my partner," he told Spinks. "Johnson doesn't believe in anything he can't smell, see, taste, or touch."

"Wrong. I don't believe half of that, either."

"Yeah, yeah." Benally jerked his chin at the reporter. "I assume you heard about the *Flint*stones versus *Flin*stones debate?"

Spinks leaned forward, discarding the pencil drawing of Charlie Manson in his hand.

"I'm not familiar with that one. Enlighten me."

"Which way do you remember it?"

"I never watched the show myself, but I always thought those vitamins said Flintstones, with a T."

"I always did, too. They're a modern *Stone* Age family, what else could possibly make sense? But guess what — it was Flinstones. No T."

Benally made an exploding gesture near his temple, complete with sound effect.

"Mind. Blown."

Spinks furrowed his brow.

"Flin? What's a Flin?"

Benally pointed a finger gun at him.

"Exactly. Now listen to this. Three, four months after the internet made this discovery? It went back to Flintstones."

"You're shitting me."

Spinks's eyes were wide.

"I do not shit you at all. It flipped. In fact, it *keeps* flipping. It'll have a T for months, then boom, no T again."

"I've got to start monitoring this." Spinks got out his phone and made a note. "If someone got some proof—"

"Nobody's going to get proof," Johnson said. "There's nothing to prove. Just a bunch of idiots with bad memories influenced by folks with too much time on their hands making up conspiracies. It's all just internet nonsense, like Pepe the Frog and Balloon Boy."

"Hey now, Balloon Boy was a real-life hoax, not an internet one."

Johnson rolled his eyes and went back to staring at his laptop.

"You know what's not a… Jesus Christ."

His brow furrowed, then he jerked back from his screen like it had burned him.

"Found him. This is our guy. It's got to be."

Chairs scraped as the three of them got up and crowded around Johnson's station.

On the screen was an email with several pornographic drawings attached, what could only be called snuff art of Andi Wayland. They depicted her death and mutilation in sickening detail. Loshak had seen a lot of disturbing fantasizing and ideation in his day, but this ranked up there with some of the most vivid and awful.

"Holy wow."

Spinks dragged a hand down his face, eyes jumping instantly away from the screen and locking on the bank of darkened windows along the far wall. The reporter grimaced.

"Dare I even ask what the email said?"

"Basically a step-by-step of the pictures," Johnson said. "But there's this weird, twisted sort of hounding her to choose him, too. Like, does he think this is going to turn her on? Get her to say, 'yes, please torture and kill me'? This has to be our guy."

"I'd definitely classify it as high threat."

Loshak leaned over Johnson's shoulder to read the text of the email. And while it was disturbing, there were no mentions or depictions of flaying.

"He does use the phrase, *It began like any other day.* We definitely want to look into him ASAP."

"What the actual fuck is wrong with people?" Benally had been silent up until then, sort of falling off Loshak's radar in the wake of this most recent discovery, but the venom in his voice made them all look his way.

"He's a serial killer, that's what's wrong with him," Johnson said.

Benally shook his head.

"I'm talking about every one of these dipshits. Like, OK, I get it, it's cool to hear creepy stories about Leonard Stump and the Zodiac." He raised his hands and waved them weakly, sarcastically pantomiming fright. "Ooh, better sleep with the lights on tonight."

He stabbed a finger at the totes of still unsorted fan mail.

"But when you've got ten thousand shitheads waxing poetic about being Ted Bundy's soulmate or painting John Wayne Gacy surrounded by roses and *RIP Pogo, Never forgotten*, something's fucking rotten in the state of Denmark. That's way too many people focusing on the wrong side of the story."

Johnson stood up and put a hand on his partner's shoulder, but Benally threw it off.

"Where the hell are the memorial drawings of the victims? Who's remembering them for just being a good person and never murdering anybody? That's a hell of an accomplishment, you ask me. That's worth never forgetting."

"Dude," Johnson said, when Benally finally ran out of steam. "Let's go get some coffee."

He cocked his head toward the door.

"The good stuff. Not that muddy shit in the coffeemaker. Pretty sure the desk sarge is just recycling it at this point."

Benally huffed a laugh, his shoulders dropping an inch or two. The tension ran out of the room like water.

"Fine. But you're buying this time." He pointed from Loshak to Spinks. "You guys up for a cup of Denver's best joe? It's on this dork."

CHAPTER 14

The officers returned half an hour later and passed out steaming cups plastered with the silhouette of a raven on the side.

"Can't beat Corvus." Benally settled back at his computer, clearly back to his jovial self. "It's got a little extra *je ne sais quoi.*"

Johnson snorted.

"How's that semester of high school French treating you?"

His partner took a sip of coffee and sighed.

"Muy bueno."

They worked in silence for a while with no new major finds. Loshak felt surprisingly fresh in spite of the fact that it was approaching midnight local time. The only sign of fatigue was the stiffness settling into his lower back.

He finished logging the latest piece of fan art, then stood and stretched. Took a lap around the conference room. He stopped at the window and looked out through the slatted blinds into a sky gone black, the stars MIA, hidden by the yellow glow of the streetlights.

Spinks sat back in his chair, rubbing his eyes.

"What about Fruit Loops?"

Loshak raised an eyebrow.

"Fruit Loops? Like the cereal?"

"What about them?" Johnson asked.

Benally, on the other hand, apparently understood

Spinks's question and perked up immediately.

"Don't even get me started on Fruit Loops. That one got so bad that they put an internet hit out on it. Posts pointing out how it changed from F-R-O-O-T fruit to F-R-U-I-T fruit started disappearing all over the place. Even worse when people realized they'd changed it back."

He shook his head.

"We got too close to the truth on that one."

"Oh my God." Johnson sighed without looking up from his typing. "Let this Mandela thing die already."

"This is how they pull them over on us, Johnson. People like you turning a blind eye."

"To a cereal name."

"Today it's a cereal, tomorrow it could be your life."

The conference room door burst open, bouncing off the doorstop with a twang. Postal Inspector Randall blinked excitedly, his cheeks jiggling, his face splotched with red.

"You're not going to believe— Completely unexpected—"

He blinked, looking around the room at each one of them.

"It's not from the same location."

Loshak turned to fully face the man.

"You've traced the second package?"

Instead of answering, Randall wove and twisted through the chairs, taking the least direct route to the glossy map of the city pinned to the wall. He snagged the dry-erase marker hanging from a piece of yarn alongside.

"We traced it alright. And the second package was sent from a different post office altogether."

He made a wild circle on the upper portion of the map.

"Here's Globeville, our first mailing location."

He dropped down to the bottom-right side of the map, searching. Apparently, he didn't find what he was looking for. He tapped the wall.

"Our second location is way out here — Aurora."

Benally scribbled something on a Post-it note and peeled it off.

"Here."

He handed the sticky note up to Randall.

The Postal Inspector slapped the pink square on the wall and circled the name, the dry-erase marker struggling to write on the paper.

Johnson frowned.

"That's about thirty minutes outside of Denver. Worse if there's traffic."

"Doesn't exactly narrow down the radius of where the unsub might live," Loshak said, cupping his chin as he studied the city map.

"Nope," Spinks agreed. "Guess our haystack just got bigger."

CHAPTER 15

Cold emptiness filled Sam Crozier as he shuffled down the street. A brittleness. He wasn't shaking anymore, but he could still feel where that trembling had passed through him.

He was swallowing a lot, though. As if his throat were trying to push down what had happened. Digest it. Process the pieces.

He noted the cross streets as he walked. Vine. Decatur. Lansing. Only three more blocks to go. He had to get his head clear before he arrived.

Another swallow. There was that old phrase "the heat of the moment." It was a cliché for a reason. He could remember it happening, that second when scalding water filled his head, flushed his cheeks, thrashed up the walls of his skull.

Rage. Something clean about it. Pure.

For those few moments, as he jammed the knife in, it had all made sense. His life. His thoughts. Existence. It all made sense.

Hot blood flooded his head. A fever that gave him a purpose. Drove him with passion. Suffused all of reality with intense meaning. He could feel music again. See colors with that same living vibrancy he used to.

But the heat had faded. Flowed away, chasing after that fleeting moment. The world had gone cold again.

The passion drained. Meaning broke down. Purpose

scattered to the wind.

Color, music, meaning. They all left him behind. Left him empty, lonely, confused.

As the fire had died away — in the cool of the moment, one might say — he'd hidden the body. Tucked it back behind the dumpster, folded it up in the same corner where he'd been sleeping, and covered it over with a scrap of cardboard from the dumpster.

It hadn't looked much different from one of the bums seeking shelter for the night. A carpet remnant would have made a better makeshift blanket, but when you didn't hit the jackpot like that, a piece of cardboard or some old industrial plastic wrap did the trick.

It could be days before anybody disturbed the body. Tried to wake it up and shoo it out.

No one cared about the living bodies who slept on the streets. Why should they care about a dead one?

Security lights from locked-up storefronts shined out onto him, neon *Closed* signs. The occasional bright beacon of the night owl flooded the sidewalk with its twenty-four-hour flood of illumination.

He slowed down in front of the big glass windows of a diner. Checked himself over again.

He'd ditched his t-shirt and hoodie. Blood-drenched. Dropped the wad of cloth in a dumpster a few blocks away from the body. Switched to one of the backups in his backpack. His jeans were still good. They'd taken surprisingly little spray.

Shame about the face, though. It hadn't come off clean like it should have. He'd been in too much of a rush. Botched it. Had to ditch the wet flap of skin in a recycling can along the way.

Maybe he should've stuck around and tried a different body part. A tongue had a lot of symbolic significance. Something to think about.

He held up his hands, turned them over in the diffuse light that made it through the tinted, UV-blocking windows of the diner. Flexed his fingers.

Clean. Good.

He took a breath. Strode forward again. Left the light of the diner, flashed through the shadow, and slid back into the almost-green glow coming from the street door of the film lab.

The security guard jumped a little. Eyes going wide, then landing on Crozier.

"Oh, it's just you."

Dennis knew Crozier wasn't going to rat him out for sleeping on the job. Under-the-table employees were quiet like that.

"Another day, another dollar, huh?"

"Think so?" Crozier stopped off at the drip coffee machine for a drink. "Feels like less than that."

Dennis huffed a polite fake laugh and stretched, the stool screeching as his head and arms pushed against the wall, shoving him out a few inches.

And that would be the extent of their conversation until Crozier's next shift the day after tomorrow. Three nights a week, they made pseudo-coworker noises at each other, then went their separate ways. The shallow, mindless *open sesame* that allowed Crozier entry into the magical cave of midnight photo development.

Coffee in hand, Crozier headed for the darkroom. Off

to go develop snapshots of other people's lives, or the moments they assigned with enough importance to take photos of, at least.

They seemed so desperate to photograph it all, capture their time in the camera's lens. Like maybe they could keep it that way. Like the camera's flash would hold back the darkness, keep that moment alive in an eight-by-ten glossy.

But he knew better. Knew that once a moment was over, it was gone forever.

CHAPTER 16

The conference room went quiet at Spinks's comment.

Loshak swallowed. Thought. Found his mind oddly blank.

The second package had been sent from a different post office. Part of Denver's urban sprawl, but technically another city altogether.

Why?

"Different guy?" suggested Benally. "Two sickos working in tandem?"

"Or at least a second victim," Johnson said. "The same guy finds his second vic in Aurora, cuts the ears off there, mails it from the second post office."

Benally tapped a pen on his teeth.

"But it'd have to be on the same day, right? Both packages were delivered today."

Randall's mustache wiggled.

"According to the records, this package was mailed the morning after our first package. The mail from Globeville and Aurora is processed through different sorting facilities, so Package Two just happened to be delivered the same day Package One was picked up from the PO box."

"So probably just the one victim," Spinks said. "But it still might be two guys. Leonard Lake and Charles Ng style. One does the first drop in Globeville while the other hops a bus to Aurora. Coordinate the efforts for maximum confusion."

Loshak didn't pitch in yet. All he could think about these theories was *Maybe*. Something didn't fit. But he didn't have a hunch of his own. Hard to contribute when you were coming up empty.

While they were talking, Loshak glided up to the map on the wall. He could smell the ink from the dry-erase marker, that familiar perfume somewhere between chemical-laced bubble gum and a rotten apple.

He stopped a foot short and let his eyes wander, tracing the black and red and blue lines of streets like a warped grid of arteries. Crossing. Flowing into each other.

He started from the Globeville post office and slowly picked out a path to the southeast corner of the map. Behind him, the officers, postal inspector, and reporter were really getting caught up in the debate, digging into the theories. He caught snippets, but nothing that stuck.

Loshak pulled out his phone and searched their second post office. Zoomed in on the street, trying to suss out something — anything — that had meaning. He read through the street names and switched to a satellite view to get a better idea of the neighborhood. It looked like an average suburb, swallowed up by the endless expansion of a growing city. And then he found what he'd been looking for.

After a minute, he tapped his finger on the map, a crinkling sound ringing out.

"Globeville has a prominent homeless population, doesn't it?"

The conversation died down behind him. There was a pause.

"Well, yeah, there's a lot of vagrants there," Benally

said. "But that's like saying, 'There's prominent traffic downtown.' There are vagrants everywhere in this city. At last count, the homeless population has tripled over the past two years."

"But there's a shelter in Globeville," Loshak said. "Not far from the post office where Package One was dropped."

"That's true," Johnson said. "You see a lot of them sleeping near the bus station around the corner from that. They pile up there when the shelter's full."

Benally was nodding.

"And there's that tent community by Alvarado Park."

Loshak glanced down at the map on his phone.

"And Aurora? Are there homeless there as well?"

The pause this time was thick, pregnant. Johnson broke the silence.

"Yeah. Yeah, there's another major shelter there. And a train station that seems like a popular hangout spot."

Loshak checked the map on his phone again. The bus stop symbols dotting the swallowed suburb.

"And it wouldn't be too uncommon for a homeless person to sleep one night in this neighborhood, hop a bus, and sleep another night in that one, would it?"

The room held quiet while they rolled the theory around, testing it out for themselves.

"You think the killer is homeless," Benally finally said.

Loshak turned around to face them. It fit the element of the profile that suggested their killer was nomadic, always drifting, never staying in one place for long.

"I think it's a distinct possibility."

The detective pushed back his chair and plopped his white cowboy hat on his head.

"Then we're going to need to talk to Wash."

CHAPTER 17

They found Detective Washburn on his way out the door for the night. Benally jogged after him.

"Hold up, Wash! We, uh, need your expertise on the face case," the detective said. "It'll take five minutes."

Wash checked the time on his phone.

"It better. I already missed my oldest's harp recital today. If I'm not in before one, Marie's going to think I'm off starting a second family."

Loshak's response fell somewhere between a laugh and a wince. He knew from experience the detective was only half joking. If you let it, the job would eat away at your personal life until there was nothing left.

Loshak hated to be part of that ravenous monster, demanding more just when Washburn was about to leave. They had to catch this guy before he killed again. That much was true.

But when this murderer was dealt with, another one would pop up. And another. The job was never done. There would only be one family, and they tended to stick around for only so long before they finally got fed up always playing second fiddle to murderers.

"I'll try not to take up too much of your time. Detective Benally here said you were the one to see about canvassing Denver's homeless population."

Benally slapped the other detective's shoulder.

"Wash is our go-to guy for vagrant questions. He's

steeped in their culture, you might say. Works with 'em more than anybody on the force. He's got eyes and ears in every camp and shelter and soup kitchen in the city."

In as succinct terms as possible, Loshak laid out his homeless theory about their unsub.

Washburn leaned a hip against a deserted desk and poked the corner of his phone into his chin while he listened.

"Tell you what, I've got some CI's among the homeless I can reach out to in the morning. Might get you somewhere to start from."

"Do you think it holds water, though?" Johnson hadn't been quite so on board with Loshak's hypothesis. "A homeless guy who listens to podcasts and uses the post office?"

"I've seen vagrants with blogs, websites, social media. Some shelters have computers nowadays, and pretty much everybody's got a phone." The detective pulled his own cell away from his face to illustrate the point, leaving behind a dent in his chin. "Failing that, you've got libraries where pretty much anybody can sign up for computer time."

"Still, we gotta be talking a small percentage of terminally online homeless people."

Wash shrugged.

"Times have changed. A big chunk of the current homeless population belongs to generations who grew up with computers, social media, smart phones. And when you take into account the mailing locations, Agent Loshak's theory isn't bad at all. The shelter there in Aurora's top-of-the-line. Get a night when the shelters are full, and the overflow will spill out into the surrounding area, sleep on benches at parks nearby or at the bus stops around the corner, wherever. When you're homeless, sleep is more of a survival thing, so they take what they can get, but there's also a minor element of comfort to it. Up off the ground is good, especially in the winter. Under some type of roof when it rains. Your basic human needs stuff.

"Then we've got the tent cities. You'll see them on the green areas around overpasses, in the parks, on the edge of the city. A new one went up in this abandoned parking lot on Ridgeline, outside what used to be the Kmart. The owners of the tents tend to be fairly stationary. They've got something relatively good going, so not a lot of movement around the city from them."

"And the ones who sleep at the shelters or on the street?" Spinks prompted.

"That's where things get pretty fluid." Washburn shifted his weight to a more comfortable position and dropped his phone into the pocket of his suit jacket. "Most of the shelters have stay limits — three days to a week — except during winter. And a subset are constantly being kicked out for violating shelter rules like no needles, no weapons, no stealing. Lots of turnover there. If you mapped it, you'd come up with a sort of circuit around the city for the habitual shelter guests. Go here until they reach the stay limit or get kicked out, then on to the next one.

"The street sleepers, on the other hand, come in two varieties. You get the ones you see on the same corner every day for years, then you have the others who roam all over the city."

Johnson crossed his arms.

"What about the fact that this guy is dropping twenty

bucks to priority ship a face or a bagful of ears? Where are they supposed to get the money for that?"

"You'd be surprised," Washburn said. "People tend to think in stereotypes: the wino spending every dollar he gets panhandling on booze or drugs. But you see a lot of money hoarding, especially within the mentally ill contingent. Folks who starve to death or freeze with a couple thousand dollars in ones wadded up in their various pockets. They may never spend a dime of it. In their mind, it doesn't equate with food or housing or booze or whatever. That money's for something else."

Benally whistled.

"Hell of a missed connection."

Wash shrugged.

"And then there's the fact that not every person living on the street is unemployed. Believe it or not, some of these folks have jobs."

Loshak considered their next moves for a moment before speaking up again.

"If you were looking for our guy, where would you start?" he asked the detective.

"I'd ask around at the soup kitchens and the shelters. You get your most outgoing personalities there. The folks who want to be around other people, want to visit and be friendly. Those are the ones most likely to talk to you. You still get some folks who are just there for a good night's sleep out of the cold, but for the most part, the loners avoid the major gathering places, rough it full time. Tent cities are about a fifty-fifty mix. Some gregarious, some loners blowing through."

"Do you get a lot of violent types out here?" Spinks

asked. "In Miami, the violent crime rate among our homeless population is higher, both victimizing other homeless and non-homeless. Time of year and spikes in cartel activity seem to have some correlation with it. Just wondering if you see any of that here."

Washburn seesawed his head back and forth.

"I mean, yes and no. A high percentage of homeless folks around Denver are peaceful. I hesitate to say 'the stable ones,' but the ones you see day in and day out are just looking to live their lives like anybody else. Your violent types tend to wind up in jail sooner or later, so it sorts itself out rather quickly."

"OK, so here's the million-dollar question," Johnson broke in. "If there is a violent type out there cutting people's faces off, do you think one of the peaceful ones will snitch to the cops? Or do you think they'll close ranks, sort of protect their own?"

"That's going to depend on who you're talking to."

Washburn's phone chirped. He checked it, then stood up and shrugged his coat on before he finished his thought.

"Let me put some feelers out. I'll get back with you tomorrow and see if we can't get an idea of areas to canvass. Anyway, that's my five minutes."

Loshak shook the detective's hand.

"Thanks for making time for us."

"Not a problem. The sooner this guy's off the streets, the better. I don't want to come off as some sort of old softie, but I don't like to see the homeless victimized. They're citizens, too. They deserve protection as much as anybody else."

CHAPTER 18

It was after two when Loshak and Spinks made it to the hotel, and Loshak was definitely dragging. Maybe it was a sign of his age, but pour enough coffee over enough hours and the caffeine stopped having a wakeful effect on him and started pushing him down the opposite slope.

They hit a minor snag checking in. There was a convention in town — something to do with geology students from colleges across the country — and their rooms had been downgraded, which included dropping a bed size and being switched to smoking.

"I'm so sorry," she said. "We've been trying to get in contact with you, but the calls kept going to voicemail."

Loshak glanced down at his phone screen. Sure enough, he'd missed three calls and had a text from Jan since their General Pickled's stop.

After a second, he realized he hadn't responded to the concierge.

"That's fine."

She smiled apologetically.

"We are refunding the price difference. That should show up on your next credit card statement."

At the moment, Loshak could honestly say he wasn't too concerned about the bill. It was the Bureau's problem, anyway. The only thing he cared about right now was getting to his room.

He was so tired that he actually ached. Even that twinge

of arthritis in his wrist was worse than usual. Getting older every day, apparently. Making a scene in front of the handful of college kids loitering near the lobby vending machines wasn't high on his priority list.

They got their key cards and took the elevator up to their floor. Loshak's room was butted up against one side of the lift, Spinks's was snugged up to the other.

"The previous occupants must've asked to be moved to get away from the noise of the elevator mechanism." Spinks yawned and hefted the strap of his laptop bag higher on his shoulder. "Can't blame 'em. I do the same when I'm traveling."

Loshak tapped his card to the RFID reader and pushed the door open.

"Is it just me, or would most college students be too drunk to notice that kind of thing? Is it a generational thing? Am I finally so old that getting wasted in a hotel isn't cool anymore?"

"The key is in the major," Spinks said, popping his own door open. "Geology students are what is referred to in the scientific community as 'a bunch of nerds.' Believe me. As someone who was very nerdy back in my school days, I'm something of an expert. It takes one to know one."

"Somehow I can't imagine you hanging around a hotel lobby staring at a rock at two in the morning."

"And yet it's disturbingly accurate. Imagine, if you will, a young Jevon and his fellow journalism students going hog wild over a well-written feature finished just seconds before the midnight deadline for the university paper." Spinks sighed. "Those were the days."

Loshak chuckled and headed into his room.

Lone Wolf

He didn't bother turning the lights on, just dropped his stuff in the closet niche and kept walking until his knees hit mattress. He plopped onto the nylon bedspread. His body collided with the bed, but his head kept going, dangling out over the edge.

Right. The downgrade to full, which in hotels was more often a super single than a true full-sized mattress.

Well, at least it wasn't a twin.

With a groan, Loshak turned his body until he found an orientation that supported the greatest amount of him at one time. He needed to check Jan's message. Take a shower. Find the little cardboard cup and get a big drink. He was parched. Which reminded him that he'd forgotten to grab that ChapStick when they gassed up the rental.

The elevator mechanism creaked and whined in the walls. The car sounded like a squawking closet door swooshing past.

He drifted off to sleep imagining Shelly and some generic college friends calling a hotel elevator to the lobby to pick them up because they were done nerding out over a handful of sedimentary rocks.

CHAPTER 19

Sam Crozier stood alone in the dark room, sneakers making that weird rubbery sound as they shifted on the non-slip floor mat. Kendra, the night manager, had already taken off, headed for wherever she went during those three- or four-hour stretches he came in to cover chunks of her shift.

She never stayed longer than the thirty minutes it took her to sort the machine rolls from the dip and dunk projects, and sometimes even stick the twin-check serial numbers to each order's leader cards. Maybe that tiny amount of effort made her feel like she was actually doing something to earn her paycheck.

When she returned at the end of the night, she would slip Crozier a twenty or two, depending on how guilty she felt. Money under the table. It might be way below the minimum wage, but hey, it was tax-free, right?

She said that several times a week. Like taxes were such a burden that Crozier should be thankful not to deal with them.

And he was, actually. He didn't need much, couldn't fool himself into wanting the empty useless junk the common rabble seemed willing to auction off hours of their life to grasp after. Four-bedroom houses, HOAs, in-ground pools. The occasional eighty or hundred bucks a week got him by just swell.

Nobody on the night shift asked questions. They

probably assumed Crozier had wanted to make a little extra cash for all those things they deemed so important. Kendra just considered herself lucky that she'd found someone with enough photography electives from high school to scrape by in an industrial photo lab with barely any training from her.

The machine orders went by the fastest, in spite of being significantly more popular than the dip and dunks. Little flashes of people's lives fed into the processing machine, shuttled from one bath to the next without Crozier's input, then dropped out the other side for him to slide into envelopes and slap on the sticker with matching serial number.

The hand-processed orders took considerably longer, moving every photo from bath to bath, hanging to dry, inspecting at every step. It cost more, so fewer people used it, but it also got the better result. Less irregularities, less chance of a calibration error, less damage to the negatives. And if the power went out? No machine to get stuck in. The professional photographers preferred it. The ones who didn't develop their work themselves, that is.

Old ladies were the big market in the industry these days, taking their trusty 35mms to weddings, reunions, to the hospital to see newborn grandkids. Buying the occasional disposable, sprinkling in pictures of their fat little dogs with life's most important events. The spoiled, piss-poor attitude of the mutts somehow showed through the gloss. The pictures of their grandkids showed attitudes not much better, though as far as Crozier could tell, there seemed to be a sliding scale with those. The babies were probably fine, but by the time the kids were toddler-age, the brattiness came through loud and clear.

Then you had the photos of elderly groups. Fifty-year class reunions or one last Christmas with all the aging brothers and sisters gathered together.

Of course, any day could be your last together. It didn't matter how old or young you were. You would make all these plans for tomorrow, and next week, and next year, and then suddenly the person you planned to do everything with was gone. No reason. No hint that it was coming. No chance to say goodbye. Just cut off mid-sentence.

Maybe that was why people took photos. Because instinctively they knew it could all be gone tomorrow, and they wanted to hold on.

Despite the hit the analog photography industry had taken with the shift to digital, some of the younger generation was starting to get into it now, too. Tweens whose parents wouldn't buy them a phone yet. Hipsters who were in it for the kitsch, the flash and ratchet and whine.

Crozier wondered if there wasn't an element of desperation to it. A need to have something physical to touch in a world where evidence that someone had lived and died was becoming increasingly intangible. A dropped phone or power surge and every shining second of life you had captured in that tiny computer could disappear.

But you could touch a roll of film. Hold processed negatives up to the light to see what had passed before the lens. Hang an eight-by-ten on the wall or stuff it in a box for the grandkids, so that one day, they could see that grandpa once went to a bar with his best hipster buddies or grandma once did a kickflip in skinny jeans and a flat-billed skater hat.

Short-term archeology, it was. Proof that they had once lived, and so had their friends, so had their family. Screaming into the future, "We were real!"

He handled those pieces of evidence for three or four hours at a time, a couple nights a week. Watched the lives roll by. The moments of warmth and happiness. And every time, the same questions came back to him.

Why was he different from all of those smiling faces? Why the dark impulses, that savage heat that filled him?

He felt like a different species from these beings on the photo paper. He looked the same, but inside he was alien. He couldn't feel what they felt.

He thought maybe he used to, a long time ago, but he couldn't be sure. Most of the time, he couldn't remember what it had felt like, his version of it. It was like trying to remember a smell. He could remember impressions of it but not the actual thing. Maybe he'd never had it, and what he dreamed of, that comfort and warmth and love and belonging, maybe it was all just that — a dream.

He shook his head and took a few deep breaths. In. Out. Tried to clear his mind.

The whir of the machines faded back in around him, the photo lab becoming real again. He went back to work.

He wasn't here to ponder existence. He was here to make a few bucks for drugs.

He started the dips on the next order. A young couple faded in on the blank photo paper.

The colors hadn't developed fully yet, but already as he moved them from solution to solution, he could make out the tan guy and the porcelain girl. Laughing. Eyes crinkling. Her big white teeth glowing like gems.

In one photo, their cheeks mashed together. In another, he kissed her on those big teeth.

Crozier stopped at the stabilizer bath. Realized he was clenching his jaw. Molars quivering. Eyelids narrowed to slits. Glaring down at the happy, laughing couple coming to life in the photo solution, but seeing Shiv again.

Her corpse with foam spilling out of the side of her mouth. Her face going as gray as a pigeon's wing. An image of death that had imprinted itself on the glossy paper somewhere behind his eyes, ready to present itself whenever he so much as blinked.

Now there was a picture he wished he could erase.

But he couldn't. Not ever.

That picture couldn't be thrown out, wiped away, burned to ash.

It would be inside him, forever. Or close enough.

CHAPTER 20

When Loshak and Spinks arrived at the station the next morning, Washburn was out talking to his informants, but he'd left a message with the desk sergeant that he would get in touch with them as soon as he had something to report.

At the morning meeting, Belte had a troubling update.

"DNA profiles on the face and ears will obviously take a while, but in the meantime, I had the lab do blood typing. The face came back as type B. The ears are type AB."

"Meaning we officially have two separate victims," Aque said.

Belte gave a curt nod.

"That's correct. Not exactly good news, but news nonetheless."

She gave them a moment to process this new information before asking each task force member to give a rundown of their particular portion of the investigation. Benally and Johnson discussed the fan mail situation; they would spend the day following up on the pieces tagged "high threat."

Aque and Schrader had come up empty interviewing the other podcasters from *All Murder*.

"My money was on our comic relief man James Nez-Kelly," Schrader said, "but he's a big boy. Goes about five-eight, three hundred pounds. You can't mistake him for our guy in the security footage."

Their next move was to track down Darren Jacob

Bowden, the self-proclaimed prophet and only real person in the matrix, who had been harassing Jessica Caine. From the fan mail investigation, Bowden's name had come up in comments on *All Murder*'s online spaces as well. A quick check had confirmed Caine's allegation that Bowden was a presence in most true crime and horror communities, leveling bizarre accusations and sending pornographic photos of himself to the female members. And even better still, he was a Denver native.

Aque read off the notes in his phone. "Former head honcho and programmer for a few strategy game apps. Worth about two-point-one mil at nineteen years old. Then he went off the rails. Started making these wild claims about Google putting his brain in a jar and using it for its processing power. By twenty-one he's got a string of minor offenses — shoplifting, assault, public indecency. His current delusion is that he's being gang-stalked by the big tech monopolies who are just fronts for the New World Order's shadow government."

"He's a better match for our lanky guy from the footage," Schrader added. "Skinny, white, late twenties. And according to the manifestos he posts in every comment section he can find, we're all fake people, so if he kills one of us, it won't matter. We'll just respawn like video game characters."

Loshak had to admit that Bowden seemed like a decent lead, but he didn't want to get too set on one suspect so early in the investigation. Better to see how the homeless investigation shook out before jumping to any conclusions.

Up front, an officer was giving a report on the anonymous tip line.

"After airing the photo on the news, we got the usual influx of calls. No major red flags yet, but anybody who wants to volunteer some time listening to the messages would be appreciated."

The conference room door cracked, and Washburn slipped in and found a seat on the opposite side of Spinks from Loshak.

Wash leaned around the reporter.

"Got a few places for you boys to start canvassing if you're interested."

The tip line officer gave way to Postal Inspector Randall, who assured them all — in what Loshak found to be a somewhat condescending tone — that every post office worker and superintendent in the Denver area was on high alert.

"By the end of the week, I'll have armed PIs in every post office in the metro area," he said, hand coming to rest on his sidearm for emphasis. "Right now, we're concentrating our limited presence in a series of likely mailing locations."

Spinks raised his eyebrows at Loshak.

"Sounds like our mail is safe with him."

Loshak turned to Wash.

"Where do you suggest we start?"

CHAPTER 21

Wash suggested starting their canvassing efforts on the fringes. They needed time to hone their technique before jumping into the middle of the homeless community. Later, they could tackle the encampment in the abandoned Kmart parking lot.

Loshak and Spinks followed the detective's directions to a busy intersection in Globeville where he'd said there was always a panhandler or two working.

In spite of the early hour, a skeletal woman in an army surplus jacket and torn jeans was leaning against the light pole, holding a creased cardboard sign with *Please. One Of God's Children. Bless YOU!* in dark Sharpie. At the light opposite, a bearded man with a dirty yellow dog that looked better fed than he was took a similar approach, shuffling down the line of cars, holding up a sign Loshak couldn't see.

A few rolled down their windows and held out bills. Mostly out-of-state plates, Loshak noted. The folks who lived here and drove through the intersection every day were more likely to have become blind to the homeless, the signs and leathery faces fading into the scenery of their morning commute.

Spinks found parking on a side street and shut off the rental.

Loshak took a second to button his suit jacket after he climbed out. There was a chill in the air this morning, but if yesterday was any indication, that would burn off before noon under the blistering sun. In Virginia, the cooler air would have been accompanied by a certain level of dampness. The lack of humidity here mingled with the lowered temperature to create a strange sensation, a confusion of nerve endings questioning whether he was too cold or just right.

"Hey." Spinks rested one arm on his open car door and gestured down the sidewalk with the other. "Maybe we should start there."

Coming toward them was a hunched man pushing a shopping cart full of blankets and crushed cans. The cart's left front wheel wobbled so hard it looked like it was going to fall off, and a dent had pushed in the corner of the basket, wires curving around the point of impact.

Loshak nodded and headed toward the pedestrian. As they got closer, he could hear the man speaking to himself in a low voice, but he couldn't make out the words. He was extremely tall, far too tall to be their suspect. Probably taller than either Loshak or Spinks if he were standing up straight, but a combination of poor nutrition and scoliosis had bent his spine into a painful-looking curve.

"Excuse me, sir. We'd like to ask you a few questions."

The man's head snapped up, the whites of his eyes showing all around the irises, bright against his rugged face.

With a grunt of effort, he shoved his shopping cart into Loshak's legs and took off sprinting in the opposite direction. The wheel bar hit Loshak just above the ankle, and the wire basket ricocheted off his knees, folding him forward over the dented cart. He grabbed for the sides, some instinctual revulsion wanting to avoid going face down in that pile of ratty, mildewing blankets.

Spinks ran a few steps, leather shoes pounding on the concrete, then stopped and shook his head.

"He's long gone. Way he's moving, he'll be in Utah by noon."

Loshak got himself straightened up and shoved the shopping cart aside. The spot above his ankle throbbed. Twenty years ago, he would have shrugged an obstacle like that off, crashed right through it, and run the guy down. Now he could already imagine the swirl of blues and purples and yellows the burst veins would paint onto the joint tomorrow.

"That went well." He sighed and looked up the street toward the intersection with the panhandlers. "Maybe we should have stuck to the original plan."

They headed up to the light.

The traffic flowed by. The lady with the "God's Children" sign stood with one foot in the bike path, one in the street, looking into the passing cars.

Loshak was more cautious in his approach this time. She didn't have anything to shove at him, but he checked for bicyclists before stepping out beside her.

"Excuse me, ma'am?"

She looked over her shoulder, looked from him to Spinks, then turned back to the cars.

"No."

Loshak stopped.

"We'd just like to ask you a few questions."

"I said no, pig."

Spinks tried his luck.

"See, there's this murderer going around Denver cutting people's faces off—"

"Good, I hope he cuts your piggy faces off. I ain't no snitch."

An SUV stopped alongside the bike path with its window down, a hand holding a bill sticking out. She shuffled up to it and took the money.

"Thank you. God bless you."

When she got back out of traffic and saw that they were still there, she flapped her cardboard at them.

"Go. Leave. Vamoose. Nobody wants you here."

Things didn't go much better with the guy and his dog on the other corner.

"You gonna arrest me for panhandling?"

Up close, Loshak was surprised by how young the guy was, probably the same age as Darger. Living on the streets had sun-charred his cheeks and the bridge of his nose, turning him into an old man before his time.

"No, we just want to know if you've seen this man around town recently."

He held out the screenshot of their suspect.

The guy didn't even glance at it.

"I don't talk to cops, and if you won't leave, I'll sic Snape on you."

Spinks's brows went up.

"Your dog's name is Snape?"

The guy rolled his eyes.

"It's from *Harry Potter*. Ever heard of it?"

It was a long walk back to the car.

"Feels like Goldilocks," Loshak said. "We've talked to three people, gotten zero results, and none of them could be our suspect. One was too tall, the other one was too thin and too female, the last one had too long of a beard to grow in two days."

"What's the world coming to?" Spinks shook his head in disbelief. "We've got *Harry Potter* fans living on the streets. I don't care whether it's from the books or the movies, that's surreal."

"Yo. Police bros. Over here."

The salutation came from across the street, a girl leaning one hip on the corner of a bus stop seat, waving them over.

Loshak thought of her as a "girl," at least, but she was probably in her early-to-mid twenties. The layers of shirts and jackets and necklaces she was swimming in might have made her look a little younger, but there was also the fact that everyone under thirty was starting to fall under the classification of "kids" to him. Next thing he knew, he'd be yelling at them to get off his lawn.

When they didn't immediately cross the street to come to her, the girl jogged over to them. Her mass of necklaces bounced and jingled audibly.

"Yo," she repeated. "I noticed y'all were creeping around, hitting up people for info. Whatever you're looking for, you ain't gonna find it."

Spinks had on his charming smile.

"And why's that?"

"Cause y'all cops don't know the streets."

She pulled the sides of her beanie down, straightening it, and dozens of rings caught the sunlight. A few had left green marks on her tanned fingers. Others were turned sideways enough to show the bottom sizing pieces pinched together far enough for the sides to go past one another. A closer look at the necklaces showed a similar level of cheapness. It all came together in a look that was strangely endearing. Like a child who'd hit the costume jewelry jackpot at a garage sale and wanted to wear the entire score at once.

"But you do," the reporter prompted.

Her grin widened.

"I live here, bro. These streets're my veins. This city's my heart. The folks you're harassing? Those are my folks. You want to know something about anything out here, you ask me."

Loshak slipped the photo of their suspect from his pocket.

"Have you ever seen this man?"

She took the paper and studied it, nodding.

"Yeah. Yeah, I know him."

She glanced up at Loshak and made eye contact. A tiny grin curved the corners of her lips.

"Y'all are looking for him?"

"What can you tell us about him?" Loshak asked.

She laughed.

"I can tell you a lot about old Jacky-boy here. Don't even get me started. But you're not really looking for secondhand info, are you? You're looking for an up-close-and-personal encounter, am I right? A little two-on-one chat?"

Not wanting to tip anyone off more than they had to, Loshak proceeded with caution.

"He might have witnessed a murder. We're just hoping he can tell us what he saw."

"Anything he knows that might help us get a killer off the streets," Spinks chimed in.

The girl was nodding along.

"Well, you ain't gonna find Jack looking like that, that's for sure. I mean, everything about y'all screams *cop*. The suit, the shoes, the hair— well, his hair," she said, hitching a thumb toward Loshak. She smirked at Spinks. "Your chrome dome's a dead giveaway, too. A little too manicured for this crowd, if you know what I mean. If they see you coming, they're gonna scatter."

She held up a beringed hand and made a dropping motion, fingers spreading and fluttering away to illustrate her point.

"What y'all need is a guide. Somebody who can get you in close. Somebody who can vouch."

"Is that somebody you?" Spinks asked.

"For a small fee, yeah, I can walk you right up to Jacky and introduce y'all."

On paper, the FBI had outlawed paying informants — the information gained more often than not had been made up for the cash — but it was one of those rules that got ignored all the time, like *don't throw your gum wrappers in the potted plants* and *don't try to murder the agents who trace human trafficking back to your doorstep*. In Loshak's experience, nobody in the Bureau really paid attention to it.

And given the fact that none of the people they'd approached had been willing to talk so far, it was worth a shot.

"How small a fee are we talking?"

She shrugged, her gray-blue eyes never leaving his face.

"Fifty seems fair. Serious work, serious pay."

Loshak slipped his wallet out and checked its contents. Since the advent of debit cards, he didn't carry around the cash that he used to on these trips.

"I've got a twenty and three ones."

He plucked the bills out.

"Dang. Sorry, bro."

She started to leave.

"Hang on," Spinks said. He was digging through his wallet. "Give her your twenty, and I've got these."

He pulled out another twenty and a ten.

"Alright, now we can do business."

She took the bills and folded them into an unnecessarily tiny rectangle that she stuck in her right shoe.

"Come on, this way to talk to Jack."

She spun around and headed back the way she came, toward the bus stop across the street, without looking either way. The light at the intersection had just turned green, and horns blared as she jogged through the rush hour traffic, seemingly oblivious to the multi-ton death machines speeding her way.

"Wait," he called out, but she kept going.

Loshak followed, some reflex in his mind throwing him after her. He jogged into the stream of vehicles, looking for gaps.

People screamed obscenities at them from their windows. Horns bent and warped in full Doppler Effect. Engines rattled and tires hissed against the asphalt what felt like mere inches from him.

He jerked up short on the rubber-marked paint at the edge of a lane, narrowly missing a collision with a black

SUV's fender. He felt the hot wind coming off the engine. Heard the rattle in the leaf springs. Saw the shadows of little heads in the tinted back windows, probably kids on their way to school. The hot exhaust from the tailpipe flapped his pant legs against his shins.

What the hell was he thinking? Running after an informant into oncoming traffic like this? If he died right now, it would go down in Bureau history as the dumbest thing an agent had ever done. He would be an object lesson they taught at Quantico.

Finally, the light changed. The last of the commuters held a middle finger high as his rusting sedan rattled past.

Loshak ran the last few steps and hopped up onto the curb. His heart was pounding so hard it was making him light-headed. Sweat soaked through his button-up shirt and turned the environment inside his jacket hot, humid, and swamp-like.

Spinks joined him a second later. The reporter had had the sense to stay where he was and wait for the light. He blew out a loud breath and grabbed his heart.

"That was some serious derring-do, partner."

"She's gone," Loshak said, gesturing at the empty sidewalk. "The whole thing was a con."

"Yeah, I kinda figured, the way she took off like that. On the bright side, at least you're still in one piece. I don't know if your life was flashing before your eyes, but it was flashing before mine. At least, what I've imagined of it. Phew."

Spinks whistled and shook his head.

"Let's all pinky-swear to never, ever scare me like that again."

CHAPTER 22

They stopped in at a diner afterward. A nice, quiet piece of pie and some coffee seemed like a pretty great idea in the afterglow of the adrenaline.

Loshak cut the end triangle from his strawberry-rhubarb and lifted it with his fork.

"We used to call that the Idiot Tax. Some rookie would come in all mad, because he thought he was going to blow a case wide open by greasing some palms, and ended up just getting conned."

"OK, so we lost fifty bucks," Spinks said. "Call us idiots if you want, but I say we were still reeling from that *Harry Potter* fan homeless revelation. And anyway, we did learn something."

"What's that?"

"We need to change tactics. Think about it — everybody we talked to picked you out as law enforcement. They all knew on sight that you were a cop."

"She actually pegged *both* of us for cops," Loshak pointed out, but Spinks wasn't listening.

"What we need is to go undercover. Not both of us, obviously. They'll see you coming a mile away."

"What? Why me?"

"With that hair?" Spinks shook his head like it was obvious. "I've got to be our man on the street. A little sprucing down, a little dirt, a little getting into character."

"What's wrong with my hair?" Loshak muttered.

"And we'll have to swing by a thrift store."

The waitress came by and refilled their coffees.

"I don't know about this," Loshak said after she'd left.

"Come on, partner, I'm great at this stuff. Remember Trufant's secret club in Kansas City?"

"I remember getting into a fight in the entryway trying to get you out."

"There's no getting me out this time. I'll already be on the street. I can run if I have to, but I won't have to, because I'll blend in perfectly. You'll see."

Before Loshak could put up another protest, his phone trilled. It was District Commander Belte.

"Aque and Schrader just brought in Bowden, our serial podcast harasser," she said. "And get this. He confessed to everything."

CHAPTER 23

The observation room was crowded by the time Loshak and Spinks made it back to the station. Word had gotten around that they had a confession in the face case, and people were crowded around the monitor showing the live feed from Interrogation like a bunch of football die-hards trying to watch the Super Bowl on a backup TV after the big screen went out.

Darren Jacob Bowden sat alone in the interrogation room. On the monitor, Loshak watched him cross his arms and shift back in his seat, scowling like a man waiting for a bus that was running late.

He was young enough to be their suspect. Clean-shaven. Right build. His hair was bleached bright yellow, which could have been a recent attempt at disguising himself. Maybe he'd seen the spot on the news.

The nose-mouth-eyes configuration was close to that of the mailer on the footage, but something about it wasn't right. Maybe that could be accounted for by the slight distortion of video. Maybe.

Loshak made a quick note to himself to get on the horn with the facial recognition software guy at the Bureau and send over the mugshot and the footage.

Bowden's eyes locked on the camera. He let out a bark of annoyed laughter and shook his head.

"He hasn't lawyered up?" Loshak asked.

Schrader shook his head.

"Said it wouldn't do any good. We've got a public defender on her way over to talk to him anyway, just to make sure. One time, we had a guy waive his right to an attorney and then sue us claiming that we asked, but not *nicely*. We had him on tape telling us to shove our lawyer up our asses, but we're extra careful about it nowadays."

"Top brass commandment number one," Aque grumbled.

Schrader translated for them.

"*Always cover thine ass.*"

"Do you mind if I talk to him?" Loshak asked.

"Knock yourself out."

Loshak left the detectives, stepped out into the hall, and rapped his knuckles on the door of the interrogation room. Without waiting for a response, he let himself in. The move always reminded him of a doctor's office; the quick knock followed by the ready-or-not entry.

Bowden threw up his hands.

"Oh good, Agent Smith's here. Nice of you to make time to spawn in. Let's get on with it, buddy."

"It's Special Agent Loshak, actually, with the FBI. Sorry to keep you waiting."

Loshak pulled out the chair opposite their suspect.

"Anyway, what exactly are we getting on with?"

"The proceedings. The kangaroo court leading to my execution — *again*. This'll be the fifteenth time you assholes have snuffed me out, by the way, so if you think I'm going begging and pleading to the chair this time, you can hop back to Judge Mama Roo crying, little joey."

On the drive back to the station, Loshak had read entries on Bowden's website. Jessica Caine had described him as going on long screeds, and from what Loshak had seen, that was the most accurate way of describing it.

For the past three years, Bowden had put out an almost daily rant ranging from five thousand to sometimes over thirty thousand words, all of them apparently proof that the world was a giant simulation built with the express purpose of torturing him to create a chemical in his brain that helped increase Big Tech's processing power.

Bowden's creativity was both staggering and chilling. Anything from a piece of trash he passed on the sidewalk to someone holding the coffee shop door for him was elaborately woven into his delusions.

At the same time, anyone he met could be justified as a target for murderous rage — elderly, children, pregnant women — they were nothing but set dressing in the simulation, a moving piece in the plot to destroy him. They weren't human, as he so often repeated in his rants, so killing or molesting them wouldn't be any more an act of deviance than deleting a word in an email.

In the interrogation room, Loshak sat back in his chair, mirroring Bowden's posture.

"I've read some of the accusations on your website."

"Oh, what a shock, the sim is monitoring what I put out there for the masses."

"I thought there were no masses. Aren't you the only human being in this simulation?"

In Loshak's experience, there were two major types of reactions to pointing out the inconsistency in paranoid delusions. Some people shut down and refused to talk any more. Others folded the inconsistency into their delusions like egg whites into cake batter.

Bowden rolled his eyes.

"Do you think I'm stupid? I know about the millions trapped in simulations outside mine, every one of us in our own little hellhole. Or is it billions now, Smith? How many people are your Nanos torturing right this second?"

"Let's talk about Jessica Caine," Loshak said. "She's the host of the *Scene of the Crime* podcast."

"Yeah, I know your little honey pot traps and their *supposed* occupations."

"You were sending her explicit photos of yourself?"

Bowden scoffed.

"Sure, yeah. Conveniently forget to mention that you people were broadcasting high-frequency trigger waves at me until I did what you wanted."

"The host of *All Murder,* Andi Wayland, reported you for similar harassment."

"Sure, I'm the one harassing everybody. Pile it on, Smith. I sent them a bunch of body parts, too, right? Supposedly from 'people' I 'murdered.'"

Bowden leaned forward over the table as he said it, fingers making exaggerated quotation marks in the air.

Loshak kept his face neutral. This interview could either tell them a lot or lead them off on a wild goose chase the investigation might not recover from.

"What did you send them?"

Bowden flapped a hand in the air.

"Body parts. Dismembered. Probably horrendous. That's how these games go, isn't it? The more gory and disturbing, the better for you assholes to get off on."

"Specifically, Darren. What specifically did you send to each of them?"

"I don't know, Smith," he sneered. "What did the mainframe tell you I sent them? A dismembered penis, because you want everyone to speculate that I'm impotent? Is that it? Get a good laugh at me? Demoralize me even more?"

Loshak glanced down at his notes.

"How did you pay for shipping, Darren?"

"Ass, grass, cash, or credit, what you take you can't always edit, leddit roll on Reddit, I said it, you maybe don't head it, I mean think, drink, making a stink—"

Rather than let the improvised rhyming session continue, Loshak interrupted. Delusional types could often go on for minutes or even hours spitting out meaningless word salad, as Bowden's website proved almost every day.

"I'm going to have some techs check your laptop's history."

As he said it, Loshak looked into the camera to make sure somebody in the observation room would get the hint and start the process.

Bowden rolled his eyes.

"Right, and tomorrow I'll be brought up on child porn charges for stuff you install on my hard drive. I know how this incriminating process works."

"No, tomorrow we'll know whether you've actually ever checked the mailing addresses for *Scene of the Crime* or *All Murder.* Because I have a feeling you haven't. My theory is your harassment of these women is all online right now and hasn't bled into the real world yet. So, here's the big question: why confess to something you didn't do?"

"Ding, ding, ding!" Bowden pointed at Loshak. "We have a winner! Agent Smith's programming finally caught up. No wonder you bots need my brain's processing power."

Bowden sat back in his chair, a smug look on his face.

"I've been through this so many times that I know how it works. You bring me in on trumped-up charges, I tell the truth, but you've got supposed 'evidence.' I cry and beg and plead, but you just keep laying on the lies, discrediting me, burying me. Still no confession from me, so we start the torture. Finally, when I'm broken down and there's nothing else I can take, I tell you what you want to hear, and then? Blam-O! Old Darren rides the electric bullet all the way to hell, screaming and writhing in pain. Next morning, I wake up back here, ready to do it all again. Well, fuck your standard procedure, pal, I'm skipping the cutscene this time."

He looked over his shoulders like a gunman was going to step out of thin air.

"I confessed. Now let's get the execution over with so I can wake up again already."

"Have you seen this man?" Loshak slid the screenshot from the footage across the table.

Bowden glanced at the photo.

"So what if I have? Is this some new phase of the torture, try to get me to incriminate an NPC? Show me how low I'll stoop?"

He threw up his hands, and then rocked back and forth in his chair, grinning like a chimp.

"I already confessed for shit's sake. So let's talk about options for my last meal."

CHAPTER 24

They didn't get as far as having the techs check out the computer. Benally and Johnson met Loshak in the hallway as he stepped out of Interrogation. Spinks, Aque, and Schrader came out of the observation room along with Belte. Apparently, the district commander had joined while Loshak was interviewing Bowden.

"Bowden was in the county hospital when our packages were mailed," Johnson said. "They think he was bitten by a spider. They're sending over the medical records now, but if we need proof, they said we can just check his right thigh."

Benally screwed up his face.

"Hope it wasn't a brown recluse. I got bit by one of those bastards on a camping trip when I was a kid. Killed off all the skin about as big as a quarter and left this dead piece in the middle. Looked like a rotten canned oyster inlaid into my butt cheek. Nasty as hell. I've still got the scar."

"Nobody wants to hear about your butt scars, Benally," Johnson said.

"When they're not relevant, no, but this time, they're vital to the case."

The commander blew out an annoyed breath.

"So this fucker's still out there, probably looking for his next vic." She frowned at Loshak. "How'd you know Bowden wasn't our murderer? Lucky guess?"

Loshak dipped his head to the side for a second.

"Something like that. He shares a lot of the right traits with our killer, but his style of harassment didn't quite fit. In his delusions, everything is aimed inward, toward him. I think he's *too* self-obsessed to kill anyone, as strange as that may sound." Loshak shrugged. "He also has multiple posts on his website explaining that he's figured out how to avoid torture from the shadow authorities by confessing to everything up front."

Benally laughed.

"Making hypotheses based on evidence? That's cheating."

"You, back to checking out those lists of fan mail creepers," Belte said. "I want some movement on this goddamn case that doesn't lead to one dead end after another."

The cowboy-hatted officer and his partner headed back down the hall toward their computers.

Belte sighed.

"Well, Agent, if you've got any other ideas or guidance, I'm all ears."

"We were actually working on a plan for canvassing the homeless population, Commander," Spinks said. "Running up on them in fed gear doesn't seem to be working, so I'll be going incognito to have some conversations."

At her raised brow, the reporter put up his hands in a placating gesture.

"Don't worry. I've gone undercover for investigations before. It's kind of my specialty."

CHAPTER 25

"Your specialty?" Loshak asked.

"The trick is in the layering."

Spinks either wasn't listening or was purposely ignoring the incredulity. Hangers squealed along the thrift shop's metal racks as the reporter dug through the old sweaters, college sweatshirts, knitted Christmas cardigans, and chunky sweater vests.

"Something comfortable, but not too clean," Spinks said. "You want that lived-in look."

Loshak checked the tags on a moth-eaten wool sweater and whistled. The price of secondhand clothes had really gone up. Of course, he hadn't been in a thrift shop in years. Not since Shelly was eleven or twelve, when she'd first decided she needed to put together her own Halloween costumes, not buy the cheap ready-made polyester ones.

"Jackpot."

Spinks pulled out a Colorado State hoodie with frayed, discolored cuffs that looked like its last owner had spent every day in class chewing on them. He added it to the pile of clothes hanging over his shoulder. He already had an old army jacket, a ratty t-shirt endorsing Ross Perot for President in '92, and a handful of lint-covered scarves.

"Now on to pants. This is where we're really going to tie it all together."

Loshak picked up a threadbare Metallica hoodie.

"Maybe I should get in on this."

Spinks snorted.

"No offense, partner, but this isn't really your forte. When you come around, I feel like I'm about to get arrested or audited. Or both."

He threw a pair of worn, teal long johns over his shoulder, then followed them with a ripped pair of flannel-lined jeans. Then he bobbed an index finger at Loshak.

"If that kid this morning taught us anything, it's that these people can smell a cop a mile away, and buddy, you reek of it."

"Apparently because of my hair."

Spinks stopped shopping for a second and put a hand on Loshak's shoulder.

"It's good hair, partner, it's just not the hair we need right now. You did your profiling mind tricks on Bowden and proved that he wasn't our killer. Now it's time to let me work *my* magic — and my magic is charming people. The salt of the Earth kind of folks, not the murderers."

Loshak still wasn't convinced that letting Spinks go out on his own was the best idea, but the reporter did have a way with people.

"Well, you're going to need a hat."

He grabbed an old Carhartt beanie off the shelf.

"Here. This'll kind of hide that manicured, waxed look the kid mentioned. Maybe some of these gloves, too. Make it look like you're out there at night when the temperature drops."

Spinks grinned.

"That's the spirit."

"Do you think you're going to smell too clean?"

Loshak thought back to the particular unwashed scent

that hung around the homeless woman and man they'd briefly spoken to that morning. Even the girl with the rings and necklaces had a certain funk. Subtler, but still there.

"Nah, that's not going to be a problem at all. I've got a two-pronged attack. First, smell this."

Spinks held out a handful of sleeves from the rack.

Loshak gave a minor sniff.

"Smells like every secondhand store ever."

"That, my friend, is the frankenstink of a hundred different laundry soaps and perfumes and deodorants mixing together, with a touch of must and dust and maybe just a smidge of B.O. to top it off. You'd think they'd wash all this stuff before selling it, but they don't. Not the big chain thrift stores, anyway. Of course, the volunteers who pick through the piles will trash the worst smelling and most heavily damaged clothing, but can you imagine the laundry bill for washing the millions of pounds of clothes they get every year?"

He stopped suddenly. His eyes swiveled toward Loshak and narrowed.

"You know what, I bet thrift shop folks see a lot of Mandela Effect items come through. Now that would be an interesting study. 'How many alternate spellings have you seen of Berenstein?'"

"So what's the other 'prong.'"

Loshak picked through the bin of gloves while he talked to see if he could find anything appropriate.

"I assumed the second one was also related to smell."

"Oh yeah, second, I'm going to smell these puppies up."

"Smell them up?"

"With dumpster juice. There's one between our hotel

and that Denny's that'll be perfect for the job."

With the full gamut of homeless chic over his shoulder, Spinks ducked into the strangely undersized door of the thrift shop's changing room.

Loshak leaned against a rack of kid's pajamas and waited, trying to figure out where this place had gotten a door at least a foot shorter than standard. It didn't look quite square, either. He would've guessed salvage from a house old enough to have had doors handmade on site, but the cheap veneer cracking into strips from the bottom proved it had to be less than fifty years old. So the question was, who was prefabricating doors that short, and why were people still buying them?

The changing room opened, and Spinks stepped out. Loshak blinked.

"Wow."

The transformation was impressive. Spinks hadn't just changed clothes, he was hunching a little to one side, keeping a hand tucked close as if he were trying to comfort a pain in his abdomen. Instead of the usual long-legged stride, he shuffled, something a little less certain in his footing, even when he was standing still. Nothing fit him quite right, but that only helped sell the look. Especially in the dirty fluorescent light of the thrift shop.

"Pretty good, right?"

He raised a pleased eyebrow at Loshak and broke the spell.

The agent nodded.

"I think we've got a winner."

"Agreed. Let's hit the street."

CHAPTER 26

As a reporter, Spinks had gone into dozens of situations incognito. It wasn't as if he were a nationally recognizable face — that sort of celebrity didn't grace the writers of criminal features or even the authors of best-selling novels about FBI profilers — so most of the time he was able to just walk in anonymously. He rarely had to pretend he was someone else to get the information he needed.

Even back in Kansas City, during the operation he was hanging his undercover career on, Spinks had been more in a "head down/ears open" situation. Going out on the street in his homeless getup was completely different. He couldn't just layer it on, be Spinks the Homeless Man. This time, he had to become someone completely different.

New name, new identity, new thought process.

Loshak had offered to drop him off close to the location Detective Washburn had suggested for their second foray, but Spinks wanted more time than that to get into character. Instead, he had the agent let him out at a gas station almost ten blocks away.

"You're sure about this?"

From the driver's seat, Loshak leaned over the console to better see out the passenger side door.

Spinks didn't feel quite as sure about it as he had ten minutes previous, but he didn't let that show.

"Are you kidding? This is the perfect opportunity to try out my street persona — J."

145

"J?"

"From Florida originally, then a little while in Georgia, out to LA, Vegas, now playing in a Denver near you."

He hiked up the collar of the army jacket around his hoodie and shrugged his shoulders a few times before he finished his thought.

"He ain't too big on these winters out here, but ol' J's managing, he's managing."

"Alright. Well."

Loshak looked down at the phone in the cup holder and gritted his teeth.

Spinks wasn't taking the phone with him. J wouldn't have something like that. Although with that guy's bit earlier about *Harry Potter*, and with what Washburn had said about phones and other tech not exactly being a rare occurrence on the streets, Spinks did think twice.

No. Technology only wired you into The Man's conspiracy. Ol' J knew better than to mess with that shit.

"I guess I'll see you at the diner on 38th, then," Loshak said.

Spinks nodded.

"I'll be there with all the information I can carry."

He let the door of the rental fall shut and moved at a shuffle toward the gas pumps.

Show time.

All the pumps were full, folks headed out of town stopping to drain the bladder, top off the tanks, and grab some road snacks. An older man was gassing up his RV at one of the diesels. Khaki cargo shorts despite the relative chill in the air, white New Balance sneakers, orange-verging-on-salmon polo tucked under a moderate-to-severe retiree gut.

That was stop number one.

Spinks's pulse sped up. He shifted his trajectory, aimed himself a little more clearly toward the old man. His mouth went instantly dry.

Play it cool. Like you've been here a thousand times before. The first step's always the hardest, right?

The old man caught sight of the hooded, homeless figure shuffling his way. Backed up a step. Not far enough to let go of the pump, but still obvious.

Spinks realized he must look fairly imposing, given his height and the extra bulk the layers of clothes added. Maybe he should've gone hood-down for ol' J's debut. Look a little less like Death come callin'.

Too late, he'd have to fix it in post — a.k.a., in the ten blocks between the gas station and the corner next to the homeless shelter.

He lowered his head and hunched his shoulders and spine a little, trying to bring his height down every bit he could.

"'Scuse me, sir, 'scuse me."

The nerves were really firing now. His face burned. He felt lightheaded, and his tongue kept sticking to his teeth and the inside of his cheeks, making every word come out sounding sticky. Damn, he should've grabbed his water bottle out of the car.

Spinks pushed through, laying on the heaviest, deepest Florida cracker accent he could dredge up.

"Bless you, sir, sorry to bother ya, but I gotta ask a minute of your time. I gotta get back to Florida, my sister's real sick, and she probably ain't gonna make it. I just need a couple bucks, whatever you can spare, to get on the Amtrak, go back'n see her one last time. If you gimme your address, write it down for me, Ol' J'll send the money right back to you soon as I get there."

"Sorry, I don't carry cash," the old fogie said.

Spinks resisted an urge to wince.

Who knew getting rejected for something you didn't even want could sting the pride so deeply? How would Ol' J feel about something like that? Would he be used to it by now? Hardened to the rebuffs? Callous?

The old man clicked the pump a few times, trying to get the price to a whole number.

"But are you hungry? If you'd like some summer sausage and crackers, I can get you a ziplock full of 'em."

Spinks considered it. Nah, J wouldn't take that. He had his pride. And he wanted money, not conciliatory snacks. But he also wouldn't be a dick about turning it down.

"That's OK, sir." He skirted past the old man and backed toward the far sidewalk, doing a sort of half bow, half nod. "Thank you, anyway. Bless you."

The old man nodded.

"Take care."

"Thank you, sir. You, too."

Spinks shuffled on down the street. About a block away, the endorphins kicked in. Spinks grinned. He'd done it. Ol' J had passed the first test. The hard part was over, the debut made, the ice broken neatly beneath J's perfect combination of obvious lies and overly gracious responses.

He made some adjustments — namely, pushed the hood back and resituated the stocking cap on his head, pulling it down over his ears and all around to make sure there was no trace of the chrome dome their street urchin con artist had mentioned that morning.

There were lots of folks out walking today. He wasn't really up on the tourist districts of Colorado, but this street in particular seemed pretty crowded.

He made up his mind, and the next person Ol' J passed, he held out a gloved hand and asked for spare change. It was a younger guy. He pushed past without acknowledging that he'd heard.

Spinks raised his eyes to the next person in line.

"Spare change? Ma'am? Spare change?"

She didn't have any cash on her. That was OK. This was the age of the debit card, after all. On he went.

One kid, probably just eight or nine, ran over from his mom and gave Spinks a wadded-up five-dollar bill.

That hurt in a new and different way. Cut into his heart a little too much.

Davin had been that way, too. Spinks couldn't count the number of times his son had hung out the window with everything he'd had in his allowance and handed it to some bum at a light.

Spinks watched the kid disappear with his mom into the foot traffic. He wished he could run after them and stick the money back in the kid's hand. Tell him, "Good job, that was really nice of you, but I'm actually an undercover consultant with the FBI. Take your five back, but keep that good heart of yours."

But that wasn't how this worked. He was too close now to the target corner, anyone could be watching him. And anyway, he would probably never catch up. That mom had been on a mission to get her kid out of there; she'd really

E.M. Smith, L.T. Vargus & Tim McBain

been moving.

So on he went. Keep on truckin'. Ol' J's motto. Keep on a-keepin' on.

The foot traffic thinned out a bit. Up ahead, he caught sight of the bus stop Wash had mentioned. That brick building behind it with the wheelchair ramp winding around the side would be the shelter. A couple of people hung around out front, a hunched old lady dressed not too unlike Spinks himself, hashing something out with a younger woman in a pink tracksuit.

At first glance, he was pretty sure the younger woman wasn't homeless. A volunteer or maybe shelter management? The old lady gestured violently with something at the building. Was that a stick or—

It caught the sun. It was a meat tenderizer. One of the old solid-metal ones.

As he drew closer, he started to pick up snippets of their conversation.

"And I told him, I said, don't you touch my pillow, you son of a bitch—"

"Miss Jeanie." The younger woman had her hands up, patting the air. "Shelter policy doesn't depend on whether you told someone once or a hundred times. No violence or weapons are allowed on shelter property. No extenuating circumstances."

"But I told him!"

"I'm informing you now, Miss Jeanie, that you are trespassed from this place for one week. Don't come back until next Tuesday. Got it? If you do, I'm just going to have to turn you away."

"And that son of a bitch gets to stay? When he's in there

stealing pillows?"

"I'll see you next Tuesday, Miss Jeanie. If you get rid of the weapon."

The younger woman turned and headed inside.

"Over my cold dead fat lumps."

The bent little woman stuffed the meat tenderizer into the pocket of her huge black duster. Pieces of the fake leather flaked away and drifted down the sidewalk on the breeze. Her words sounded like she was muttering to herself, but her tone was sharper than that. Louder, too.

"You want my 'weapon' gone? I want my pillow back. Son of a bitch."

Spinks shoved his hands into his pockets. He understood Ol' J a little better now from the time he'd spent begging, and he thought he knew what the Florida émigré would do here. In the presence of such a big personality as Miss Jeanie, Ol' J would take a more submissive role. He lowered his head into something of a dog-scared-of-a-kick posture.

"'Scuse me, honey," he said, laying on the swamp talk heavy once again. He nodded up to the shelter without actually lifting his head up all the way. "This place up yonder here got any empty beds?"

"Got one goddamn empty bed now, I'll tell you that much. And it's gonna stay empty! See if they ever get my business again."

Spinks sucked his teeth.

"Kinda assholes in there, huh?"

"And thieving sons of bitches!"

"Damn. Here I was hoping to find something for tonight. I can't be having folks stealing my shit, though."

"Nobody can," Miss Jeanie snapped. "It's a disgrace!"

Spinks let out a weary sigh.

"Well, shit. Guess I'm gonna have to take my friend up on his offer. You know a guy around here — young guy, about yea tall?"

He went quiet for a second and held his hand out for reference, measuring off where their mailer's five-foot-eight- or nine-inch stature would come to on him, right about his shoulder. Then he launched into the rest of the description.

"Dark hair, kinda pale kid. Skinny. Met him a few days ago up in Globeville. He was wearing a black hoodie and jeans."

Spinks wasn't sure what sort of signifiers homeless folks looked for in one another, so he decided to go for broke.

"He was packing around a cardboard box, said he had to go mail it, but to look him up later."

Miss Jeanie shook her head.

"No, I don't know any sons of bitches with cardboard boxes. Some of the younger ones stay in the tents out by the Kmart, though. He probably wanted you to look him up there."

"Thanks, honey, I'm gonna go poke around inside just in case somebody else saw him."

She grunted.

"Suit yourself."

It wasn't necessarily progress, but she had accepted him as one of her own. The disguise had passed the second, and more important, test.

Spinks gave the disgruntled old woman a friendly smile, then started his shuffle up the wheelchair ramp toward the door.

Time to drop Ol' J into the deep end.

CHAPTER 27

In the soup kitchen portion of the shelter, Ol' J found his people.

"Never knew there was a name for it!"

Whitey was an older black man with that shock-white hair writers so often referred to but Spinks had never seen in person before. It was truly shocking.

"Back in the sixties that shit kept happening to me. First you had your O'Dool's with two O's, and then the name changed to O'Doul's on me out of nowhere — O-U — and nobody but me noticed! Then you had the parkway out here, over on the west side, you know the one. It was there, then for about five years, there was nothing. Now it's back!"

Spinks nodded along.

"It's everywhere, if folks would just pay attention."

"That ain't nothing."

Loogie, their fellow Mandela Effect enthusiast, looked like an aging moonshiner, craggy face hung with a long dirty beard of indeterminate color, worn Big Smith overalls and shitkicker boots. He even had on one of those floppy felt hats, the brim drooping with age.

"I fuckin' drowned when I was a kid. Lifeguard at the city pool wasn't watching, and I was down at the bottom of the deep end for ten minutes before anybody noticed. I remember sinking down there, staring up, choking and coughing and thinking, 'Nobody knows I'm down here.

154

I'm dying.' Everything went black, and I felt bugs swarm all over me, biting me, then I woke up in the hospital. Docs said I'd been dead for four minutes, and they had to revive me. But guess what? I wake up the next morning, and my folks don't remember a thing. My brother's the only one who remembered. Then he starts forgetting about it, like bits and chunks, until poof, it was all gone."

"Now, if I'm recollecting right," Spinks said, tipping a pointer finger toward Loogie, "that's Quantum Immortality, not a Mandela Effect."

"Quantum what now?"

"Quantum Immortality. It's this thing where your consciousness can't exist in a universe where you don't exist, so if the You in this universe dies, your consciousness is shifted over to another universe where you survived the drowning."

"I'll be damned."

Loogie's upper body jumped when he said it, a seated hop, something satisfied in the motion and his tone.

"Yeah. Mandela Effect is large scale, Quantum Immortality only happens to one person who went through a deadly situation — and *supposedly* survived." Spinks shrugged. "Least that's the way I heard it."

"My brother died in a house fire back in '93," Loogie said. "Think he's out there somewhere in another universe where I don't even remember a fire?"

Spinks shifted in his plastic chair. Playing Ol' J was one thing, but messing with somebody's emotions on such a painful subject was not something he wanted to do.

But Whitey threw in his two cents before Spinks had a chance to think of an answer.

155

"No, buddy, your brother's in heaven," Whitey said. "No one's immortal. That's just made-up stuff somebody thought up so they don't have to face the fact that someday they're gonna die, just like all the rest of us. I mean, think about it — getting your brain jumped from universe to universe? Do you keep jumping even when you're old? Is there some universe out there where everybody lives forever? And if there is, why wouldn't you just jump to that in the first place? And what are all these other bodies doing while your brain's in that first universe? Do they have alternate Yous that get kicked out to another universe when your brain kicks into theirs? It'd be a never-ending chain of kicking out one brain for another. Nope, it don't follow. It don't follow at all."

Spinks grinned.

"I got a friend from back East you'd get along real well with, Whitey. He's always poking holes in my fancy ideas, too."

The old man chuckled, his hard round belly jerking beneath layers of jacket and suspenders.

"I just tell it like it is, boy-o."

"But you gotta admit there's a certain draw to Quantum Immortality. 'Specially considering the way things've been around here lately. Folks mutilating corpses and whatnot."

Spinks let that suggestion hang in the air. Over the years, he'd found that silence was the ultimate question. Most people felt like they had to answer it.

Loogie was no exception.

"Heard about that. Prob'ly bath salt smokers. I never tried the stuff myself — they say it turns you into a cannibal."

Whitey huffed, a half-annoyed sound.

"Tell you what it is, it's somebody messed up in the mind. And not just because of drugs or bath salts or whatever. There's no call for doing something like that. Desecrating a corpse. Sometimes you end up with your back against a wall, and there's nothing you can do but survive, you know? And I get that. But you never have to go that far, to cutting someone up just for kicks." He crossed his arms over his old-man gut. "That's psychological."

Spinks nodded along. Ol' J would agree with Whitey, because he knew what it was like living on the streets, too. But the Miami reporter with the mortgage on a house in the suburbs with attached two-car garage was thinking, *Is this old man saying he's had to kill folk to stay alive out here on the streets? There's a hell of a story right there. Maybe a whole damn book. Maybe when I'm done with this case, I should come back and find my buddy Whitey...*

That was a rabbit trail for another day, though. He had to focus on the now. Getting a killer off the streets was the most important, most pressing issue. Sometimes his writer brain just ran away with him.

"I'm telling you, it ain't tweakers," Whitey insisted. Then he rethought his stance. "Well, maybe this guy tweaks, too, I don't know. But Cali didn't make it sound like any tweaker I ever heard of, way she told it."

Loogie blew a raspberry.

"Cali? What would she know?"

"Says she seen it."

"Someone saw something? Did she witness the murder?"

Spinks leaned his elbows on the table as he asked the twin questions, Ol' J's cool attitude forgotten, something in his instincts trying to pull him closer to the source of information. Luckily, the other men seemed to take this as natural morbid curiosity.

"Man, you can't listen to nothing Cali Girl tells you," Loogie said, shaking his head. "That girl's crazier than a shithouse rat. Nothing comes outta her mouth is real. She's what you call a compulsive liar. She just lays it on and lays it on."

"Maybe if you'd listen, you'd realize there was a grain of truth at the bottom of all those lies," Whitey said.

"Must be a pretty damn small grain."

"Bah."

Whitey waved a hand at Loogie's sneer.

"True or not, I wanna hear what she seen," Spinks said, remembering just in time to fall back into Ol' J's deep Florida accent. "Y'all see much of her around here?"

Loogie snorted.

"She ain't allowed in the shelter anymore — brought in a box cutter one too many times and got kicked out for good."

"Always got to screw up a good thing." Whitey sighed and shook his head. "She's not a bad kid, overall. Just got some problems. But who doesn't?"

Spinks nodded.

"Ain't that the truth."

Maybe tracking down this Cali Girl was a waste of time. It could turn out that Loogie was right, and talking to her would give them nothing but a headache of attention-seeking lies. But if there was any possibility she'd seen something, Spinks knew they had to find her. Even the smallest amount of progress was one step closer to getting this guy off the streets.

CHAPTER 28

Loshak sat at the diner, picking at the Pike's Peak Roast from the daily special. It was just after two, and he hadn't had lunch yet, but he hadn't been able to eat more than a few bites so far. His stomach gnawed and squirmed. Not hungry. Or maybe too anxious to tell the underlying hunger apart.

He set his fork down and picked up his phone for the hundredth time. The lock screen showed no new texts, but he opened it and checked his messages anyway. Spinks had left his phone in the car, but if there was any trouble, the Denver PD might call or text to let Loshak know. At least, he hoped they would. Surely if something had happened to his partner…

There was nothing, though. That could mean Spinks was doing well, finding lots of leads to follow. Or it could mean he'd ended up in some sort of trouble, and the DPD hadn't thought to notify Loshak.

"Everything OK?"

The waitress looked down at his mostly untouched food like she expected him to complain.

She was young, late teens, early twenties, and in the time she'd waited on him, Loshak had developed the opinion that she wasn't cut out for this sort of work. She lacked that aggressive cheerfulness waitresses and waiters tended to have. In its place, she seemed to have a greater than average desire to curl into herself and disappear.

But maybe she was just new here.

"Yeah, it's great." Loshak looked behind her toward the pie case. "I was just thinking I'd skip lunch and go straight to dessert. Could I have a piece of that chocolate pie over there?"

She looked where he was pointing, then hunched in on herself a little more.

"Sorry, sir, that's just a display piece. It's not real pie. Our pies today are apple, juneberry, and lemon meringue."

"What's a juneberry?"

She blinked.

"I— I don't know."

He tried to put her at ease by smiling.

"Well, I guess I'll try that out."

She scuttled back toward the kitchen. At the opening in the counter, she stepped back and scooted to the side to give one of the other waitresses an unnecessarily large berth.

Loshak checked his phone. Still nothing. And his coffee was cold now, too. He drained the last of it and turned up the ringer on his phone to full blast. He knew it was stupid — he was right there, he had the phone in hand, he would feel it vibrate — but the lack of communication was causing all sorts of doubts about how he might miss a call or text.

"Sir, I'm so sorry." His waitress was back. "We're out of the juneberry pie. And the apple."

"That leaves lemon meringue?"

She nodded.

"Then I'll take a piece of that." Loshak smiled and lifted his empty coffee cup. "And when you get a second, could I have a warm-up?"

"Oh, sorry, yeah, I'll be right back with the coffee. And the pie."

"Thank you."

Loshak didn't know why he'd ordered the lemon meringue. He'd never really liked that type of pie. Maybe something about being too invested in maintaining the illusion of wanting pie instead of lunch food. There was a weird feeling of owing the waitress something now that he'd sent her running back to the kitchen to check on pies for him.

It had been a while since he'd had a lemon meringue pie, though. When was the last time he'd had a slice? A decade ago? Two? During Desert Storm? No idea. He couldn't remember what it actually tasted like. Maybe he would like it this time around.

He did remember the first and last time Shelly tried lemon meringue. She'd been about ten at the time, the two of them out together without Jan for some reason. When Shelly saw the perfect little curls of meringue, toasted golden brown, on top of the smooth and shiny yellow pie filling, she'd been entranced. Colors and novel designs drew that kid in like nothing else. Loshak couldn't guess how much he — and later, when she had her own allowance to spend, she — had thrown away on square water bottles and exotic supermarket fruits for her just because they were strange and different.

They'd both gotten a slice, and it came just as beautiful as the piece in the display case. Unfortunately, father and daughter had the same taste in pie. Shelly had been just as disappointed in the flavor as he was.

"It tastes like Pine-Sol," she had said.

A paternal warning bell had gone off in his mind, making him forget for a moment the pie on his fork.

"You've tasted Pine-Sol?"

"No, but I smelled it, and my teacher said that's just tasting with your nose." Shelly had sighed and scraped the meringue off the top and the crust off the bottom, spooning the lemony center into a goopy yellow mound at the corner of her plate. "The rest of it's good. Too bad they made the middle part, though."

Loshak flipped over his phone and unlocked it again. This time he went to his texts with Jan.

How do you feel about lemon meringue pie? he sent.

A few minutes ticked by without a response. It was the middle of the day. She was probably busy with her new project, repainting the front door. He scrolled up to their conversation from the previous night, looking for the ridiculous name of the color she'd chosen.

Vernal Cedar Rain — that was it. The nerve of these paint companies.

His phone chirped, making him jump. He'd forgotten he had turned the ringer on high. He shut the sound back off.

It's no pumpkin, was Jan's opinion on the pie.

No juneberry, either, he replied.

Didn't take her long to get back that time.

What's a juneberry?

My guess is it's the new blue raspberry. How's the door going?

Just left the paint place. I switched colors at the last minute. We're going with Midnight Emerald instead. I think it's going to go better with the brickwork.

She sent him a photo of the dark green swipe on the lid of the paint bucket. It looked the exact same as the Cedar Rain version of dark green, but he'd had that conversation before with Jan about the different shades of Cream. Apparently there was more than one.

Midnight Emerald? Sounds like a perfume, he sent back.

I'll let you know if the fumes attract French-speaking models. How's Denver?

A plate tapped down on his table with a ceramic clunk and scrape. His waitress sped away without a word and before he could thank her, maybe afraid she was interrupting an important conversation.

Loshak cut off the triangular tip of the pie and tried it.

Yep, the Pine-Sol flavor was universal, and he still didn't like it.

He levered his fork between the layers and lifted off the fluffy meringue top. It came off in a single piece, the little amber beads of sugar sweat glistening in the dimples. With that resting on the edge of his plate, he scraped out the Pine-Sol center, then stuck the meringue to the crust.

He sent Jan a photo of his Frankensteined slice of pie.

Workin' hard or hardly workin'? she responded. As he read it, he could see the wry smile on her face.

Workin' my pie to the crust, he sent.

They continued texting while Loshak ate the now-just-meringue pie. He never did get that refill, but with Jan to talk to, the lack of coffee and the anxiety over Spinks faded to a dull hum in the background.

CHAPTER 29

The swirling, spiraling thoughts didn't disappear with the daylight. Crozier had left the photo lab and gone straight to looking for a dealer, but he hadn't been able to find anybody today.

Tintin was MIA and probably dead. Roso was in a holding cell looking at five to ten in the state pen. And according to Markie-Mark's crack house roomies, he was off at a family reunion. Three strikes, and Sam Crozier was out.

Unbelievable. Tintin's death was no surprise, but he had just seen Roso two days ago. The thought of him locked in a cage was a shocking one.

Strange how much harder it was to fathom that someone could suddenly wind up in prison than in the morgue. He suspected that most people couldn't really get a handle on either scenario until they had the rug pulled out from under them, that bit of security and certainty of well-being, the belief that everything would work out in the end.

It didn't. When confronted with that truth, you either adjusted your expectations or you slipped the blindfold back down and went on with your life, trying to stay blissfully unaware.

He could see how they did it, sometimes, how they kept up the mental distance between themselves and the grave. Social media. Games. Movies and shows. Audiobooks.

Podcasts. Digital content delivered at the speed of light to small rectangles of plastic and precious metals in the palms of their hands.

It seemed the crux of human existence in this age. The trash that was actively destroying the Earth bound up with gold and lithium. Screens aglow with distraction. An endless TikTok scroll to help us all tune out the real world.

He looked up at the redbud trees lining the sidewalk, their pinkish-purple blossoms just starting to dot the branches, somehow highlighting the dry hanging seedpods from the previous fall. Life and vibrancy reemerging from the dark, deathlike sleep of winter.

There were harsh truths out there, yes, but there was also beauty. The problem was nobody wanted to see it unless it came through the screen of a phone.

Of course, you couldn't bask too long without the shit of the world invading your space. Even here, in the shade of the redbuds, there was the stink of exhaust fumes from the street, the roar of the traffic and honking drivers cutting each other off as if getting to their next destination was all they'd ever wanted, as if even a single second lost was devastating. Everyone in a big rush to get back to their screens.

One time he'd watched an old lady in a Lexus SUV lay on the horn at an intersection, a sneer curling her lip. He wondered why she was in such a hurry and could only imagine her screaming, *"I'M MEETING PHYLLIS FOR FUCKING BRUNCH!"*

The foot traffic out today wasn't much better. People pushing past each other, elbowing, bustling to the job, the appointment, the vacation. Hurry up so you can get where you're going and hurry some more.

Up ahead, a group of ten or fifteen people waited for the light to change so they could cross. He considered dodging traffic to get away from them, but as he got closer, something different in the crowd noise caught his attention. An excitement, a buzz he didn't usually hear among the tourists and foot commuters.

As he got closer, he realized a vehicle was stopped at the corner, a small Ford compact, and the people were all pushed back from the curb. No impatient toes perched on the very edge of the concrete, desperate for their chance to pull out ahead of the crowd.

Crozier shouldered his way through. He broke clear of the mob, and it was there in the street.

A body. Facedown. Uniform coveralls from a factory or maybe a sanitation department.

The front end of the Escort still hovered over him slightly, the light dent in the hood the only real sign that the car had been involved.

And all at once he could see it, picture it as it must have been.

The car slamming the guy, his grease- and dirt-covered body — weary from a day's hard labor — folding over the hood, slapping down with a crunch of bone and clunk of metal.

This man getting tossed, broken body flailing, tumbling across the asphalt like a crumpled candy wrapper in high wind.

Blood puddling as it pumped out of the guy's broken head for a few seconds, then slowing to nothing.

The car braking in time to not run over the sprawled

figure, albeit just barely.

Too late. The factory worker was already dead. A few more broken bones weren't going to hurt him anymore.

Crozier stood there, skin prickling, breath lightly shaking. He stared down at the shiny pool of blood.

It looked glossy black against the street. Asphalt pebbles stuck up in it like islands in a gelatinous sea.

The man's face was smashed flat, the bones collapsed in a way that felt cartoonish, impossible.

And there was something detached in the people standing around. A distance. Unimpressed.

They'd seen this all before in higher definition on TV. They swiped their phones, glowing screens pressed close to their faces. Probably messaging their friends about the accident. *Some idiot got hit by a car. LOL.* Making memes out of the dead man's photo and posting first-on-the-scene selfies with emoji prayer hands and false sympathies for this guy's family, who didn't even know yet that a vital chunk had just been ripped out of their lives.

Some guy had just gotten his head caved in, brain smashed inside its protective case like a dropped egg, and the people couldn't even be bothered to panic about it. Nobody getting worked up, nobody shedding a tear, nobody even bending down to the man's side to give that basic level of human comfort and dignity to a body that wasn't even cold yet.

At best, they looked bored.

Life. Death. The universe. It was nothing to them. Meaningless.

A disturbing feeling crawled across the surface of his skin like an itch. A feeling that he needed to start walking again, get away, put a safe distance between himself and this crowd of creatures with hearts as cold as frozen tubes of ground beef.

He pressed back through the throng. Strode away from the scene of the accident.

It was too strange to stand there among them, to stand and stare into the ultimate meaninglessness they took from it all. Shoulder to shoulder. Gazing into their void, into their abyss.

It seemed like the shock of death would wake the masses up somehow. Some violent, permanent thing to shake them out of whatever fantasy they were hiding in.

But he was pretty sure nothing could shake them anymore. Maybe nothing could touch them at all.

CHAPTER 30

Evening was coming up fast when Spinks left the shelter for the tent city. He didn't realize he'd spent so long talking, but some of those shelter folks were real characters. It'd almost been hard to tear himself away.

Between the time of year and the mountains, the sun was setting fast. He tucked his ears into his stocking cap, yanked up his hood, and zipped his outer jacket. The temperature outside was already dropping. Thankfully, homeless fashion leaned more toward function than form.

It was only eight blocks to the abandoned Kmart, but the streetlights were winking on by the time he got there. He took in the scene from a distance as he neared the lot.

The building looked bombed out, with mortar crumbling out from between the bricks like tooth decay. The bollards in front of the entrance hunched and tilted, their yellow paint all chipped. The beige metal near the roof had been dented on one side as if somebody had dropped a car on it from above.

Between Spinks and the former department store stood a mishmash of tents — spikes of colored vinyl and canvas poking up from the blacktop. Everything from the long, low one-man bivouac to the brightly colored family tent. He even saw a canvas teepee over by the pedestal of a removed light pole. Nothing near the size of tipis he'd seen in journalism school when he'd gone to a special event at a reservation in Oklahoma — some of those monsters stretched thirty feet high and could easily sleep fifty adults — but if you were sleeping alone and packing your home with you when you moved on, less was probably more.

Lanterns of various ages and wear shined here and there, making the tents look as if they were all glowing at different intensity levels. Judging by the color of the light they gave off, several were the Coleman propane version, but a lot more were the pure white of LED.

Bodies flitted through the spheres of yellow and white light. Silhouettes darting and fluttering.

If Spinks hadn't known better, he would've said the scene looked cozy.

But he was freezing his nads off, and he had to assume the rest of them were, too. Hard to feel cozy when you were trying to stave off hypothermia.

The closer he got, the more the encampment put him in mind of the old European cities. Cities that hadn't been planned but had grown organically as more people settled the area. As a result, many modern-day French or Italian streets were tangled pavement or even cobblestone jobs of what had once been cow paths — meandering, narrow, and rarely in any sort of discernible pattern.

The tent city was set up in the same way. He could almost see where the initial settlement had been and how it had expanded, but every layer melded into two or three others, blurring the lines and creating footpaths with switchbacks, squeeze points, and dead ends.

It was going to be hard to find his way around once he was inside. But Ol' J would've waltzed through a hundred tent cities like this one before. Nothing to be nervous about. This was just another day in the life. If J wanted to find somebody, J had to ask around, that was all. No big deal.

Once he got talking to somebody, Spinks knew he would forget his nerves. He was a people person. Interactions were his bread and butter. He just had to find somebody to strike up a conversation with.

No one was moving around outside at the edge of the tent city as he drew up on the perimeter. Still, he could see the shadows shifting farther in. Maybe it was a primeval piece of survival knowledge at play: keep to the middle of the settlement for safety; on the edges danger lurks.

Spinks picked the closest lantern bubble — a warm yellow indicative of propane — and moseyed over. He got stuck at a dead end when a pair of tents in his path were set up unnecessarily close but quickly discovered the roadblock wasn't the barrier it had seemed. The corners of the tents were touching, but just at the bottom. He grabbed onto one of the thin tent poles and levered his long legs over. The whole obstacle was a minor inconvenience at best.

Around his target lantern, an elderly woman with hollow cheeks sat on a battered five-gallon bucket. A guy in a magenta puff coat with a fur-lined hood hung out talking with her, sipping from a fifth of Popov.

"Hey, hey, hey, how y'all doin' tonight?" Spinks said in Ol' J's just-stumbled-out-of-the-Everglades accent. "Beautiful weather, ain't it?"

The woman grunted, sizing him up with pale blue eyes tinged yellow with jaundice. The vodka disappeared into the man's puff coat pocket.

"Could always be worse," he said, shrugging. "Could be

snowing."

"No, it couldn't. I already told you." The older woman massaged swollen red knuckles. "We're not getting any more snow this year."

"Listen, Mabel, if joints were accurate weather indicators, they'd have old geezers like you doing the weather reports and throw away all that expensive meteorology crap. Doppler and whatnot."

"You wait," she muttered. "You'll see."

"Ah, they couldn't have somebody actually get the weather right," Spinks said. "That would mess up their record of predicting the wrong thing all the time. I figure they're in league with the umbrella companies. Keep peeps walking around without theirs so's they have to buy new ones all the time."

Mabel let out a chuckle and rocked slightly on her bucket, still rubbing those painful-looking hands. Spinks tried not to stare, but him and Ol' J were softies at heart.

"Don't you got any gloves, ma?" he asked.

She nodded, staring into the lantern light.

"Can't get 'em pulled on."

The way her fingers were twisted it was no wonder.

"That's some shit."

He sucked his teeth.

"Don't get old, that's all I have to say."

"Give 'em here, and I can get 'em on for ya," he offered, holding out a hand.

The guy in the puff jacket drifted away from their lantern while Spinks helped Mabel wrestle her gloves on over the swollen hands.

Spinks straightened back up and shoved his own hands

down into his pockets.

"How is it, staying here?" He jerked his chin toward the center of the encampment. "What do you think?"

Mabel blinked at him.

"Why? Are you thinking about moving in?"

He seesawed his head.

"Keepin' my options open at the moment, but you never know."

"It isn't too bad. It gets smaller over winter. But I made it through, so this place must be good for something, huh?"

"Must be."

"I want to head for Baja California one of these years. They say it doesn't get too cold down there. Nobody ever runs you off, either, because anybody can camp down there on the beach."

Mabel pulled a dented McDonald's fry container from her pocket and stuck one salty golden stick in her mouth, working it over with her toothless jaws before she spoke again.

"My Terry and I were going to buy an RV and travel out there. See the ocean."

Spinks swallowed hard. He wanted to know how Mabel had ended up here. She seemed perfectly coherent, not plagued with the untreated mental health issues that drove so many onto the streets. Drugs weren't out of the question.

But what about her Terry? Why hadn't he helped get her clean? An unexpected death, maybe. Heart attack on the factory floor or out on a long haul in his semi.

Unfortunately, as much as he wanted to get to the bottom of things and help, delving into someone's tragic past wasn't why he was there.

"Cali's nice this time of year," he made himself say. "I'm actually looking for a friend of mine named after the Golden State. Cali Girl and me's supposed to meet up tonight, but she never told me where. Just said to find her."

An uproar across camp caught Mabel's attention briefly. Spinks glanced over his shoulder to see who was yelling, but from their angle it was all just dark shapes against lantern light.

"Slinky, willowy girl?" Mabel asked, turning her jaundiced blue eyes back on him. "Got that blonde hair?"

Excitement made Spinks's pulse speed up. He wasn't sure what slinky meant in describing people, but Mabel sounded like she knew exactly who she was talking about.

"Yeah, that's Cali."

"I didn't think she was going to stay up here much longer," Mabel said. "Might check down at the shelter in Aurora—"

"Hey, no!" Tent material rustled and slapped together as a tall form stormed through the dead end Spinks had gotten hung up in earlier. "Don't talk to this guy! He's a cop — he's a fucking cop!"

It took Spinks's brain a second to switch gears from their potential witness's whereabouts to this new threat, but when it finally did, he realized the yeller was the tall, hunched guy who had pushed the shopping cart into Loshak that morning.

And the livid shopping cart pusher wasn't alone. The guy in the fur-lined puff jacket was back, and more shapes were coming out of the darkness, slipping between the tents toward Spinks. The lanterns painted their furious scowls in sharp shadows and sallow yellow illumination.

Spinks caught the dull gleam of metal in at least one fist. A guy in an old Buffalo Bills hoodie had a blade tucked into his hand, half hidden by his ratty sleeve. And he got the feeling this guy wasn't the only one in the encampment with a weapon.

Spinks tried to back away, but more were coming up behind him, cinching him in.

He was surrounded.

CHAPTER 31

Loshak's plate of lemon meringue goop had just been whisked away when a familiar white cowboy hat and uniform came into the diner. Benally headed up to the counter without seeing Loshak and spoke to the middle-aged woman running the cash register. Over the last few hours, Loshak had inferred that this was the diner's owner.

Benally joked around with the owner for a minute before craning his neck to call out a hello to the cook through the order window. An older waitress with the voice of a multi-decade smoker — she had eventually refilled Loshak's coffee when she realized the young girl on his table had forgotten about him — gave the detective a friendly slap on the shoulder with her order pad as she passed.

"Don't think I forgot about you, Kathleen," Benally said, turning around and leaning an elbow on the counter.

The old smoker let out a growling laugh.

"Don't you get smart with me, Joseph Andrew. I'll call your mother."

The detective spotted Loshak in his booth by the window. Loshak nodded. Benally sent him a conspiratorial smirk.

"Mean Kathleen, we call her," Benally told him, hooking a thumb at the waitress's back. "She's a drag racer from way back. Can't keep her foot off the gas pedal."

Kathleen shook her head and stopped at another table

to refill some empty cups.

"I'm about to put my foot about ankle deep somewhere the sun don't shine."

"Can you believe the mouth on this woman?" The detective pulled a mock shocked face. "She's curling my ear hairs, Donna. I can't believe you let her waltz around this place bluein' up the air like that."

The diner owner chuckled.

"Don't drag me into this."

Benally came over to Loshak's table and leaned his hip against the opposite seat back.

"How does it go, agent?"

"Not bad." Loshak gestured with his coffee cup. "You're welcome to sit down if you've got time."

"Nah, I can't stay long. I was going to pick up a piece of pie for my wife — she loves their juneberry — but apparently they're all out."

"I tried to get the same thing earlier," Loshak said. "Ended up having to go with lemon meringue."

"Oh lord!" Benally tipped his head back. "The worst of all the pie flavors. Annette—" He pronounced the name with the emphasis on the first syllable, as if the 'ette' was just an afterthought. That was a new one on Loshak. "—my wife, she won't eat a meringue of any kind. Absolutely hates that fluffy stuff. She says it sticks to the roof of her mouth and her tongue all weird. Can't say as I blame her. I'm a pecan or pumpkin man myself."

Loshak let out a thoughtful grunt.

"Pecan — that's one I didn't think of. I don't suppose they have that here?"

"Only around Thanksgiving, unfortunately." Despite

what he'd claimed earlier about not being able to stay, Benally slipped into the booth and sat his cowboy hat on the table. "So what brings you here? Heard about Donna's famous juneberry pie?"

"I'd never heard of it before. What exactly is a juneberry?"

"Never heard of juneberry!" Benally slapped his forehead, again feigning shock. "What are they teaching you on that East coast?"

Loshak shifted forward in his seat.

"You're telling me juneberry is a real berry? It's not a made-up flavor like blue raspberry or blue coconut?"

"No way. They're something of a state specialty. Hell, me and the wife used to find great big patches of 'em when we went hiking. You can find U-Pick farms for 'em all over. They flourish around here. Something in the soil."

Kathleen brought Benally a coffee in a large to-go cup.

"Donna said to come back in an hour or so. She's got a pie coming out of the oven right now, but it needs to cool before we can cut it."

"Aw, tell her she didn't have to do that."

"We're pulling for Annette. You tell her that. Everybody here's pulling for her."

The old waitress's voice gained gravel as she said this. Loshak caught a hint of wetness in her eyes. She cleared her throat and opened her mouth to say something else but stopped herself short. Instead, she gave Benally's shoulder a squeeze and headed for the kitchen.

Benally turned back to face Loshak, his grin fading to a sad smile. He stared down at the to-go cup in his hands.

"She's got pancreatic cancer. Annette, I mean. That's

actually the reason we found this place." He tipped his head toward the window. "Her new specialist is up the street a ways."

Loshak nodded.

"Been there. We went through several specialists when our daughter got sick."

There had always been the hope that the next doctor would know something the rest hadn't. Right up until the end.

"Costs a pretty penny, doesn't it?" Benally said, putting his cheerful face back on.

Loshak couldn't help noticing that the man's veneer of joviality was wearing thin around the edges. A tiredness pulled at the skin around the detective's eyes and muted the smile as he talked.

"When they diagnosed her, they said she had less than three months left, but she's been kicking for eight and a half now. Maybe she's living on borrowed time, but it's a miracle she made it this long. That's how we're looking at it."

"Staying positive."

Loshak had heard the phrase repeated over and over during Shelly's downhill slide.

"Yep." Benally stared down at his to-go cup. "Yep, staying positive. Sometimes that's all you can do. The world's got enough negatives in it already without adding more."

A few seconds passed with nothing but the low rumble of conversation from the other diners and the hiss of something on the grill. A door banged shut somewhere in the back of the place.

"She's got a plan for her funeral and everything," Benally said. "We worked it all out. I didn't want to, but…" He shrugged. Then he chuckled. "She's got Donna here conned into catering the dessert table. Juneberry pies only. If one of the attendees wants something else, they're shit outta luck."

Loshak thumbed a brown drip of coffee off the rim of his mug. He'd forgotten about Shelly making requests like that at the end. A certain song she wanted played. A silly joke she'd wanted the funeral director to make.

Maybe the truth was that he hadn't forgotten. Maybe he'd blocked it out because every new funerary request had cut out a little more of his heart. It must've hurt Jan even worse, because she shushed Shelly every time and said it wouldn't come to that. But Loshak had agreed to everything she'd asked for. It'd been one last thing he could do for his daughter, one last way to spoil her.

"I think it helps, that planning," he told Benally. "Makes them feel in control. Makes us feel like we're doing something."

The detective messed with the cardboard sleeve of his cup.

"Yeah, I can see that."

For a while, they sat there listening to an older couple over by the door argue about whether they should sit at the counter or one of the four-tops.

"Well!" Benally slapped his thighs and slid out of the booth. "Can't avoid work all day."

He grabbed his to-go coffee and stuck his hat on his head. His posture seemed to straighten as he kept talking, his own words puffing him back up physically.

"Bad guys to catch. Partners to exasperate. You know the drill. Speaking of, how did your undercover homeless thing go?"

Loshak shrugged.

"Spinks is supposed to stop in any time now. Won't know until then."

The detective nodded.

"Anyhow. Be seein' ya."

With a two-fingered wave, Benally headed for the door, calling out goodbyes to his diner acquaintances.

His phone started ringing as he stepped onto the nonslip mat in front of the entrance.

"Yeh-llo." Benally stopped with his hand on the door's push bar. "Where at?"

He held still for a second, the phone still pressed to his ear. Then he swiveled around and locked eyes with a Loshak.

"Don't bother," he said. "I'm with him right now."

He pulled the phone away from his face.

"It's your partner. We need to go. Now."

CHAPTER 32

Crozier woke up to a muffled commotion nearby, the sound coming through the garbage bag taped up in the busted-out window of his car. Something happening over in the tent village.

He stretched as much as the back seat would allow him, feet pushing on the creaking door panel, elbows overhead bumping the window, hands in his hair, scratching awake the cells of his scalp as his spine arched and popped.

The yelling went on across the street. A fight of some sort.

It didn't happen all the time, but he'd heard a few disagreements turn into uproars over in the homeless hamlet since he moved in. He was parked diagonal from the abandoned Kmart, in the cracked concrete parking lot of what used to be a strip club. Cheeks had been the name of the place, according to the faded pink sign that still stood guard over it. The building had been torn down with a level of over-the-top caution that made him wonder whether the building itself had tested positive for syphilis and HPV. Razed to a dirt patch by, one assumed, the CDC, probably with the appropriate sowing of salt so nothing would ever grow there again.

His car, an old Dodge Stratus, had been parked there for three months now on two flat tires. He kept expecting to come back and find it gone, towed away by the city for imposing on private, diseased property, but the wrathful eye of the public works department had yet to fall on his four-door abode. He slept there a couple nights a week, and he'd continue to do so as long as it stayed there.

Being more than twenty years old at this point, the Stratus wasn't much to look at. Sitting between the dirt patch formerly known as Cheeks and the forgotten Kmart, its scratched, rusting passenger side doors and flapping black plastic window added to the post-apocalyptic look of the area, as if the beater car had been abandoned there the day the world ended.

In the orange glow of the streetlights, he could see the shine of the black electrical tape holding the garbage bag to the back door's frame, a darker, smoother black than the plastic. The patch job wasn't pretty, but it kept out the wet. What it didn't do squat against was the cold. It got chilly as hell in there some nights.

Still, this was as close as he had to a home.

Little trinkets lay on the dashboard and in the back window, things he'd found around the city — some battered books, a bracelet, a handful of brightly colored bottlecaps from Denver microbreweries all in a row, a scuffed and bent hood ornament from a BMW, an antique glass milk bottle, a dark blue cat's eye marble with a chip out of it, a keychain that looked like a mini copy of the *Call of the Wild* but flipped open to hold stuff.

That was where he kept the less important stuff. The décor. Up in the sunlight on the dash, fading like the Stratus's paint job. The real treasures, the relics, the vital detritus, were shoved under the front seats.

Voices shrilled and strained like violins across the street. Sounded like the fighting in the tent city was getting heated.

This didn't sound like the usual accusation of theft or random paranoid rantings. Crozier sat up and wiped a spot in the condensation to try to see.

No good. Too blurry. He climbed over the console into the passenger seat and leaned forward, looking out the cracked windshield.

Looked like things were kicking off out there on the fringes of the tent city. Two tall guys screaming at each other, one jabbing a finger at the other.

The accuser was a tall, hunched guy Crozier saw around from time to time. He always reminded Crozier of a sasquatch.

The accused was backing away, palms held high in the lantern light. But he wasn't going to get far. Friends and allies were crowding around to support Sasquatch as he and his jabbing finger inched closer.

The guy must've done something that required communal censure, then. Hard to say what that might've been. The rules out in the Land of the Vagrants were different from the rules in a settled, traditionally housed community.

"—fuckin' cop!"

Crozier froze, ears straining. Had he heard Sasquatch right?

He watched the accused. Read his body language.

The man's mouth was moving fast, maybe trying to talk his way out of this, but Sasquatch advanced again, stalking forward with choppy steps, still yelling.

And there was that word again, clear as day. *Cop.*

A prickle of nervousness ran down Crozier's spine and

bloomed in his belly.

It came again two more times — cop. Sasquatch was hitting that note hard, making sure everybody in the encampment knew. More people joined the crowd surrounding the alleged cop, metal glinting here and there in half-hidden fists.

Crozier dug under his own seat, pushing aside bits and pieces until he found the knife. He stuck the blade in his jacket.

He usually steered clear of the big gatherings of the homeless types. Didn't find their company tolerable in groups.

One on one, they were generally fine. Get too many of them together, and a bunch of 'em turned into chatty, smiling, warm people despite their lots in life. Cheery in a way that got under his skin.

But tonight he climbed out of the car and headed across the street toward the commotion.

He needed to get closer, check this out.

CHAPTER 33

"Whoa, whoa, whoa." Spinks backed up, hands held high as if the tall man had pulled a gun on him. "I ain't no cop. I don't know what you're talkin' about, man, but—"

"Liar!"

Cords stood out down the man's neck. He lurched forward, stabbing his finger at Spinks as he yelled again.

"You're a fucking cop, I fucking saw you down by the recycling place on Eighth!"

Something snagged Spinks's ankle, and he almost went down. He caught himself. It was a tent corner. He stepped backward over it, scanning for an escape route. Two rings of tents stood between him and safety.

But so did a line of people. One of whom had a knife.

Spinks edged away from him.

"Listen, man, let's just be reasonable about this. That couldn't've been me because I wasn't by the recycling place today."

The tall man wasn't listening. He started yelling, "Cop! Cop! Cop!" like a guy trying to start a chant in a stadium, stabbing his finger at Spinks with every shout.

Someone in the crowd joined in with him. The voice was a little off-kilter, sort of wrong in a way that made Spinks think the joiner wasn't necessarily agreeing but more likely had a mental issue that made them echo words. Still, it had the effect of getting more of the homeless folks gathered around to chant with the tall man.

187

If anybody in camp hadn't heard the yelling before, they would know what was going on now. His cover was completely blown. Even the sweet old lady he'd been building rapport with before was glaring at him now, yelling "Cop!" with the rest of them.

"You know what, I don't need this," Spinks yelled.

He couldn't get loud enough for anybody to hear him, but he stuck to it, some part of him desperate to maintain the illusion of Ol' J that he'd started with.

"They don't treat me this way at the shelter! I'm outta here, man!"

He picked a spot in the crowd that looked thinner and went for it, the street visible through a narrow gap between a guy in a ski mask and a heavyset bearded man. As he got closer to them, Spinks shoved his hands in his pockets and pulled his head down, instinctively bracing for impact.

But just when collision looked unavoidable, the guy in the ski mask shuffled aside. Either he was afraid that Spinks would run smack into him, or he just wasn't as interested in keeping the outsider in if it meant he had to personally do something to stop him.

"Yeah, run away, cop!" the tall man yelled. "Tuck your piggy tail between your legs and run back to your donut-eating buddies!"

Spinks swerved between the side of a tent and the concrete pillar from a light pole, and he was out in the open again. He hadn't realized how hemmed in he'd felt until he was pounding across the Kmart parking lot with nothing else blocking his way. Felt like he'd just shed a belt that was on too tight.

He hit the street and turned toward the diner.

Hopefully, they could get working on this Cali Girl angle tonight.

Things were settling down behind him. A few last shouts and some murmuring, then presumably they'd decided they were done with him.

The street was quiet. Empty. Still.

He rounded a corner, curling his fingers in the pockets of the thrift store jacket. A little grit got under his nails as he scraped the seam.

He peeled back his hood and took his beanie off. Cold air swirled around his shaved head. Open. Refreshing. It felt good.

A deep breath rushed some of that night air into the core of him, and that felt even better.

Well, he couldn't do any more undercover assignments for this particular case, but at least he'd come up with some potentially useful information. A nickname for their possible witness, a potential hangout. Even if Cali Girl turned out to be a bust as an eyewitness, she might have some new leads for them to look into. See what shook loose, as his partner would say.

Spinks was so absorbed in his thoughts that he didn't notice the dark figure drifting through the shadows behind him, following.

CHAPTER 34

Above the tall buildings of Denver's cityscape, the night sky yawned — a black mouth full of stars.

Benally led the way to his car, and Loshak followed. The detective explained as they jogged.

"A uniform making the rounds spotted a disturbance in the tent city outside the old Kmart. Couple guys hollering and shouting. I guess these things usually resolve themselves pretty fast out there, so she called it in as she drove by, figures she'll circle back later and check up on things. But Washburn heard the call come in, and he remembered you two were doing your undercover canvas today. So she goes back, but the guys making the ruckus are gone, and of course nobody there is saying boo about it."

Loshak yanked the door open and dropped into the passenger seat. His mind was going a hundred miles a minute, circling back to how he should've made Spinks take his phone, staying in character be damned. It sure as hell wasn't doing any good sitting in the cup holder in the rental.

Benally's car was unmarked, but he pulled out a suction-cupped LED dash light and lit it up before swerving into traffic.

"How long ago did the call come in?" Loshak asked.

"Ten to fifteen minutes ago."

Loshak's stomach sank. A lot could happen in that

much time.

But worrying about what might have gone down wasn't going to find Spinks. He had to focus on the most efficient way to search for a missing person.

Start at the last known point. They were already speeding toward the encampment, Benally's lips pressed in a tight line as he squeezed the car through the gap left in the evening traffic.

The uniform had already presumably searched the tent city itself. They had to spread out, widen their search area.

"Get me a block away from the Kmart, and let me out," Loshak said.

Benally shot him a sidelong glance before returning his eyes to the road.

"You sure about that?"

"There'll be places a car can't get into. You cruise around the block, and then drop back another block. Move in concentric rings, keeping your eye out. I'll do the same, but focusing on alleys and the backs of buildings."

The diner was less than a mile from the tent city, but at the moment, it felt much farther away.

Benally pulled cautiously through a red light, making sure they weren't going to get T-boned, then gunned the engine again.

"Plenty of abandoned lots around here, too. Don't forget to take a look in those. Never know if he might've gotten hurt and crawled into one. Had something like that last year with an informant. Didn't find his body for a week."

The detective swung around a turn and shrugged his shoulders before he went on.

"Guess that's not very cheerful, but I'd feel like shit if I didn't mention it and, y'know, something like that happened here."

"Understood."

"We're pretty close now. Let me get past…"

He trailed off as he veered around a bus and didn't pick the thread up again. A block later, he hit the blinker and pulled onto a side street. He half-swiveled his torso toward the passenger seat, eyes meeting the agent's.

"Ready?"

Loshak nodded, unbuckling his seatbelt and wrapping his fingers around the door handle. Benally rolled the car up beside a hydrant at the next intersection.

The detective hit the brakes harder than expected, and Loshak had to throw a hand out to catch himself against the dash. Little jags of pain sizzled up his wrist.

Damn arthritis. It wouldn't be a hindrance unless there was a scuffle or he had to carry someone or push something heavy for some reason. All problems he wouldn't have had to think twice about ten years ago.

"Call to update every ten minutes," Loshak said, climbing out.

Benally turned off the dash strobe.

"Got it. Stay safe."

Loshak shut the door and watched the detective speed away.

Then he was alone. It took him a second to get oriented.

The side street he'd been left on was devoid of life. No traffic passed down it at this hour. The buildings looked industrial, an impenetrable wall without any outlets between, all of their reinforced pull-down doors closed and locked up for the night.

He pulled up a map of the area on his phone to make sure he wouldn't get turned around. The blue lines of the streets crisscrossed on the glowing screen.

He started walking.

CHAPTER 35

The soles of Loshak's shoes clopped against the pavement, echoed off the buildings around him. He speedwalked, the slap and echo of his footsteps like rapid applause, his heart thudding in his chest. He could feel the blood beating in his temples, pumping in the side of his neck.

He lanced into an alley, the unadorned brick backs of businesses surrounding him. Niches all over that a person could disappear into. Dumpsters they could hide behind. He'd even found an open manhole cover at one of the intersections.

Loshak shined his phone into every nook and cranny as he passed, the tension mounting as he approached the shadows, then falling when he didn't find anyone there. Then it started the upward creep again as he realized that was one more alcove he hadn't found Spinks in.

His eyes scanned everywhere. Head on a swivel.

Another recess ahead, a gap between buildings. The end of a composite picnic table stuck out, marred with scrapes, probably from delivery vehicles. From the looks of the cigarette butts littering the ground around it, the table was a popular hangout for a smoke break.

He shined his light into the gap between the buildings. No one down that way. He turned to go.

"Hey!"

Loshak's heart leaped into his throat as a shadow under the table moved. A hooded protrusion emerged from a pile of coats and broken-down cardboard boxes.

"Shut that damn light out! Can't a soul get any sleep around here?"

"Sorry," Loshak muttered, heat creeping into his face.

He turned the phone light the other way down the alley and kept moving.

He found himself gritting his teeth as he went. Grinding the molars. His posture was off, too. Head and shoulders leaning forward over his feet.

His phone rang, and he jumped again. Benally. He thumbed the answer icon.

"Find anything?"

"Nope," the detective said. "Ten-minute check-in, though. What's your status?"

"I've made two circles. No sign. I'm in an alley off—" He pulled his phone away from his ear and checked the map. "—Levarro. Heading north."

"Alright. I'm about eight blocks out from the encampment over here, about to make it ten. Check in again in ten minutes?"

"Roger that."

Loshak ended the call, feeling vaguely stupid. When was the last time he'd said "roger that" in a non-ironic way? All these jump scares were getting to him, maybe, throwing him off his stride.

He came out of the alley to the street where he'd started his circle. He took a right. Shined his light across an abandoned lot surrounded by chain-link fence. No movement in the sparse weeds that had overtaken the dirt plot.

Halfway down the block, he found another alley, this

time lined with wrought iron fire escapes. Apartments over the businesses, maybe. What did they call those? Lofts.

In the darkness, a door down the alley banged shut. Someone was dragging something across the dingy pavement.

Loshak started toward them. A light flipped on in one of the apartment windows overhead, illuminating a faded army jacket with a gray hoodie. His pulse fluttered, and he broke into a run.

"Spinks—"

The army jacket turned toward Loshak, but it wasn't the reporter. White male, mid-to-late thirties, patchy facial hair.

"Huh?"

The man spun around and shifted his cargo in front of him like a shield. It was a twin mattress, yellowed and pocked with cigarette burns like a back covered in acne.

Loshak shook his head, apologizing for the second time.

"Never mind. Thought you were someone else. Sorry."

He gave the man a wide berth, not wanting to make him feel any more threatened. The guy had already had someone run up on him in the dark while he was trying to lug his old mattress to the dumpster. That was probably enough shock for one night.

This alley was shorter than the previous one, and soon Loshak spilled out onto another street. The breeze cut through his jacket and caught the lapels, making them flap. It was like a wind tunnel out here.

He saw why a second later. No corresponding path on the opposite side of the road, or for a good distance, just a wall of buildings shouldered up against one another. He was at a dead end. He checked his map. He needed to head east. Looked like there was another inlet there.

Half the streetlamps on this road were out, one of them with wires hanging from the lamp head. Loshak switched his phone to the other hand, sticking the frozen right hand in his pocket, and kept walking.

His left wouldn't be able to bear the chill for long — that pang of arthritis, for whatever reason, made it more susceptible to the cold — but he just needed time to warm up the right before he switched back. He should've grabbed some gloves for himself at the thrift shop. And while he was wishing, a couple of those HotHands packets he'd seen at all the gas stations out here.

A pain was drilling into his left shoulder blade, only partly from the cold. The rest of it was tension, the result of mounting stress and worry over a prolonged period.

Where the hell was Spinks?

Movement down the street brought his attention back on the street, sharpened, searching.

There was a person out there, shambling his way. Big. Bulky clothes. Shoes scuffing on the sidewalk. But too deep in the shadows to make out any key identifiers.

"Well, well, well, Special Agent Loshak," the shape called.

Loshak stopped where he was.

A second later, Spinks stepped into the light of one of the working lamps, all smiles.

"As I live and breathe."

Loshak gulped, his head going dizzy with relief. His scalp prickled, and his hands tingled, though some of that might have been the cold. He wanted to say something but found he couldn't.

"Good news, partner," Spinks said cheerfully. "I got run out of the tent city before I could really get to asking folks about our guy, but I did get us a possible eyewitness, and her possible whereabouts."

Loshak swallowed hard.

"I heard there was some sort of disturbance. Couple of tall guys yelling at each other, one of them in an army surplus jacket?"

"More like getting yelled *at*. But I got out of there unscathed. Anyway, I'm thinking we head to the shelter in Aurora, do a little snooping around there. That's where she's supposed to be hanging out these days."

As hesitant as Loshak was to let Spinks jump back into this near-disastrous undercover mission, he had to admit a potential eyewitness was a good lead.

"Alright," he said, nodding. "Let's head back to the station, check in, then we'll—"

Something gritted on the concrete behind Spinks, and Loshak fell silent. He narrowed his eyes, straining to see into the shadows.

There was someone out there. Drifting closer.

Mouth hanging slightly open, Spinks turned to see what Loshak was looking at, eyes darting around the dark street.

The shape moved into the light. It was a man in a bright fuchsia puff coat.

"So you really are a cop. I fuckin' knew it."

He pulled a fifth of vodka from his coat and took a swig.

"That why you left when I was talking to Mabel?" Spinks asked.

The man shrugged.

"Y'all are looking for that killer, right? The one who steals faces?"

Loshak caught Spinks's eye. The reporter's eyebrows bounced in a *we might have something here* sort of motion.

"Do you know anything about him?" Loshak asked.

Another pull on the vodka. Then he smeared his cuff across his lips.

"No, but I think I know where the body is."

CHAPTER 36

Work lights illuminated the space between two dumpsters, red and blue flashers adding the occasional strobe of color to the scene. A flattened box dotted with oil stains had been placed over the body wedged there between the steel boxes.

The techs were moving that out of the way now, carefully peeling the soggy cardboard aside, laying the corpse bare to the harsh white glare of their work lights.

Female, Loshak noted as she appeared. *Petite.* Swallowed up in the fabric of an oversized t-shirt and jeans. Could be one of the junkies slowly going emaciated out on the streets, their clothes seemingly growing larger and larger around them, but it was hard to be certain at this point.

The flesh of her face had been peeled off, exposing bone and sinew and bulbous eyes that looked too white against the browning red of the muscle tissue. Brown irises stared up at nothing.

Flies buzzed around, woken by the untimely lighting. Circling from the dumpsters to the woman, landing on what had been a cheek or a lip, making a meal of it, then flitting back to the refuse containers.

The blood around the body looked gummy and black. Adhered to the rough texture of the asphalt like some sort of gory Halloween glue. A congealing pudding crusting to the sides of the bowl.

There was more blood closer to the entrance of the alley, likely where the actual killing had taken place.

A camera bulb flashed. The techs were really getting into the swing of things now. Taking the endless videos and photos required for evidence. Scribbling on clipboards, documenting every aspect of the crime scene. Squatting next to the body at one angle and then another. Arranging numbered evidence cards.

No bunny suits tonight. The CSIs were all in regular attire, the occasional business casual topped with a coat or jacket, a few polos peeking out with the name of the department stitched on the left breast.

The choice of clothing said something about the lack of mess at the scene. The techs only wore the Tyvek when they had to.

A large, heavy tech without a jacket stood under a work light, steam rising from his shaved head, documenting the victim's wallet on some forms and adding the contents to an evidence baggie.

Loshak had already searched that particular dead end when they arrived. She hadn't been carrying a driver's license. The only thing in it besides a handful of small bills was a faded and crinkled cardboard punch card for Dutch Bros. Coffee. Six punches toward a free coffee and the surname *McClintic* in looping Sharpie.

Someone would check it out, but the odds they would get an ID from an old-fashioned loyalty card were low. Loshak hadn't even realized anyone still did paper punch cards. Seemed like everything was digital now. On the app, as the kids say.

He imagined the face Darger would make if he ever said

that in front of her and almost chuckled. Then he remembered where he was. The grisly work surrounding him. He winced.

"Think she's the face Andi Wayland got in the mail?" Spinks asked in a low voice. He wasn't looking at the body.

A tech was passing the reporter, her low heels clicking on the concrete. She stopped when she heard his question.

"We'll have to get the body back to the lab to confirm our findings, but she's too fresh to have been killed on the twenty-ninth. We're looking at a day, thirty-six hours at the most."

Loshak grunted.

"So this is victim number three."

Now Spinks was the one grimacing.

They fell silent again as the body was bagged and removed to the waiting transport. Loshak eyed the place where the body had been.

There was a sense of improvisation here. This guy was winging it, at least with the murders themselves, if not the mailings. The facts of the case file all pointed to that spontaneity, but seeing it up close, actually standing in the presence of the corpse, the impression hit even harder. The reality was just a few feet away, staring him in the face.

He took a few steps back and let his gaze roam around the scene.

A body covered in stab wounds covered with a crooked flap of cardboard, probably snatched out of one of these dumpsters right here. There was something childish about it. A kid covering a grape juice stain on the couch with a throw pillow.

Slapdash. Thrown together. Those were the phrases

that came to him.

"Check this out," a tech in a windbreaker said, waving a purple latex-covered finger at the side of the far dumpster.

Loshak blinked several times, feeling like he'd been pulled out of another world. For a second there, he'd been alone in the alley with the corpse.

The tech was indicating dried streaks of blood, their vivid ruddiness just barely visible until a flashlight shone directly on them. They looked like drying ketchup, smeared thin on the metal surface.

But as the flashlight beam swept up, the marks turned from dark to red, widening. They came to the lip of the dumpster. This, Loshak thought, was where the streaks started. Started here and trailed down, the impressions becoming uneven at the bottom.

Their unsub had tried to throw the body in but couldn't get her center of gravity over the breach.

The image came unbidden to mind, a small man trying to hoist the dead body. Struggling with dead weight, limp arms and legs dangling.

Loshak shifted his weight, considering the logistics. How would you even grip a body you were trying to toss into a dumpster? Like that guy with the mattress had been holding it, by the sides? Hands cupping the armpits? One hand in the crotch and the other under the arm or neck?

With each subsequent scenario, though, the scene played out the same in his mind — the body slapped the edge of the dumpster, then slipped down to the asphalt in a belly flop.

Given the petite nature of their victim, he doubted the weight was the real problem. She couldn't weigh more than a hundred and forty or a hundred and fifty pounds. It would be the gangling floppiness of the body that would present the primary problem.

Rigor wouldn't start setting in until two to six hours after death, so the body would have felt like a big awkward trash bag of meat when he moved it. Lolling head, and all that long blonde hair getting in the way, too. A big guy might have managed it. Of course, they had the footage to show that their unsub was far from large.

The failure at hiding the body in the dumpster fit the profile, too.

A shrill scream from Loshak's pocket made him and a few of the CSIs jump. He pulled it out and answered.

"We found Cali," Detective Washburn said. "Holed up at the Aurora shelter. And get this — she says she knows where our killer lives."

CHAPTER 37

Loshak, Spinks, and Detective Washburn stood to the side of a broken-down sedan leaning on two flat tires, waiting for DC Belte to call to let them know she'd gotten the proper paperwork for an abandoned vehicle search. The car was a 2006 Dodge Stratus according to its windshield VIN, but they were still waiting for registration to come back. Lots of waiting.

The tent city Spinks had made his escape from just a few hours before sat just across the street, shapes still moving through the spheres of yellow lantern light despite the early morning hour. None of the inhabitants seemed eager to get too close, but now and again, Loshak caught sight of a head and neck stretching up over the vinyl domes to see what all the fuss was about.

"Just keep in mind that this could be nothing," Wash told them.

His hands were shoved deep into his pockets, and he bounced on the balls of his feet, as if trying to stay warm. He ticked his chin toward the car.

"I've had dealings with Cali before. Although, to tell the truth, I always thought it was 'Callie,' like the girl's name, not the state. Anyway, she's something of… let's say a compulsive liar. She claims to see hit-and-runs, bank robberies, hostage situations, all kinds of shit."

Washburn paused and sucked his teeth.

"I think she likes the attention of being an eyewitness.

Everybody's hanging on her every word, you know? But every now and then she'll say something that makes me think she's not just making stuff up."

"You get that with tip lines," Loshak said, his words hitting the air as misty ghosts and drifting apart. "Certain people will call in for every crime, no matter what it is. Some of them are trying to get revenge on neighbors or genuinely think the guy across the street is in on everything, but some of them just want someone to listen."

There was an element of deep loneliness and desperation to the lies. In some ways, it wasn't unlike their killer's profile — seeking that attention, no matter how negative, because it was the only way they could think to get human contact.

"Like the old folks who call the Butterball hotlines around Thanksgiving just to talk," Spinks said.

"Well, some of this could be conditioning, too," Wash said. "If you believe Cali, she and her mom were hostages in a convenience store hold-up when she was a kid. That got her a lot of attention, interviews for the papers and the local news talking about what happened. That might be where the fame bug bit her."

"The folks I talked to were pretty skeptical of her." Spinks pulled down the strings of his hoodie, tightening it around his face. "Do you think she's for real this time?"

Wash *hmm*ed, the sound steaming out of his nose.

"I had my doubts, especially when she only offered details that were released to the media. But when we showed her the photo you all got from the footage, she was like, 'Hey, I know him. He sleeps in the broken-down car across from the Kmart.' Sounded surprised, too. Like she hadn't expected to see him is how I took it. Of course, she could've been bullshitting me. If there's one thing most compulsive liars have down pat, it's sincerity."

The trill of the detective's phone cut off their musings. Belte had the paperwork greenlighting the abandoned vehicle search.

Spinks rubbed his hands together.

"Let's get in there. See if this Cali Girl knows what she's talking about."

The car was locked, but with the busted-out back passenger window, that didn't prove much of an obstacle. Loshak slipped an arm through the bottom corner of the garbage bag, where the electrical tape was already pulling away, and opened the door from the inside. Within a minute, all three of them were hunched through one of the doors and sifting through the contents of the Stratus.

Through the front windshield, Loshak had already seen the collection of beer caps, a milk bottle, some little trinkets like marbles and keychains arranged on the dash. There were even more in the back window, where he was searching. Battered, water-stained books, comics with the covers ripped off, a handful of mussel shells, maybe from a local lake or river. A small teddy bear holding a Valentine's heart. A metallic purple iPhone case from who knew how many generations back. A pair of those shiny magnetic rocks and a small pile of crystals and iron pyrite, the kind of thing a kid would get playing at panning for gold at the gift shop of an old mine or cave.

The hoard was raccoon-like in its shininess and meaninglessness. A random assortment of things that had caught the occupant's eye, be they expensive or junk. Once again, Loshak found himself comparing their killer to a child. A kid wouldn't care whether the bottle caps were trash. They were small and colorful and shiny, therefore they were treasure.

The question remained, however, as to whether this hoard actually belonged to their killer.

The car's location wasn't far from the Globeville post office the first package had originated from, but that meant little without any solid evidence to back it up. The truth was, anybody could be the owner, and any number of mental disorders might inspire someone to hoard small, seemingly insignificant items. At least so far as he had seen, there was nothing here to tie the inhabitant to any crime. The car could very well turn out to be a dead end, like Wash had warned them.

"Oh boy. I might have something."

Spinks's latex gloves creaked as he pushed himself up in the driver's seat. He hesitated before he spoke again.

"This still has some hair in it."

He held up a pink scrunchy. A few long dark hairs were tangled around the hair tie.

"Bag it."

Wash handed an evidence baggie over the console.

Loshak went back to searching. The scrunchy could be a trophy. But it could also be another random found object. Hell, they hadn't thought to ask Cali Girl if anyone else slept in the car besides their suspect.

"Uh." Spinks's head rose over the seat again. "Now we've got a wallet. Louis Vuitton knockoff."

He flipped it around to show them the driver's license.

"She's got long, black hair, looks like. Could be a match

for the scrunchy."

Loshak read the vitals printed on the card.

The girl was just twenty-two. Five-four, a hundred eleven pounds. Petite, like their most recent victim. But with long, dark hair instead of the blonde of the body in the alley. Her name was Alita Simms.

Only after he'd taken in the data did he study the photo.

There was something Bohemian about her. The dark makeup around the eyes and the peasant blouse with the brightly colored scarf she was using as a headband. It gave Loshak the impression of wrists full of bangles and a long, swishing, brightly colored skirt.

There was something tranquil, peaceful in the expression. Soft, dark eyes. A half-smile. A pointy, almost elfin nose.

"Do we think…?" Spinks swallowed. "I mean, this could be one of our victims, right?"

Loshak looked down at the floor mats in the backseat, taking this in. If he'd learned one thing in all these years, it was that anyone could wind up dead, the victim of a knife or a gun or an improvised noose. But seeing her posing for her driver's license photo, barely an adult, still essentially a child trying to fit into the world, made it feel as if gravity in the vehicle had doubled.

There was something sticking out from beneath a edge of the floor mat behind the driver's seat, he realized. It looked like the plasticky, rounded corner of another license.

He reached down, fumbled with it for a second, his glove refusing to pull up the edge of the sleek plastic material. Then he finally got it in hand.

It wasn't actually a license. It had been clearly stamped with the Non-Driver mark, just a state ID. Mississippi issue. He flipped it over. The owner was a blonde girl, a year older than the Bohemian license holder, but same build. Small, almost elfin.

Her name seemed to jump off the card at him.

McClintic, Cassandra L.

It matched the name on the loyalty card they'd found with the body dumped in the alley.

His eyes went back to the floor mat. Something else tucked down there. Another card of some sort, from the look of it. He plucked the laminated rectangle from its hiding place.

Same name as the Mississippi ID card. Same face in the photo. A student card for the Department of Geosciences at MSU.

Loshak's mouth went suddenly dry. Jesus. This girl could have been in the hotel lobby with those college kids the night before, nerding out over rocks.

"I think we've got an ID for the body we found in the alley," he said, all thoughts of dead ends and coincidences evaporating.

Up in the front seat, Washburn sucked his teeth.

"I'll do you one better, agent."

He disappeared below the seat line, going quiet for a second. Then he bobbed back into view.

"We've also got a possible murder weapon."

When his hand came up, he was holding a long, shining butcher knife flecked with brown.

CHAPTER 38

There were a lot of bleary faces in the conference room by the time the task force had been called together for the meeting at nine that morning. Loshak had managed to grab a shower and about an hour's sleep after searching their unsub's car, but most of the other folks looked like they hadn't been as lucky. The coffee machine over on the snack table was really getting a workout.

Spinks, in spite of getting the same scant rest, was bright-eyed and unnaturally chipper.

When Loshak had brought this up on the ride over to the station, the reporter explained, "Our undercover mission paid off. We got inside info, and it led us straight to our killer's lair. I don't know how a mission could be any more successful than that."

"Meaning you've convinced yourself now that going undercover really is your specialty."

"Let's just say, if I ever need to apply for a new job, it's definitely going at the top of my resume."

In the conference room, Belte stopped by to congratulate them on their find.

"Looks like that lead from your UC canvassing panned out, Jevon," she told Spinks, slapping him on the shoulder with a sheaf of papers.

Spinks shrugged.

"You can take the investigative reporter out of the street, but you can't take the street out of the investigative

211

reporter."

She rolled her eyes conspiratorially at Loshak.

"He's going to be insufferable now, you know that, right?"

"I think you mean *even more* insufferable," Loshak said. "Any word on the murder weapon?"

"I got them to bump our knife to the head of the line. Definitely human blood, but it's going to take a while to compare the DNA on the knife to that of our victims. Don't want a rush job on something like that."

She bobbed her head to the side in a sort of above-the-shoulders shrug.

"But I think we can be reasonably sure there'll be a match. Might get something from the hair scrunchy, too, if there's any follicle attached." She checked her watch. "Anyway, time to get this show on the road."

Loshak settled back in his chair as the district commander headed up to the front of the room. The last stragglers at the coffee pot snatched a cup and found a seat.

"Most of you should already be caught up on our finds last night," Belte began, the murmur of conversation subsiding. "An informant tipped us off to a potential victim. White female, early twenties, found in an alley off East 29th. Her face had been cut off. We're waiting to confirm an ID for her, but we think we've got a pretty good idea.

"In case anyone's lost count, we're up to three victims now. If the stakes were high before, they're astronomical now. But it's not all bad news. A second informant gave us a potential home for our suspect — an abandoned 2006 Dodge Stratus in Highland near the Globeville post office.

Expired plates out of Oklahoma. What do we know about it, Johnson?"

The detective shifted in his seat.

"Registered to a Persephone Gunderson of Oklahoma City, plates expired a year ago. No match for the IDs found in the car. We put a call in to the local sheriff's office, but they haven't gotten back to us yet on Miss Gunderson. We cross-referenced the name with our fan mail list. Two Gundersons, one out of Wisconsin, the other from South Dakota. Neither fan mail Gunderson was marked 'high threat,' and neither one was related to a Persephone Gunderson."

Belte nodded and went back to her handful of notes.

"Since you mentioned the IDs, a search of the vehicle brought up a Colorado driver's license and a Mississippi non-driver ID, both issued to females with no priors. Also found in the car was a potential murder weapon, a fourteen-inch stainless steel butcher's knife, Chicago Cutlery. Lots of prints, no match in our database. Forensics show human blood on the blade and handle, but we're still waiting on the DNA comparison."

She looked at Aque.

"Any contact with the family of the girls on the IDs?"

"District Three's doing a welfare check at the address on Alita Simms's driver's license." Alita Simms, Loshak remembered, was the name of their dark-haired Bohemian girl. "And the issuing office for the Mississippi ID got back to us with the numbers on file for Cassandra McClintic — hers and next of kin. No answer yet, but it was early when we started calling. Given the tip from Agent Spinks on her major and the geo convention in town, Jerry drove over to the College of the Mines to see if he could turn anything up," Aque finished, jerking his head toward the door, presumably in the direction of the college.

"Sounds like we've got more than enough waiting to go around," Belte said, tapping her papers on her thigh impatiently. "Let's not waste it sitting around with our thumbs up our asses. What do we want to move on in the meantime?"

Loshak stuck up a hand.

"We could stake out the car and a few spots in the neighborhood, hope he comes back tonight."

"You don't think somebody will have tipped him off to his car being searched?" a uniform in the front row asked.

"It's possible." Loshak cupped his chin. "But you have to remember our guy is extremely isolated from other people, probably even other homeless in his area. Based on what we found, there's the possibility that he'll want to see just how much we messed up his hoard. The ID cards are trophies of his kills. I think he might have an almost compulsive urge to go back, assess the damage to his sacred space."

"I like it." Belte nodded. "Any volunteers for stakeout teams?"

Loshak and Spinks put their hands in the air. They were in good company. Despite the exhaustion evident in most of the task force that morning, it seemed there was a greater desire to see this guy caught than to get sleep.

CHAPTER 39

Most of the day went to organizing the stakeout among the varying districts and departments involved, but by one that afternoon, the teams were in place.

"It's weird to be staking out somebody in the middle of the day, right?" Spinks said, opening a package of voodoo-flavored kettle chips from a gas station.

The reporter did this with the same meticulous care that he usually reserved for napkin usage. Thumb and forefinger pinching the sides of the bag almost daintily, knuckles meeting over what would become the opening to make sure the whole thing didn't rip asunder and spray the rental with voodoo seasoning. Whatever that was.

With a crinkling squeal, the sides came neatly apart.

Loshak tore his attention away from the brightly packaged snack food and raised the binoculars to his eyes as he answered Spinks's question.

"Given that he wasn't there last night, we may have better luck in the daytime. An irregular sleep schedule would fit the profile."

He and Spinks weren't the closest team to the suspect's Dodge. They were about a block away, down the meandering curve that led to the abandoned Kmart, parked in an alley. They had a good angle on the car, although with the distance they had to pull out the binoculars to see it.

The chip bag rattled. He lowered the 'nocs to find

Spinks offering it to him.

"Fancy a taste of New Orleans, partner? It's Mardi Gras in every bite."

Loshak tried one. Kettle-cooked chips always surprised him with their hardness. They waltzed right up to that line of *too hard to chew*, stepped on it a couple of times, then pulled back just enough to make him want another.

The flavor was hard to nail down. Somewhere between a spicy barbecue and a vinegar and sea salt. And like all kettle chips, they left his tongue feeling oily.

"Weird. I was at Mardi Gras back in the eighties," he said, taking another one. "These don't taste like getting arrested for taking a leak in public or climbing up a private balcony in the French Quarter."

"What about hopping a cemetery fence and making Xs on Marie Leveau's tomb?"

Loshak nodded as he chewed.

"Yeah, I could see that with these."

They ate through the savory food over the next several hours and eventually moved on to sweet. Spinks had picked up a package of Hostess Crunch Donettes, while Loshak had gone with a KitKat.

Along with his donuts, Spinks had begun holding forth on social media.

"Do you remember when it was nothing but jokes about how, 'Sir, this is a Wendy's'? I'd call that the Golden Era of social media. That lasted about ten years, this gilded age of innocent hilarity, then it was like we stumbled onto a minefield. A digital war of attrition. The more people we saw blown apart, the more bitter and jaded we became. We lost our innocence and our sense of humor. Now it's like everybody on the internet hates everybody else. We've all got a cause, and that cause is diametrically opposed to everybody else's cause, so we've got to take up arms and fight each other to the death. You know what I mean?"

"Not really."

Loshak snapped off a rectangle of chocolate and wafer. A chunk of the bottom stayed stuck to the rest of the bar. For some reason, he'd never been able to get them apart in one long clean break. Maybe it was his technique.

"I usually just get on to watch funny videos. People falling. Cats. That sort of thing."

"Then you're one of the lucky ones. Because from what I see, seems like a lot of people these days spend their time online trying to hurt somebody else, like the perfect amount of snark or the right scathing meme will make somebody they disagree with go, 'oh, wow, I've been wrong about this and such all along.'"

Spinks paused long enough to wipe his mouth and fingers with a napkin before grabbing another mini donut.

"What they don't realize is no one can win that way. That's not how humans work. You can't change somebody's mind by beating them to death. The more you push, the more they'll push back. That's why I'm proposing we call this the War of Attrition Era. Or something along those lines. Something catchier would be better."

He lapsed into silence, maybe casting around for a more appealing name. Then he looked over at Loshak.

"You're really just watching cat videos?"

He asked it as if he'd just realized what Loshak had said. Loshak shrugged.

"They're funny. I saw a pretty good one the other day

where a cat got into some wrapped ham. The owner was trying to tear it away, but the cat was hanging on for dear life, claws and teeth all sunk in. Growling like it was going to have to fight some stray cat to the death."

Spinks huffed that silent nose-laugh.

"What?"

"Nothing."

The reporter went back to his donuts.

"I sent it to Jan," Loshak said, feeling weirdly like he should defend his stance on this video. "She thought it was hilarious, too, so…"

Spinks shook his head, still grinning.

"Just when I think I've reached the bottom of the 'Shaknado, something like cats eating ham comes up and reveals hidden depths. It's refreshing."

That didn't make Loshak feel any less defensive. If anything, it highlighted that he was under the microscope around Spinks — something he'd always suspected. He broke off another piece of the KitKat unevenly, trying to remember how casually he'd done it the first time, back when he wasn't thinking about being observed.

On the upside, though, he'd have a pretty decent chunk of bonus chocolate when he got to that last rectangle. That was one good thing about not being able to break it along the lines.

An electronic *blip* interrupted his attempt to shake off the hyper self-awareness.

Spinks checked his phone.

"Wasn't me."

Loshak frowned.

"I've never heard my phone make that sound before."

He dug it out of his pocket, wondering if he'd somehow changed the notification sound when he turned it off and then back on earlier.

It was an email from Detective Aque.

"Huh. Who knew I had a sound set up for emails."

Loshak opened it.

Found another of our guy's vics. Somebody called in a body with missing ears. Caucasian, female, age 57. Report and photos attached.

The message was short and to the point, almost verging on gruff. As far as Loshak had seen, that was pretty in line with the detective's personality. He hit the attachments and waited as the files downloaded.

"Looks like they might have found Victim Two," Loshak said.

Spinks looked intrigued, then confused.

"Hold up, we're getting this update via email?" He blinked. "There are a lot of 'this could have been an email' scenarios, but I don't think this is one of them. A body is phone call material. *Maybe* a text."

"I guess Detective Aque felt an email would be more efficient."

Spinks nodded.

"Ah, that explains it. Aque's right in the 'elder millennial' age range. I think that entire generation would rather set themselves on fire over having to make a phone call."

When the report finished downloading, Loshak opened it.

Their victim was Barbara Wickham. She'd been found face down in her luxury apartment in Cherry Creek that morning, covered in stab wounds to the torso and throat, both ears removed.

She may have been there for up to five days. Her husband had been on a business trip to Europe and hadn't been able to reach her, but apparently this wasn't unusual. They had a cabin out in the mountains where the cell reception was awful, and he'd assumed she'd gone out there for the week. That was, until he'd returned home.

Though he'd only read about half of the report to Spinks so far, Loshak's eyes were starting to blur. Lack of sleep, maybe some dehydration. He definitely hadn't been drinking enough water to combat the moisture-sapping ability of the climate and altitude.

He handed the phone off to Spinks, rubbing at his eyes and wondering when the last time was that he'd called Jan. Was it just yesterday he'd texted with her in the diner? Seemed longer. The side effect of getting almost zero sleep was the illusion of more time passing than had actually elapsed. A twinge of guilt made him wish he still had the phone in hand to text her.

Spinks picked up reading aloud where Loshak had left off.

According to the medical examiner's preliminary findings, the wounds on Wickham were similar to those inflicted on Cassandra McClintic. Time of death was in the four-to-seven day range, which was consistent with the date on their ear package. Additionally, Wickham's husband confirmed that her blood type was AB, which matched the blood type of the ears.

Over the next few minutes, the photos came in. The apartment showed obvious signs of a struggle. Blood splashed and smeared across white carpet and furniture. Pooled on the floor where she'd lain.

Loshak found it interesting and strangely tasteful that Aque had chosen to only include one picture of the actual crime scene. The rest showed the victim in life. Her driver's license photo with a faint, somehow refined smile. Another picture that looked like something she'd gotten taken at Sears — her, her husband, an embarrassed-looking kid in a letterman jacket.

There was something in Barbara Wickham's subtle air of sophistication that reminded him of Jan. A sort of effortless elegance.

Or maybe that resemblance was a manifestation of his own fears and insecurities. He made up his mind to give Jan a call as soon as they finished going through the info on their latest victim, trying not to think about how many days Barbara Wickham's husband had told himself she was just out of cell reception.

Loshak rubbed at his eyes again. He could already feel a headache coming on from too little sleep and too much coffee.

"That tells us where the ears came from, but what about the package Andi Wayland got? We still have a yet-to-be-located victim out there with no face," Spinks said, tapping a finger on the bottom of the steering wheel. "Do you think we should head back to the station?"

Loshak shifted in his seat. Let his mind sift through the range of possible outcomes.

"I can't see that there's much we'd be able to do at the moment," he said after a few seconds. "Probably best to stay on the stakeout until we hear otherwise."

The reporter nodded.

"Yeah. Be proactive instead of reactive."

The crime scene photo was still glaring in red and white on the screen of the phone. Loshak leaned over to look at it closer.

He knew they were right in staying on the stakeout, but it still made him itch not to walk the scene. To soak up the details in person. To see and smell and hear what their killer and victim had experienced.

"How do you think he managed to get into a place like this?" Spinks asked, tilting the phone so Loshak could see better. "From the looks of him, he wasn't exactly the kind of dresser I could see a wealthy woman of advanced years inviting up to her penthouse."

"Advanced years?"

Wickham wasn't much older than Loshak.

Spinks chuckled.

"Excuse me, I forgot I was in mixed age company. But you've got to admit, there's a major discrepancy here. Homeless guy in his mid-to-late twenties living out of a trashed car versus a fifty-something who keeps her apartment looking like something out of *Better Homes & Gardens*."

He had a point. Loshak kicked that around for a minute. There was the girl from the alley, too. Cassandra McClintic, college student.

"He's got to have a way he's getting access to these victims. Knowledge of their whereabouts… their life…" Loshak frowned. "Maybe some way of getting them to open the door."

"A uniform maybe, like that hitman down in Tucson?"

Spinks suggested. "It'd be a hell of a blow to Postal Inspector Randall if our killer was dressing up like a mailman, pretending to deliver a package."

His eyebrows jumped up.

"Oh, what if he was an actual mailman, and he delivered those packages to the podcasters?"

"If that was the case, why mail them at all? He would know the place was covered in security cameras. Not to mention the fact that he risked the staff at the post office recognizing him."

"You said in your profile that he loves the attention," Spinks said. "Maybe he wants to be caught."

Loshak leaned back in his seat and checked through the binoculars again.

"I don't know. Package delivery is a high-stress, high-pressure job. You've got a really small window to get all your deliveries made. They're all guaranteed by that day, so you can't go home until it's done. Most of the companies nowadays have routes you're required to follow, time demands you're required to stick to. If you miss a turn or blow past a hidden mailbox, you're behind. I don't see him holding down a job like that for long."

"Maybe he just got hired. Maybe that was part of his plan."

But planning like that didn't fit, either.

"With all the publicity his post office video footage is getting, someone would have recognized his face. They'd have to; those spots are running ten times a day, and his photo is up in every post office between here and Aurora."

Spinks *hmm*ed.

"Yeah, I guess the chances nobody has turned him in

yet would be slim to none if he worked in the postal industry. But that doesn't negate the possibility of him posing as a delivery man."

"We're ignoring the fact that Cassandra McClintic was found in an alley. She didn't have to open a door to him; *he* found *her.*"

As he said the words, Loshak felt them settle in his gut like a stone. He found her.

He pawed at his jaw, his early five o'clock shadow rasping a little.

"What we need to be looking for is a commonality between a college student in town for a geology conference, a wealthy older woman, and our as-yet-unidentified victim — who may or may not be Alita Simms. Some thread that ties them all together."

Spinks sighed and leaned his arm on his window ledge.

"Well, it's not location. So far, we're all over the map for bodies and deliveries. The most we can say is that he's in the greater metropolitan area. Doesn't seem like it's age or appearance, either."

There was something they were missing, a key piece that would make the rest of the puzzle fall into place. Loshak stared down that empty alley toward their suspect's vehicle, possibilities bouncing around in his head.

Nothing jumped out at him. Until they had more information, they were spinning their wheels.

The afternoon stole away, evening bleeding into the landscape. Set as a backdrop against the urban sprawl, the tops of the Rockies were still lit a bright gold, but even that was creeping toward darkness. The traffic cramming the nearest road slowed and slowed until the street was completely dead.

The killer was out there somewhere tonight, maybe even stalking his next victim. But wherever he was, he wasn't here.

CHAPTER 40

Day faded to night, and the Stratus blurred into a lump of shadow outlined by streetlights. Loshak stared through the lenses of the binoculars periodically. Something about the bulky shape of the vehicle made him think of the carcass of some huge beast brought down by ancient predators, picked over and abandoned to desiccate in the harsh climate.

The stakeout had reached the point where both he and Spinks were silent, lost in thought, similar to the wee hours of the morning on an overnight drive where conversation died out and road hypnosis set one's consciousness adrift on some other plane.

Lights went on in the upper floors across the way, neat squares of yellow shining into the darkness. From inside their narrow alleyway, it felt like he was looking down a long tunnel passing through the tall buildings on each side. It reminded him of those chunks of interstate cut right through the mountains. Hard rock chiseled into straight lines.

Thinking of all those tunnels brought to mind something Loshak had read recently. He rested the binoculars on his knee.

"Did you ever hear about that train tunnel through the mountains where the clearance is only like an inch on either side of the cars?"

Spinks shifted in his seat as if he were coming awake.

226

"An inch? That'd be a nerve-wracking squeeze."

"It might be two inches," Loshak admitted. "The point is, it's incredibly tight in there. When they were blasting and digging it out, the rock of that mountain was so hard that they didn't leave any extra space, just made it barely wide enough for the tracks they were laying. That tunnel is the main reason they don't build train cars any wider to this day, even though it might ultimately be more efficient."

"Huh. You'd think they would go back in and widen it out some more if it was that important to them."

"But do you know why train tracks in the US are the size they are?"

A hint of a smile appeared on the reporter's face.

"Based on the other weights and measures we use, I'd say it must be because we wanted to be different from the rest of the world."

"Actually, our tracks are the same width as the tracks in Britain."

"So we based it on ye olde English train measurement?"

"Sure did. Now guess why the UK's train tracks are that wide."

Spinks inhaled deeply, squinting out at the night like a man puzzling out a riddle. After a few seconds, he let the breath out and shook his head.

"No idea. They used some sovereign's height?"

"Actually, that was the standard distance between the wheels of their animal-driven carts. Coal wagons, milk wagons, old-timey fire engines and such. And *that* standard measurement came because of the ruts worn into the land by the Roman chariots of old back in Hadrian's day."

He glanced sidelong at Spinks, finally coming to the culmination of this history lesson.

"But here's the kicker — Roman chariot wheels were only positioned that far apart because that was the width of two horses' backsides when they were harnessed together to pull the chariot. So some tunnel in the southwestern United States, now, in the present day, is considered the most dangerous train tunnel in the country, because two thousand years ago, chariot makers decided the ideal distance between their wheels was two horse butts wide."

Spinks stared at him for a second, mouth open.

"Seriously?"

"I don't know."

Loshak shrugged and raised the binoculars to his eyes again. Still no movement on the Stratus.

"You were talking about social media earlier. I read it on one of those sites, so probably not."

"'One of those sites?'" The reporter huffed that breathy laugh through his nose. "How many profiles do you have, partner?"

"A couple, I guess."

"Just for the cat videos?"

"And the apocryphal history facts."

"Well, it definitely sounds like something that would be floating around the internet. Just the other day, I read this thing about Frida Kahlo..."

When Spinks didn't go on, Loshak looked over. The reporter was staring out the window.

Loshak's stomach jumped.

A dark shape was loping down the alley toward them.

Impossible to tell the gender or any other identifying characteristics because of the baggy coat they wore, but they were running toward the car in a sort of animalistic, rolling jog that was almost graceful.

Loshak's pulse sped up, preparing for some unknown confrontation with the runner.

But whoever they were, they passed by the rental car without stopping.

The men watched in the rearview and door mirrors until the runner stopped near the back of the alley, dug around in a pocket, pulled out a key, and let themselves into the building at the end. The door slammed shut with a bang.

"Phew," Spinks breathed. "False alarm."

Loshak grabbed his cardboard cup from the cup holder and took a swig of cold, bitter coffee. He was down to the dregs, and a good dose of grounds came with it, scratching his throat on their way down and making him cough.

"Gonna make it?" Spinks asked.

Loshak nodded and cleared his throat. His eyes watered. He didn't have anything in the car to wash that down with except the last bit of his coffee, so he swallowed another more careful mouthful. That helped a little.

The shock of the surprise runner seemed to liven things up in the rental. Rather than lapsing back into thoughtful silence, they moved onto the subject of killers.

"There's that old cliché of, 'he was such a quiet man,' and 'he was so nice, I never would have guessed he would go nuts and murder a hundred people.'"

Spinks bounced one long leg back and forth while he spoke, his knee bumping against the driver's side of the control panel and gently shaking the car.

"Take John Wayne Gacy. His family was always talking about how it was like there were two Johns — the good John and the bad John. Like there were two versions of him sharing the same body. Mostly, from their point of view, he was a gregarious family man who loved nothing better than to throw a cookout for everybody in the neighborhood, but then they got these glimpses of another guy, these scary moments when he seemed cold and detached, almost inhuman. Moments when they didn't even recognize the person they thought they knew."

"You get that a lot from the people closest to serial killers," Loshak said. "I mean, you've heard of that graphic novel *My Friend Dahmer*. That could've been about any unpopular high school kid getting bullied and acting out. And people forget that Ted Bundy had a series of girlfriends and a wife. The kid of one of his girlfriends described him as a father figure.

"I think we like to paint these murderers as monsters, just monsters and nothing else, because it's easier to understand such heinous crimes in black and white. But in reality, these monsters are also still people. They do awful, unforgivable things, but they have internal worlds and feelings, and they experience life not so differently than we do in a lot of ways. At least part of the time."

Loshak thumbed the binocular's textured grip. The words poured out of him now.

"I think it's easier to see them as The Other. Cast them out of the rest of humanity. Ultimately, that's less scary than accepting that they're part of us, they walk among us, and some of the insights that we learn from their psychology point to the same ugly things we might find in ourselves if we were brave enough to look.

"I mean, every day, we've got one-off murders, assaults, rapes taking place, but serial killers are like the id of humanity. Something is broken in them, something that fully releases the violent urges. Some of those dark impulses are in all of us, to some extent. The desire for control, for power. Serial killers lay bare some of the primal parts of our psychology, show us some kind of logical conclusion — our worst selves pushed to the extreme.

"It boils down to power and control. Universal human desires, to some degree. You don't have to cut a girl's face off and mail it to somebody to have those selfish impulses. They can be expressed in so many ways — some of them quite subtle — but I think ultimately the psychology behind the yearning to control others is often the same, whether the expression of it comes in the form of rape or abuse or conniving to have more influence at the PTA meeting.

"Even just arguing with someone to prove you're right or all that stuff you were talking about on social media, trying to hurt one another, trying to prove superiority and righteousness by beating somebody over the head with your cause. It's all part of a ubiquitous human phenomenon.

"But it's too painful to lump ourselves in with someone like Ted Bundy, so we cast him out instead. Say that we're different, and that could never be us."

Spinks was quiet for a minute, chewing this over. Processing.

"OK, so if—"

Spinks stopped talking abruptly, not trailing off like he'd done before with his Frida Kahlo anecdote. He leaned forward, narrowed eyes squinting out into the night.

Startled, Loshak frowned. He followed the reporter's gaze.

There was someone drifting down the street, crossing diagonally toward the Dodge Stratus. Someone in a dark zip-up hoodie.

Feeling like he was moving on autopilot, Loshak raised the binoculars to his eyes.

The person had their hood up, the zipper pulled all the way to their chin so that their face was almost completely obscured by the dark material. Just like they'd seen in the post office footage. The build seemed about the right size. And thin, really thin.

Spinks held out a hand.

"Can I…?"

Loshak passed the lenses over.

The hooded person hesitated a few paces from the abandoned car. Not a full-on stop, just a bobble in the sure-footed gait while they looked up and down the street, hood swiveling as though they sensed they were being watched.

Just then the cops in the car posted closest to the Stratus burst out of their vehicle, weapons drawn. Loshak could hear their muffled shouts echoing down the street.

The hooded figure staggered backward a step. Hands coming toward the face, then balling into fists.

They spun and broke into a sprint, feet kicking up dust on the empty dirt lot next to the abandoned car. With forearms braced out in front, they crashed through a barrier of dead-looking landscaping hedge and disappeared from view.

CHAPTER 41

For a second, both Loshak and Spinks sat in silent shock.

It was really him. Their killer. Their killer had just run into the bushes.

"Drive," Loshak said, his throat suddenly dry. "Go."

Spinks's face scrunched up as if he hadn't quite heard what Loshak had said.

"Go!"

Loshak craned his neck as if he could see around the corner and watch for oncoming traffic.

"We can catch him on the next block, maybe."

"Right, yeah."

Spinks's hands fumbled on the keys, jangling them against the steering column, then finally cranking them.

The rental roared to life, and he jammed the shifter into reverse. The tires squealed, throwing grit. They shot backward down the alley.

Loshak winced a little as the car wavered, Spinks fighting to straighten them out. Though it was counterintuitive, it would've been faster to go out the front of the alley and around. Faster and safer. But they were already at the end of the alley, Spinks palming the wheel to pull them out into the empty side street. They bumped up on the sidewalk and narrowly missed a hydrant.

Spinks dropped them into drive and put the pedal to the metal again. The rental, formerly mild-mannered, seemed to leap into the chase, engine building volume as they sped up.

Both Spinks and Loshak cranked their heads left to look for movement at the back of the landscaped hedge row.

Needled branches formed stark silhouettes in the foreground. Dark brickwork blurred past in the background.

Nothing there.

No human shape blacker than the rest of the bushes. No telltale shivering branches to show where he'd been.

Nothing.

Loshak whipped his head around to check across the street. Nothing there, either.

"Where do I go?" Spinks asked, voice choked with adrenaline.

"Straight." But there was no sign of anyone ahead, either.

They pressed onward. The agent could feel his pulse battering away in his temples.

"Left at the turn," Loshak guessed.

Spinks whipped them through the turn, the centrifugal force mashing Loshak's shoulder against the door.

"Wait!" Loshak had caught sight of something in the side mirror. Movement behind them. "It was back there."

Spinks slammed on the brakes and moved for the shifter, but Loshak stopped him.

"No, just park it."

Already, the agent was ripping off his seatbelt with one hand and throwing open the door with the other.

The wind cut through the stale warmth of his suit jacket, and a matching chill radiated up from the cold concrete. He hit the street running.

Up ahead, he could still see the commotion. Shadows leaping everywhere. Multiple people moving. Struggling. Confusion.

He heard Spinks's door bang shut behind him, but he didn't slow down.

"They've got him," he yelled back to Spinks.

It wasn't until Loshak said the words that the image up ahead came clear to him. The details sharpened into focus all at once.

The perp lay face down on the asphalt. A frail thing mashed into the crook of the gutter.

The two cops who'd initiated the chase on foot hovered over him. One of the officers had his gun out, while the other was wrangling the cuffs onto their writhing suspect.

Loshak's middle seemed to go numb. Stomach floating. Airy. Feet slapping the ground with strange force considering how light he felt in the center. Shock waves jolted up his knees with every slap.

Together the cops scooped the suspect up, one under each arm, and lifted him to his feet. They ripped the hood off as Loshak and Spinks jogged to a stop in front of them.

The killer sneered at them. Lips snarled up like he might try to lunge and bite like a rabid dog.

Except it wasn't him.

But Loshak did recognize the crinkly green hair, the big doe eyes. Remembered how the podcaster had started to hyperventilate when he'd interviewed her.

It was Jessica Caine.

CHAPTER 42

Sam Crozier ghosted down the sidewalk, his hood pulled up against that killing wind, hands shoved deep into the pockets of his jacket. The threadbare material of his hoodie wasn't enough to keep him warm, but the icy numbness in his fingers and windburn on his face barely registered.

Ahead of him by maybe ten yards walked a small form. A girl of maybe twenty with her fur-lined hood thrown back, long coat open to the elements.

He'd seen her face when she passed a stoop where he was curled up for the night, his eyes capturing the image like all those photos he processed at the lab. One slice of her time searched and seized. Kept.

Pointy nose. Wide-set eyes. Pale, slender, widow's peak. A red bandanna wrapped like a headband against her dark hair.

It was her clothes that had caught his eye. The vintage calf-length tapestry coat. The too-big jeans hanging on her hips and layers upon layers of worn henley shirts. She looked like she'd just stepped out of her studio in the middle of painting some Hieronymus Bosch–esque scene boiling with demons and the pathetic human quarry they consumed.

A car flashed past on his right, its wheels hissing on the asphalt. The streets were mostly empty of traffic tonight, and he hadn't seen another soul in blocks.

Just her.

Now and then, the artist ahead stumbled. Soles of her shoes scuffing on the sidewalk. She could be drunk.

In his mind's eye, Crozier saw a bottle of absinthe next to the easel, a color-splattered palette knife lying to the side of an array of mixed paints in shades only a tortured and brilliant mind could bring to life. Purple sheened with gold. An orange so red that it felt like the dawning sun had been born in its depths. The deep and fathomless green of pine needles beneath a midnight sky.

Works that meant something, like art used to. Spoke like the classical masters.

These days, you nailed a banana to a wall or cut a hole in your jeans and pissed in a tin can in front of people and called it art. Works that existed only to denigrate the onlooker, to tell them what a dumbshit they were to search for beauty or truth.

To her, that crap would be just as senseless and idiotic as a McDonald's commercial. He could see her in front of her easel, lips and eyes set in a serious, soulful attitude, face glowing with the act of creation, the scene burning her from the inside out as she transferred it to the canvas.

Evidently, she wasn't in any big hurry to get where she was going. She meandered down the sidewalk, head occasionally lolling back on her shoulders to stare up at the sky.

Now, she stopped walking altogether and looked around. He ducked behind the corner of a cinderblock wall just in time to keep her from seeing him.

He peeked out after a few seconds. He couldn't resist.

Her head tilted back in a slow-motion drift. Gaze gliding up the brick façades set around them like tunnel walls. Finally, her neck reached its apex.

She stared at the starry sky for what felt like a long time. Rapt. Gone still, save for the slightest sway.

After some forty seconds, she started moving again. Something loose-jointed and rolling in her walk confirmed the drunkenness for him. He pulled himself out from behind the wall and sped up.

The city seemed like an open thing before them. Endless blocks of apartment buildings flecked with smaller homes. The dots of the streetlights trailed off into the dark horizon. The asphalt itself like a river snaking through all the structures.

Her breath fogged into the air and disappeared, that warmth coming from deep inside, deeper than words, as deep and hot as the heart's blood.

His skin tingled as he got closer to her, arms and legs and gut sending back the giddy sensation of floating. A childlike rapture filled him — the thrill of sneaking up on someone to scare them. The urge to giggle stuck like a bubble in his throat.

Of course he could be wrong about the painting. He could also see her working with her hands.

An artist majoring in something solid and physical. Sculpting. Bringing the clay to life with the tips of her delicate fingers.

The image of a pottery wheel spun in his mind, a lump of gray mush whirling and whirling as pale, slender fingers ran up its sides.

There was something poetic about shaping a singular work of art out of a shapeless lump. Bringing form from formlessness. The clay would be just a blob when she took hold of it. Meaningless. But from the nothing, she created something. From the void she brought forth beauty.

These fantasies exploded in his mind as he weaved in and out of barriers and around trashcans and bags left piled at the edge of the street for the early morning pickup. When there were no alcoves or fences to hide behind, he ducked down behind parked cars along the curb.

Her silhouette was drawing closer, coming into perfect definition. The individual hairs on her fur-lined hood stood out in the streetlamps. He could see a cigarette burn in the material of one sleeve, some of the lining showing through, white against the colorful weave. Fine dark flyaway hairs that had escaped from her bandanna headband whipped silently against her head. Earrings, half a dozen in each lobe, all mismatched with artsy precision.

He ducked one last time, got low behind a stand of newspaper machines and a blue mail collection box on the corner. One knee and both hands touched down on the cold concrete of the sidewalk, rough and dry.

She was close now. He could feel her movement somehow, like puppet strings connecting her to his pounding heart.

He stayed down, eyes wide, face stretched into a grin, some electric current sizzling like a filament burning bright in his skull. Unable to hold it in anymore, an almost silent laugh puffed white clouds of his breath into the air.

He swallowed the gaiety and dipped out of his hiding spot.

She wasn't there.

The sidewalk stood still. Empty cells of cement trailing away from him.

He stood up straight and gaped at the vacant path.

No rustle of her coat. No plumes of soul-deep breath dissipating into the cold night air.

He held his own breath and listened. The silence whispered in his ears.

She was gone. Just gone.

Impossible.

The word sounded in his head as if someone else had said it.

It's impossible.

A mechanical shriek of brakes cut through the silence. A bus creeping past the intersection down the street.

Its headlights swept over the buildings, a glowing tunnel advancing. The yellow strips of light on the sides made it look like a passing ship somehow, glowing dots drifting through the darkness.

The movement seemed to unfasten his feet from the ground. He shuffled around the side of the newspaper machines, and then he was plunging down the sidewalk again. Slower now. Careful. Like a child whose prized treasure had been ripped away by some unknown evil. This had to be approached with caution.

She could still be close.

She had to be.

Didn't she?

A shaky breath entered his chest, cold and strange. The rhythm was off, a hitch to it, but then his breathing evened out.

He pressed forward, eyes flitting over everything as he passed. The glass storefront of a bookshop. A house with a porch light casting a sphere of yellow over the swing and rail there.

Something scraped to his left. A drawn-out sound. Raspy and close. Low to the ground.

His shoulders jumped. He stutter-stepped backward.

A voice spoke from the darkness.

"Hey."

CHAPTER 43

Loshak stood in the station's observation room with Spinks and Detectives Aque and Schrader, all of their gazes locked on the green-haired podcaster framed on the monitor. A timestamp ticked in the corner, marking the early morning off in hours, minutes, seconds. Jessica Caine stewed, running her hands over the tabletop, chewing the cuff of her hoodie, unable to keep still.

Commander Belte came through the door, shaking her head.

"I ran everything I could on her. Nothing but a parking ticket, and she paid for that in a timely fashion. Has she said anything yet?"

"Nothing."

Aque stared into the screen like he was trying to nail down what exactly this girl was.

"Apart from giving her name and date of birth, she hasn't said a word. Never asked if she was under arrest, for a lawyer, anything. She just went mute."

Spinks shook a finger in the air.

"She's gotta be doing some amateur investigating of her own, right? Trying to dig up a juicy lead or two for her podcast."

Loshak had considered this possibility himself. But the longer he thought about it, the less he liked the explanation.

"Why bother stonewalling, in that case?" he said. "It's

not like she was caught trespassing or something. She was walking down the street. No laws against that."

Schrader frowned.

"So, just to be clear… we *don't* think she's the killer? I mean, she could have had someone else mail the packages for her, right? And she could've sent one to herself to throw off the scent."

"She could have," Loshak admitted, "but she doesn't fit the profile. From what we've seen, Caine is steady and organized enough to hold down a full-time job and keep up her apartment. Hosting a podcast aside, when we interviewed her about the ears, she didn't show the sort of excitement and eagerness you get from someone who's dying to be the center of attention."

"Could've been acting."

Loshak nodded slowly, but not really committing to it.

"You get slips in those situations, though. Little glimmers of the real thoughts beneath the façade. Stuff that you can edit out of a movie but not real life."

"Like when that mother back in the 90s was on TV begging for her children to be returned from a carjacking, when she had actually drowned them herself and run the car into the lake," Belte supplied. "I remember studying the tapes on that. Our psych teacher pointed out all the smug twinges in her facial expressions."

She shivered.

"It was creepy."

Schrader let out a long breath through his nose.

"So we're back to square one."

There'd been a half-formed thought in the back of Loshak's mind ever since he'd stepped into the observation room, and suddenly it revealed itself to him.

"Not this time," Loshak said. "She's not our killer, but she knows him."

As he said the words, a feeling of certainty settled around him. A sense of them finally being on the right track.

"*That's* why she won't talk. She's protecting someone."

Silence fell in the observation room as they all studied her face on the monitor.

CHAPTER 44

She was there. The artist girl. His artist girl. Crouched on the ground to his left, the hem of her coat puddled on the concrete.

She scraped a match across the sidewalk beside her shoe, letting out another long scratching sound. The head sparked over the rough concrete, but it didn't flare to life.

"You got a light?"

The cigarette perched between her lips bobbed as she spoke. It was a Camel Light 100. An absurdly long white tube protruding from her tiny elfin face.

Crozier blinked, trying to catch up.

"Are those— Are you using kitchen matches?"

She sniffed out a laugh.

"I'm trying to. Supposed to be strike anywhere, but… turns out they kinda blow ass at striking anywhere." She shrugged and the material of her coat rustled. "They're all my friend Pablo had. Not a smoker, that one."

Up close, framed by the yellow porch light, he could tell for sure now that she was drunk. Not wasted, but feeling good all the same. Something about the way she looked around, the looseness in her neck and hands, the way she tilted her head, the openness in her gaze — it all seemed too free, too uninhibited for her to be sober.

A party. That made sense. She was walking home from a party — at Pablo's, apparently.

Crozier fished a lighter out of his pocket and handed it

over.

"Thanks."

She sniffed again, this time like someone whose nose was running in the cold, and took it.

The wheel ratcheted, and the flame popped from the lighter. Almost magical. Sufficiently advanced technology, and all that. That and the calm, quiet chill of the night didn't hurt, either.

The mile-long cigarette glowed like an ember, bathing her eyes and nose in red. Those wispy strands of hair whipped around her face as the breeze picked up. She handed the lighter back, then held out her empty hand to him, palm up, fingers faintly cupped.

Crozier's brow furrowed. He stared down at her outstretched limb like it was some exotic language he couldn't read.

She's... asking me to help her up?

As if she'd heard his thought, she stretched her arm out a little farther and waggled her fingers. Something good-natured and amused that said *Well?*

He took her hand.

It was warm and soft. Silky. The image of those delicate fingers shaping the clay came back to him.

How long had it been since he'd been touched by another person? A long time, for sure. But was it weeks? Or months?

A breath squeezed out of his lungs. Abrupt, like a dog huffing. Was he alarmed? Confused? Definitely confused. He didn't know what to feel.

Something prickled in her touch. Some strange energy like static electricity arcing between their palms. A connection. A silent tug at somewhere deep inside.

He pulled her to her feet.

She looked around on that floppy neck again. Took a drag from the Camel and exhaled the smoke. The plume eased into the frozen air and disintegrated.

"Thanks," she said again.

There was an edge to the word that made him think either she wasn't sure whether she had thanked him for the light earlier or she wanted him to respond. He couldn't remember, but he didn't think he'd acknowledged her thanks the first time.

This time, he nodded.

Suddenly, she went almost rigid, that loose neck straightening for a heartbeat. She squinted up at him.

He tried to break eye contact, to look at the ground, the porch light, anything to push off the uncomfortable feeling of being exposed, of being stripped down to the bone. But he couldn't.

Her small, pointed chin tipped up. She was going to say something. Declare judgment on him, reject him, cast him out.

Her lips quirked. The words came spilling free like she was pouring them out.

"Not a big talker, huh?"

He shrugged.

She laughed. She was close enough that he could smell the smoke on her breath. The scent was slower to dissipate than the clouds of white.

She hit her cigarette again and pointed two fingers and the smoldering tube of tobacco at the open road in front of them.

"You want to go get a coffee or something? Night's still young and shit."

CHAPTER 45

"What were you doing out by the tent city tonight?" Aque asked.

He and Loshak had moved into the interrogation room with Jessica Caine, the detective's chair parked sideways along the table in front of her. Loshak leaned against the wall in the corner, observing.

Caine was even paler tonight than she'd been in her apartment the day she'd unwrapped the package containing the ears. Brownish shadows stood out beneath those big eyes. She slipped her fingers under her green hair, scratching just behind her ear.

"I was looking for someone."

"Who?" Aque demanded. "Do you know the person that lives in the Stratus?"

Loshak hid his grimace. Either out of inexperience with interrogations or eagerness to catch their killer, the detective had jumped in too fast. Caine was retracting from the conversation, burrowing into herself. She pulled the sleeves of her hoodie down over her fingers and wrapped them tighter around her body, like she'd done with that knitted comfort wrap she'd been wearing in her apartment.

"Is it a friend? Boyfriend?"

Caine stared over his shoulder at the wall.

"You were a long way from home," Aque tried a different tack. "And in the middle of the night. Were you doing some on-the-street investigations for your podcast?"

Nothing.

"Here's what I think," Loshak said.

Caine's eyes focused on him, but he stayed in his corner, a hunch telling him this was the better move. Keep the physical distance, distract her attention away from the guy putting pressure on her from close up, draw her out.

"I think you know the person who sleeps in that car. I think you care about him, and I think you're worried about him. But I think you're also worried about getting the police involved, getting that person in trouble. Is that right?"

Her big dark eyes held Loshak's steadily for a few seconds. Then she nodded in slow motion. Somewhere in that look, somewhere behind the fear was a deep concern for someone. She felt bad for their killer. Worried about him.

Loshak knew he had to go slow and easy here, keep her moving forward. He went out on a limb based on that look of pity.

"You don't want the cops in on this because this friend, he's had it hard enough already, hasn't he?"

Another hesitant nod.

"You don't have to tell us a name," Loshak said.

Aque shifted in his seat, but thankfully didn't try to wrestle the interview back from him.

"But what's got you so worried about him that you're trying to find him in the middle of the night?"

She looked down at the cuff of her jacket.

"It's a bad neighborhood, and… I heard some talk. I was grabbing some food earlier, and I overheard people saying that something went down in the encampment by the old Kmart, cops everywhere. I got worried something happened."

The words came out choked, and her eyes started to water.

"You were checking up on him," Loshak said.

She swallowed audibly and shrugged one shoulder.

"It's my ex. But we've known each other forever, since high school. It wasn't one of those breakups where everybody hates everybody. We were just kids, and we just kind of fizzled out as a couple, but we've always been friends."

Caine paused, and Loshak held his breath, hoping Aque would sense that this was no time to interrupt. They had to let her keep talking.

"He's a good guy." She said it as if she'd been repeating it since high school to anybody who would listen. "You wouldn't believe how smart he is. Hilarious, too. He's got this way of looking at the world that just… It makes you see it in a whole new light.

"But he's been living on the street for a few months now. Sort of spiraling since this girl — his girlfriend — died." She let out a breath. "I think he needs help. Like psychiatric help."

She tried to laugh and missed it by a mile, falling somewhere closer to a pained groan.

"But they say all the greatest geniuses are a little broken, right? I mean, look at Van Gogh."

Bringing up that example out of nowhere threatened to break through the carefully empathetic face Loshak was projecting. Talking about an artist famous for cutting his own ear off to impress a girl when just two days ago, she'd received a pair of dismembered ears in the mail? Completely unbidden? That had to indicate some kind of powerful subconscious tug-of-war going on in her mind.

Caine didn't seem to notice the irony. She kept talking, some of the tension draining from her pale face as she went on, her body language loosening, shoulders lowering. It was like lancing a boil to talk about this stuff, all the pressure giving way as the infected fluid gushed out.

"He's such a passionate person, but he could never get that excitement and... I don't know, verve for life turned toward something that would benefit him. It's like he's more sensitive than the rest of the world, like just living hurts him. Of course, he tries all the usual suspects to drown out the pain — drinking, I know he's done drugs. And then Siobhan... They were really in love."

Her dark eyes bored into Loshak's as if she could make him understand the significance through sheer intensity.

"When Shiv overdosed, he just fell apart. I couldn't even get him to go back to the apartment to get his stuff. He said to let her stupid fucking parents take it all."

Caine sniffed and wiped at her eye with her sleeve.

"Of course, they didn't want it, either. They took what she'd left behind, and I paid some movers to put all his stuff in storage for him." She shook her head. "They were already months behind on rent when she died. That was the last straw for their landlord. He kicked S— He kicked my friend out."

"Is that when he moved into the car?"

Again she hesitated. Then a nod.

"Did anyone tell you the reason that car was being watched?" Loshak asked.

"No one's told me anything," Caine said in a voice that wavered between accusation and hysteria. "God, this whole week's just been fucking insane."

Loshak waited for her to run herself out, then in a gentle voice he said, "The person who stays in that car is a person of interest in some serious crimes."

She stared at him; this time, her expressive eyes were giving him nothing. He was going to have to risk it.

"Obviously, you know about the mail stuff," he said. "Have you seen the footage on the news?"

She frowned.

"I don't have a TV, I just stream stuff on my phone."

"Well, the thing is, your friend is in danger, and we think other people are in danger, too. We could be looking at multiple deaths if you don't help us. I don't want to shift any blame for what's happened, but I do have to give you the reality of the situation. A serial killer, that's what we're talking about here."

Her watery eyes stared into space. She wasn't going to say anything. She was going to clam up again.

Internally, Loshak scrambled. How could he get through to her? Get her to open up the rest of the way? There had to be a right approach here, a perfect turn of phrase.

He could tell she was highly empathetic, the type of overly kind person Loshak had seen dragged into the wake of these killers dozens of times, before and after their convictions. They saw some potential for good in the perpetrator that the rest of the world didn't recognize, which only ever seemed to make their loyalty to the killer even stronger.

His tongue stabbed into the roof of his mouth, poised to speak. But the perfect turn of phrase didn't come to him.

Think.

Maybe if he drove home the humanity of the victims, put them in the same light as her friend. Talk about how Barbara Wickham was a loving mother and wife, Cassandra McClintic a promising young student who fostered kittens in her spare time. Loshak took a quick breath to dive in.

"Jessica, you saw the—"

Before he could even bring up the body parts taken from the victims, Jessica Caine buried her head in her hands and started sobbing.

CHAPTER 46

First there was the all-night diner with the amazing coffee. Sumatran, the waitress said when the artist complemented it, as if she, the waitress, had hand-picked the beans herself.

He and the artist — she said her name was Blaine, but he couldn't stop thinking that she'd probably changed it from something less exciting, like Jennifer or Kelly or maybe Brooke so she could keep her initials — he and Blaine sat in the cracked seat of the red booth, laughing and drinking Sumatran coffee. The knife pressed warm against his side. She shucked off her coat, revealing narrow, fragile-looking shoulders and arms made longer by the sleeves falling over her wrists.

The diner had those napkin dispenser–slash–jukeboxes that were supposed to play music, but when she bummed a quarter from him, theirs didn't work.

"Dammit," she muttered. "I wanted to hear *Surfin' Safari*."

"Seriously?"

He couldn't reconcile that with her clothes, her personality, the air that hung around her like a cloud.

She smirked.

"Hey man, fuck you if you don't like the Beach Boys. I know what's good, and they're good."

Then they were on the street, walking and carrying on about politics and the fuckers who ran the city, the state, and the world. Blaine had opinions on all of it, and he was just aware enough of current events to be part of the conversation. Sometimes he agreed, and sometimes he took the opposite view, needling her just to see how she would react.

"I live in my car," he said once, abruptly, while she was talking about greed.

She stopped talking for a second, stopped walking. Stared at him.

He swallowed.

"I'm homeless."

The words floated away on those clouds of condensation, born in his lungs, released into the wild, and gone.

After a second of stunned silence, she said, "That's really something to spring on somebody."

"Sorry."

"But that's what I'm talking about." She started moving again. "This city, man. It grinds you down and spits you out. You don't even matter to it, because it's not a living, breathing thing that thinks and feels…"

They cut through a park at one point, traipsing along the frozen edges of a pond. No one there to witness her death. And it would be a beautiful place for an artist to die. Something about the urge to take a last breath in a semblance of nature trapped within the ugliness of the city. He could see the wounds steaming, an elfin face laid bare to the cold, red draining onto the pebbly shore while the last of the heat escaped into the sky.

They stopped there for a while, skipping rocks.

"You suck at this," he said, trying out her blunt way of stating facts.

He could do it, too, be straightforward and zany and shit.

She laughed and chucked another rock out into the water. Instead of jumping across the surface of the pond, it *thunk*ed into the black depths.

"Oh yeah, Mr. Fucking Rock-Skipping Genius? I'd like to see you do better."

He reared back and winged his rock. It skittered across the growing ice at the edges first, then skipped three, eight, fifteen times, finally clattering onto the rocks on the far shore.

"Please," he said, "Mr. Fucking Rock-Skipping Genius was my father. You can just call me Genius."

Still chuckling, she threw another one and got two skips out of it. Then she stood up.

"You never said what your name was."

The lamps were too far away from the pond to see the expression on her face, but he thought he heard fear in her voice. Could just be surprise, though. Hard to say. He wasn't getting fear from her posture. She let out a laugh that could have been forced.

"Listen man, I'm not that kind of girl. I like to know who the fuck I'm skipping rocks with."

"Sammy."

He wasn't quite sure why he'd gone with the diminutive instead of just saying "Sam." Something about it being less threatening, maybe.

"Sammy Fucking Rock-Skipper," she said, nodding. "Yeah, that tracks."

Then there was another street, this time with her hand in his. Her phone went off, and she checked it.

"Apparently Pablo's party is still going strong," she said. "Want to check it out?"

He hesitated.

"It's kind of dumb." She shrugged. "Just a bunch of writing majors drinking and talking shit, but it could be fun or could be stupid."

So she *was* an artist, like he'd thought. Not of the canvas or the clay, but the written word. He could imagine her engrossed in Dostoevsky or Tolstoy, dense and meaningful, dissecting every word they wrote, unfurling meaning and truth with that sharp little knife of her wit.

"Last time, Pablo and Jason — this guy from my lit classics class — they hit each other in the head with a hammer. Not like a fight, but like…" She rolled her eyes and took a drag from her latest Camel, smoke rolling out of her mouth and nose as she went on. "They're crazy sometimes. I think they both want to die. I mean, who writes who *doesn't* want to die sometimes? But they can both be pretty effed up. Fun, but you know… Anyway, they took turns smacking each other in the head with a hammer last time."

That idea of wanting to die lurched something loose in his gut. He didn't like thinking about her that way.

But then what the hell had he been fantasizing about when he stalked her? Ducking into hiding spots and crouching behind mailboxes like some kind of monster trailing its prey. Some kind of psycho. A freak. When he caught up to her, hadn't he planned to…

He pulled back from the thought.

"Anyway. It was just an idea," she said.

She turned away and blew a lungful of smoke into the

breeze. It rolled back over her face and hair before slipping away. Something about the embarrassment, not really in her voice but in the set of her tiny shoulders and the motion of the Camel between her fingers, got to him.

"Hammer to the head?" He nodded. "Sounds like a blast. Let's go."

She grinned.

"Pablo's is this way."

On the walk over, they found a low retaining wall alongside a strip mall. It was only about three feet high, but she picked her way up the stair-step portion to the top like she was walking a tightrope over the Grand Canyon and held her hands out for balance while he walked alongside just below her on the sidewalk. Neither of them talking, just grinning.

At the end of the wall, she stuck her hand out again, this time reaching down to him for help.

He held his hand out, palm up. She grabbed it as she hopped down, landing right next to him. Her coat brushed the front of his hoodie.

Still not talking, she stretched up and kissed him. Her lips were soft, warm. She smelled like smoke and coffee and some kind of flowery shampoo or lotion. Those flyaway hairs tickled his face, but in a good way. In a way that said this was really happening, someone really wanted his help and his comfort and his touch. He closed his eyes and leaned his forehead against hers, feeling the cold tip of her nose poking into his cheekbone.

I wonder if she'll still be alive when the sun comes up, he thought.

CHAPTER 47

"I saw it, OK?"

Jessica Caine sniffed hard, scrubbing at the tears still pouring from her eyes. Makeup smeared the dark sleeve balled around her fist.

"The picture they had of him on the news. I knew it was him, obviously, but I didn't believe it at first. I couldn't. He wouldn't do that. He just wouldn't. You don't know him. It's some kind of mistake.

"And if he did — mailing it?" She shook her head. "No way. He would never do that to somebody. He would never do that to *me*. I'm the only friend he's got, the only person who's stuck by him."

Loshak nodded along, keeping his face neutral. Now that Caine had started speaking again, she was gaining momentum, and he didn't want to give her any reason to stop.

"Back when we were kids, I mean, everybody was sort of in awe of him. He just had that kind of personality. You knew he was going to go on to do big things. Probably even be famous. A couple of his poems won writing contests — one from UC Denver — and he even had a poem published in *McSweeney's*. That was all while we were still in high school."

Her mouth sagged open for a second, and her chest rose and fell, while she stared down at the table in front of her as if she couldn't figure out where things had gone so wrong.

"When I saw it — the news, I mean, I didn't know what to do," she said in a small voice. "I called the tip line. But I couldn't do it. I hung up. It didn't feel right."

She stopped, shook her head, then restarted.

"See, I hadn't actually talked to him in a while, not since right after he got kicked out of his apartment, but I've been keeping tabs. I— I know this is going to sound like I'm stalking him, but I was worried, you know. I was afraid he'd hurt himself. Or maybe that he would overdose, too.

"Then one week, I couldn't find him anywhere. I started asking around, panicking a little. I almost lost my job because I spent three days driving around the city looking. It took a while, but I finally found him."

She shrugged.

"But when I did, he didn't seem very interested in talking to me. This was a couple of months ago. I took him to get something to eat — it looked like he wasn't eating, sometimes he did that, just stopped doing all the necessary stuff to stay alive, but before it was always because he was so involved in other things…" She tapered off. "But he barely said two words to me, and then he just took off before our food even came. He hasn't talked to me since."

That hung in the air for a second. A slight shift in Caine's expression made Loshak's stomach tighten. It looked like she regretted revealing so much. If she cut them off now…

But she went on, anger undercutting her words.

"And maybe this makes me a bitch, but I have my own life to live, too. I've tried everything I can, but I can't always be running out to save him, right? You can try to

keep people going, but you can't make them want to live."
Her voice wavered on the last line. "No matter how much
you love them, they've got to want it too, or you're just…"

She trailed off and shook her head.

"It sounds as if you've gone above and beyond what
most friends would do," Loshak said. "You're right, you're
entitled to live your life, too."

That brought up a fresh wave of tears. Loshak grabbed
the tissues and set them in front of her. He couldn't help
but feel bad for Caine. He'd met too many people suffering
under the weight of pain that belonged to the ones they
loved — loved ones who often wouldn't look up from their
own self-absorption long enough to see the suffering
around them.

After blowing her nose and scrubbing at her eyes again,
Caine pursed her lips and blew out a shaky breath.

"I went to talk to him tonight because I didn't want to
believe it out of hand, you know? I wanted to find out for
myself what the truth was. Give him a chance to tell his
side of the story." She pressed the folded tissue on the table,
flattening the creases beneath her fingertips. "I don't know
why I'd go through all that. I guess I still love him, you
know?"

This time, she didn't go on.

"The thing is," Loshak said, modulating his voice so
that it stayed low, understanding, "what you're doing now,
telling us this, talking to us — it's for his own good, Jessica.
You're doing the right thing. Saving innocent lives. And
not just other people, but most likely his life, too. You're
still looking out for him."

She nodded but didn't look up from smoothing out the

tissue.

"We need to find him, Jessica, before anybody else gets hurt."

"I don't know where he is," she whispered.

"Anything you know helps," Loshak said, careful to avoid going directly to questioning or phrases like *anything you can give us*, things that might make it seem like she was betraying him in favor of them.

"I… I know he hangs out on the street most of the time, but he's not big on being around other people. Kind of a lone wolf, I guess. A homeless guy I talked to — back when I was searching for him that week, you know — he said he hung out in a park near the aquarium, that he saw him sleeping around there sometimes."

She rolled her eyes and gave a little disdainful shake of the head.

Aque, who had skillfully bled into the background of the interrogation room, now started scrawling on a yellow legal pad. Loshak wished he could do the same, but he hadn't brought anything to write with. He was used to documenting many interviews with his memory alone — it wasn't uncommon for the serial killers he'd interviewed over the years to insist there be no camera, no notes, no audio recorder.

But Caine's interview was being recorded. He could come back and rewatch it to take notes later if he needed to.

"You've seen him," she said. "Obviously you've got the pictures of him mailing those packages. But those didn't show the tattoo he's got on the side of his neck. It says Siobhan. She has one of his name, too. Or… had one, I

264

mean."

Aque's pen stopped moving on the paper. Loshak held his breath. The tiny room seemed to swell with anticipation, hanging on her next words.

"Sam," she said, not looking at either of them. "His name is Sam Crozier."

CHAPTER 48

Pablo's was not all it was cracked up to be. Instead of the noisy rager Crozier had been imagining, it was a dozen pretentious twenty-somethings crammed into a small apartment, all of them obnoxiously drunk. Bottles had been crowded onto every inch of a coffee table that looked too new and expensive for Pablo's raggedy and yet still perfectly matched 1800s newsie attire.

All the furniture was like that — a little too nice for a struggling college kid, much like the neighborhood the apartment was in. His rich mommy must've bought it for him. She'd probably bought him those Bowery Boys clothes, too.

The place smelled like stale weed and cigarettes, booze, and B.O., which Crozier quickly learned was emanating from Jason, the other half of the hammer bros.

"Gotta love the Avatar movies, am I right?" Jason ground his teeth side to side.

He was a tall, coked-out, fussily dressed douchebag, with horn-rimmed glasses that he probably didn't even need, and a sheen of sweat covering his face.

Crozier hadn't been looking for a conversation, just refilling his Solo cup, when Jason cornered him. And once Jason started talking, it was impossible to get away from him.

"Pinnacle of filmmaking, in my opinion. Can't do better than it. I mean, James Cameron. You pretty much can't go wrong with James Cameron. You walk into one of his movies, you know you're gonna get your money's worth. I mean, *Titanic, Avatar…*" More tooth grinding. "The peak of cinematic prowess. He goes for it every time. The scale. The spectacle. Just absolutely goes for it. We're never gonna top that, not in our lifetimes. Absolute. Pinnacle."

There was an aggressiveness to Jason's monologue that made Crozier want to hit him, something that called up a primal, animalistic hatred. But maybe that had to do with Smelly Jason's height, the way he was almost leaning over Crozier, plus the constant bearing of his teeth, the better to grind them with.

Unfortunately, none of the promised hammers were lying around. Somebody must've made sure they were hidden ahead of time. Either that, or Crozier had already missed the skull-bashing portion of the festivities.

Here and there, people were passing out. The party was on its last legs. Not Jason, though. He was still going strong. Chattering like a fucking squirrel.

"Now you take something like the *Avatar* movies, for example. You've got yourself a perfect first movie and the rarest of unicorns — an excellent sequel. Nobody but Cameron could've pulled that off, nobody. Tell you what, every other director in Hollywood is in this for the money, but James Cameron, he doesn't give a fuck about their money. He's there for the art."

Eventually, Crozier scraped Jason off by going into the bathroom and shutting the door in his annoying face.

When he came back out, Jason was chatting up a girl with cat-shaped blue eyes and long wavy hair, who was clutching a clove cigarette and a craft beer in a long neck. She was nodding, but the way she kept blinking hard and squinting made it look like there was no way she was actually hearing him. She was long gone.

Blaine was on the couch, a seat cushion away from the snoring Pablo. Crozier squeezed in next to her. She leaned her head on his shoulder.

"We got in on the end of it. I was right, it kinda sucks." There was a dreamy quality to her voice. "Probably shoulda stayed out, just us."

He shrugged, keeping the motion of his shoulder small so she wouldn't move her head.

"I'm glad we're here together. In this moment." She snuggled into his side, warm and cozy against him, and so soft. "In this turn of the earth."

"Yeah." He drank some of his hard-earned vodka. His taste buds were too dead by then to feel it, but that simmering cold dribbled down his throat and bloomed its warmth in his stomach. "Me, too."

She sighed.

"All because you gave me a light on a dark street. It could've been anyone, but it was you."

"You're right," he said. "Any girl could have come down that street. I could've followed anyone. There's no order to it, life. You could be dead in an hour."

He looked around at the passed-out forms.

"Any one of these assholes might not wake up. Alcohol poisoning. Stabbed in their sleep."

He caught sight of sweaty Jason grinding his teeth again, heading around the corner toward the kitchen.

"Overdose. Car wreck. It just happens. The world is a

tangle of events without meaning. We think death is all significant because it's *our* puny life that stops, but… Anybody could die at any second."

He raised the vodka to his lips again, but this time, the weight on his shoulder was different. Her head pressed more heavily on him, her tiny body loose against his side.

She was asleep, mouth hanging open a little, cigarette filter burning between her fingers.

He rubbed his cheek against her hair, feeling the tickle of those fine strands again. The knife handle pushed warm and solid against his side. He knocked back the rest of his vodka and stood up. She lolled over onto the arm of the couch.

It was easy to see her as just a body now, gone floppy and limp as though in death. All that literature and art, all those opinions and that blunt sarcastic personality drained from her in an outpouring of blood that lasted only a few seconds.

Her phone was on her thigh near a limp hand. He could leave her his number, punch it in for when she woke up.

But he didn't.

He left the cramped apartment behind, walked down a few flights of stairs, and out into a sky going golden-gray with oncoming dawn. The cold hit him as soon as he stepped through the door, some frigid barrier hung up around the building.

Sam Crozier padded down the sidewalk, his steps clapping in the emptiness. The city looked dead. Still. A blank canvas for the moment.

Within the hour, cars would be lining these streets, backed up for miles, honking and cutting each other off and putting out greasy exhaust fumes. The endless repeat of days where the teeming animals crawled all over each other trying to get to the top of this concrete bucket.

A huge rat stirred in a pile of garbage bags next to the curb. Its back arched, tail slithering through the waste. Plastic crinkled, and aluminum cans and glass clinked.

Yeah. Just another day in paradise.

CHAPTER 49

As the last of the task force filtered into the conference
room, Belte asked a uniform to pull the shades while she
got the overhead projector connected to her laptop. One by
one, the blinds shut out the glare from the early morning
sun.

A police radio babbled from the table in the corner.
Patrol cars were out sweeping the areas Jessica Caine had
tipped them off to, but so far there had been no sightings.

"Alright, let's get to it," Belte said.

She had a sheaf of papers in one hand, and the remote
from the projector in the other. A projection of the
computer screen appeared on the wall, along with a picture
of Belte and her husband in kayaks, two life-jacketed
children grinning and leaning over the sides behind them.
She clicked the remote.

"Right out of the gate, we've got a mugshot of our
suspect."

Loshak had elected to stand along the wall during the
task force meeting. After two nights with little to no sleep,
he was running out of gas, and even the dense black brew
from the station coffee maker wasn't putting much of a
dent in the exhaustion.

Maybe he should look into energy drinks again. He
knew some folks from a bomb team who swore by
Monster.

When the family photo was replaced by the mugshot, a

jolt of shaky energy shot through him. Sam Crozier was bony, almost emaciated in the image. His long neck showed a hint of the tattoo Jessica Caine had told them about. Roses sprouting from the end of a swirling cursive letter Loshak wouldn't have been able to guess at without knowing ahead of time that it was supposed to say Siobhan.

After decades on the job, Loshak didn't usually react to this kind of thing. He'd looked into the eyes of hundreds of murderers over the years.

But there was something about Crozier that made his skin contract, a chill crawling over the surface of him. Something flat in the eyes that reminded him of an alligator or snapping turtle. Cold. Reptilian. Looking into those eyes, Loshak felt the same sort of unease he'd felt when they were revealed in the HALO footage.

"Samuel Aaron Crozier," Commander Belte read from her notes. "Twenty-five, formerly of Aurora. He moved to Denver four years ago with Siobhan Connelly to an apartment in the Baker area. One incident of assault and battery with the Aurora PD. He bashed in a guy's face with a skateboard. Broke his front teeth. But Crozier plead it down to a misdemeanor, served a few months in county, then got out again.

"Crozier doesn't show up in our records again until nine months ago. Several counts of basic possession. In August, it was meth. December, oxy. February, meth again. Two weeks ago, heroin. He's all over the board. This all came after the death of Connelly, the live-in girlfriend, last June."

Belte looked over the heads of the detectives and uniforms in the chairs, locking eyes with Loshak.

"I could go on, but I think this would be a good time to have Agent Loshak speak about our suspect and what impact this new information might have on the case." She shrugged. "Basically whatever you think is pertinent, Agent."

Loshak nodded and wound around the outside of the room, coming to a stop at the edge of the projected mugshot. He ached for a podium or lectern or even a table to rest his elbows on but had to settle for crossing his arms.

He turned to face the task force, noting the slumped postures, dark under-eye circles, and lined faces. He wasn't the only one dragging today.

"If you wouldn't mind pulling up the next slide, Commander?"

He realized they didn't call them slides anymore, but at the moment, he couldn't pull the correct term from the fuzz in his brain.

"Right."

Belte clicked it over.

The mugshot was replaced by a photo of Crozier and a girl with a curtain of long black hair spilling around her shoulders. The pair of them grinned into the camera, her frail-looking arm around his neck, her cheek pressed against his hair.

"Sam Crozier and Siobhan Connelly," Loshak said. "This photo was taken a few months before Connelly's death and posted to a mutual friend's social media. According to our informant, Sam was as stable as he'd ever been with Siobhan, but in time, they both started sliding into addiction. Sam lost his job first, then Siobhan stopped showing up for work. We see the rent start piling up, bills going unpaid. Mid-June last year, Siobhan died of a heroin overdose."

Loshak paused there, thinking about the stark, cold language of the coroner's report they had turned up.

"Crozier slept next to his dead girlfriend for a few hours. Woke up to find her body gone icy, foam still frothing at her mouth and nose."

For the second time that morning, he got chills. It all sounded so detached, but what it boiled down to was a man losing someone he loved.

"It's the sort of trauma that would be scarring to anybody," Loshak went on, "but it falls in line with our killer's profile. Connelly's death acted as a sort of trigger to Crozier. When an unstable person feels out of control, that's when they're most apt to lash out, to attempt to regain a sense of power over their situation once again."

CHAPTER 50

Crozier walked the last of the night away and into the morning. The gray horizon turned gold, and then the sky hit a red-orange he hadn't expected. The sun must have been just about to come over the mountains.

Somehow it felt colder now than it had overnight. A biting chill that cut right through the clothes and saturated the flesh. Sank into the bones until they felt achy and frozen, down to the marrow.

Looking back, he couldn't figure out how he had ended up spending so much time with that artist girl. It felt like some kind of dream or a parallel universe. Something he'd stumbled into and finally backed out of. Laughing at a diner, skipping rocks in a park.

It was too much like that part of his life that was gone. Lost forever. He could even see Shiv crouching to scrape that match over the concrete, a wry smile on her face.

But one way or another, that door always closed. Always left him cold and lonely in the end, walking with no place to go.

He clenched his jaw. Tried to push the bad feelings away.

Cars whooshed past on the road. The morning rush. All the ants filing around to do their duty.

Looking at the traffic, the body in the street came back to him. The accident victim flashing in his head.

The guy in coveralls laid out in the road beneath the

Escort. Face down on the asphalt, blood pooling around his head. That tiny dent in the hood. He died surrounded by strangers, just a blip of entertainment on their radar, something for them to barf back up at the water cooler later.

And he couldn't see how any of it could be real. The ball of fire hanging in the sky above the cold wind. The concrete sprawl they scurried over until something stopped them. The blood that poured out of them for other creatures to stare at or lick up. The smells, the sounds, the sensations drilling into their skin.

How could any of it be there? Where did it come from? What was this instinct to hold onto it, to snap pictures, to keep living when none of it mattered?

A gust of cold wind ripped the thoughts away. Planted him back on the sidewalk, coming up on a busy intersection.

A few early morning commuters had gathered on the corner, waiting for the light to change so they could cross. Only two or three. One of them was a smaller woman with dark hair. She wore a green parka, and the fur-lined hood made him think of Blaine again.

The woman saw him looking her way and smiled.

"Cold enough for you?"

Her question took him by surprise. Being noticed and even acknowledged somehow shattered the alienation he'd been lost in. It left little shards of it lying around, while the warmth of her openness sank into him.

After a second, he found his voice.

"Yeah, it's been a chilly week."

"Tell me about it." She nodded at his hoodie. "You're a

lot tougher than I am; I couldn't survive in something like that. I've got to have my winter coat until it's sunny and seventy-five every day for a month."

He took a step closer. Her cheerful friendliness drew him in. Made him want to be friendly, too. Filled him with an urge to forge a connection with another human being.

He shrugged.

"I'm hot-blooded. Always have been."

The woman laughed and started to say something else, but just then a couple of assholes in puffy coats walked up talking loudly about the Nuggets–Bulls game and how refs across the board should handle egregious fouling. That shut down the conversation with the woman, made it impossible to continue without screaming.

They waited at the corner for what seemed like a long time. Traffic thrashed past violently on the street inches from them. Cars chopped at the wind. The puffy-coated Nugget fanatics hollered at each other to be heard.

Finally, the light changed. The loud talkers streamed away, leaving just three of them on the corner — him, the smiley lady in the parka, and some beanpole in a suit and pea coat shivering and glued to his phone. They had all shuffled a little at the light change, a sort of jockeying for position. The woman was in front of Crozier now and to his right. Beanpole had slotted into the space beside him.

And something throbbed in his skull then. A restless beat of blood. A counter-rhythm to the rush and thump of the traffic.

That movie played in his head again. That dribble of beige vomit trailing out of Shiv's mouth. Her cold skin going blue.

And he couldn't blot it out anymore. Couldn't contain the image, the feelings that came with it.

He waited. Watched the cages of metal and glass scream past. Timing it.

Then he stepped forward and shoved the woman.

The heels of his hands punched out, catching her in the upper back, connecting solidly. His arms reached full extension.

Her head snapped back hard on her neck. Whiplash.

And she flew away from him. Thrown. Pitched into the street.

Limbs wobbling. Legs churning, trying to catch herself.

The oncoming BMW didn't slow down even a little. It caught her in stride.

From his point of view, it looked like she just cracked in half. She went from mostly upright to snapped sideways, toppled onto the hood in an instant. Chopped down.

Then she was thrown again. Lifted from the ground and tossed into the intersection.

Her legs lifted up higher than her head. The top half of her pitched to the ground.

She touched down face first. Bouncing. Sliding. Shaking. A limp rag skidding over the asphalt.

The BMW's brakes squealed. The car jerked to a stop just in front of Crozier.

The slack figure on the roadway slowed to a stop. Belly down. Not unlike the broken man in the factory coveralls.

White gashes slit the dark green of her fur-lined parka, wide leering mouths frothing with polyester insulation.

A little flattened, she was now, some wrongness inherent in her pose. A certain flimsiness evident in the awkward angles of her arms and neck.

The BMW driver popped out of his vehicle, standing in the open door. His head bobbed over the roof like a buoy on a stormy sea. Some kind of businessman. Tailored suit. Overly groomed eyebrows and hair, bleached teeth.

"Fuck. Oh fuck. She just jumped right out in front of me!"

His phone was already pressed to his ear, probably calling 9-1-1.

"You all saw it, right?"

He looked at Crozier and the beanpole on the corner without really seeing them. Eyes big and blinking a lot.

"Jesus! Why did she do that?"

Crozier ignored him, turning back to the beanpole, expecting to find the fucker still transfixed by his phone. Mildly amused like the people at the scene of yesterday's wreck.

But the guy was staring at Crozier. Eyes blank. Body rigid.

He saw.

"Yeah, I'm on the corner of Federal and Louisiana," the driver of the BMW yell-talked into his phone. "There's been a, uh, an accident. A pedestrian got hit by a car — it was my car. I don't think… um… I mean, Jesus, I think she's dead."

Crozier lurched forward, hand whipping out to grab.

But the beanpole was already off and running. Barreling down the sidewalk like somebody had fired him out of a cannon.

Crozier didn't even try to pull out of his dive. He put his head down and sprinted after the guy.

CHAPTER 51

Brandon Carver raced down the sidewalk, his pea coat flapping against his hips and thighs. His wingtips made firecracker pops with every churn of his long legs.

He swerved and juked his way through a small crowd of people waiting at a bus stop. Crashed into one and almost went down. Managed to save it by wheeling his arms, smacking off the building.

He's crazy.

Fucking crazy.

Pushed that lady into traffic right in front of me and everyone.

The series of images bloomed in his head unbidden. Fevered pictures that plagued him as he ran. Instant replay.

The psycho jolting forward. Shoving.

The woman tilted out into the road. Back arched funny.

Then the car. The collision. The body skittering over the asphalt, limbs all aflutter.

And the sound. My God, he'd never forget that sound.

He skirted around a glut of newspaper machines outside of an office building. Heart thudding. Cheeks flushed with heat that somehow made the cold morning air feel wet and heavy.

The sense of disbelief pushed to the front of his thoughts.

Five minutes ago, he'd been on his way to work, nervous because of that stupid presentation. Jitters in his belly from the campaign he was about to pitch. And he'd known all along that the pitch was DOA, known that the clients were too uptight for it. He'd gone funny and edgy because that was the best angle with this product, this demographic. Energy drinks? The copy basically wrote itself.

But he could already hear their marketing liaison saying it was too much like a beer commercial and wouldn't fit their brand, could already see the constipated look on Diane's face, telling him she was giving the account to Steve.

Two weeks now he'd had trouble sleeping over this shit. Woke up nervous and sweaty, all stressed out.

And suddenly the presentation, the rejection, the uptight boss — none of it meant anything.

Crazy how running for your life changed your perspective. Real quick.

He plunged headlong through the urban sprawl of Denver, desperately trying to escape a psycho who had just pushed a woman into oncoming traffic.

Can't stop and ask for help.

If the crazy fucker can push a lady into traffic out in the open, he could do anything.

Brandon cranked his neck to check back over his shoulder. The killer was still back there. And was he mistaken, or was the guy smiling?

Jesus.

A fresh wave of panic made Brandon's long legs churn faster, arms pumping, adrenaline all cold in his hands, the icy chill roiling in the tip of his nose. Frozen air ripped in and out of his lungs.

That look at his pursuer seemed to wipe his mind blank. No more jumbled memories of the conference room or ad copy.

Just shoes slapping concrete. Chest heaving. Wind ragged in ears.

That sense of forward momentum was the only thing that mattered.

Pop-pop-pop, a rhythm that his life depended on.

Gotta do... something.

Brandon veered right. Tramped down off the curb. Sliced diagonally across a clogged intersection without slowing down.

Horns screamed at him. Tires screeched.

If the psycho wanted to finish him off by shoving him into traffic too, then he was doing the job for him running out in the road like this. But he couldn't fight the instinct to shake this guy off.

He wheeled his head. Scanned the way forward.

Over there. On the opposite side of four lanes of roaring traffic, past the median of grass and low evergreen hedges — an oasis.

Neon lights glowing in a bakery window. Pink pooling on the concrete in front.

It felt so far away. Miles. Light years. Like looking at a promised land he might never reach.

Oncoming cars roared around him. Buffeted him with wind so hard that the currents knifed through his jacket, through his suit, through him. Cold.

He dodged a small white sedan. Cut hard to his left. Ran right up the strip of dotted lines. Then he sidestepped behind a red SUV to make it to the median.

He jumped up onto the raised center divider, poised on the strip of grass like a balance beam. Treaded along it.

The smooth sole of his right wingtip slipped, and he lost his footing. His upper half wavered back into traffic, hanging out in front of the flat nose of a bus.

Its horn blatted. Flat front end racing for him.

He saw the driver through the glass, a heavy black woman, her face scrunched into a disbelieving frown, mouth moving as if to warn him.

His arms windmilled, flapping and flagging, swimming at the air like that could save him.

And it did.

He pulled himself upright. Caught himself just short of the passing city vehicle.

Wind blasted his face as the side of the bus passed inches from his cheek. The scarf draped around the shoulders of his pea coat ripped free and disappeared under the wheels.

Can't stop. Gotta keep moving.

The bakery was right over there. He had to reach it.

He leaped off the median and into the opposite side of the road, traffic flying in the other direction. A whole new game.

He slid behind a sports car, caught a stretch of empty road, and took it, huffing and wheezing as he sprinted across the final lane and jumped onto the far curb.

The toe of his shoes caught a pile of wood mulch around the base of a tree, kicking the chips out ahead of him. He stumbled for a few steps, but righted himself again, finally jogging onto the sidewalk.

He sprinted into that puddle of pink neon light before

the bakery like a runner lunging forward into the tape at the finish line. The soft glow enveloped him.

Did he dare look back?

He did a kind of spin mid-step. Saw only the cars still rushing around.

His field of vision panned left and then right as his head turned.

No psycho. Not yet.

Nothing but the constant flow of rush hour traffic. Business as usual.

He turned back around, still jogging. Something drew his gaze down.

His phone was still in his hand, still open to that stupid firm-wide memo about not leaving food in the break room for more than a week.

He had to call the police. Immediately. No dicking around.

But he couldn't get his legs to stop moving. Something inside him was propelling him onward, telling him to get out of the open. Panic. Shock. Terror.

Damn it, he should've holed up in that bakery.

Maybe.

But what if he'd gotten stuck inside? Cornered?

A nutcase like that wouldn't care if there was a whole crowd of witnesses. Not when he'd chucked a woman to her death out in the open where everybody could see.

The motherfucker has nothing to lose.

Better to keep running, then. Keep his possible exit strategies open.

He came to a block of brick-front buildings. Generic names plastered across glass windows, investment corps,

CPA services, a law office. The parking here was angled, with tails of spotless trucks and cars poking out toward the street.

That was it, that was what he needed.

He ducked in between a yellow Hummer and a gray Cadillac. He was too tall to just stand upright, so he crouched, leaning up against the Hummer's tire.

His whole arm and shoulder shook as he brought the phone up. Swiped out of the emailed memo and brought up the keypad.

Each breath seemed to rasp in his throat, rattle in his chest. He was really sucking wind.

And fresh panic told him he wasn't going to have enough breath to tell them where he was, what was going on. That he'd just wheeze into the phone. Powerless.

"No," he muttered out loud, voice small.

There. Stupid. He could talk. It was just fear.

Still, he forced a labored inhale and let it seep out, tried to slow down his breathing. His eyes snapped back to the glowing screen in his hand.

With clumsy fingers, he dialed 9-1-1. Then he put the phone to his ear.

CHAPTER 52

Loshak tilted his head to the side, studying the glossy map of the city. Already on the map were their pair of mailing locations, the alley where Cassandra McClintic's faceless body was found, and the apartment that had concealed the earless corpse of Barbara Wickham.

While Loshak watched, Detective Johnson circled the places Jessica Caine had listed as Crozier's known hangouts. There was the broken-down Stratus next to the tent city. A café in Globeville that had a community "pay it forward" program where people prepaid for meals for anyone who came in unable to afford food. A city park near the river where he sometimes slept. A film processing lab where he used to pick up under-the-table work; she wasn't sure whether he still did. A uniformed officer had talked to a couple of the employees there and would get in touch if they saw Crozier. Meanwhile, cruisers on patrol were running by the place on a regular basis.

Nothing marked on the map was near their Aurora mailing location, but Caine had admitted that her contact with Crozier lately had been patchy at best. Crozier could've found a new hangout in the area. Or he could have been looking for a post office farther from his usual haunts to throw them off the trail.

"Now taking all bets, get your tickets before betting closes, ladies and gents," Benally said, doing a nasally imitation of an old-timey racetrack announcer. "Where do

286

you think we're going to find him?"

Johnson tapped the map.

"My money's on Globeville."

"Mr. FBI Consultant, Esquire?" Benally asked, turning to Spinks.

The reporter was leaning a hip against the back of one of the chairs left behind from the task force meeting.

"How much is on the line here?" Spinks asked.

Benally scratched his forehead.

"Snickers bar, fresh from the vending machine."

"Just what I've always wanted." The reporter shifted his weight, making the chair creak. "I like long shots. I want the photo lab."

"Cars have already cruised past twice. Nothing doing."

"Yet," Spinks said, pointing at the detective. He shot a look at Loshak. "What do you think, partner?"

Loshak pressed his lips together, still staring at the map.

"The problem with killers like this is their unpredictability. There's always the chance that he'll pop up somewhere we've never seen him before."

"Nah, I don't buy it," Johnson said, shaking his head. "Criminals always want to look like they're all over the place, but no one's capable of true randomness. It's human nature to start falling into patterns and habits."

"With more data points, maybe we'd start to see a better pattern emerging," Loshak agreed. "But what we're looking at now already has one outlier — the post office in Aurora. I wouldn't be surprised to see—"

A uniformed officer whipped into the conference room as if he'd grabbed the door frame and swung himself inside. His eyes were wide, excitement bright in his slightly oily face.

"We just got word about a girl being pushed intentionally into traffic. Corner of South Federal and Louisiana. But here's the interesting thing: the dude who did the pushing? He's got a tat on the side of his neck."

He went quiet for a moment as he poked his own jugular to demonstrate.

"Our witness couldn't read it, but he said it looked like fancy cursive lettering."

"Holy shit," Johnson muttered.

The uniform nodded.

"He's chasing our witness slash 9-1-1 caller right now. Foot pursuit. Last I heard, they're running down West Florida Ave. near South Eliot. Units headed that way, calls going out to choppers and SWAT, the whole nine yards."

Johnson's head rocked back on his shoulders like he'd been slapped.

"Holy shit," he said again.

"Yeah."

The uniform's chest puffed out as if he were proud of having brought the message.

Benally snatched his hat off the podium.

"Well, what are we waiting for? Let's get a move on."

While the rest of the room went into a mild uproar around him, Loshak's eyes snapped back to the map. He found the wide vein of West Florida Avenue, dragging across it until he spotted Eliot Street.

He's there right now.

Loshak locked in on that tiny stretch of street, a single city block, fixing the point in an imaginary bullseye.

Right there.

Lone Wolf

We're about to get him.

CHAPTER 53

Crozier scanned the street for Beanpole. Feet shuffling over concrete in a rolling jog. Eyes flitting everywhere.

The guy had switched gears. Picked up those scrawny legs and transformed into some kind of Olympic sprinter. Gliding over the sidewalk even with his dress shoes.

Adrenaline. Crozier had seen it before. Like a mother lifting a car off her baby. Except this was just a tall, gangly business douche saving his own skin.

A hero for our times.

Crozier Froggered his way through traffic, ignoring the blaring horns and curses screamed out car windows. The lanky frame in the flapping pea coat had almost made it across the street now, and Crozier was hot on his heels.

Then a city bus came barreling through, making Crozier stop short. Cutting off his line of sight.

It was only a few seconds at most, but by the time the bus had passed by, Beanpole was gone.

Crozier finally hit the sidewalk and spilled through a circle of pink light. A fluorescent bloom the shade of cotton candy angling over the cement in front of a bakery.

Now he broke onto a mostly empty block. Traffic distant. Pedestrians nonexistent.

No Beanpole here.

No movement.

Nothing but the building fronts. Concrete façades that looked gray and dead like a corpse's teeth.

After all the bustle and running, the sudden emptiness made his scalp prickle. His breath felt cold and itchy in his throat.

He pressed forward. Slower than before. Senses heightened. Hackles up.

Listening. Watching.

His heart clawed at the walls of his chest. A muscle in his upper lip ticked.

Cars flicked by on the intersection two blocks down, something casual in their passing. Careless things. Unaware.

His focus drew back to his immediate surroundings. Waiting for any movement.

The details along the sides of the street drifted by him. Slow motion. Brick and concrete walls sliding. Storefronts shiny with glass.

Instinct pulled him. Directed him. An invisible line between him and the Beanpole.

He obeyed the tug. Veered left at its urging, slowing even more as he reached the next block.

He was barely making a sound now. Feet gritting just louder than his breath with every step. The muscles in his shoulders were strung so tight it felt like they could snap.

His eyes roved his surroundings, scanning everything, everywhere. Near and far. High and low.

No movement.

But Beanpole was there. Nearby.

He felt it the way a wolf might sense the presence of a rabbit in the long grass. It wasn't a sight or smell or sound that told him, but some sixth sense a predator had for prey.

Up ahead, the sidewalk curved away from the road,

made way for one of those angled parking lots in front of a strip of businesses. All the vehicles parked there at matching forty-five-degree angles from the curb, shining and spotless.

He could picture Beanpole squatted down between the vehicles. Trying to get small, hide his tall, lanky frame.

Crozier glided toward the cars, eyes searching the space beneath for feet, for shadows. His mind flashed forward. Different versions of how this might play out opened in his head:

Beanpole leaned over but on his feet. Something athletic about the pose, like a sprinter about to take off.

Then he pictured him huddled against a tire, arms wrapped around his long legs. Like a kid playing hide and seek.

Next sitting directly on the asphalt, head between his knees, arms covering the back of his neck like he was in some elementary school bombing drill.

Crouched and duck-walking, with his phone pressed to his ear, whispering into it, begging for help.

Maybe even curled into a ball. Gone fetal.

Crozier ran the last few steps to get around the cars. Blank spaces between vehicles flitted past, black lines of naked asphalt making columns in his field of vision.

Empty.

Empty.

Empty.

Empty?

All the gaps were bare. No Beanpole. No one at all.

What the fuck?

Crozier stood still. Stared into the last strip of parking

lot laid bare. Breathed.

Then something clinked off to his left. His ears perked up, and his head snapped around.

Black woolen material flashed behind the wrought iron fencing around the side of the brick building. The Beanpole disappearing into the alley there.

Crozier smiled to himself.

CHAPTER 54

Brandon Carver sprinted once more. Arms pumping. Legs churning.

The concrete squares of the sidewalk flitted past, a blur beneath his wingtips. He chewed up ground like that, pointed toes flung out in front, the sides of his suit jacket flapping against his flanks. Breath burning in and out.

It felt like this was his life now. The running. Nothing before or after this moment existed anymore. Not fully. The ten years he'd been working for the ad firm reduced to a hazy memory, disjointed, more like a dream than something that had really happened.

Still, some fresh wind seemed to lift him now — his spirits bobbing back up. New faith rising. Belief tingling along with the frigid air ripping through his chest cavity.

He would run. He would keep going as long as it took. He would survive.

A lightness spread through him. A runner's high, maybe.

It felt like he could go indefinitely. Forever, if it was the only way.

And then the image thrust itself into his head again — the psycho closing in.

He'd seen the half scowl, half grin on his pursuer's face as the killer crept along the parked cars. Stalking the gaps like a hound on the scent. Enjoying the hunt.

Something about that smile made it worse. The joy in it.

The idea of this all being a game, his life being a joke to this guy, something to rip and tear and destroy and laugh while he did it.

The alley spat him out on a street full of restaurants and strip malls. Squat buildings and wide-open parking lots in front of impenetrable walls of shitty chain stores and gyms pushing their hot yoga classes.

How was it so dead at this hour of the morning? How were half of these places closed?

Barely any cars. No customers. Nowhere to hide.

Too open. Some instinct hammered in his skull, shouting at him about being the only thing moving on a wide-open plain. Exposure was a death sentence. A primal urge. He had to get out of there. Had to.

Brandon pounded diagonally over the pavement in front of a Dollar Tree/Family Dollar combo unit, past a laundromat butted up against a retaining wall. Through the gap, he could see a break in the barricade of businesses. A cleft. A flash of green space visible on the other side of the wall.

He leaped. Hooked his arms over the top of the wall and toed the mortar between the cinder blocks. Those wingtips slipped at first, and then found purchase, propelling him up the barrier.

His chest skidded up onto the top of the wall. Cold. Legs folding up and over a second later.

He teetered on the precipice. His knee scraped against the edge as he spilled over the concrete lip, tearing a hole in his suit pants.

Then he was falling. Shoes slamming cement. Both hands likewise bracing the ground. His whole body folding up into a superhero squat.

He shot upright. Bolted for the green.

He vented that last tunnel of pavement and came out in a residential neighborhood. Rows of ranch-style houses hugged up close to one another, manicured landscaping, porches, privacy fences. A narrow sea of grass lapping up on the shores of it all.

Footsteps tramped the ground somewhere behind him. And then he heard the puff of the psycho's breath, harsh, rhythmic. Too fast, too close.

Brandon barreled across another street. Ducked through an empty carport and shuttled into a backyard.

The shadows thickened here. His head whipped around.

Up close, it was more of a patio with a strip of grass around it than a real yard. Small. Closed in by a low stone wall. Neighbor's yard chock full of kid's toys visible on the other side.

He hopped the wall. Dodged around an orange and blue plastic slide and a Power Wheels Jeep.

The wood fence on the other side of the yard was too high to jump, but there was an alleyway running behind the houses. Small, more of an easement for public utility vehicles.

He vaulted back there, wingtips kicking up gravel. He followed the ribbon of tar cutting through the yards for some fifty yards.

Then he veered off down another narrow driveway. Traced it all the way past the house to where it let out on another street.

He kept running. Kept going. Couldn't hear the

footsteps behind him anymore.

A block passed underfoot. Then another.

And heat flushed his face. Boiling water poured into his cheeks. Flashing to steam behind his eyes.

The neighborhood morphed around him. Houses cinching tighter and tighter together, choking the land. Some of these homes barely had gaps wide enough between them to squeeze his shoulders through.

Where was he? He squinted at the nearest intersection but couldn't make out the letters on the street sign.

The yards he passed were likewise tiny. Closet-sized swaths of land that bore patchy, weed-choked grass, concrete slabs, bare dirt surrounded by chain-link.

He fled the street, darting down the nearest driveway. Needled through the tight spaces between the homes.

It felt insane. Like running through a maze. Twice he had to turn sideways just to get around a house, his coat scraping and catching on the stucco walls.

But the claustrophobia meant cover, too. He was blocked out. Hidden by his surroundings.

Still that voice in his head told him to keep moving. Keep moving. Don't stop.

The houses took a turn. Even more rundown. Boarded up. Concrete sidewalks cracked. Bars gating doors and windows.

He had to slow down to climb over a pile of asphalt shingles. He scrabbled over the hump, scratchy tiles sliding around under his feet. Sandpaper sounds rasping under the wing tips.

He let his gaze shoot down the pathway between the houses ahead. So close. Three footsteps would propel him over a fence and shuttle him into that shadowy space, cover him once more.

Instead, the next step stopped him short.

His foot came down, and he froze. Pain surged up his ankle, spiraled into the meat of his calf.

Something stabbed into the arch of his foot.

A tar-covered roofing nail.

CHAPTER 55

The pain hit a second after Brandon saw the nail protruding from his foot. Piercing the sole of his shoe. Impaling the flesh of the foot within. Pinning the flap of roof shingle to him. It felt as wide as a railroad spike even if he could see it wasn't.

He clenched his teeth. Let out an agonized wheeze. Then he tried to hop a little ways on one foot. Tried to shake it. But that didn't work.

Too slow.

Have to think.

He stopped. Put a hand on the peeling clapboard siding of the rundown house and hauled his foot up onto his knee.

His fingers crawled over the shoe. Snagged the piece of shingle, the gritty pebbles scoring his fingertips, and yanked it off his shoe.

The nail didn't come with it.

"Shit."

He lifted his head, scanning the street for movement. Nothing. Not yet.

But he knew the psycho was coming. It was just a matter of time.

He swung his good leg over a waist-high chain-link fence. Dragged the bad leg behind. Lanced into another yard that way.

The house looked crooked, its porch leaning and

299

covered in old couches and a couple of old washing machines. The front yard stank with the overwhelming air of dog shit.

The front door had been replaced with a piece of plywood with a little swing-window cut in it, the screws sticking out the front. Crack house if he'd ever seen one.

But there was an ancient-looking central air unit parked at the corner of the house, more rust than metal nowadays. Still, it might be enough cover to give him time to get this nail out of his foot.

He limped over to it and dropped next to the dusty metal cage covering the unit's fins. Tucked his legs behind it and once again pulled his foot up onto his knee.

The nail stuck out, gummy with roofing tar, but not far enough to get his fingers around the shaft. He pinched the head between his thumb and forefinger. Hesitated.

A feeling of fiery mucus had built up in his lungs, somehow both frigid and burning. He fought off the urge to start coughing.

He pulled. The nail fought him. Slipped through his fingers.

It was stuck.

His breath scraped his throat and nostrils as he tried to work the metal spike out, his pulse punching at his temples. He tried to slow his breathing down, listen for the psycho.

There was a loud hissing rush next to him. His stomach jumped into his throat.

Steam rolled out of a vent to his right and a little ways above him, mingling the yard's stench of dog shit with that of dryer sheets.

He swallowed, went back to digging at the nail, twisting, desperately trying to make it wiggle loose. His foot twitched and flexed. The nail didn't budge.

All at once, the silence grew tense. Huge. Pulled taut the skin of his chest and prickled along his arms.

His fingers fell away from the nail.

He strained his ears, listening for footfalls. Waiting for the silence to be broken. The chase to resume.

His heartbeat thrummed in his head. Blood squishing everywhere inside him. He listened past it. Focused.

The quiet stretched out, filling the space around him. Growing. Expanding.

He leaned forward, watching the street, waiting for the psycho to appear.

Nothing moved.

No one.

He was alone. Getting away. Escaping.

He slid back against the wall and went back to working the nail, up, down, up, down, twist. His foot twitched again like he was plucking the nerves in there like harp strings. Maybe he was.

Finally, it gave. The nail slid out for what felt like six or eight inches. Popped free.

He chucked it into the bare dirt of the crack house yard. It skittered past a weed, bounced over a dried-up white turd, and landed next to a beer can.

He was safe. No longer hunted. He'd lost his pursuer.

He climbed onto his hands and knees, still not quite able to shake the need for caution, then pushed to his feet. A bolt of pain shot up from where the nail had penetrated him, but the hurt mostly died quickly.

OK.

OK good.

A jingling sound caught his ear over the sound from the vent.

Familiar. Not wind chimes.

It cut out.

He froze. Listening.

The jingling came again. Close. Panting. Thumps.

The rottweiler leaped as though from nowhere. A hulking blur that launched at him about chest high.

CHAPTER 56

A hundred and thirty pounds of dog thumped into Brandon Carver's ribcage. The impact knocked him back a half step.

The air woofed out of him. Expelled in a single heave. Chest locked taut after that.

And then the dog was on him. Pressing. Bulling into him. Mouth lurching.

Its nails scratched his neck. The shiny chain collar jangling.

Brandon tumbled off balance. He threw up a hand out of instinct, catching the beast under the chin. He tried to shove the head back.

But the thick skull held steady. Stout. A flat thing anchored on a neck made of steel.

And some inches above his hand the mouth worked. Teeth clacking. Ropelike strands of drool looping out of the corners of its lips.

The dog fell back. Gathered itself and lurched again. Legs springing, extending.

It launched itself under his chin. Raced for him.

The words *leaping for the jugular* occurred to some distant part of him.

He kept that hand clutched to the thing's throat. Tried to brace its advance. But the dog was too much, too strong. His arm folded up at the elbow.

Those slabs of muscle bashed him in the chest once

more. Knocked him straight back. He lost his footing.

And together, they went sprawling backward.

The whole world seemed to twist. A kaleidoscope of grays. His vision whirled from the concrete to the houses to the sky.

Falling.

Jaws snapped at his face even as he fell, the dog clotheslining itself on his forearm. Thrashing and scrabbling. Hatred rolling off of it like heat.

He came down on his side, the air *woofing* out of him again. A sound torn from him somewhere between a cough and a grunt.

The dog thudded on top of him then, paws clawing at his stomach and stamping on his groin. The muscular beast jerking and heaving.

Stinking drool flung into Brandon's face. He could feel the growl thrum through his skin, vibrate through his muscles, rumble into his bones.

He lost his grip. Its head pressed close.

He swung his elbows. Tried to shield himself.

Razor teeth pierced his forearm. Ripped to the side. Jerking his arm.

The pain shot through the meat of him. A bright hot bolt lancing from the wound up into his shoulder.

And then new hurts erupted. Pain tore through his ear, raked down his cheek.

Two dogs.

As if one hadn't been bad enough.

The dogs blotted out the sunlight now. Their bodies smothering him.

He writhed beneath them. Tried to turn onto his belly

and crawl. The fucker on his chest was so heavy, he could only move when the dog lurched up and slammed back down again.

He spun. Belly touching down on cold concrete.

Teeth dug into his upper back, stony bits puncturing his flesh. More snagged on his cheek again, and this time he heard the flesh rip like cloth.

He was going to die here. Die to the sound of his own skin being torn off. Ripped apart by crack house dogs.

Paws slammed into his back, and this time the dog didn't come up again. Its weight held him down, crushing him, while the teeth ripped chunks from his shoulder and chewed toward his neck.

He screamed.

CHAPTER 57

"What the fuck?" The voice was coming from the porch. "Hey, who are you? What the fuck are you—"

The rottweilers pulled back. Hesitated. Chain collars jingling, ears perking up.

Gray daylight reached Brandon again. Hot slobber and cooling blood dripped into his hair.

He could feel the dogs breathing above him. Waiting. Listening.

"*Aus!*" the voice shouted. "*Aus,* you stupid sonsabitches! *Platz!*"

The dogs moved back a step each. A blob of red drool hit the ground beside Brandon's face with a thick splat.

"Yo, are you a cop? You have to tell me if you're a cop."

Brandon crawled. Scrabbled down the passageway between the houses, past the air conditioning unit.

Collars jingled again, dogs lunging.

"*Foos, foos!*"

The thuds of dog footpads on the dirt, then nails on concrete.

"Tell me, or I'll sic them on you again."

He didn't think he could answer. He could feel air coming through the side of his face with every puff of breath.

He coiled his fingers into the chain-link fence. Pulled himself to his feet. Legs shaking.

A dizziness swirled in his head as he hauled himself

over the barrier. Blackness creeping in at the edges. He slammed hard to the ground on the other side.

Through the fence, he saw the dogs on the porch, a fat guy in a Broncos jersey standing between them. He blinked and all three were thick, blocky slabs of meat. Red covered the dogs' muzzles.

Mine. That's my blood.

Then he spun his head to gaze down the alley toward the street. Eyes flitting everywhere for any sign of the psycho in the narrow gap.

An SUV sped past unperturbed. Nothing else moved out there.

"And don't fucking come back!" The man was still yelling at the top of his lungs. "I don't call my dogs off twice! That's a promise."

Stop, Brandon thought.

Wetness caught in his throat. Choking. Water flooding his eyes, blurring the scene.

Be quiet. You're telling him right where I am.

The man spat off the porch, then turned around. The plywood door screeched open, then slammed shut. More noise. More blaring alarms, telling the psycho where to find him.

He had to get up. Keep running. It wasn't safe here.

But the best he could do was to prop himself up on his elbows. Inch forward, shoes scraping on the dirt.

He looked up just as the silhouette stepped into the end of the alley.

CHAPTER 58

Loshak rode in the back of the unmarked Crown Victoria, Johnson driving and Spinks in the passenger seat. It was a boat of a car to use as a patrol vehicle, but the agent had to admit that the long, whipping antenna looked less obvious on an antique like that, more like a car show display piece than a modern police vehicle.

Apparently Spinks was thinking along the same lines.

"Hell of a ghetto cruiser," he said. "I always thought I'd like to have something like this when I retired. Long and chrome. Seats like soft leather couches. Plenty of leg room."

The corner of Johnson's mouth lifted.

"I figured I might not live long enough to retire; why not go for it while I'm still on the force?"

Spinks shrugged.

"Can't argue with logic like that."

They fell silent then, listening to the radio chatter. Coordinating flight paths for the choppers, outlining the SWAT team's route. A dispatcher reeled off blocks and unit numbers. Officers responded that they were en route or asked for repeats. Breaking up the search area bit by bit, an invisible grid cutting the city into bite-sized pieces.

Johnson had the light flashing on the roof, but he'd kept the siren off until they approached an intersection. Now he reached over, flipped the screamer on, eyes focused on the stopping cross traffic as they hurtled through. Then, when they were safe on the other side, the detective flipped it off again.

"Can't stand that noise," the detective said by way of explanation. "It's as bad as an alarm clock."

"No complaints here," Loshak said. "I've got enough tinnitus from the last thirty years. I'll take the quiet whenever I can."

Spinks lifted a finger.

"Did you know that there are two proper pronunciations of tinnitus?" The reporter's eyebrows waggled. "Medical professionals say, '*tin*-uh-tus,' with the stress on the first syllable and a soft vowel sound for that middle 'i.' Regular folks say, 'ti-*night*-us,' stressing the second syllable and going for the hard 'i.'"

Everyone held quiet for a beat.

"Fun fact," Loshak said, finally.

Spinks shrugged.

"I think I only know because my mom used to say it completely wrong. 'Tin-tin-*night*-us.' Not sure where that extra syllable came from."

The conversation died out again, and the city blurred by on either side of the vehicle. A throbbing, shapeless thing outside of the windows, punctuated by flashes of glaring morning sun between the buildings.

Loshak squirmed in his seat. The bottom of the bulletproof vest they'd given him was digging into his thighs, the neckline chafing the underside of his Adam's apple. These things never rode quite right when he was seated.

He tugged the front of the vest away from his throat, imagining some comedian from the late eighties tugging at his collar and asking whether this thing was on.

"Point of clarification on this bet," Spinks said. "It's where the arrest is made, right? Not where the call came in from and not where the initial sighting occurs."

"What?"

Loshak blinked, unable to pull sense from the reporter's words. It felt like he'd strung together a bunch of manhunt vocab with no rhyme or reason.

"I'm saying, if a Snickers is on the line here, I'd like to know at exactly what point we're calling the finish line. Come on, it's got to be where he gets arrested. That's what decides who wins the bet."

"Oh, I get it," Johnson said without taking his eyes from the road. "You're the Benally."

Spinks raised his brows.

"Excuse me?"

"You're the joker. The one keeping it light." The detective was nodding as if everything made sense now. "I couldn't peg you down before, but I get it now."

"Where *is* your partner?" Loshak asked, realizing he'd lost track of the white-hatted detective somewhere in the excitement and confusion of the manhunt.

Johnson licked his lips. His expression didn't change, but there was a grimness to his voice when he answered.

"Got a call just as we were heading out that Annette was in the ER with a high fever. That's his wife. You heard she's got cancer?" he said while checking the rearview mirror.

Loshak nodded.

"Anyway, she's under observation at the university cancer center."

That silence roiled again, stronger than before.

"They're supposed to be really good. The doctors there," Johnson said. "Tops in the nation. Lots of experimental medicine and stuff."

Despite the detective's poker face, he sounded as if he were looking for some reassurance.

Loshak nodded.

"That's good."

"Yeah."

Another beat of silence unfolded. Something heavier in it now.

Suddenly, the chatter on the radio picked up, voices going louder, harder, cutting across each other in their excitement.

Johnson unhooked the handset from the radio and lifted it to his mouth.

"Did not copy. Repeat that last bit, Dispatch."

"Repeating," said the staticky voice. "Chopper Two has eyes on our suspect."

CHAPTER 59

Crozier followed the sounds of shouting and barking dogs, jogging down the middle of the street, head swiveling. He couldn't see anything yet, just a bunch of still houses up and down the block.

The barks made his skin crawl as he got closer. Deep, growling woofs that made him think of something big and bad. Violent. A beast that knew an intruder when it saw one. Something that liked saying hello by way of ripping someone's genitals off.

He smiled a little to himself. Close now. Close.

He crossed the street, moving toward the noise, picking up into a sprint. Weeds sprouted up through the cracks in the sidewalk underfoot.

The barking went harsh as he got to within a hundred feet or so. Raspy and loud. Another sound churned in the background, threatening to drown it out, but he blocked the noise, focused in on the canine's warning call.

He veered to the right. Let instinct carry him. The sound coming to him on the wind.

Closer now. Soon he could hear the little growls between the barks, the deep rumble in the chest of some homicidal monster.

He crossed dirt yards and hopped low cinder block fences. Fixed his gaze on the way ahead.

It's here. Right here. It has to be.

His eyes locked on a target ahead. He licked his lips.

The barking was coming from up ahead, pouring forth from an alley, the rundown houses on either side amplifying it like a bullhorn.

And as he ran, his panting breath seemed to even out. Pumping heart slowing to a deep bass throb in his chest. Anticipation building in his head like static.

He edged around the corner of the house. Stepped into the cleft.

There was Beanpole. Crumpled on the ground like a littered candy wrapper, shrouded in the shade of the alley. He was walled in by the house and a chain-link fence.

Trapped.

As Crozier watched, the guy turned onto his stomach, arms pushing him up into a shitty imitation of an army crawl, his long legs and body stretched out like taffy.

Blood covered Beanpole's face and hair, a red hole punched into his cheek. His mouth hung open like he was trying to catch flies.

A pair of rottweilers patrolled the fence line. The bigger one padded heavily along its side of the barrier, collar jingling, barking now and again at the man who lay just out of its reach.

The slightly smaller dog lunged at the fence, snapping and growling, trying to tear his way through to Beanpole. Its eyes showed whites all around, crazy with blood lust. Hatred seethed from its body language.

The grin pulled Crozier's face tight, reflecting the bared teeth of the monster on the opposite side of the fence. He felt the knife come out, dangling there at the end of his hand all at once, as though it had a mind and will of its own.

Trapped. You're trapped between hateful creatures now. Superior beings that mean you all the harm in the world.

The hunt is over.

He took a step forward, feet crunching on the rocky dirt.

That low, churning sound grew louder all at once, details filling in the spaces he was trying to block out. A mechanical chopping rhythm. A chuffing like…

Crozier craned his neck. Turned his face skyward.

Churning clouds choked the thin strip of heavens visible between the houses, the swaybacked eaves of each roof reaching out to try to block even that out. Nothing up there but endless gray gauze.

He twisted his whole upper body now, half turning back the way he came. The opening out there over the street showed him more.

Something black stood out in the sky, bold against the listless gray. Drifting closer.

The thing fluttered like a dragonfly over the street behind him. Rotors slicing the air over and over.

Then the helicopter wheeled suddenly, jerked as if it had seen him seeing it. Jumping like he'd spooked it.

Its back end rotated smoothly around, exposing a shiny black flank. Then it just hovered there.

He turned around the rest of the way. Squared his shoulders to keep the chopper in his sights.

Then on second thought, he backpedaled into the alley, ducking in beneath the eaves of the house on his side of the fence.

They can't see me, can they? Not in here.

By now, the smile was long gone. He couldn't

remember feeling it slip away, but his cheeks had gone slack. That victorious feeling fleeing him all at once. Some vortex of emptiness swirled inside his chest, filling the place where the bubble of triumph had vacated.

He waited. Stared the chopper down. Some kind of standoff was happening just now. He felt so close to understanding it. So close to knowing how to defeat that flying metal monster.

Nothing moved but the swirling wind. The tension swelled like a feeding tick. Bigger. Bigger.

Go, he willed it. *Move on. Fly away.*

It felt like a violation. This was something no one should see. This was secret.

But the machine held steady. Levitating over the street. Sunlight glinted on its glass as it turned just slightly.

Then he could see inside. See the pilot, the helmet, the shades, the safety belts.

And a passenger. *STATE TROOPER* stood out in yellow text on his bulky bulletproof vest.

Both their heads were cranked hard to the right. Staring right at him.

The trooper raised a hand to his face, some dark bulk clutched in it.

A radio.

Calling in his location.

CHAPTER 60

On their assigned street, Johnson parked his gleaming Crown Vic at the opposite end of the block from a District 4 SUV. They snugged up to the curb, and the engine's rumble cut off.

Loshak climbed out and spent a few seconds adjusting his vest. The chill burned in his nostrils. Unseasonably cold for such a bright and sunny morning, but from what he'd heard, that was springtime in the mountains.

A dry breeze blew into his eyes, making them water. He rubbed at them, something rough in the touch, a cold stiffness in his fingers.

The houses lining this street were all squat single-story ranches, most with carports butted up against them. The last they'd heard over the radio, their killer was spotted near a gulley called Sanderson Gulch several streets over, and moving in the opposite direction, so there wasn't much chance they would see him out here. SWAT had taken the primo real estate around the last known location.

But they weren't the only team assigned to the dead spot. The four uniformed LEOs from District 4 were already fanning out through the neighborhood, weapons drawn. One spotted them, stowed his sidearm, and jogged down to meet them. He jerked his head at Loshak, Spinks, and Johnson in greeting.

"We're taking the west side. If you all could cover the east side, that would be great. And watch yourselves.

There's a lotta damn hiding spots through here."

Johnson nodded.

"Chopper pinned him down some. If we get eyes all over, he'll poke his head out sooner or later."

The uniform returned to the search, and Johnson, Spinks, and Loshak all picked a yard to start with. The reporter was the first to take off, his long legs eating up ground as he darted between the houses to check the backyard.

Johnson stopped on the front walk of his yard, pulling his badge. It took Loshak a second to spot why — a young woman with a baby was standing in the screen door, looking out. A toddler hung behind her, his arm wrapped around her leg.

The breeze whipped the detective's words away, but Loshak knew he would be telling the woman that there was a manhunt in the area and asking her to remain inside. Something lurched in Loshak's gut, and he found himself imagining what might happen if their killer barged into a house with occupants at home.

The woman shuffled her toddler back inside, closing the inner door behind her. Through the window, Loshak saw her turning on a huge television; a children's show featuring characters in garish primary colors bouncing around like coked-out grasshoppers flickered on the screen. The toddler climbed onto the coffee table and started bending this way and that. Dancing along to the music, apparently.

The dark shape of Johnson jogging past the window broke Loshak's momentary hypnosis. The detective disappeared around the corner of the house.

Get a move on.

Loshak darted off to the yard he'd chosen. Its windows were black, the empty carport testifying to the vacancy.

No cover in the sliver of front yard to hide their suspect. Fastest route around back looked to be through the carport. The privacy fence between houses sat flush against the side of the metal structure, blocking out the sun's rays.

As Loshak crossed into the shadows, the small warmth he'd been getting from the sunlight retreated, cut off. He shivered.

He'd kicked down countless doors over the years, been part of SWAT operations that took entire apartment buildings by force, but something about going into someone's yard unannounced still made him nervous. Hard to pin down a logical reason for it. It just felt wrong going onto someone's land. Some primordial taboo that must date back to his ancestors' days when defending grazing land and your livestock literally meant life or death for your family unit.

Something smelled like mildew back here. The cracks going black around the house's foundation were probably the culprit.

He held his breath instinctively. He wasn't easily grossed out, but mold was high on his list of disgusting life-forms. The idea that the amorphous gunk could take up residence in your lungs had always disturbed him. Nasty.

He came to a wood gate, reached over and triggered the release to let himself into the backyard.

At the back, he swept his gun over the area. Noted the concrete patio with a grill in its corner. On the opposite end sat a patio table with a propane fire pit set into the top, mesh chairs loosely gathered around it.

No one there.

Then he checked behind the central air unit and in a storage box, but found nothing but a refill for the fire pit and some lime green cushions for the chairs.

Coming to the back of the yard, it occurred to him that he should've picked one of the houses with lower fencing. The high cedar planks were hemming him in, and he wasn't the fence-climber he used to be.

After a few seconds' consideration, he grabbed one of the chairs, set it next to the fence, then hauled one leg over. Straddled the lumber. Not a seat he wanted to keep for any amount of time, the thin planks digging into his butt and groin.

He swung the other leg over and dropped to his feet in the adjacent backyard, faint white sparks of shock popping in his knees. He'd landed a bit too stiff-legged.

These folks had a nearly identical patio setup. The main difference was the color of the outdoor furniture and the placement of the grill. This whole neighborhood must've been built up in spec houses during one of Denver's population booms.

He cleared the yard, then headed for the front of the house. The gap here was barely wide enough for his shoulders. His shirtsleeves snagged on the rough stucco coating the wall.

Another carport up ahead, this one lined with a fence on one side and a stack of storage totes on the other, creating a blind corner. The sun ducked behind a cloud.

Loshak's breath went quiet and shaky as he stepped

toward the corner where the stair-stepped totes cut off in shadow. The gun extended before him.

He swung himself into the dark passage and trudged forward.

CHAPTER 61

Now Crozier's feet were the ones pounding the ground. He tore past Beanpole, skirting close enough to the fence for the snarling, lunging rottweiler to spew hot breath onto his hand as he passed.

He ducked out of the narrow passage between the houses and loped across the next yard. Shot down another gap.

The barking behind him trailed away, shrank. Bulky air conditioning units dotted the spaces between houses. He darted around them, jumped over bikes stacked up against fences. Hopped a low wall and came to a much higher fence.

He panicked for a second, unable to see a way forward. Then he spotted the bike propped in the corner. He got a leg up on the seat and pulled himself the rest of the way over, dropping to his feet on the other side.

Finally, he spilled out into the street again. Stumbled and fell forward.

Concrete tore through the knees of his jeans. He pushed off with his hands, scrabbling back to his feet and taking off again.

The open street felt vast and strange after all that time pinned between houses. He ran into the emptiness.

The ground sloped downward beneath his feet. He let it carry him down the hill, adding momentum, building up his speed.

The land evened out into a rocky ditch, littered with trash. A trickle of water ran between the uneven stones.

He chanced a look over his shoulder, expecting to see the chopper looming right behind him, but from this angle, the sky over the hill looked empty.

His heart leaped like a trout fighting upstream. Holy shit, he was actually getting away. He was doing it. The elation only spurred him on.

His legs churned. His heart galloped in his chest.

Excitement burst inside his skull. The forward momentum felt incredible. Made him feel alive.

The ground blurred beneath him. Scrolling past.

But he could still hear the chopper. Loud as ever.

He swallowed, blinked. Cast his vision that direction again.

The helicopter swooped into view, cresting the hill, gliding into the frame of his vision. It was lower now. Just skimming above the rooftops it was passing.

That chopping thud of the rotors thumped against his eardrums.

He turned and ran, tripping and sliding on the stones. Barely keeping his feet.

That thing was closing in. Police units would be flooding the block any second now.

Get gone, he told himself.

But how was he supposed to do that?

He spotted another chain-link fence ahead. A sign warning him to keep out.

SANDERSON WATER TREATMENT FACILITY - NO TRESPASSING.

He grabbed the fence, fingers twisting in the wire, shoes

fumbling on the links. But no. This was taking too long.

He dropped and ran again, climbing up the far bank, sprinting across the greening spring grass of the park. His feet pounded on a concrete walking path, a narrow loop between a fountain and a statue, then he was spilling back onto a quiet side street. A row of townhouses that seemed annoyed by his harsh breathing and the clap of his feet on the asphalt.

Then he saw it.

The round disk set in the road ahead.

He ran to it, squatted down. Sweat sluiced down his forehead as he leaned over the metallic circle. He worked the tip of his blade into the opening there and pried.

The edge popped up.

He got his fingers under it, felt serrated metal pricking the skin. It was heavier than he expected. He heaved, back and thighs burning with the motion, jagged bits of steel scraping his hands.

The manhole cover hauled free and clanged onto the street, rolling a short distance, then spinning in place like a dropped penny.

The hole gaped up at him. A black vacancy trailing into the earth. It looked wrong, the asphalt cleaving off into this perfect circular cavity.

Behind him, the chopper crept closer. The wind from the rotors tore at him again, sighing through the hole and down into the void.

He took a breath and leaped into the darkness.

CHAPTER 62

The air in the sewers felt heavy. Dank and oddly warm.

A smell like rotten seafood hung in the air. Like someone in this neighborhood had been flushing old crab legs down their toilet.

Something dripped in the darkness. Crozier could hear the constant *plip* of the drops, wetness slapping wetness, but he couldn't tell which way they were coming from or how close he was standing to the splash zone.

The relief he felt at getting out of the helicopter's sight was quickly eaten away by the atmosphere.

The dark, the stench. The wet air, uncomfortably warm, smearing itself on his sweat-slick skin.

It was only warmer in sewers because of bacteria, he'd read once. Little single-celled monsters eating up the shit and rotten food and whatever else people poured down their drains, their microbial metabolisms raising the temperature.

Couldn't do anything about that. But he *could* do something about the dark.

Crozier pulled his phone from his pocket. Tried to turn it on. Nothing happened.

He'd meant to charge it the last time he was at the photo lab, but he must have forgotten.

Fuck.

It was OK, though. He had options.

He dug into his pocket, fumbling at the bulk there.

Then pulling out his lighter, he flicked the wheel.

The tiny flame pushed at the darkness, carving a sphere of light in the gloom. Crozier thrust the lighter out in front, holding it higher, poking it up over his head in a Statue of Liberty pose. He'd been hoping that would help him see farther into the tunnels, but moving it around didn't help much. He got the same sphere of visibility either way.

Now he saw the source of the drip — a leaking pipe about ten feet in front of him. A wide puddle lay under it like some kind of underground lake. Even though he knew it couldn't be more than a few inches deep, the oily blackness of the water, impenetrable to his lighter, seemed to go down fathoms, hiding who knew what in its depths.

He'd been expecting walls of that corrugated metal piping, but the underground passages were lined with red brick or maybe tile, covered in a slick sheen of algae or just straight-up slime, some green and some black, all shiny. He could see the grooves between the segments but couldn't tell what exactly they were made of.

Something thumped aboveground, the sound kind of funny as it traveled through the manhole. Could have been a car door.

Instantly he pictured flashlights slicing into the darkness. Loud cop voices calling out strident orders. The clicks and clacks of drawn weapons.

His heart thumped faster in response to the fantasy, almost matching the time of that dripping. He had to keep moving.

He broke into a jog, shoes squelching in the sewer sludge, flinging up black water from the puddle. As his body picked up speed, his mind raced ahead all the faster, leaping to the next move and the next.

The key was going to be getting out of the tunnels quickly. Getting down here had bought him time, but they would figure out where he was before long, if they didn't already know.

A tunnel chase was no good. Too many places where he could be cornered, trapped.

And he wanted out now, in truth. Some darkened corner of his mind reeled at the wrongness of this maze of underground tubes. It felt like he could get lost down here forever, starving to death in the darkness and crab-stank. Unrealistic, the rational part of him knew, but it didn't feel that way in the moment.

The lighter flickered, the air currents in his rush trying to put out the flame. He stuck a hand out in front of it as a shield, then had to adjust his grip so he could still get enough illumination to see by.

A spike of pain flared up his thumb and into his arm. Some spinal reaction jerked his hand back, ripped his thumb away from the heat.

The fire winked out. All was darkness again, save for the floating pink spot in his retina where the flame had been.

Fuck.

He stopped running. Winced and stuck the burnt pad of his thumb into his mouth, breath sizzling in and out of his nose. Then he pulled it out and blew on it. The cool air soothed the pain momentarily before the last of his spit was dried up and the burn bored into his skin again.

The pain wasn't the real concern here, though. The light was the problem. He needed to keep moving.

The lighter was still clawed up in his fingers. Maybe if he switched hands and, for fuck's sake, kept his skin away from the hot metal.

He traded the lighter off to the other hand and flicked it. Quick to minimize contact with that blazing metal wheel.

Then he took off again. Sloshing and stomping.

He passed two sets of steel rungs leading upward. He left those behind, chugging onward.

But after another minute or two, he started to get nervous. Seemed like he'd passed that last set a long time back. What if there weren't any more coming? What if those had been his only options for getting out of here?

Finally, a rusty ladder appeared up on his right, steel loops jutting from the wall. He jogged to a stop, put one hand on a chest-high rung, then let the lighter go out.

He didn't want to pocket that red-hot piece of metal, so he kept it wrapped in his fingers and stepped onto the ladder, giving his free hand most of the climbing duties and only using the lighter hand as a hook, looping it over the rungs while he grabbed the next highest and pulled himself up.

At the top of the ladder, he crooked an arm over the rung and tested the metal of the lighter head. Still hot, but not enough to burn him. He shoved it into his pocket and adjusted his stance on the ladder. Reached overhead, into the infinite blackness.

His palms found cold metal. Rough. He pressed his whole hand flat to the surface like a starfish.

Heavy, but some movement. It fought him at first, then with a metallic scraping, shifted out of the hole's grasp.

A golden glow spilled around the curved edge, strange in the darkness, like a crescent moon waxing into fullness before his eyes.

He stepped up another rung. Felt his arm shaking from the strain of lifting the weight of the manhole cover, the tension strongest in his shoulders. Then his whole torso was rattling, back and abs, a quiver running through him like he was a plucked guitar string, all those muscles trying to sing out in harmony.

He heaved. The circle of metal cranked his wrist, the spiky edge scraping along his palm as the steel slab slid off to the side. The glow spread to fill his vision, a bright and burning world waiting to receive him.

Sam reached through the rim, hands finding and gripping the asphalt edge on the other side. He pushed off the steel rung and climbed into the light, hauling himself up until he got a hip on the street. He turned around and sat down, legs dangling into the nothingness, the sole of one sneaker scraping a rung below.

But then something came to him. A new idea shot through his skull like a bolt of lightning, zinging down his spine.

Yes.

Yes.

He climbed back down into the dark.

CHAPTER 63

Loshak checked in the shadows beneath a fifth wheel camper, then squeezed between it and another house, his vest squealing as it rubbed along the vinyl siding. He had his radio volume turned down to a whisper, but he caught bits and pieces as the helicopter tracked the suspect and chatter from the other teams on the ground. SWAT made up the majority of it, coordinating their search of the hot zone. So far, he hadn't heard anything from Johnson or Spinks.

He slipped out of the narrow passage, finally able to square his shoulders again, and swept the backyard.

A big fire pit sat on the edge of the cracked concrete slab. This one had those novelty skull-shaped fire stones stacked neatly at the center, blackened and grinning.

Charming.

Crossing the faux cannibal's patio, he made for the next yard back. Luckily these two houses had marked their boundaries with a low concrete wall rather than the eight-foot privacy fences that seemed to be all the rage in this neighborhood.

He stepped over, a hand on the cold, rough concrete to stabilize himself.

Something clanged in the distance. Metallic. Heavy.

Loshak froze. Sounded like it had come from the street behind him.

He pulled his leg back into the cannibal yard and spun

around, sprinting for the driveway. Then he turned sideways and shuffled between the house and camper this time, mostly leaning on the house and making his vest scream out again.

One last squish, and then the camper released him. He broke out the other side of the squeeze into the open street.

Jogging to a stop at the edge of the driveway, Loshak scanned the strip of asphalt. Left, then right.

A quiet block lay in front of him. All still in both directions.

Could it have been a metal garbage can lid? Did anybody still use those galvanized steel cans? He'd thought trash can technology had moved on in the late eighties.

No, the sound he'd heard was too heavy to be one of those stupid lids. Dense. Thick.

There was nothing there. Nothing stirring. Even the wind had died down.

But his gut wouldn't let it go.

Loshak strode onto the street. Choppy steps. Still jittery from the burst of adrenaline. He had to be sure about this before he moved on.

He climbed the gentle asphalt slope, going uphill from the house. Within ten paces, something came clear on the road ahead.

A sliver of some round object was sticking up there, poking over the top of that black hill.

A manhole cover. That's what he'd heard. That metallic clanging as the thing was dropped on the ground.

He drew up to it and stared into the open place in the street.

What the hell?

Did he come up out of this thing?

Loshak turned, studying the neighborhood more closely this time and returning both hands to his gun as he did.

Movement caught the corner of his eye. He whirled and lifted the gun.

Then he saw the bright yellow lettering across the black vest. He swung his arm down so his gun was pointed at the ground.

Aque. He and Schrader must've been assigned to one of the neighboring streets.

"Might have something here," Loshak said, nodding down at the hole opened up in the earth.

"What do—"

Aque's radio blared out from his belt. Not only was the detective's set to a louder volume than Loshak's, but the voice calling out the warning was close to shouting, wavering between fear and exhilaration.

"SWAT has entered the storm drain beneath West Gunnison Drive and is headed southwest in pursuit of the suspect. Do not approach. Stay clear of the sewers and let SWAT apprehend. Repeat, do not approach!"

CHAPTER 64

The minutes ticked by before they had another update.

"Visual contact lost."

With this announcement, the voice on the radio sounded deflated. No shouting now. "Repeat, visual contact of the suspect was lost."

Loshak stared down into the darkness within the circle cut out of the street. It seemed as if the light of day couldn't reach down there, like some invisible field of energy stopped it at ground level.

Aque snatched his radio off his belt. Brought it to his lips.

"This is Aque on South Tejon." He glanced at the houses. "Fourteen-hundred block. We have an open manhole cover."

"What's going on?" Schrader jogged onto the street to join them.

Loshak gestured to the manhole cover.

"I heard this being tossed aside a minute ago, two at most. He was right here. If he'd come out, one of us would've seen him. I got here thirty seconds after the clang."

Schrader nodded, but he seemed unsure.

Aque put the radio to his face again.

"Requesting a map of the drainage system. Forward it to Detective Aque. Over."

The detective's phone chirped a second later. He'd

barely had a chance to look at the map when Loshak snagged the blocky screen away from him.

He looked at the tunnel map, spotted West Gunnison right away. Fingered the glass to scan around to find his own position.

There.

Crozier had given his pursuers the shake somewhere between those two points. There were a number of places he could've done it, the map of those tunnels was all branching routes.

"It's one hell of a maze down there," Schrader said, leaning over Loshak's shoulder. "There are almost four hundred miles of sewer line under the Denver metro area. Well, I'm not sure how much of that's still standing, but there's still seventy miles of it in operation. That's a lot of damn pipe to search."

He shook his head and poked at the screen.

"We're actually pretty close to the early stuff here. See, you've got the brick mains from back in the eighteen-seventies, then your turn-of-the-century concrete lines. We're pretty close to where the first storm sewers were laid. After that, they put in interceptors. Hell, where we are right now, there are twenty sewer subdistricts alone. Obviously, this spot would've been farmland back when the drains were laid, and most of it was for irrigation, but still."

Aque shot his partner a flat look.

"What are you, the History Channel?"

"My mom was working in the office for Yarmer Construction back when everyone was bidding for the Ruby Hill improvements contract — and again during the waterway initiative. You wouldn't believe the boring shit I know about this city's plumbing."

"Where does this ultimately come out?" Loshak asked.

"South Platte River, over here." Schrader shaded the screen so he could see better, then moved the map. "There's a new industrial drainage system they put in to reduce the load on the Marston plant. It's supposedly the third largest in Denver now."

Loshak eyed the series of concrete waterways, pumps, clearwells, and tanks.

"That's only what, five, six blocks away? Were any search teams assigned to that area?"

Schrader shook his head.

"Aque and me were the farthest east."

"This has to be where he's headed," Loshak said. "See how the largest tunnels below us are all sort of flowing into it? This is where we need to go."

Schrader frowned down at the map without answering, that pinched expression of uncertainty still on his face.

But Aque nodded.

"Then let's move."

Loshak might not have endeared himself to the prickly detective from their first impressions, but apparently when an arrest was on the line, he didn't let a little thing such as dislike hold him back.

CHAPTER 65

After radioing Johnson and Spinks, Loshak and his search
team loaded into Johnson's shining Crown Vic and
followed Schrader and Aque to the water processing plant.
Aque had the station call ahead, and security let them in
through the rolling chain-link gate. The spiral of razor wire
over the top shook as the gate groaned open.

Johnson eyed the wire as they drove through.

"Place is locked down like a prison."

"You've gotta keep the water *in*," Spinks said, grinning.

"Ever read *Dreamcatcher*?" Loshak tugged down the
neck of his vest. "I'd be tightening security around my
water supply, too."

The reporter made a face.

"I never read that one. Lisa — my wife —" he explained
for Johnson's benefit, "spoiled the ending for me. She
didn't mean to, but she was so appalled that it just slipped
out."

"Huh," Loshak said with a shrug. "I don't know. Maybe
not King's best, but I liked it."

"Wait a second. Hold up." Spinks twisted in his seat so
he could look back at Loshak. "You're a closet Stephen
King fan? Why are you just now letting this bomb drop?
This whole time we could've been discussing his books and
short stories and the movies — both good and awful —
based on them."

"I don't know if I was closeted, per se. It just never

came up." He realized something. "You know, earlier today, I was wondering where I got this intense disgust for mildew and any kind of spreading, fuzzy fungus. But maybe it was that book. *Dreamcatcher,* I mean."

"Fuzzy mold and mildew?" Spinks shook his head. "I feel like I'm meeting you all over again, partner."

They parked the cars at the edge of the drainage site and met with the commissioner of the water district. She brought out a tablet with the most up-to-date maps of the neighborhood.

"We've got construction here and here," she said, pointing out yellow triangles on the map, "which is effectively going to funnel him this way. If he doesn't leave via manhole, he'll have to come out in the subsection behind us. During heavy load season, this whole place gushes like a dirty river, but we've got subsections four, seven, ten, and eleven dry 'til the middle of next month. All clear down there right now."

Johnson went back to his car, waiting to brief the auxiliary teams when they arrived. Meanwhile, Loshak, Spinks, Schrader, and Aque followed the commissioner's directions into the drainage site.

The sloped, scrubby land led them down to a dry concrete spillway that let out onto the dusty canal below. Their shoes scuffed through the powdery grit, the only sound in the canals. It was quiet down here. A little eerie.

Despite the lack of water and the commissioner's assurance that they had weeks until the subsection was in full use, Loshak got the squirming feeling in his stomach that he usually got standing below the flood line at dams, that nagging knowledge that the gates could open up or break at any moment and sweep away everything in its path.

A myriad of grates drained into this silent manmade basin, concrete tunnels that looked like waterslides trailing down from higher ground.

"Our boy should have come from that one up there."

Schrader's voice bounced off the concrete, the echoing sound evoking something metallic in spite of the stone that surrounded them.

Loshak cringed at the volume.

Schrader checked the map on his phone, apparently oblivious to how loud he was talking.

"That's the main line for this section, full-sized and everything."

"Keep it down," Loshak snapped.

The detective looked surprised.

"Should I not talk at all?" he whispered.

"Well, no, that's not what I meant," Loshak said, realizing how harsh he'd just sounded. That had been kind of shitty, snapping at the detective like Gandalf calling that one hobbit a fool. "I just meant we should keep our voices low. He might already be watching us, but… if not, we don't want to warn him we're here. That's all."

Schrader nodded.

"Got it. So, what are we thinking about that pipe?"

The only sign of wetness in the place was coming from that round concrete tube, a tiny trickle smaller than Loshak's pinkie, oozing down the slope and making a puddle at the bottom that was rapidly baking away at the edges. The tunnel itself had a steel grate over it, but a chunk of the bottom had been cut away, the edges weathered and rusted as if it had been that way for a while.

Aque turned in a circle, scanning up and down the canal. It was as straight as a ruler for what looked like miles.

Then he gestured at the muddy grit below the pipe. "No footprints."

"You think we beat him here?" Spinks asked.

"It's looking like it."

Loshak realized a second later what that meant, what was about to happen, and he groaned under his breath.

They were going in.

CHAPTER 66

The tunnel poked out of the rocky slope like a pooched mouth as the five of them posted up at its edge. Loshak felt like he was staring into the thing's throat.

Aque ducked through the grate first and disappeared into the gloom. It felt wrong to watch the shadows swallow him. Something between indecent and creepy.

Then a second later, his flashlight clicked on. Aque aimed it at the floor in front of the grate's opening. Glossy green tile shined back at them. A layer of slime coating an infected tongue.

Up until then, Loshak hadn't noticed the funk. But looking down at that slippery, almost stringy carpeting, the smell bloomed in his nose. A fine bouquet of human sewage, chemicals, and that brown stink of old riverbank mud.

The rest of them filed in one by one. No one spoke now. The scrape and slosh of their shoes seemed loud in the enclosed space, echoing down the hole like bat wings fluttering in a cave.

Loshak felt his gut clamping down. Cold sweat formed on his upper lip and dampened his pits. More beaded on the back of his neck.

They shuffled into the dark, flashlight beams from Aque and Spinks pointing their way. The rest of them had their weapons drawn.

The farther in they traveled, the more their tunnel

339

began to branch off. Narrower lines stretched away from the central one, veering off in the distance. Alcoves had been placed at regular intervals, control boxes blinking with red and green and yellow lights.

"Something moved down there!" Schrader swung his gun toward a tunnel. "Get a light over here!"

Spinks poked his flashlight beam in that direction.

Shining green eyes appeared. Black and white fur. Loshak's heart felt like it stopped mid-beat.

Then the skunk let out a hissing scream and scrabbled away, rounding the bend of the side tunnel in a waddle. They could hear it skittering for a long time.

The guns lowered one by one, and then it was as if they all breathed out at the same time.

Spinks chuckled. Shook his head.

Loshak laughed a beat later, both from relief and at the momentary skunk terror he'd felt. The realization that they were trapped in an enclosed space, seemingly about to get sprayed with a faceful of stink, had shaken him. Somehow, for that split second, he'd been more afraid than he could remember ever feeling on a manhunt.

"It sounded bigger," Schrader said defensively.

His partner let out a snort.

"We're all just glad you didn't shoot this one. It wouldn't be the first time the great Detective Schrader tried to put down a wild animal, would it?"

They began to shuffle forward again, lights scanning the tunnels.

"Hey man, when a vicious bunch of raccoons with murder in their beady eyes are charging out of a dumpster your suspect just climbed into, you've only got a split second to decide. Me or these rabid fuzzballs. I picked me."

"That's not what it looked like." Aque's flashlight illuminated a tunnel so Loshak could clear it. "I heard you screamed like a girl and almost shot yourself in the leg."

Loshak was only half-listening as he eyed the shadowy holes on either side of the main line ahead of them. Nothing stirred in any direction. He was starting to think they weren't going to find anything down here.

Maybe he'd been wrong about the suspect going back down into the tunnels. He could've been mistaken at how long it had taken him to get to the manhole after hearing it clang, adrenaline messing with his sense of time. Their guy could've taken off and hidden in or behind one of the houses they'd already searched.

The more he thought about it, the more it dawned on him that if Crozier was smart, he would've climbed out of any random manhole and made a run for it. Crozier could be anywhere in the city by then, and their search would have gotten them nowhere. They'd be back to square one.

"Look, I'm an animal lover," Schrader was saying. "But I'll be damned if I'm going to let a bunch of disease-infested—"

Motion blurred in the maintenance alcove just to their right. A shape lunging out of the shadows.

An arm.

That's all Loshak saw at first.

A thin, pale limb partially shrouded in a dark hoodie. It swooped out of the murk. Lunged for Schrader's throat.

The blade ripped to the side. One quick motion.

And the detective's neck fell open. The shadowy slit yawing like a slack jaw.

Loshak only had time to blink before the blood was spraying. Jetting in clean spurts.

In almost the same move as the throat slash, the man ripped the gun away from Schrader. Then he fell back into the shadows.

The detective choked and then gurgled. Staggered forward one step. Empty hands groping at his neck. Trying to hold in blood that spritzed between his fingers like twin sprinklers.

Behind Schrader, Spinks stumbled back a step. His flashlight scraped tunnel wall, then fell, winking out when it hit the floor.

The beam of Aque's light seared across Loshak's retinas, then swung uselessly to the ceiling as he leaped forward to help his partner.

Chaos roiled. A jumble of shouts and choking, light and darkness shifting over slimy green walls.

Loshak scooted back and to the side, blinking rapidly, sweeping his gun toward where the killer had been.

He saw motion there. Details coming to him one by one.

A flash of white forearm beneath the pushed-up sleeves of the hoodie.

The glint of the knife.

The dark blocky shape of the gun.

Loshak squeezed the trigger.

His shot went off a split second before Crozier's. The two blasts ringing out right on top of one another.

A second light hit the ground, still on, and then Aque landed on top of it.

Everything went dark.

CHAPTER 67

Sam Crozier sprinted through the darkness toward that little grid of daylight and bars in the distance. The caged wall of steel with the smile cut right where the mouth would be.

The gunshots still roared in his ears. High-pitched shrieks piercing without end.

His footsteps were muffled. Thumps that felt like they were coming from inside him rather than out. A second heartbeat.

He'd never imagined something that painful could come from a sound. So loud in that enclosed space. He was pretty sure one or both of his eardrums had burst.

Crozier zoomed toward the opening, full speed ahead. He could only sort of feel the gun pumping along at his side, an alien object clutched in his right hand.

From behind, he could make out snatches of the confusion he'd left in his wake. Voices tangling over each other.

Another shot blasted through the tube. The crack and whoosh echoing everywhere, fluttering closer.

Without thinking, he dove for the cut in the grate. Felt metal rip and poke in his chest, grabbing at him, trying to hold him in, trap him.

And for just a second, he saw Shiv in his mind's eye again. Dead and cold. Laid to eternal rest on her half of their bed.

The image seared itself into his imagination. A bright hot fantasy blotting out reality for a moment, projecting itself onto the last of the shadows around him.

But he didn't slow down.

He wriggled through the opening in the grate and wormed his way into the brightness.

CHAPTER 68

Loshak blinked. Tottered two steps forward on legs gone numb.

Shock ran through him like an electrical current. A cold buzz in his veins, in his skull.

Schrader was dead. Probably gone within seconds at the rate his neck had been gushing.

Aque was a fountain of blood in his own right. So much red flowing that it seeped between Spinks's fingers.

The detective slumped, half-propped against the curved wall of the tunnel, while the reporter adjusted his hands and leaned into him, trying to stanch the blood.

"OK, it's OK," Spinks was saying, his tone low and soothing in spite of the fact that he was now soaked in blood. Between each word, Loshak could hear the chattering of the detective's teeth. "You're going to be alright. We're going to get this bleeding stopped and get you out of here."

Loshak suddenly felt the gun clutched in his icy fist. He stared down at it. Blinking again. He only half-remembered firing after Crozier as he disappeared down the tunnel.

It was only instinct that pushed him to grab the radio. He lifted the black box to his lips. He could hear the adrenaline as a slight waver in his voice.

"This is team twelve, secondary search location, water processing plant. We just made contact with the suspect.

He left the tunnels, heading into the canals below the spillway. We've got two officers down. Requesting backup and medical ASAP."

Dispatch asked for confirmation, but Loshak was looking down the tunnel toward its mouth, that tiny bit of illumination still visible in the distance.

A dark blot flitted in front of it, arms and legs pumping. The killer had reached the grate.

Loshak let his radio drop and squeezed off another shot.

The bullet sparked off metal, ricocheted with a skirling whine. The killer did a superman dive through the gap and disappeared.

Loshak took a few running steps, then stopped, turning back.

"Go on," Spinks said, his voice still modulated and soothing. "Aque and I have this under control. Go get him."

Loshak sprinted toward the light.

CHAPTER 69

As he reached the mouth of the tunnel, Loshak slowed to a creep, listening. A voice on the radio had taken up communication with the dispatcher, hurrying the paramedics and the backup along. The agent recognized it after a second. Johnson, safe in the parking lot.

If he hadn't agreed to wait for the other teams, it could've been Johnson who'd gotten his throat cut.

Loshak swallowed.

It could've been me.

Crozier could have hidden on the opposite side of the tunnel. Or Loshak could have been in Schrader's place. Why hadn't he been? Under normal circumstances, default would've made Spinks his flashlight man. At what point had they decided who would pair up with who while they cleared the tunnels?

It was all a jumble of randomness in his head, a tangle of lurching shadows, narrow misses, and what might have been.

Loshak padded the last few steps toward the brightness. He felt lighter on his feet now. Crazy what a spurt of adrenaline could do.

He eased closer to the grate. His heart squeezed, rapid-fire bursts quivering in his chest.

The sun glimmered through the torn grating, making the interior of the tunnel seem all the more shadowy around him. He couldn't see anyone on the other side of the steel mesh. Still, he slowed down a few steps shy of the threshold.

The scene to come played in Loshak's mind, ducking through the tunnel mouth and finding himself on the wrong end of Crozier's knife. Streams of blood flying as it drained his life into a Colorado sewer.

No.

Worse.

He has Schrader's gun now.

He mopped the back of his wrist over his top lip. His eyes traced the edges of the opening, pulse swishing in his ears, sweat pouring down his back and from his hairline.

Waiting. Waiting for Crozier to pop out of nowhere again.

But then…

With a dive like the one Crozier had taken, the killer should have tumbled down the slope and dropped to the canal below. He'd probably sprinted away from there.

And yet, against all reason, Loshak felt it in his viscera that Sam Crozier was just outside, listening for him, ready to spring.

The agent swallowed. His mouth and throat were dry. His breath scraped through them, loud and hot.

He eased that last step up to the grate, neck craning as if he could get the perfect angle to see around the corner without actually poking his head out.

Nope. He was just going to have to do it.

He nodded to himself, alone in the tunnel of death.

There was no way around it. He had to go for it.

On three.

One.

The breath hissed in and out of him, almost panting as he ramped up to the dreaded move.

Two.

He bent at the knees. Felt like his whole body was shaking.

Three.

Loshak ducked through the grate into the sunshine, one fell swoop, neck tensed enough to snap.

Brightness surrounded him. Open air suddenly shooting up into the heavens.

He almost lost his footing on the slope, but he widened his stance and swept his gun around, searching for the dark hoodie in all that light.

The canal was deserted.

What the hell?

He turned around and around. Held his breath and listened.

Footsteps pounded somewhere ahead, that strangely metallic echo bouncing back to him off the concrete. Crozier was already around the bend, out of view.

Dust gritted under his feet as Loshak bolted after the sound, racing for that spot where he would be able to see around the curve.

This time, he didn't slow down when he reached the blind corner. He whipped around it, feet skidding in the powdery silt.

But there was no one there. The way ahead was empty. Even the metallic thundering of footsteps was gone.

Shit.

CHAPTER 70

Loshak shuffled forward a few paces, then stopped. He gritted his teeth. Swallowed in a throat so dry it felt sandy. Then he proceeded a few more steps.

The silence in the empty canal felt heavy. The air charged and thick.

Just get eyes on him. That's all.

Backup will be here soon.

He replayed the sounds he'd just heard in his head. Puzzled over their meaning.

It didn't make sense. He knew the running footsteps had been coming from this direction, downstream of their pipe, around the corner from the spillway. There hadn't been anywhere upstream for Crozier to go.

And yet, here was a stretch of uninterrupted canal for at least five hundred yards before it stair-stepped down to the elevation of the river.

Maybe Crozier was faster than Loshak had estimated. Maybe he'd already made it to the first of the canal's step-downs and was crouched against that concrete wall, hiding, holding his breath.

In spite of the sun beating down from overhead, Loshak's sweat had turned icy. He advanced toward the knife-edge of the first dry manmade waterfall with care.

It was so far away, though. Twice the distance between the site of the shooting and the grate Crozier had escaped through. Was it really feasible that the killer had been fast enough to hide down there before Loshak had rounded the corner?

His head rotated, eyes jumping from the step-down ahead up to the lip of the canal on his left and right.

Could Crozier have climbed up and out?

The concrete walls stood a good eight feet straight up on both sides from here. Crozier was on the smaller side.

Even with his height, Loshak wasn't sure he could haul himself up the cement these days. A couple of decades ago, with a running start, take a jump, grab the top — he could have pulled himself up there. Crozier was young enough, but was he tall enough?

Then he saw it emerge ahead and to his left.

A ladder mounted on one side of the canal. It led to a concrete platform surrounded by chain-link topped with more razor wire. From below, Loshak could see the top of a huge valve painted red, gauges sticking out from the sides. Some sort of shutoff, maybe, or a pump station.

The gate was hanging open, the padlock twisted and broken.

Loshak broke into a run again. Half jumped when he got to the ladder and grabbed on, pulling himself up, rung over rung.

He crested the top and stepped onto the strip of scrubby grass there. Scanned the area.

There was a manhole next to the shutoff.

Its cover was still partially open. A slice of darkness visible on one rounded edge.

Christ.

Not again.

Loshak headed for the gate. Metal clinked under his

shoe. He drew his leg back up to find a snapped-off portion of a large-bladed knife, warped and broken from forcing the shackle on the fence padlock.

This had to be it. Crozier must've gone underground again.

He stooped beside the manhole cover and hefted it out of the way, elbows and knees cracking with the motion.

The second he got it moving, he lurched back out of the way, waiting for a gunshot to come ripping out of the dark. Body tensed. Bracing for it.

Nothing.

He hesitated. Eyes piercing that black nothing welling up from the ground.

Then he edged to the hole again and peered down. He didn't have a flashlight on him, so he turned on the light on his phone.

The weak circle of illumination wedged into the space, shaking slightly. Adrenaline. Exertion.

The interior looked smaller than the main line the four of them had traversed. PVC tubes on one wall led to blinking instrument panels, measuring, he assumed, the complete lack of water currently running through it.

Loshak took a deep breath as if he were about to dive into the ocean. Then he climbed down into the dark, hands and feet clunking against the rungs.

As soon as his head dipped below ground, the concrete closed off the sound from above, revealing an auditory backdrop he hadn't realized was there — the faint breeze, the hum of tires and traffic from the roadways around the plant. A feeling of constriction closed in without the ambient noise to hold it back.

Lone Wolf

He stepped off the ladder, feet slipping in the thin film of slime coating the floor. He grabbed one of the rungs to steady himself. There was no running water here this time of year, but apparently there was enough moisture to keep this mossy stuff alive and well.

Keeping one hand on the ladder, he brushed his phone light to the right.

Nothing but more instrument panels and an overflow gate that opened during this wet season he kept hearing about.

He brushed the light to the left.

A dark shape swooped out of the gloom. Pain exploded across the side of his head, and then the darkness rushed in.

CHAPTER 71

Spinks knelt with his hands pressed to Aque's gut wound, one hand mashed in the soft place beneath the bottom of the detective's bulletproof vest. Blood welled up from the hole, pulsing weakly against his palms. Wet and warm. Warmer than the body he was leaning on.

Aque squirmed beneath his hands, arms and legs scraping the tunnel floor uselessly, head lolling from side to side. The detective's chest hitched as he issued forth sounds that were half groan, half sob.

"You're going to be alright. We'll get you out of here. You heard my partner, he called you in, and folks are on the way to help."

The constant stream of words poured out of Spinks. He hardly thought about what he was saying. He just let them flow.

It was strange how calm he felt. There was a man with a bullet in him who would bleed to death if he stopped pushing on the wound, and another man on the ground beside him already dead, his lifeblood puddled and cold on the floor of the tunnel.

Every time Spinks adjusted his weight so he could put more pressure on Aque, he felt his foot nudge Schrader. A bump that sent back sensations that were both too floppy and too stiff at the same time.

And yet Spinks felt somehow matter-of-fact about the whole situation. It was ironic, really. He was always sure he

354

would react badly to these high-stress, high-pressure, life-or-death emergencies. Panic. Maybe even faint. He wasn't a big fan of blood.

He'd watched Lisa get a C-section back when Davin had been born — or rather, watched her for about ten seconds — and when the docs "unzipped her," as they called it, that shining blade slicing a gaping smile into her stomach, Spinks had felt heat rush down from the top of his head, seen red close in until his vision was nothing more than a pinprick of light at the end of a darkening tunnel. He'd felt himself leaning and leaning. Then thankfully a nurse had spotted him about to collapse and led him to a chair to put his head between his legs and breathe.

Again, when Davin had broken his clavicle falling off the trampoline, and the doctor had set it. There was something about seeing the ones he loved bleeding or in pain that Spinks couldn't handle. Even minor stuff like watching them get a flu shot or blood drawn overwhelmed his system.

But now, with a man's life depending on him, everything seemed clear. Every next step rolled out in front of him, waiting for him to take it. Hard to say what would have happened if he'd been conscious in the moments after the wreck that had killed Davin. Maybe he would have felt this clarity then. Maybe he could have saved his son.

These thoughts flitted through his mind, distant and emotionless. None of them hung around long enough to dwell on. They flowed by like the constant stream of soothing nonsense he was keeping up for Aque's benefit.

Meanwhile, he had a job to do — keep pressure on the

wound until someone with better emergency medical qualifications could take over. He was the stopper in Aque's bottle. Simple as that. Easy to comprehend, easy to carry out.

"Once they get here, they'll have you fixed up in no time. I saw a hospital on the drive over. They'll probably take you there, since it's closest. Should be a fairly smooth ride. Not like our highways back in Miami. Pothole city. I once cracked a rim hitting one of those things. No joke. Had to replace the thing, it couldn't even be welded…"

While he talked, he kept an ear tuned to the detectives' radios. Finally, out came the phrase he'd been listening for.

"Team twelve: Paramedics are on the scene." Johnson's voice sounded tinny and small, echoing in chorus. "What's your location? Please advise."

He was going to have to tell them the way. Right. Should've thought of that earlier.

Spinks adjusted his grip, bearing down with his left hand and making Aque cry out, while his right swiped through the bloody, silty mud on the tunnel floor. Nothing.

"Repeating: Team twelve—"

Where the hell was the radio? He could hear the damn thing.

There should be two close by, one on Aque and one on Schrader's corpse. He patted around Aque's belt and then up his chest, feeling for the boxy contraption.

Nothing.

A vague sense of frustration built, but still nothing like panic. Just a vague annoyance that he couldn't find a single one of the damn things.

"Detective, I need you to put pressure on this for just a

second." Spinks switched from the comforting, soothing tone to something a little more commanding. Clear and confident.

Aque took a shaky breath and stuttered out two words. "I cuh-can't."

He grabbed Aque's hand and stuck it to the bullet hole. "You can, and you will."

The dying man whimpered and tried to pull his hand away, but Spinks stuck it back down and gave it a little shake for emphasis.

"I know it hurts. I just need my hands free for one second. We're going to get you out of here, but first I have to find a radio to tell them where you are."

This time he didn't wait to see whether Aque would keep the pressure on. He turned around, knees gritting on the tunnel floor, and felt around until he found Schrader's cooling torso. It rolled weirdly beneath his vest. Reminded Spinks a little of those Jell-O jigglers everybody used to love.

His fingers skimmed the blood-soaked material, bumping Velcro and pouches, until he hit hard, blocky plastic.

"Got it," he found himself telling Aque as he pulled it off the dead man's belt. Something compelled him to keep the detective updated.

Spinks fumbled around until he felt the long rectangular button. He clicked it and was rewarded with a break in the radio chatter.

"This is Jevon Spinks. I'm with the wounded officers in a tunnel beneath the spillway. Same spillway we went down into when we arrived. I think the water district commissioner said it was subsection seven... or eleven."

Shit.

Which was it? He wracked his brain, trying to remember.

He let out a frustrated breath.

"You know what? Forget it. I'll come to you, show you the way in."

"Copy, Spinks. We're on our way down the hill into the canal and will wait for a visual."

"OK." He glanced behind him, barely able to see more than the outline of the detective in the darkness. "I mean, copy."

Spinks pushed to his feet, wobbling a little with the sudden head rush. Pins and needles flared in his calves. Apparently, they'd fallen asleep while he was down there. He stuck a hand out to stabilize himself on the curve of the wall.

"I'll be right back, Detective. Keep pressure on that stomach."

Without waiting for a reply, he took off toward the pinprick of light ahead. One knee tried to give out as he ran, the circulation in his legs fighting to return to normal, but he tensed his thighs and caught himself shy of falling.

The circle of light ahead grew. Gained details like the black slashes of grating across a portion of the opening.

He sprinted at top speed. Heart and lungs filling and squeezing out their payloads as the exertion amped them up.

The radio in his hand smashed against something hard at his hip and went tumbling out of his grasp, skidding down the tunnel. In the light from the opening, he saw the offending block of plastic attached to his belt.

It was another radio. The one he'd been given at the beginning of the manhunt.

Well, ain't that some shit? as his homeless persona Ol' J would say. He'd had a radio on him this whole time. Shock did strange things to the brain.

His feet slapped to a stop in front of the grating, and he stretched out into the sunlight, waving his arm.

"Over here!" Spinks yelled.

As his eyes adjusted to the brightness, he saw the paramedic team, one of them packing their stretcher board, jogging along the canal.

"Hey! We're over here!"

Things lurched into fast-forward then. It seemed like he blinked, and the paramedics were inside the tunnel, following him into the darkness, their lights flashing this way and that.

They reeled off questions as they bent over the bodies, and he shot back answers. One gunshot wound. One throat cut. One alive, one probably dead.

No, he was fine — no wounds — nothing had touched him. All this blood was Aque's.

OK, but he should let them have a look at him when they got to the ambulance, just in case.

Then they had Aque on the stretcher board, one man at his head and another at his feet, hauling him out, while two more zipped Schrader into a body bag, his skin gone white as yogurt in the glare of their flashlights.

Spinks found himself in the dirt parking lot beside subsection seven, squinting in the brilliant glare of the daylight and dusty wind as they loaded the stretcher board onto a Flight for Life helicopter. Schrader didn't get the helo treatment. He got put in the back of an ambulance, its lights dark and its siren off.

Johnson had sidled up beside Spinks at some point.

"Glad I didn't mention I only have twenty-five years until retirement," the detective said.

Spinks gave a grim snort.

"I can tell you with full confidence right now, Detective, I'm getting too old for this shit."

Gravel scraped as Johnson scuffed a booted foot in the dirt. He hooked his hands into the armholes of his vest.

"I almost hate to ask, given the circumstances, but…" Johnson looked over his shoulder toward the canals. "Where's your partner?"

CHAPTER 72

Plink.

Plink.

Plink.

The steady dripping of water was the first thing Loshak noticed as he swam up out of the depths of unconsciousness. Pain throbbed in his temple in time with the sound. A mini heartbeat pulsing beneath a sticky substance drying down the side of his face, pulling the skin taut.

He grimaced, the motion of his facial muscles aggravating that throbbing lump. That thumping was so insistent that it took him longer to realize his left shoulder hurt as well. Familiar. The same lance of pain he felt when he slept on his side with his head propped on his arm.

But he wasn't lying down. He was upright.

And he couldn't actually feel his arms. But he could feel the toes of one shoe scraping the ground, the side of the other smashed flat with the ankle turned limply.

Metal clinked and scraped as he shifted his legs under him and opened his eyes.

He was hanging like a side of beef, hands cuffed around a pipe over his head.

He shifted his shoulders the best he could. The muscles arched funny along the side of his neck.

All at once, his arms came to life. Prickling jolts of pain shot up the lengths of them in unison, the sensation especially loud in his palms and fingertips. His arthritic wrist wasn't going to like that once it got circulation back.

He squinted. Focused on the space around himself.

He was in a small concrete room. More like a box.

The electronic instruments he'd seen before were winking on and off in red, yellow, and green, measuring God only knew what. It was probably too much to hope that they were measuring extraneous weight put on pipes. Then maybe LEO or waterworks employees would come bursting in at any moment to let him down.

His eyes stopped at an object resting on top of one of the control boxes. His gun. Out of reach for the moment. But he had a visual. That was something.

The dripping went on, *plink, plink, plink*. Small. He couldn't locate its source, but he did find where the light was coming from.

A smartphone balanced on a pipe hugging the wall. Its flashlight slanted over one corner of the room and gave the rest a ghostly gray glow.

OK. He was alone, unarmed, underground, in a concrete box.

Straight ahead, just outside the phone's sphere of light, was something out of a submarine movie. A bulkhead door — rounded edges, porthole, wheeled handle — everything. Except through this door was nothing but blackness.

Some kind of sealed-off chamber in the water treatment facility, then. Maybe just off the tunnel he'd climbed into.

The word *vault* came to mind. The concrete box they lowered caskets into.

He should've radioed somebody before he went in. In the heat of the chase, he hadn't been thinking. Now there was no way in hell anybody knew where he was. With the sheer linear footage of tunnel he'd seen on the commissioner's tablet, it could be days before they found him.

Or his body.

Something shifted behind him, the soft rustle of cloth and grit of shoes announcing that Loshak wasn't alone after all.

Sam Crozier stepped in front of him, the phone light blasting the right side of that pale face, throwing shadows across the rest from his lips and nose and hair.

Breath rasping in the enclosed space, he grabbed the phone off the pipe and shined the light in Loshak's eyes.

The agent winced, screwing up his eyelids to escape from the sudden spike in his already throbbing temple. Just as quickly, the light withdrew, but the pulsing in his head remained. His breath whistled between his clenched teeth.

Louder than that, however, was the unmistakable sound of his phone being unlocked. Crozier had been scanning his face.

"OK, asshole," the killer said, lowering the phone.

Past the afterimages seared into his retinas, Loshak could see Crozier pawing at the glowing screen.

"I'm going to tell you this one time. I dial. You talk. When they answer, you're going to tell them to get the police out of the tunnels. Every one of them. Fuck it up, and I shoot you in the face."

Already, Loshak could hear the muffled ringing from the earpiece.

Crozier stuck the square of glass and plastic to his ear. The ringing got louder.

Loshak swallowed. Licked his lips.

And tasted blood. That sticky substance on the side of his face was blood. Was it his or a spray of Schrader's that had gone unnoticed in the chaos of the death tunnel?

"Denver 9-1-1. What's your emergency?"

Loshak's breath breezed out of his mouth, silently drying out his chapped, blood-spotted lips.

"Tell her," Crozier hissed, shoving the muzzle of the gun to Loshak's forehead.

His voice remained even, but a vein stood out in the younger man's neck, as if it were taking all his effort not to immediately paint the walls with Loshak's brains.

"Hello? Hello?"

The muzzle pushed harder, twisting the skin of Loshak's forehead a little.

"Do. It."

"Hello, this is 9-1-1. If you can, please speak up, or I'll have to send a unit to your location for a welfare check…"

With a snarl, Crozier snatched the phone away and jammed the screen to hang up. He stomped a few feet away, the light from the front of the phone sliding across the floor and over the bottom few inches of the bulkhead door.

Loshak swayed on the spot, then caught himself. If he let his muscles go slack, he'd wrench his shoulder more, and it already hurt like hell. He stretched up onto his toes, a measure of relief flowing along with the pins and needles in his arms.

Crozier growled. In the shadows above the phone light, he scrubbed his face with the back of his gun hand. He stopped, spun around.

Loshak tensed himself for a blow, but nothing came. Crozier swept past him, into the darkness behind him. He tried to look over his shoulder to where the killer had gone, but the cuffs stopped him before he could twist far enough.

His ears perked up, snatching onto every sound he could hear now. The plinking. The scuff of Crozier's feet.

Something scraped. Again. Three times. Friction. The groan of metal or maybe hard plastic.

The broken-off knife came to mind, though Loshak couldn't imagine it making that sound unless Crozier was trying to pry something open. Maybe twisting off another padlock?

Then something clunked, and there was a scuff of hinges, and everything fell silent. Everything save for that *plink, plink, plink*ing.

The quiet stretched out. Time melting past. Maybe just a few minutes. Maybe longer.

Loshak found his mind wandering out into nothing. Heavy eyelids drooping, drooping.

More sounds woke him from the daze. A scrabbling sound followed by a grunt of effort from Crozier.

Loshak tried again to twist around, pain shooting down his wrists and into the cranked shoulder, but still he couldn't see what the killer was doing.

A hiss that reminded Loshak of yanking a garden hose out of its coil, hearing it slip across the nylon. Then a sizzle.

Lightning struck the back of Loshak's neck, a blue-hot bomb of electricity detonating in his body.

CHAPTER 73

"No thank you," Spinks said, pulling away from the EMTs trying to check him over. "I'm fine. None of this blood is mine. I need to go find my partner."

He broke into a jog, leaving the ambulances behind and heading for the spot on one side of the parking lot where LEOs were gathering around the water commissioner.

A white cowboy hat at the edge of the crowd of vests caught the reporter's attention. He moved for it.

Benally was there. He and Johnson were leaning over a phone, like several others around them.

"Hey, you made it."

Spinks slapped Benally on the shoulder and stopped between the partners.

"I wouldn't miss this," the white-hatted detective said. "Besides, they got Annette's fever down finally, so…"

Spinks leaned over the phone.

"What are we looking at?"

"It's an app the maintenance crews use so they don't get turned around in the tunnels," Johnson said. He pointed to a marker, then scrolled over so they could see the spillway and the canals. "We're here, and this is the tunnel where the gunfight happened."

Spinks nodded, though it hadn't been much of a gunfight. More like an ambush.

A SWAT leader was at the center of the group, half-yelling out what they knew and what they didn't. Nobody had been able to raise Loshak on the radio, and the choppers hadn't caught sight of him or their killer in the area. The working theory was that the killer had gone underground again. He didn't mention any theories relating to where Loshak was.

"We'll spread out across subsections three, four, and five," he said. "These are the closest ones to our suspect's last known location. Three and five are in operation right now, so take extra care if you're searching there. We don't want this to turn from a manhunt into a water rescue."

As the teams were divided up and sent searching, Spinks split off with the detectives. They'd been assigned to subsection four again, the series of dry canals Spinks had just come out of.

After what had happened in the tunnels, he felt extremely conspicuous creeping along without a gun. He kept noticing spots along the canal's edge where the killer could be lurking, hiding, ready to pick them off.

"What do you think the odds are he stuck around here?" Spinks asked as they headed downstream in the dusty man-made riverbed.

Benally shrugged, eyes scanning the lip of the concrete.

"I figure pretty good if he found somewhere to hole up or if he's just a big dipshit. Otherwise, not great."

The radios crackled.

"9-1-1 call center just received a call from the vicinity of the water treatment plant," the dispatcher updated them. "Cell phone, emergency location service on. No response from the caller, but the number it came from belongs to Special Agent Loshak."

CHAPTER 74

Loshak hung from the pipe, unable to pull himself up anymore. He could feel the electrical burns peppering his body. After that first one on his back had knocked him out, Crozier had gotten smarter. Moved around to spots that wouldn't immediately kill or incapacitate him.

Unless my heart gives out, Loshak thought.

Cardiac arrest was always a possibility with electricity. And heart failure happened to even healthy people under torture. As Spinks had once pointed out, with the way he ate, Loshak wasn't exactly the healthiest profiler at the FBI.

"Here's what's going to happen," Crozier said.

He'd set the gun aside, and now he was holding the phone in one hand and the power supply cord to those electronic instruments in the other. Bare wires poked out of the end.

"Looks like you've got some influential folks in your contacts — detectives, commanders. We'll go in alphabetical order. I call, you tell them to stop the search and get out of the tunnels. Fuck up and say nothing, and we get serious about this."

He lifted the live wire for emphasis.

"Won't work."

Loshak swallowed the blood in his mouth after he spoke. One of the most recent blasts had made his teeth clamp down on the inside of his cheek.

"I didn't ask for editorializing."

Crozier advanced on him with the wires.

Loshak twisted weakly out of the way, talking as fast as he could.

"You need a hostage!" Blood sprayed between his teeth on the *s* sound.

Crozier hesitated.

Loshak tried to slow the flow of words pouring out of himself, tried to sound calm.

"They'll agree to whatever you say, but it's all lies. They'll be waiting for you the second you stick your head out."

Crozier held still, the hand with the wire hovering before him, fingers strangely dainty on the cord, as if he were offering Loshak a chance to hold it.

He was listening. Glaring.

"It's standard procedure for a negotiation," Loshak said. "Agree to anything the suspect wants to get him out in the open, then open fire. Unless..." He paused long enough to swallow. "Unless they have a hostage."

"Hostage?"

"Completely flips the script. Law enforcement won't take the shot if there's a chance of hitting—" He avoided the phrase *innocent bystander* just in time. "—someone other than you. It's how they're trained. Drilled into their heads from day one in the police academy."

Crozier stood there, staring into Loshak's eyes. His mouth hung slightly open, as if he wanted to ask a question but couldn't quite form the words.

"I've done a hundred hostage negotiations," Loshak said. "And the only guys who get away are the ones who use their hostages as a shield. They won't come near you if you've got someone out front."

"Yeah?" Crozier's eyes narrowed with suspicion. "And I guess you're offering yourself as a hostage, huh, asshole? Suddenly you're not scared to throw yourself into the line of fire?"

Loshak shook his head.

"I'm telling you, that's how safe it is. Not one of them is going to pull the trigger with someone out in front of you."

Crozier digested that for a second. Then he blinked hard.

"Oh sure, and this is all the honest truth. You're suddenly on my side. Can't wait to help a guy out."

"I'm on the side that keeps me from getting shocked anymore," Loshak said, taking a gamble and nodding at the seemingly forgotten electrical wires in Crozier's hand. "One hundred percent self-preservation, I won't deny it. If I've got to tell you how to get away so I can live — well, I get to live."

"Prove it," Crozier said, thumbing the phone screen again. "When this Commander Belte guy answers, you tell him to call off the cops. If he agrees, we'll give them ten minutes. Then we come out, you first."

He let the electrical cable fall to the floor, the wires sparking as they bounced against one another. He kicked it carelessly aside and pulled the gun from his waistband. He gestured with the muzzle as he spoke.

"But in case you get any funny fucking ideas, I'll have this snugged up to the back of your skull."

Cowed was what Crozier was looking for. Loshak nodded emphatically, keeping his eyes on the gun, hoping the killer was buying it.

Crozier mashed the ringing phone to Loshak's ear again.

"Belte."

"Commander Belte, this is Special Agent Loshak. I'm with our suspect." He paused to lick his chapped lips. "You might say I'm at his mercy here. He's asking that you call off the search of the tunnels around the water treatment facility."

There was a pause.

"Can he hear me?"

She had unknowingly asked the perfect question.

Loshak locked eyes with Crozier.

"Yes."

Another pause.

"Tell him we'll give him anything he wants."

The faintest smile touched Loshak's lips. He stared at Crozier for a full second before he responded to Belte.

"He wants the place emptied of LEO in ten minutes."

"Consider it done."

"And a van," Loshak added, looking to Crozier.

The gun jabbed painfully into his cheek.

"Fuck your getaway van and the extraneous shit. Stick to the script, or I'll light you up again."

Belte was saying, "A van's going to take time—"

"No van," Loshak cut across her response. "Just get everyone out."

"OK, forget the van. But tell him I need fifteen minutes to—"

Crozier snatched the phone away from Loshak.

"You've got ten minutes, fuckface. That's it. And just know that if anybody tries to come after me in the meantime, I've got a plan for every one of them. Come after me, and everybody leaves in a body bag — you, this guy, and me — everybody."

Then he pitched the phone at the bulkhead door as hard as he could. The screen shattered, and the flashlight guttered out.

CHAPTER 75

Spinks kept swallowing, his eyes roving from one side of the canal to the other. He didn't want to show how badly he was panicking inside, but that swallow reflex wouldn't let him be.

Concrete walls brushed past on either side. The cement spillway funneled back toward the tunnel mouth with the busted grate.

The 9-1-1 dispatch center hadn't been able to pinpoint the spot where Loshak's call was coming from, and knowing the approximate location was almost as worthless as knowing nothing. Narrowed it down to 400 miles of tunnel and however many more of dry canal bed. Something like that, anyway. Spinks couldn't remember the actual numbers anymore.

Both the detectives with him had gone silent, feet gritting in the dust. The three of them searched with renewed determination, a grim cloud of quiet hanging over them.

They'd come around the canal's bend and found exactly nothing. Spinks wondered if they shouldn't turn back, start at the tunnel mouth, and try again.

Maybe they had missed something. Maybe they would find a blood trail or casing or some other clue telling them which way Loshak and the killer had gone.

There was a high-pitched whistle, and Benally waved them over.

"Might have something."

Spinks and Johnson jogged to join him. He was squatted down, the big white hat concealing his face. He pointed out the depressions in the dust.

"Footprints. Looks like they head that-a-way."

CHAPTER 76

In the pitch blackness, Loshak heard Crozier moving. The flat of the gun barrel shoved against his Adam's apple, pain shooting into his neck. He grunted and tried to pull away.

The gun went with him, pushing harder.

"Move and die," Crozier growled.

Loshak went limp. His only chance now was to play along.

"I thought you said ten minutes," he said.

"Do you think I'm stupid enough to let them set up their snipers and shields and shit? We go now."

Crozier's breath was harsh so close to his ear. The killer grunted, leaning on Loshak, stretching up next to him.

The gun wavered, digging a channel into Loshak's throat. Metal clinked and sneakers squeaked. Crozier's hand grazed his arm, elbow bumping elbow, fingers poking around wrists as he pulled himself up.

Crozier wasn't a big guy. Small was the word that kept coming to the agent's mind. Almost petite. Reaching the cuffs so far over Loshak's head was a struggle for him, and Loshak was sure from the sounds that he'd climbed onto something — a pipe or electrical box — close behind him.

And with the way he was leaning and turning...

Loshak's pulse doubled, seemed to synchronize itself with the steady *plink, plink, plink* of the water. His original plan had been to wait until they were out of the concrete box, up in the sunlight and open air, where he could run, but he might have to go at this sooner rather than later. Take the opportunities where they presented themselves, as it were.

Crozier grunted and fumbled with the cuffs. Loshak swallowed, trying to seem as limp and frightened as possible.

Metal ratcheted. The left cuff released. The chain slid over the pipe.

Loshak's shoulders screamed in relief as his arms came loose and dropped, stinging and prickling, to his sides. The cuffs dangled from his right wrist, twirling at the end of his dead arm.

Crozier let out a puff of breath and started to move.

The gun shifted, just enough.

Loshak jerked backward and threw both tingling hands at the place where it had been.

"Hey!"

The gun went off, a sharp bark and flash of light. Orange glitter strobed over everything. The bullet struck a spark on concrete.

In the flash, Loshak could still see the young man perched precariously on the instrument panel, one thin arm hanging over the pipe where the cuffs had been.

Then it was midnight in the concrete box again.

Loshak threw himself, shoulder-first, into the darkness. Crozier had moved a little, but not much.

He struck him below the ribs, a sharp hip digging into the side of his face. The gun went off again. Screaming.

They slammed into a tangle of pipes and wall and blinking instrument panels. The air woofed out of Crozier's lungs with the impact, and pain cracked through

Loshak's shoulder, the hurt radiating out of the joint like spokes.

Another gunshot. Muffled by the two that had gone before.

How many rounds left?

Loshak scrabbled at him, clawing up his scrawny chest for his arms, flailing for the weapon. He had to get control of it.

But he couldn't even get to his knees. Blocky equipment and endless coils of metal and PVC snaked around this side of the concrete box, tripping up any chance at regaining his footing.

And somewhere — a disconnected portion of Loshak's brain said — there was a live wire, hanging out on the floor waiting to fry one of them.

His fingertips skimmed over the gun, thumbnail catching for a second on what he was sure was the slide. Then a dull pain hit as the gun was torn away.

Another boom and flash, this time barely audible.

Loshak crawled up Crozier's chest, feet kicking at the jumble of legs and equipment as he went.

A fist grazed his cheek. Rocked his head and pulled at the skin there.

His chapped bottom lip popped open, and blood oozed out.

Loshak retaliated with a punch. Felt it hit a bony shoulder.

That was it, that was the appendage he needed. The muscles in his arm and chest strained as Loshak leaned on the killer's arm. Grappled for the gun at the end. His middle finger slipped into a hole in the ratty hoodie, and the sleeve ripped as he kept reaching.

Then he was lying on his back on Crozier's face and chest, wrestling with the smaller man's arm. He wrenched it. Leaned. Used the leverage of their awkward position. Torqued it like Crozier's arm was a crowbar.

Crozier's free hand tangled in Loshak's hair, jerked, flailed. When that didn't work, it tore free and started battering his head and shoulders.

Loshak grunted, tucking his head the best he could. Salty blood entered the corners of his mouth.

He slammed Crozier's gun hand into the closest hard surface. Once, twice, three times.

Red tinged the edges of the dark now. A ruddy blur pulsing in time with his heart.

Loshak felt his arm lurch. His fingers finding smooth polymer.

He snatched the barrel of the gun and twisted it, still smashing the hand against that pipe. Something snapped beneath his fingers, and he thought he heard Crozier yell.

Loshak yanked the gun free of the killer's broken fingers. He scrambled backward. Something like a crab walk.

He pulled free of the wreckage of the smaller man's body and the water treatment equipment, onto the open ground, and knocked his head against that metal bulkhead door.

The dull thud sounded wrong. Dense. Not the right noise if the chamber were empty on the other side.

Where the back of his scalp pressed against the door, he could feel the thrum of rushing water. And though he couldn't hear the *plink, plink, plink* of water anymore, he felt it dripping steadily onto the bloody side of his face.

The concrete box must be some sort of side-flow then, the waterway behind the bulkhead door releasing its payload in a constant gushing roar into the river.

"Don't move," Loshak warned Crozier.

His voice sounded so muffled and far away that he could barely hear it. He doubted the killer could either.

He adjusted his grip on the gun, then braced a hand on the floor to push himself up.

His palm pressed against shattered glass.

His phone screen lit up as he brushed it, glowing weakly through the damage.

The dying phone bathed Crozier's form in pale bluish light. On his hands and knees, loping toward Loshak like some kind of wild dog.

"Stop!" Loshak warned, leveling the gun.

Crozier's lips pulled back, bearing his teeth in a feral grin. He leaped.

Loshak squeezed the trigger twice. Then Crozier was on him, hot air hissing against Loshak's face.

The killer reached up and yanked something.

The bulkhead door crashed open, battering Loshak into the concrete wall.

Thousands of gallons of black water came rushing in.

CHAPTER 77

Spinks felt the hairs he tried to keep shaved smooth at the back of his neck prickle as the radio crackled. The skin there tightened as the voices came forth from the speaker.

"All units be advised that the water district is reporting an unauthorized opening of flood vault 21 in subsection 3. Possibly a failed emergency release. Repeat, unauthorized opening of flood vault 21 in subsection 3. Consider this area extremely dangerous until it has been closed off again."

Johnson pulled out his phone and checked the maintenance app. A long finger swiping and flicking the screen.

He looked up at the far side of the canal.

"That's just over there, by the dam."

Another voice cut through the static on the radio, one Spinks recognized.

"This is District Six Commander Belte," Katie Belte said, a hard edge in her voice. "I just received a call from Agent Loshak. Crozier is holding him hostage, demanding all teams pull out of the water treatment facility in the next ten minutes. Suspect threatened to kill anyone who came after him."

Spinks's shoulders jerked. His mouth popped open.

"What if Crozier's the one who opened that flood vault gate? They could be there right now."

"Hell, what are we waiting for?" Benally jerked his head

toward subsection 3. "Let's go get your partner, buddy."

Spinks's long legs ate up the distance to the ladder. He hauled himself up, arms yanking and legs shoving, reaching the top before Johnson or Benally had even started climbing.

"Which way?" Spinks called back down to them.

Johnson panted as he stepped onto the grass and dug his phone out again, checking the maps. Before he could answer, however, water sprayed in small arcs around the edges of a hatch in the top of a concrete platform.

Spinks sprinted toward it.

CHAPTER 78

Icy water smashed into Loshak. Shoved him back against the concrete wall.

The black fluid enveloped him. A fist clenching his torso. It closed around his ears and squelched out all sound.

The shock of the cold gripped his chest next. Pulled his skin taut.

He choked then. Sinuses and throat and lungs flushed with liquid. Mucus membranes stinging everywhere.

He thrashed in the darkness. Water slowing his limbs to a strange drift. Already numbing him.

He raked his fingers through empty water. Reached out for—

But the gun was long gone, lost in the torrent. Swallowed by the dark.

The concrete box filled within seconds, and the currents seemed to strengthen as the water deepencd. Slabs of water flexing like muscles along his flanks.

And then he was untethered from solid ground. Spinning in the darkness.

He touched down for a second. Shoes scraping hard concrete below.

But a swell grabbed him and yanked him away again. Pulled him off his feet. Tossed him around like a limp rag in a washing machine.

A leg crashed against Loshak's neck. He grabbed it,

wrapped an arm around it. His shoulder protested, throbbing dully, but he held on.

They had to get out. Escape this death trap. Somehow. He tried to think.

He had climbed down through a hatch in the ceiling. There was a ladder. Somewhere. But he couldn't tell which way was up anymore.

His hip slammed into a pipe. Pain burst out from that knob of bone.

And then the ground was there again, real again. He planted a foot and pushed as hard as he could, the sole of his shoe slipping in decades' worth of slime.

His body knifed upward. Pierced the current. Fighting it like a salmon swimming upstream.

His shoulder smacked against the edge of something. Then the surge was ripping him forward without a chance of resisting, turning him as it did.

He grabbed onto Crozier with both arms. Pulled him along.

Darkness. Wetness. No sound. Gallons of blackness twisting around him, wrenching him in a crooked spiral.

Loshak broke the surface. He coughed and spluttered, bobbing like an apple. What seemed like a gallon of water spewed out of his mouth and nose.

Then the top of his head grazed concrete. The ceiling.

It was dark here. But a lighter dark.

He could see shapes in the softer black. The walls. Maybe some pipes protruding from them.

He breathed. Coughed some more and breathed.

Instinct kept his arms wrapped around Crozier. The killer's head lolled on his neck. Floating face down.

Unconscious or dead?

He fumbled with the floating body, going under again as he tried to get the smaller man's head above water. He kicked at the water below him, finally coming up again.

Loshak had to believe the killer was just unconscious. Had to proceed as if he were.

It was important now. He didn't know why.

Everyone leaves in a body bag, Crozier had said. Meaning all along, he hadn't cared whether he lived or died.

They were being dragged forward now, without that sickening tornado of turning.

He looked around. Scanned for anything familiar. No blinking lights just here. The walls seemed too far away.

They must have been pulled out into the main tunnel.

Panic prickled along his spine. He pictured what would happen if they were flushed into a pipe with no headroom. No way to breathe.

Couldn't think about that. Had to keep going, fighting forward.

Up ahead, Loshak spotted a half-moon sitting in the darkness.

The outflow.

He hooked one arm under the smaller man's armpits, pushing him higher in his grasp until Crozier was over his bad shoulder.

Loshak kicked, his legs cramping with effort, and wheeled his free arm through the water. He wrenched his neck sideways to gasp in a deep breath, repeated the motion every few seconds like an Olympic swimmer.

The current dragged them along at top speed.

The sliver of light grew until Loshak could see the concrete overhead and the black water turned a translucent green. His hand, scraped but bloodless, became visible raking through the treated water.

The swell surged as they neared the corrugated pipe. Faster. Sucking.

Christ. Hope this leads out.

The water pulled them under again. Ripped them along.

Loshak's ears filled with that empty sound again. The ocean snuffling in a shell.

The pipe winnowed into something smaller, tighter. He could feel it somehow. The walls closing in.

His lungs grew tight. He ached for breath.

He gripped Crozier tighter.

And then the pipe was gone. The sky burst open overhead. Sunlight shattering all of the darkness.

They rushed out of the pipe into the lazy flow of a concrete canal. Drifted to the surface.

Loshak let out a cry of relief at seeing the openness overhead. All that empty space reaching out for eternity. Warm and dry.

He didn't try to fight the currents. He angled himself toward one wall, kicking and pulling Crozier along.

Finally, he banged against the concrete. Scraped along it, the rough surface abrading his chest and arm as he struggled to grab hold of the lip.

Loshak's hand slipped off. The current dragged him and the killer downstream, bumping along the wall.

He relaxed then. Let them drift. Watched the way ahead.

A ladder.

The water shoved them toward it. Loshak caught it and hooked his arm through a rung.

But he didn't have the strength to pull them up. Not anymore.

He made sure Crozier's head was above water. Then he leaned his head against the cold metal.

He panted. His throat hurt. But he was alive.

No additional thoughts came to him. He focused on his breathing. Found the emptiness inside a strange comfort.

"Need a hand, partner?"

Loshak raised his eyes, head falling back on the exhausted muscles of his neck, to find Spinks grinning down at him.

CHAPTER 79

Loshak sat on the back gate of an open ambulance. One of the paramedics had wrapped him in an emergency blanket, and bandages made his right shoulder bulge.

He'd thought he'd broken it in the scuffle, but he'd actually been grazed by a ricochet. It hadn't hit bone, just torn open the skin.

Spinks sat next to him, one leg folded onto the diamond grating, as they watched the other ambulance drive silently away, carrying Crozier's corpse to the morgue. Not a bullet in him, after all that.

Loshak stared holes in the back of the emergency vehicle. Watched it shrink into the horizon.

Crozier had gotten what he wanted. Escaped justice in his own way, even if it meant forfeiting his life. A final act of control.

He remembered dragging the killer's limp form through those flooded tunnels. Holding onto him that whole time as the currents ripped them along.

What had been the point?

To drag him to justice? To keep him alive so he could pay?

To make all of this mean something?

Maybe so.

Maybe so.

And maybe that was the wrong approach, and maybe it wasn't. He didn't know. He had a feeling he'd keep trying, anyway.

Loshak turned to Spinks.

"Can I borrow your phone? Mine's somewhere at the bottom of the South Platte by now."

"Sure."

The reporter dug out the electronic rectangle and handed it to Loshak.

"Who you gonna call? Besides *Ghostbusters*, I mean. Obviously."

Loshak opened up the contacts list.

"Do people still make that joke?"

"Cool guys do," Spinks said, shrugging.

Loshak huffed a laugh. He found Jan's name and hit Call.

EPILOGUE

The day after Detective Schrader's funeral, Alita Simms's parents came down to the District Six station.

In the interview room, Lucia Simms, Alita's mother, opened her handbag and pulled out a padded envelope. Loshak had to resist an urge to recoil, unable to ignore the strange parallel between this envelope and the one that had started all of this. And when Mrs. Simms thrust her hand inside and pulled out Alita's face, a shiver ran up his spine.

The portrait was framed, a posed shot that Loshak thought was probably her senior picture from high school.

He doubted anything out of the ordinary had occurred to Mrs. Simms when she'd slid the print of her daughter's face into that envelope. She and her husband were, after all, still holding out hope that the dismembered face in the morgue wouldn't belong to their daughter. Alita was missing, yes, and had been for nearly two weeks, but, "We think she's probably on her way home. She's a bright girl, but she can be a little scatterbrained at times. I'm sure she went off somewhere and forgot her phone charger. It would be just like her to not realize how worried we'd be, not hearing from her for so long." Their optimism was heartbreaking.

The framed photo wasn't the only one in the envelope, either. There was a whole pile of loose snapshots of Alita throughout her life — riding an elephant at the zoo, standing on a cliff edge on a mountaintop somewhere, posing like Charlie's Angels with a group of friends.

Looking at the pictures, Loshak understood how the girl's parents could continue holding out hope the way they were. It was almost impossible to look at the bright, smiling young woman in the photos, full of such vitality and zeal, and imagine that she was dead. Lying faceless somewhere in a ditch or shallow grave.

Loshak was there when Commander Belte broke the news to them: the lab had matched a DNA sample from Lucia Simms to DNA from the dismembered face in the mailer.

Belte told them that their daughter's murderer wouldn't hurt anyone ever again, but Loshak could see how little comfort that gave them. Their baby girl was still dead. They would never get her back, never hug her again, never see her age another day, or pass another milestone.

The task force members gathered at a local bar that afternoon to celebrate Detective Aque's discharge from the hospital. As prickly as the detective had been throughout the investigation, Loshak was glad to see him back on his feet. But the memory of Mrs. Simms's wailing sobs from that morning echoed in his mind as the men and women around him made toasts and patted one another on the back for closing the case. He couldn't truly enjoy himself or revel in the victory.

"I can't decide whether he got what he deserved or basically got away with it," Loshak told Spinks that night, while they waited for the taxi to the airport. "Crozier."

Spinks's lips pressed into a thin line, thinking it over.

"Depends on what you think happens after death, I guess," he said. "After some of the things we've seen, personally, I'm hoping there's some grand celestial payback for guys like him. And some kind of cosmic compensation for the victims. I want to believe all scales balance out in the end."

He grinned somewhat sheepishly.

"But maybe that's just the writer in me, the guy who's always looking for a neat bow to tie up the story of our lives. Maybe there's nothing coming to us after death. Or maybe it's like a great big tent city in the sky, where the only comfort you get is the comfort you're willing to give. The old ladies you're willing to help, and the friends who help you."

Loshak blew out a long breath. "Guess the possibilities are endless."

The cab pulled up to the curb.

"That they are, partner," Spinks said, heading for the far side of the car. "That they are."

THANK YOU

Thanks so much for reading *Lone Wolf*. Want another Loshak novel? Leave a review on Amazon and let us know.

MORE LOSHAK

But wait! How will you find out about more Loshak?

It's a sad fact that Amazon won't magically beam news of upcoming Loshak books into your head. (I wish.) Don't miss out! Choose one of the options below to keep up with Loshak, Jan, and Spinks:

1) You can join our Facebook Fan group. Then you'll hear all about our new and upcoming releases. Join at: **http://facebook.com/groups/mcbainvargus**

2) You can follow us on Amazon. Just go to one of our author pages and click on the **FOLLOW** button under our pictures. That way Amazon will send you an email whenever we publish something new.

3) You can join our mailing list. In fact, we'll give you a free copy of *The Good Life Crisis (A Victor Loshak Novella)* if you partake in this one. Just visit: **http://ltvargus.com/emfreebook**

See where it all started for Loshak in the *Violet Darger* series...

Her body is broken. Wrapped in plastic. Dumped on the side of the road. She is the first. There will be more.

The serial killer thriller that "refuses to let go until you've read the last sentence."

The most recent body was discovered in the grease dumpster behind a Burger King. Dismembered. Shoved into two garbage bags and lowered into the murky oil.

Now rookie agent **Violet Darger** gets the most important assignment of her career. She travels to the Midwest to face a killer unlike anything she's seen. Aggressive. Territorial. Deranged and driven.

Another mutilated corpse was found next to a roller rink. A third in the gutter in a residential neighborhood.

These bold displays of violence shock the rural community and rattle local law enforcement.

Who could carry out such brutality? And why?

Unfortunately for Agent Darger, there's little physical evidence to work with, and the only witnesses prove to be unreliable. The case seems hopeless.

If she fails, more will die. He will kill again and again.

The victims harbor dark secrets. The clues twist and writhe and refuse to keep still. And the killer watches the investigation on the nightly news, gleeful to relive the violence, knowing that he can't be stopped.

Get your copy now: **http://mybook.to/DeadEndGirl**

ABOUT THE AUTHORS

E.M. Smith came by his redneck roots honestly, his barbwire tattoo dishonestly, and his sobriety slowly. Recovery isn't a sprint, according to his friends, it's a marathon. That's probably why he turned into such a fitness geek when he quit drinking.

L.T. Vargus grew up in Hell, Michigan, which is a lot smaller, quieter, and less fiery than one might imagine. When not glued to her computer, she can be found sewing, fantasizing about food, and rotting her brain in front of the TV.

    If you want to wax poetic about pizza or cats, you can contact L.T. (the L is for Lex) at ltvargus9@gmail.com or on Twitter @ltvargus.

Tim McBain writes because life is short, and he wants to make something awesome before he dies. Additionally, he likes to move it, move it.

    You can connect with Tim via email at tim@timmcbain.com.

Made in the USA
Las Vegas, NV
17 March 2024

87337740R10223